DAUGHTER OF THE REEF

Carried from her homeland, a chieftain's beautiful daughter discovers peril and passion in the eyes of strangers, in a land so different from her own. This is where Tepua's story begins . . .

"BRIMS WITH EXOTIC SPICE . . . FULL OF ENTRANCING DETAIL THAT CATAPULTS THE READER TO THE ANCIENT PACIFIC."
—LYNN ARMISTEAD McKEE, author of <u>Woman of the Mists</u> and <u>Touches the Stars</u>

"The author's masterful grasp of the history of the South Pacific—the ancient rituals and customs— suffuses this exciting romantic novel of Tahiti . . . The cruelty of the time comes through, but so does the magic."
—SHIRLEY STRESHINSKY, bestselling author of <u>Hers the Kingdom</u> and <u>The Shores of Paradise</u>

SISTER OF THE SUN

The woman warrior Tepua returns to her native island to follow a bold passion—and to lead her people into the dark clouds of war that threaten their destiny . . .

*　　*　　*　　*　　*

SPECIAL PREVIEW INCLUDED IN THIS BOOK!
Don't miss the next magnificent novel by Clare Coleman, continuing the acclaimed saga of <u>Daughter of the Reef</u>

CHILD O

Coming

Also by Clare Coleman from Jove

DAUGHTER OF THE REEF

SISTER OF THE SUN

CLARE COLEMAN

JOVE BOOKS, NEW YORK

SISTER OF THE SUN

A Jove Book / published by arrangement with
the authors

PRINTING HISTORY
Jove edition / September 1993

ISBN: 0-515-11186-4

Jove Books are published by The Berkley Publishing Group,
200 Madison Avenue, New York, New York 10016.
The name "JOVE" and the "J" logo
are trademarks belonging to Jove Publications, Inc.

PRINTED IN THE UNITED STATES OF AMERICA

10 9 8 7 6 5 4 3 2 1

PRONUNCIATION

The vowels are pronounced approximately as follows:

a - as the "a" in "father"
e - as the "a" in "say"
i - as the "e" in "me"
o - as the "o" in "so"
u - as the "u" in "rule"

The "ng" has a nasal sound, somewhat like that in "singer."

When two vowels are adjacent, each is pronounced as a separate sound. The accent on a word usually falls on the next-to-last syllable. The presence of an apostrophe in a word indicates a break or glottal stop.

NOTE: A glossary of unfamiliar terms appears in the back.

ACKNOWLEDGMENTS

I am grateful to the following for help with research: San Jose City Library, San Jose State University Library, Trigger Hill Trading Post, anthropologist Kauraka Kauraka, author Sven Wahlroos, Cultural Village of Rarotonga, and the many Polynesians I met in my travels.

I also thank readers Kevin J. Anderson, Michael Berch, Michael Meltzer, Dan'l Danehy-Oakes, Avis Minger, Dorothy Wall, and Lori Ann White.

ONE

Wave after great wave buffeted a two-hulled voyaging canoe that was beating its way windward. The craft was tossing so violently that only its sturdy master dared remain standing. Heavy sheets of spray hit the plaited sails and swept across the platform that crossed the hulls. Brine drenched the crewmen, who crouched, waiting for orders. But the canoe-master, wearing only a narrow loincloth, stood fast at the bow. Sinewy legs spread wide, knees flexed, he peered out over the heaving water for signs of land.

Beneath a small thatched canopy that was lashed to the deck sat the principal passenger, Tepua-mua, daughter of an atoll chief. Almost as tall as a man, she was lightly and gracefully built, as supple as a young coconut palm. Training in the dance had sculpted and defined the muscles in her arms, thighs, and calves. The swell of her breasts and hips showed that she had reached womanhood.

Her eyes were large and lively, surrounded by black lashes beneath angular eyebrows. Strong, wide cheekbones tapered down to a pointed chin. A mane of blue-black hair spilled back from her high forehead.

As the double canoe, the *pahi*, pitched and rolled, she felt her pearl-shell necklace sliding against the bare skin below her throat. She was wrapped in a garment of finely plaited matting to protect her against the wind and spray. Even so, the chill of sudden gusts set her teeth on edge.

1

"Aue!" one crewman shouted in dismay as a huge wave lifted the *pahi*. Tepua tightened her grip and tried not to think about her last sea voyage. It would be cruel of the gods, she thought, to bring her so close to home, only to toss her into the ocean again.

She had known worse sailing than this. Some time ago a squall had swept her overboard, taking her away from friends and kin. Only through the aid of the gods had she survived, finding refuge in far-off Tahiti. And now, despite misgivings, she was finally returning home.

"Aue!" came another cry, this one filled with hope. Tepua looked up to see the canoe-master pointing to something far ahead.

Paruru, her father's chief warrior, hurried forward to stand with him. Bared to the waist, Paruru seemed indifferent to the cold. His powerful shoulders and back were slick from spray.

She fought her impulse to join the men, knowing that she was expected to remain confidently seated under the shelter. Straining her eyes at the gray horizon that rose and fell with the deck, she saw only whitecaps. Waves crashed against the hull, and wind whistled through the thatch, drowning all voices.

Then, at last, she glimpsed a few black specks that set her pulse racing. The dots grew until she could see that they were feathery tops of palm trees. Others appeared, in a familiar pattern. The canoe-master called orders excitedly to the men. The sails had to be changed now, for the present course would take them far past their destination.

Tepua tried to fight her impatience. After so many days of travel she was eager for the journey to end. She ached to stretch her legs, to run free, to taste fresh food.

She had been away nearly two years. At first she had been treated with scorn in Tahiti, yet she had found a place for herself in that unfamiliar land. She had joined a society of dancers and performers who celebrated their patron god Oro. For a long time she had believed that she could never return to her home island, because she had lost the virginity required of a chief's unwed daughter.

But then Paruru arrived and invited her back for a visit. Her father, now ill, understood that she had been cleansed by a priest of Tahiti of all her offenses against the gods. Paruru brought the pearl-shell necklace as a gift from her relatives, and assured her that she would be welcome. . . .

With land in view, Tepua's thoughts filled with the people who awaited her. The spirit of her mother had long ago departed on its journey. But Ehi, who had been her feeding mother, would be waiting to welcome Tepua in her ample arms. And Ehi's daughter Maukiri, closer than a sister, would have tales to keep Tepua awake for many nights. As for her father, she could only hope that he still lived.

She glanced out again, this time seeing foam shooting high on the horizon as breakers crashed into the outer reefs. More palms appeared, marking the length of the large islet known as Ata-mea. Soon she saw, separated by gaps, tree clusters on other islets of the atoll's coral ring. She shifted her seat and wished the *pahi* could move faster.

But the waters here were hazardous, bristling with underwater reefs, and the rough weather only made the canoe-master's task more difficult. Carefully he directed a zigzag course that ended downwind of the atoll. At his command, the *pahi* turned to approach the pass through the reefs.

The canoe was close enough now for Tepua to see details of the familiar shoreline. Great chunks of old coral, tossed up by some malevolent spirit of storms, gave a harsh look to the seaward beach. Beyond this rugged barrier lay stretches of white sand, and there she saw people gathering, waving at the boat. A few youngsters ventured onto the rough coral banks, keeping just out of reach of waves that thundered against the rock.

Now Tepua could no longer bear to remain in the shelter. She came out to sit cross-legged on the deck and watch the final maneuvers. People from shore were shouting, but it was impossible to make out their words.

With a frenzy, the crewmen began paddling, trying to bring the *pahi* into position to enter the pass. Tepua knew how fortunate her people were to have such a channel into the calm enclosed waters of their lagoon. At other atolls it was necessary to land on the outer reef, a dangerous undertaking.

But entering a pass also involved risk, and today's rough seas made the hazard far greater than usual. Tepua took a quick glance over the stern, to see what waves were gathering to carry her to shore. A huge swell was already upon her! She felt its power in the pit of her stomach as the canoe rose high above the land. She spoke a brief prayer to her ancestress, Tapahi-roro-ariki, as she began to plunge through the gap.

Steep, rough walls of ruddy coral loomed suddenly on both sides. She clutched for a new handhold and tried to keep from crying out. Once, not so long ago, she had found amusement in shooting the pass on a blustery day. She remembered cajoling her father's boatmen into taking her out and back. Now, as she raced past the jagged walls, she could not even find words of prayer to her guardian spirit. *Life on Tahiti has made me soft,* came a distant thought as the bow of the *pahi* slammed down and sent her sprawling forward on the deck.

Before she could get up, the platform was awash. Then she found herself afloat in the boiling current, flailing about for something to hold on to. She clawed at the roof of the shelter beside her, but the thatching tore away in her hand. The canoe bounced up again, tossing her behind it. Then the boat shot forward, leaving her to struggle in its foaming wake.

Tepua sputtered a she came up for air. There was no time for shock or anger. On both sides, sharp and deadly walls hemmed her in. Men were shouting to her from the *pahi,* now far ahead, but they could not stop its rush toward the lagoon. Someone—Paruru, she thought—dove in after her, but he was too far away to help.

Tepua's head went under. Perhaps life in Tahiti had indeed made her soft, but she had not forgotten how to swim. Stroking fiercely, she emerged in a mass of foam. Now the coral wall rose just in front of her, its sharp edges glistening with seawater. In a frenzy she turned away and fought the current as waves pulled her down into a deep trough, lifted her and dropped her again.

Then she was swimming underwater, heading for the center of the channel, only dimly sensing pain on the side of her leg. Ahead she saw hints of the brighter, calmer water of the lagoon, but the current was treacherous here, swirling her away from her course.

Once more the coral seemed to reach out for her, and again she felt its sting. Turning, she tried to change direction, fighting a surge of water that was dragging her down. She saw a pair of glittering fish above, tried to follow them into a gentler current. The fish raced on before her, always just beyond her fingertips.

Then, at last, she was free of the treacherous undertow, and she saw overhead the quiet surface of the lagoon. She came up, gasping, pushing strands of hair from her face. Outrigger canoes, singled-hulled *vaka* that could be quickly launched, were coming toward her.

Tepua felt weak. The sting of her coral cuts grew worse, and she saw threads of blood rising through the clear water. She knew that sharks often entered the lagoon. . . .

"Get her out! Quick!" came cries from shore.

Hands reached down to help her. She half climbed, half rolled into the bottom of a canoe, and lay back, still trying to catch her breath. "Daughter, welcome home," cried a familiar voice from shore. "I will take care of you," Ehi called. Tepua closed her eyes, content, for the moment, just to feel the gentle rocking of the canoe as it headed in.

She sat up as the craft reached shallow water. Ehi was already wading from shore, her broad face filled with affection. Someone helped Tepua out of the canoe, and she splashed into the warm embrace of the older woman. For a long moment they held on to each other.

Then Paruru rushed up to stand beside Tepua. Water streamed from his soaked hair down his cheeks and brow. He was out of breath, his broad chest heaving. Tepua realized that he had fought the deadly currents also, and only for her sake. "I was too slow," he said in an anguished voice. "If I had jumped sooner . . ."

She glanced at Paruru's strong features, the heavy brows, straight forehead, broad nose that flared about the nostrils. Blue-black tattoos of a principal warrior decorated his shoulders and swirled about his hips.

"Do not blame yourself, Paruru," Tepua answered. "There is an evil spirit dwelling in that pass. It is enough that you brought me home safely." Then she turned to Ehi to ask the question that was now uppermost in her mind. "Does my father . . . Does . . ."

"Kohekapu is waiting for you, daughter," said Ehi, leading her out of the shallows and onto the white sand beach. Ehi made a scolding sound as she crouched to inspect Tepua's legs. "But first we must put ointment on those scrapes. And find you something to wear."

With chagrin, Tepua glanced down at herself. The fine atoll wrap that Paruru had brought her, tied with a sash, hung drenched and tattered about her waist. The pearl-shell necklace, she was pleased to see, had survived.

By the time Tepua emerged from Ehi's oblong, thatched house, a large crowd had gathered. To her dismay, Tepua saw few expressions of joy on the faces of people she had known all her life. She began to wonder at this lack of an enthusiastic greeting. "Am I no longer welcome here?" she asked Ehi in a whisper.

"Everyone is worried about Kohekapu," Ehi answered quickly. "They cannot think of anything else." Tepua was not satisfied with that answer, but for now she did not press the point. She heard the deep voice of a drum and turned in the direction of her father's *marae,* his sacred open-air courtyard. She could not see it through the trees, but she knew that priests were busy petitioning the gods to restore Kohekapu's health.

"Come," said Paruru, who had been waiting by the door. Ehi stepped aside, leaving Tepua to accompany him alone. Paruru was the *kaito-nui,* the high chief's first warrior. She remembered him from childhood as a tall figure who loomed over her, and later as a man whose mere presence excited her. But during the voyage from Tahiti, with so many eyes watching, she had been cool to him.

Now Paruru strode forward, leading her onto a broad, shaded path beneath the coconut palms. She breathed the familiar fragrance, a mixture of salt spray and faint perfumes from blossoming trees. Underfoot she felt the crushed coral that covered much of the island. *Home!* Every scent was delicious; every sensation brought back an earlier time. She followed him quickly, coming out on the lagoon beach.

The booming of drums grew louder, and beyond that she heard surf pounding the outer shore. Tepua's coral cuts still stung, despite Ehi's ointment, but she tried not to notice the pain. Just ahead lay the most important dwelling on the atoll—the house of Kohekapu—oblong in shape and thatched with slender *fara* leaves. It had once seemed huge to Tepua, and she wondered if it had somehow grown smaller.

Paruru spoke to the man standing guard, then waved Tepua to go in alone. She hesitated, her pulse beating with the drums of the priests. Then she pulled aside the hanging that covered the low entranceway and ducked into the dim interior of the house.

Her father lay stretched on his thick pile of finely plaited mats, his head on the smoothed log that served as a headrest. Another mat, plaited of coarser leaves, covered him to his neck. Beside him crouched a *tahunga,* a priest of healing, who chanted and waved a small bunch of red feathers.

Kohekapu grunted a command, sending the *tahunga* back a few steps.

Tepua knelt beside her father and pressed her nose to his cheek. The sparse whiskers of his beard seemed whiter than she remembered, the wrinkles of his forehead deeper.

"Come to me, first daughter," said Kohekapu in a cracked and tired voice. "Let me see for myself that the sea gods did not take you."

Swallowing hard, she said, "I am well, Father. My guardian spirit has protected me."

He grunted assent. "Then I owe something to your protector. I will have an offering made to Tapahi-roro-ariki."

"That is kind of you."

"But speak to me, daughter. Tell me of your life in Tahiti. I heard such tales after your brother's visit that I do not know what to believe."

Recalling the incident, Tepua frowned and clenched her fist in anger. Her married brother had come to Tahiti for the Ripening Festival. When he found Tepua there, he demanded that she return with him to her father. She had refused then, earning her brother's scorn. He knew only atoll ways. He could not understand that the gods had brought her to Tahiti and wished her to remain there.

"Father," she said softly. "I have joined the Arioi sect, as you must know. I have pledged myself to serve a high-island god, Oro-of-the-laid-down-spear."

Kohekapu cleared his throat. "I am familiar with this god. The people of Tahiti make much of him. But such a power does not bother with people like us, so distant from the lands that he watches over. We must look to our ancestors in times of trouble. The great Oro will not hear us."

Tepua did not know how to answer him. In her thoughts, she was now a high-islander. While living on Tahiti, the problems of her kin had seemed remote.

"But what will become of you, my sweet flower," he

asked, "with your wild dancing and your foreign god? I know that Arioi women must not bear children. What kind of life will that be, with no sons and daughters?"

"One day, Father, when I have finished my duty, I will leave the Arioi. Then I will have sons. My children will be of the *ariki,* of the high chiefs, not only here but in Tahiti."

"Then you have a man, and one of high birth. I am glad to hear that, daughter. But I regret that he is so far away. It is important that you remain with your own people awhile. That is what the *ringoringo* seems to be telling us."

As she took in his words Tepua's mouth fell open and a chill touched her shoulders. From time to time a child-ghost, or *ringoringo,* flew out from the Vast Darkness, crying faintly beyond the roar of the surf. The voice brought a warning—that some great change was coming.

"Every morning at dawn we have heard it," said her father. "For seven days. The priests tried divination, but learned nothing of what is to come."

Tepua felt her throat tighten. She clasped her father's weathered hand, whispering, "I will stay by you. Until you have an answer, and are well."

"Ah, daughter, do not fool yourself. My body will not get well. Soon my spirit will fly from here to join the ancestors. I will learn what is coming, and then I will send you a message."

She blinked away a tear. "Go now," Kohekapu continued, giving her hand a gentle squeeze. "I must rest. We will talk later."

With a sigh Tepua turned away. Only now did she gaze down the full length of the one-room dwelling, whose thatched walls curved inward as they rose, suggesting the contours of an overturned canoe. Then she noticed, at the far end of the house, the bulky form of Natunatu, her father's second wife, sitting cross-legged as she quietly chanted her own pleas to the spirits. Tepua did not interrupt her prayers.

Long ago, after consultation with the gods, the atoll's ruling succession had been decided. Natunatu's son, Umia, was to be the next high chief. As was customary, Kohekapu retained power until the boy reached a proper age to take up his duties. Tepua frowned as she headed for the doorway, its mat covering now streaming sunlight. Young as he was, Umia might be chief sooner than anyone expected. She hoped the priests and elders had prepared him well.

Outside again, Tepua blinked, dazzled by the sudden brightness. She looked up and saw that half the clouds had blown away, leaving a stretch of blue sky and a brilliant sun. The remaining clouds were quickly vanishing.

She remembered how homesick she had been during her first days in Tahiti. The sights and smells of the atoll had never been far from her mind. Now Tepua wanted to stop for a moment just to look around.

Glancing across the lagoon, its color pale as sand in the shallows, rich azure farther out, she studied distant islets. She and Maukiri, Ehi's daughter, had a favorite. . . .

"Tepua!"

She turned, and her mood brightened at once. Here came Maukiri running along the sandy beach, sturdy brown legs flying. Tepua eagerly embraced her young cousin. "I was picking clams," Maukiri explained breathlessly. "Ehi just found me."

"Ah, it has been so long." Tepua stood back to look at her cousin, the broad face and full lips, the dark hair askew in the breeze. For decoration Maukiri wore tiny fern leaves thrust through the holes in her earlobes. A shade woven of a coconut frond kept the sun from her eyes.

"I prayed every day that the spirits would bring you back to me," said Maukiri, taking Tepua's arm and leading her along the narrow beach. "And now it will be just like before. We will go to our islet, where no one can find us. Stretch out in the shade and say whatever we please."

Tepua recalled the islet, the special *motu*, that she and Maukiri had claimed as their own. It was too small for a family to live on. Coral heads studded the surrounding waters, discouraging casual visitors from risking their canoes. But for one who knew how to get onto the tiny beach, it was a perfect refuge.

"The sun is getting hotter," said Maukiri. "We should go now, before someone finds work for us."

Tepua laughed. Maukiri was talking as if the two of them were still children. She glanced back toward Kohekapu's house.

"You have seen him?" Maukiri whispered, her expression suddenly solemn.

"Yes. He is resting now."

"And Natunatu?"

"Praying."

"Praying that her son will soon be chief," Maukiri answered harshly.

"Let's not talk about that now." Tepua and Natunatu had never gotten along. Tepua could not remember when she had last exchanged even a word of greeting with her father's second wife. But she held no grudge against Natunatu's son. Umia had been a growing youth when Tepua last saw him.

"Look," said Maukiri, pointing to a battered *vaka*, a single-hulled canoe with an outrigger float, that was drawn high up on the sand.

Tepua stared at the old canoe for a moment before she recognized it as one they had often used for paddling about the lagoon. "Have you gotten your brothers to tighten the seams yet?" she asked. Her people built their hulls from small planks, fitted edge to edge and sewn together with coconut fiber cord. After much use, the seams began to leak intolerably. She and Maukiri used to argue about who was to bail, waiting until the hull was half-filled with water before finally getting started.

"Come with me and find out," Maukiri answered in a teasing voice.

Tepua could not resist. Together, she and Maukiri pushed the small outrigger canoe into the warm, shallow water that covered the reef flat near shore. They waded a short way out over the soft bottom, then climbed into the *vaka*.

A slight breeze ruffled the surface of the lagoon as the two young women began to paddle. They were past the reef flat now. Looking down into deep, clear water, Tepua saw gardens of branching coral, a swarm of striped fish, and a baby eel. Long, maroon sea cucumbers lay motionless on the bottom.

The hot sun felt good on her back after the chill of the morning's wind. The canoe rocked gently, stabilized by the long outrigger float that was attached by slender poles. Across the water, trees of other islets stood in clusters.

Tepua glanced back toward the shallows and saw a group of women gathering clams, shucking them quickly and tossing the thick, white shells onto a heap that rose out of the lagoon. Her mouth watered for a taste.

Then she noticed that her feet were getting wet again. "So your boat is as leaky as ever!" she complained as a thin layer of water began sloshing in the bottom of the canoe.

"Not as bad as before," Maukiri protested. "But since you are the honored visitor, I will bail today." They paused, halfway to their destination, while Maukiri scooped out some of the water with a coconut shell. Tepua sat watching for a moment. Then she sighed, picked up a second shell, and began to help.

At last they reached the channel they had long ago discovered, threading their way between coral heads that broke the surface with each gentle motion of the waves. Half the small *motu* was well shaded by palms and thorny-leaved *fara* trees. On the other half, a white sand beach glistened in the afternoon sunlight.

Tepua helped her cousin pull the canoe ashore, then ran over the hot sand into the cool beneath the palms. Thirsty after her paddling, she picked up a green coconut that looked freshly fallen and shook it to listen for the water. It was a *viavia*, the best kind for drinking.

The sharp stake that she remembered still stood upright in

the ground beneath the trees. With a practiced blow, Tepua rammed the coconut's husk onto the stake and started tearing away the thick, fibrous covering.

"That is something new," said Maukiri, when she caught up with her.

Tepua realized what she was doing and felt her face burn. In the past, she recalled, she had always prevailed on Maukiri to do the heavy work of opening coconuts. Tepua had insisted that a chief's daughter must save her strength for more delicate tasks. But in Tahiti, as servant to a chiefess of the Arioi, Tepua had husked enough coconuts— more than enough—to feed everyone on her atoll.

"And I see you are good at it!" Maukiri laughed and went searching for a drinking nut of her own. Tepua paused for a moment, then continued her work. What was the point of pretending she did not know how? With a blade of seashell that was kept conveniently beside the stake, Tepua cut through the "mouth" of the nut and began to drink.

She swallowed the cool, sweet liquid greedily. Even in Tahiti, the coconuts did not taste quite as rich as this one. Within the *viavia*, the soft, white meat had a special fragrance. Tepua held the drained nut in one hand, tapped it sharply about the middle with a rock, and broke it open. With her fingers she brought out the first tender morsel.

At last, thirst and hunger satisfied, the two young women stretched out on a shady part of the beach. "Now you will tell me everything," said Maukiri. "Everything about the men of Tahiti."

Tepua laughed. "They are like our men, of course, but a little fatter. You have seen Tahitian traders."

"I am not talking about *looking* at them! Surely you have a lover by now. Tell me what their *hanihani* is like."

Tepua pursed her lips. Maukiri had reminded her of an old sore point between them. When Tepua was younger, she had been kept from the love games that Maukiri and other young people enjoyed. Because of her noble station,

Tepua's virginity had been protected by a chaperon—old Bone-needle—as well as by *tapu*.

"I do have someone . . . at least I did," said Tepua at last, recalling uncomfortably how she had listened, long ago, to Maukiri chatter about her first boyfriends. "He is called Matopahu. Brother of a high chief, and a great man of Tahiti."

"I hear some doubt in your voice."

"It is not so simple," said Tepua irritably. "He asked me to be his wife and I refused—until I can complete my service to the Arioi. He said he would wait, but now he grows impatient. Someone told me he has another *vahine*."

"Then you must find someone else," said Maukiri cheerfully.

"I can be happy without a man," Tepua retorted. "Remember how much practice I had."

"Maybe you can," said Maukiri. "But I remember how you used to talk about Paruru. When Bone-needle wasn't looking, you would waggle your hips when he passed, and see if he looked at you."

"I just spent ten days sailing with Paruru! I will be happy to see no more of him for a while."

"I think, cousin, that you are not telling me the truth. And I know for certain that now he *does* look at you."

Tepua rolled away in mock disgust. On the journey, her father's warrior had behaved toward her with formal aloofness, though she sensed his interest. And it was true that as a girl she had often thought about his dark, probing eyes and his capable fingers.

"Maukiri, I have heard enough about men. I want to ask you a serious question. Why do I see so many worried expressions? Almost no one seems happy to see me home."

Her cousin did not answer at once. Tepua turned and saw her lying on her belly, tracing patterns in the sand with her fingers. "It is because of the priest, Faka-ora, and all this talk of ghost voices," Maukiri said. "Faka-ora is telling people that a time of trial is at hand, and that Umia is not ready to lead our people through it.''

"If my father recovers, then Umia will not have to."

"And what if we lose Kohekapu? Faka-ora says that the gods may have a new plan for us."

Tepua frowned, unwilling to admit to herself that the old man's spirit might depart. "I still do not see—"

"Ah, Tepua. There is certain to be a dispute now. Here is what some priests and elders are saying. You are the oldest living child of Kohekapu. Why should *you* not be our chief?"

TWO

When Tepua and Maukiri returned, late in the day, they found that Ehi had prepared a welcoming feast. Outside Ehi's house, steam and aromas of cooking food rose from the *umu,* the shallow, circular pit oven. Beneath a covering of coconut leaf matting, fire-heated stones were baking the delicacies. The smells were tempting, but Tepua felt a gnawing in her stomach that dulled her appetite.

She looked around at the small group of guests and realized that all were close kin to her, all women of Ahiku Clan. These women came forward at once and greeted her warmly. Tepua thought she understood now why other islanders had not welcomed her return. A dispute over the ruling succession could throw the entire atoll into turmoil. Everyone expected Natunatu's son to follow Kohekapu. Tepua's arrival could only cause trouble.

"Come, daughter, to your honored place," said Ehi, after Tepua had pressed noses with all the guests. Ehi led her to mats, woven of *fara* leaves, that were spread on the sandy ground. Maukiri brought a coconut shell full of water and spilled some onto Tepua's hands for washing. Then two girls bent over the steaming oven and began uncovering the food.

This feast was for women only. Here, as in Tahiti, men and women cooked and ate in separate groups. Tepua watched silently as the food was brought to her place—a large piece of steaming fish, a pile of clams, baked taro root,

16

cakes made from fruit of the *fara*. She had eaten lightly on the long sea journey. Now she should be famished, yet her stomach felt cold and tight.

The customary silence reigned as each guest tore into the generous meal. Tepua tried to do justice to the fare, but had to force herself to swallow each morsel. She could not get Maukiri's words out of her mind.

She began to wonder, angrily, whether Paruru had deceived her. On his arrival in Tahiti he had said only that her father wanted to speak to her before he died. The warrior had mentioned nothing about the chiefhood.

Perhaps the priests had misled her, she thought. Long ago they had told her that she must give way to her younger brother. She had accepted that decision, agreeing to marry a chief of another island. But the marriage had not taken place. And now the priests seemed to be changing their minds. . . .

Tepua looked up, seeing the tangle of atoll forest that surrounded Ehi's house. Despite all her treasured memories, this island was no longer her home. But the trees seemed so close on all sides, the shadows so deep. In those shadows, the spirits of her ancestors lingered, watching over their people. The spirits might not let her go back to Tahiti.

At last the meal was done, guests packing leftovers in baskets to carry home. Nearly everyone hurried off, anxious to reach their own houses before dark. Ehi's old mother and two daughters remained—Maukiri as well as Maukiri's married sister, slender Roki. Soon Roki's young and portly husband, Adze-falling, arrived from a meal with his companions.

"I have eaten well, and now I am sleepy," Adze-falling announced. His wife looked at him scornfully. Evidently she had hoped he would keep her awake.

Maukiri readied a copra candle—chunks of dried coconut strung on a stick. She blew on some hot embers preserved from the fire until the first piece of copra began to burn.

With this as their source of light, the people of Ehi's household moved into the dark interior of the dwelling.

On such occasions as a homecoming, there would usually be singing and storytelling late into the night. Tepua sensed a less festive mood this evening. Now that the guests were gone, Ehi's expression had become thoughtful, even worried. "We must talk," she said in a low voice.

Adze-falling yawned loudly.

"This concerns Ahiku Clan," said Ehi sharply to her daughter's husband. "If *you* want to sleep, that is no matter."

"Sleep now so that later you will have some life in you," Roki added, giving him a playful slap.

Maukiri laughed, and Ehi whispered a rebuke. "You youngsters think about nothing but *hanihani*! We have serious things to discuss."

The women gathered about the copra light and sat in a circle, facing each other. Tepua, guessing what was to come, wished she could retreat into the darkness.

"I want to warn you all," said Ehi. "We must watch out for Natunatu. She is dangerous. She knows how to get rid of people who stand in her way."

Maukiri, her mood turning suddenly solemn, gave a dismayed cry of *"Aue!"*

"It is true," said Ehi. "We must be certain she cannot use sorcery against Tepua. Every morning, Maukiri, you will check Tepua's sleeping mat for fallen hairs, and dispose of them properly." Ehi held up a small, leaf-wrapped packet. "I have saved the leavings from Tepua's meal. Tomorrow, Roki, you will go with your husband and drown this in the sea. And Tepua, from now on you will take no meals with anyone but me."

Tepua protested. "I have no wish to anger Natunatu. I came only for a visit. Are we to believe idle talk? If the high priest and his friends have plans for me, then why do they say nothing to my face?"

"I know Faka-ora well," replied Ehi. "He is cautious.

He will continue to consult the spirits until he has a confirming sign. Meanwhile it is up to us to protect you.''

"I do not want to be chief. Umia is next—''

"That is not for you to decide,'' replied Ehi harshly. "Daughter,'' she added in a softer tone. "You must listen to the ancestors. They will tell you what to do.''

In the morning, when the others rose early to bathe and to begin the work of the day, Tepua feigned sleep and remained on her mat. "Let her rest,'' said Ehi. "She has crossed a wide sea to come back to us.''

Even Ehi's old mother shuffled out through the low doorway. At last Tepua was alone.

She had decided what to do now, though the prospect troubled her. She still could hear, from long ago, her attendant Bone-needle's voice warning her not to meddle in the realm of priests. Tepua had a rare gift and she was determined to use it.

Adults as well as children played with loops of string, making patterns on their fingers. The figures illustrated everyday objects or favorite tales. But for Tepua this art was far more important—it sometimes brought visions of distant or future events.

Now she looked around the interior of the house, which was lit by sunlight streaming through openings in the thatch. Small utensils—coconut cups, a wooden dish, a coral pounder for *fara* fruit—lay neatly stacked at the base of the wall. Higher up, where rolled mats hung, she found a dangling length of sennit, coconut fiber cord. It was already knotted into a loop.

This was probably a cord that Maukiri used for playing string games. But Tepua's use would not be a game. Through it, the gods might reveal to her secrets that even priests could not obtain.

After taking a glance at the doorway to see that no one was watching, Tepua looped the cord about her fingers. Kneeling, she intoned a prayer, asking for aid from her guardian spirit, Tapahi-roro-ariki, the great chiefess of long ago. Finally Tepua sat and held the loop between her hands.

She began with the ordinary play, making the shapes of an eel, a warbler, a turtle. Gradually she let her thoughts run free so that her fingers moved the strings of their own accord. She began to slip into a daze, losing track of her surroundings, aware of nothing but the tiny world before her.

Her fingers continued to work. The loops kept forming, sliding through each other. The strings crossed and re-crossed. *Now,* a whisper said. *Now the vision may come.* Yet Tepua saw only her fingers and the cord.

She forced herself to keep at it, ignoring the weariness, the heaviness of her arms, the soreness of skin. An answer had never come easily. She watched the strings until she could watch no more. Then, with a cry of despair, she fell forward on the mat. The spirits must be angry with her, for they would not show her anything of what was to come.

She dozed, woke late in the morning, and went out for a bath in the lagoon. A group of Varoa women, people from Natunatu's clan, passed her on the beach; they barely responded to her greeting cry, "May you have life!"

Of course they were angry at her. They had long waited for the son of their clan to take the chiefhood. Tepua bit her lip as she recalled old alliances among the family groups of the atoll. In case of a dispute, Rongo Clan would probably side with Varoa. The conflicts of long ago, settled when her father took Natunatu as his wife, were now on the verge of erupting again.

Tepua gazed out across the lagoon, in the direction of far-off Tahiti. What if she took a canoe now and slipped away before the trouble here grew worse? What a pleasant prospect! But she would not get far before Kohekapu sent a fleet to bring her back.

Even so, a brief escape was still possible. She waded out from shore, feeling the fine sand between her toes and warm water swirling about her knees. Here the underwater reef flat sloped gently, reaching at last a sudden drop-off. She plunged in, swimming angrily, taking out her frustration on the water. She barely noticed the sting of saltwater against the coral cuts that still marked her legs.

In the far distance she saw her little islet, the one called Ata-ruru or "Dense-shade," after a legendary dwelling. If she swam to the place, she thought, then perhaps no one would know where she had gone. Without a canoe missing, they might not even think to look for her there!

The water slid by, helping her forget her turmoil. Vaguely she thought of sharks, but she did not consider them a threat to her now. The dangerous ones usually stayed near the pass to the sea.

The motions of swimming became as repetitive as the game of string figures had been. Once more she felt herself slipping into a daze. Lulled by the rhythm of stroking and the feel of the water sliding past, she grew less and less aware of her surroundings.

Then she seemed to hear a distant murmur of voices. She glimpsed a circle of human figures, men wearing tall feathers in their hair. They were priests squatting together in the sacred precincts of the *marae*.

The men were all staring at something, arguing, moving their hands. Tepua tried to see what they were looking at, but it lay deep in shadow. She strained to make out their words but all she could hear now was a rhythmic splash, splash, splash.

Something was poking her shoulder. She tried to pull away. "Tepua!" a voice shouted, and this time the sound was unmistakable. Her eyes opened. She stopped swimming and looked up to see Maukiri and Roki in an outrigger. "We are going to our *motu*," said Maukiri. "Come in the *vaka*. It is too far for you to swim."

Tepua frowned, wishing her cousin would be quiet for a moment. She wanted to remember the vision, but it had faded. Below her, in the water, a long dark shape was circling.

"I am coming," said Tepua, glancing nervously at the shark. "I want to stay at Ata-ruru awhile." She took a place in the middle of the boat and picked up a paddle.

"We cannot stay long," said Maukiri. "Kohekapu wants to see you. Mother sent us out here only to clean up after yesterday's visit."

With three paddlers, the canoe reached the *motu* quickly. Maukiri led the way to the shady spot where she and Tepua had been sitting the previous day. The broken remains of the coconuts they had eaten lay in a heap beneath a spiky *fara* palm. Inedible parts of the orange-hued *fara* fruit were strewn with the rest.

From the canoe, Roki brought a shovel, a short pole lashed to part of a sea turtle's belly plate. She began to dig a hole in the sandy soil. When sweat ran down her back, she dropped the shovel and told Maukiri to finish the job.

Tepua watched grimly as the two sisters buried the refuse, then smoothed sand over the hole. She wondered if Ehi was taking her precautions too far. It would be bad, of course, for leavings from Tepua's meal to fall into the hands of an enemy. Natunatu might be able to fashion a powerful spell if she obtained something that had touched Tepua's lips.

Feeling downhearted over the trouble that she was causing, Tepua made no protest when Maukiri and Roki prepared to leave Ata-ruru. She had thought earlier that she might try living alone on this *motu* awhile, pulling up clams from the nearby shallows and drinking from coconuts. Now she wondered if she could be safe here.

As the three women headed back the air grew still and the surface of the lagoon became perfectly smooth. In the distance, two long canoes full of paddlers raced each other. From their cries, Tepua knew they were thinking only of their game.

She remembered other days as pleasant as this one, when she had run footraces along the beach or competed in diving for pearl shells. Now, despite the sky's brightness and the sun's warmth, she felt a chill that went deep beneath the skin. The paddle felt heavy in her hands and she had to force herself to keep stroking.

Suddenly the vision came back to her, and she understood what she had seen while swimming. The priests had been engaged in divination, trying to answer their concerns about the chiefly succession. This time she suspected that the gods had given an answer.

When she reached shore, the sun was high overhead, the glare on the sand almost blinding. Paruru emerged from the shade of the bordering palms and beckoned her to follow him. Behind the warrior Tepua saw many eyes watching her from the shadows.

Following Paruru, she approached her father's high-roofed house. To her surprise she saw Natunatu seated *outside* the long dwelling. Beside the chief's wife sat a youth Tepua did not know at once, a tall and well-made young man. *Umia!* She barely recognized him.

Umia lived with his uncle on another islet, so Tepua had not seen him often while he was growing up. In her memory he was still a youngster, running with his friends along the beach. "Life to you!" Tepua said, giving the traditional greeting, first to her father's wife, then to her half brother. Natunatu stared back in silence, her eyes seemingly unfocused. Umia responded coolly, "May you have life."

"That is no way for brother to greet sister," she said, waiting for him to stand and embrace her. He glanced uncomfortably toward Natunatu but did not rise.

Tepua lowered her voice. "None of this is my doing," she insisted. "I will not take what is yours. Even if the priests try to force me—"

"Do not make rash promises," said Umia. "Go inside. They are waiting for you."

"Brother—" She studied his downcast eyes, wishing she had some way to make him believe her. Then she heard soft voices from within the house; it seemed the same murmur she had listened to in the lagoon.

With a sigh she turned from Umia and entered the gloomy interior of the house. Leaving dazzling sunlight, at first she could not see anything within. Then her mouth opened and she nearly cried out in dismay. *So many important people*. As she came in they all grew silent.

Kohekapu remained in his bed, his covering of mats pulled up to his withered neck. He called to her in a tremulous voice. "Daughter, you must do as the priests and elders advise you. Follow their instructions and all will be well." Then he fell back, exhausted by this small effort.

Tepua turned to Faka-ora, the high priest, who sat closest to Kohekapu. His short beard was almost as gray as her father's. His body was lean, his face deeply wrinkled. His nose was like a small clam stuck in the middle of his face.

It was the wrath of this man that Tepua had feared when she first thought about returning home. But Faka-ora was evidently satisfied that the priests of Tahiti had freed her from her misdeeds. He welcomed her warmly and gazed at her with an expression of affection.

With the high priest sat the head of almost every clan of the atoll. Only Varoa and Rongo were not represented. One after another, the clan chief, man or woman, greeted her.

At last, Faka-ora began to speak. "Tepua-mua," he said in a quiet but authoritative voice. "I think you understand why we have come together for this meeting. The ancestors have given us a warning, and we cannot ignore it. Kohekapu is now too weak, and Umia too young to serve our people. But you are here—the highest born among us. It is through you that the gods will provide the leadership that we need."

He gestured toward the others. "The clan chiefs agree to accept your authority." He nodded toward Kohekapu. "Your father also wishes you to succeed him. And now that all are together in this, I urge that we do it quickly. We must invest you with the office, wrap the crimson cloth about your loins."

The mention of that sacred relic brought goose bumps to

her arms. "But—" Tepua struggled for words. "Not every clan is present here. It is wrong to act without them."

The old priest grunted. "We cannot wait for those two stubborn ones to see what is apparent to everyone else."

"I saw Umia just now. He has grown—"

"No, Tepua," the priest chided. "We have studied the signs carefully, not once but many times. Umia is not ready. Nor do we dare trust anyone to act on his behalf."

A quiet voice sounded; everyone turned toward Kohekapu. "I think I know what is troubling my daughter," he began. "She has left a man in Tahiti."

A few eyebrows lifted at that pronouncement, and Tepua felt her face burn.

"You no longer have any sacred obligation to us," the priest told her. "There is no reason now that you cannot take a man. If this Tahitian of yours is of good birth, we will welcome him among us."

She could not answer. Matopahu's ancestry was at least as honored as her own, but what did that matter? He could not leave Tahiti, where he served as adviser to his brother, high chief over a vast territory.

"If you do not wish to bring your Tahitian here," said Heka, chiefess of Piho Clan, to Tepua, "then why not choose someone from your own people? My brother Paruru is known throughout these islands as a man of courage and strength and good looks."

Other chiefs immediately began suggesting candidates. Faka-ora interrupted them. "This is no time to be discussing such questions. Tepua knows she can have her pick of consorts. We will even send canoes to the neighboring islands—"

"Enough!" said Tepua. "I will take no man here. My life is in Tahiti."

"Someday you will go back there," the priest answered in a gentle tone.

"But I am unprepared for this office!"

Faka-ora nodded his head. "Have no fear, Tepua. Have

you forgotten who watches over you? The spirit of your ancestress will enter you and make you wise.''

Her mouth opened, but now she could offer no reply. She was remembering the chant of her great forebear, who had ruled this atoll long ago. From early childhood Tepua had recited the words, even before she grasped their meaning.

> I am Tapahi-roro-ariki,
> The woman who was established on the land.

She felt gooseflesh rising as voices buzzed around her, discussing, planning. In her memory, the chant continued:

> I am Tapahi-roro-ariki,
> Who stood proudly in the *marae*.

''We need time to prepare the grand feast,'' one clan chief complained. ''It will take days.''

''We do not have days to spare,'' replied Faka-ora. ''Send your people out to fish and to gather what they can. Everything must take place tomorrow.''

''Tomorrow?'' another voice echoed with dismay.

''That is when the signs tell us to proclaim our new chief,'' said Faka-ora. ''And now that all is decided, I must go. The *marae* must be readied, the underpriests reminded of their duties.'' He stood up and left the house. Tepua stared after him in disbelief.

What about Umia? Somehow she must make him understand that she was not pushing him aside. He would be chief soon. The priests could not hold her here forever.

Tepua spent the night in a special shelter erected for her just outside the high chief's sacred courtyard. This *marae* was the most revered ceremonial place that her atoll possessed. Only the great men and a few chosen women of the land dared approached it.

All through the hours of darkness she listened to the

priests chanting as they called on the spirits, asking them to attend her investiture. All night the wind whistled through the branches of the lofty *pukatea* trees, bringing the gods' answers.

At dawn, groggy from lack of sleep, she saw a pair of young women approaching her. She emerged from the shelter and stood in deep shade under the flowering trees. The women washed her with fresh water, then rubbed her body with scented coconut oil. An underpriest, averting his eyes, brought her a garment, a simple plaited wrap, but one that had been sanctified in the *marae*.

From afar she heard a sound that made her shiver. The conch shell was being blown, its deep and resonant notes carried to her on the breeze. In every part of the atoll, she knew, people were being roused by that awesome sound.

Dressed and perfumed, she approached the *marae*. The courtyard, a neat rectangle floored with crushed white coral, stood ready for her. She glanced at the wooden coffers, the houses of god images, suspended one beside the other on poles above the stone platform at the end of the courtyard. Along the sides of the *marae* sat the elders on their four-legged stools, each man holding his carved ceremonial spear. The polished wood glinted as morning sunlight filtered through the broad-leaved *pukatea* trees.

Ahead of her, in solemn procession, marched Faka-ora and his assistants, the priests not yet arrayed in their finery. A crowd of highborn people stood watching from a respectful distance. Tepua shivered, hesitating for a moment at the low fence of woven fronds that bordered the courtyard. No woman except one of extraordinary birth could set foot in the *marae*. She had always been warned that the power of the gods would destroy a trespasser.

What if the gods did not judge her worthy? She had no time to reconsider. The priests were taking up their positions, waiting to be invested with the symbols and sacred garments of their office.

Drawing a deep breath, Tepua stepped across the line and

felt a sharp tingle as her foot pressed into the finely crushed coral. She brought the other foot across, and then she raised her head high, gazing at Faka-ora with a feeling of triumph. If she could come this far, then perhaps she could manage the rest. . . .

After that moment the ceremony seemed to blur. Priests made loud invocations. Drums and conch trumpets sounded. Finally there came a great chorus of indrawn breath as the *maro kura,* the sacred crimson loincloth, was unwound and displayed for all the notables to see. They gasped loudly at its brilliant color, elaborate fringing and fineness of its matting. With a slow and dignified tread, the priests began to wrap the *maro kura* about her waist, letting one end fall in front and the other in a regal drape behind. Then the cries rang out, *Maeva ariki!* Exalted be the chief!

From all about Tepua the tributes came. Seabirds swooped down over the *marae.* The surf boomed louder against the reef. Overhead, the *pukatea* trees waved their glossy leaves in greeting.

Later came a procession by water, a tour around the lagoon on the chief's elegantly decorated *pahi.* Along every shore the people stood and called to her, *Maeva ariki!* Children, decked in wreaths, danced on the beaches as she passed.

Even on the lands of Varoa and Rongo Clans many people waved, and hailed her as their high chief. She wondered about the people who refused to accept her. What would they do?

THREE

At midmorning several days later, on the seaward side of the island, a stiff wind was blowing. It came from the northeast, flinging spray and fine sand that stung Paruru's lips. The chief warrior stood on high ground, gazing past the white line of breakers where the sea pounded the outermost reef. Closer in, scattered about the barren tidal zone, lay tumbled blocks of pink and gray-white coral.

The tall coconut palms that lookouts climbed stood just behind him. Paruru had been summoned because of a sighting. He waited now while his men got a better look.

Shortly he heard a voice calling from the closest tree. "Canoe afar!" He frowned, glancing seaward, though he did not expect to spot anything from the ground. Then he looked up at the small figure high above him, clinging just below the fronds. "Who else sees it?" he called back.

For a moment there was a no answer. Perhaps this was a mistake, but he dared not dismiss it. What would Tepua think if he could not warn her of incoming canoes?

When he had gone to bring her home, he had never suspected that she was to be made chief. Often during the journey he had gazed at her, hoping for a glance in return. His own wife's spirit had long since gone to the ancestors, yet he had not found a woman to take her place.

He remembered how Tepua's black hair glistened as it tumbled in waves around her smooth and supple shoulders. He recalled the rich brown of her eyes and the proud way

29

she walked. Were she not chief, how eager he would be for her caresses!

Paruru's sister, Heka, had pointed out what a fine pair they would make. Heka understood nothing about men! It was bad enough that his sister was head of his own clan, which resided principally on a separate islet of the atoll. If Tepua took him as her consort, then a woman would rule his household, his clan, *and* his tribe.

He could not imagine such a life. Even so, he found himself constantly thinking about ways to please his new chief. If visitors were coming, he would make sure that she had plenty of warning.

"Canoe! I see it!" came a second lookout's voice.

"Traders?" Paruru called back eagerly, feeling a tingle of anticipation. Traders from other islands were always welcome, not only because of the goods they carried. They would bring new songs and tales from afar. Paruru would get his share of attention when he told the visitors about his recent long voyage to Tahiti.

He knew another possibility, far less pleasant. The raiders known as Pu-tahi had been sighted recently in nearby waters. They might be coming to his own atoll seeking spoils again—or human flesh for their ovens.

Scowling, Paruru shaded his eyes and peered once more at the horizon. He wished he could mount a force to stand against the Pu-tahi. His own men, brave as they were, had never proved a match for the ferocity of the raiders. Too many lives had been lost in fighting them.

If the man-eating enemies came again, he knew that he would have to withdraw. The clans would take to their canoes and hurry to distant islets of the lagoon. Perhaps the Pu-tahi would be content to plunder the abandoned houses. Or perhaps they would seek out stragglers, the weak and the old, taking them back as offerings to their gods. . . .

"What kind of canoe?" he asked impatiently. When the men did not answer, Paruru decided to look for himself. He picked up a plaited climbing loop that someone had left on

the ground. Choosing an unoccupied palm that leaned away
from him, he stretched the band between his feet, grasped
the tree with both hands and jumped onto its base, gripping
with the callused arches of both feet. Bracing the loop
against the ridged trunk for added support, he began to
climb, pulling himself up in a series of bounds.

Paruru had once been the fastest tree climber among the
island youths, but his spare frame had long since filled out.
The extra flesh, as well as reduced practice, had hurt his
agility. Today he felt even slower than usual. He hoped that
the younger men did not notice.

When he reached the top, he saw the lookout in the next
tree gesturing toward the horizon. Paruru squinted and
followed the other's extended fingers. At first he could see
nothing, but he did not wish to admit that the young man's
eyesight was keener than his own. Then a white dot
appeared, trembling against the blue sky.

"Sails!" Paruru said. An insect crawled across his bare
foot. It made an annoying tickle, but he forced himself to
concentrate on the distant horizon. Had the canoe vanished,
heading in some other direction? No, there it was again on
the crest of a blue-gray mound of ocean.

"I see just one boat," said the lookout. "A lost fisherman
or a lone visitor."

Paruru hoped that the young man was right. "Do not be
too quick to decide," he cautioned. "It may be the lead craft
of a war fleet."

The dot on the horizon grew steadily larger and its
appearance more puzzling. The boat seemed to wallow
excessively on a sea that had only moderate swells.

The lookout apparently had made the same observation.
"It cannot be Pu-tahi," he said. "Pu-tahi would not be
thrown around so. And the sail is very strange."

"Remember how tricky Pu-tahi can be," said Paruru. "I
heard they once pretended to be dismasted and adrift. After
they reached shore, they did not even bother with the usual

ceremonies. They treated the captured men like clams—cut
up their flesh and hung it to dry in the sun.''

''*Aue!*'' said the lookout in dismay as Paruru continued to
study the approaching vessel. He had seen many kinds of
craft during his lifetime and had become expert at identify-
ing them from afar. It was part of a warrior's training.

Each atoll had its own variation on the double-hulled *pahi*
and the single-hulled outrigger canoe—the *vaka*. He had
seen these from all angles, in all possible conditions, from
the fresh timber and clean lines of a new vessel to the
weathered and battered hull of a derelict. He grew frustrated
and then alarmed as he realized that the oncoming vessel
looked totally unfamiliar.

Then he heard the lookout gasp. ''This cannot be possible, *kaito-nui!* The canoe has a single hull, but no outrigger.''

Paruru strained his eyes to see the shape of the vessel
beneath the billowing sail. At first he thought that the
outrigger float had broken away. But how could a canoe
stay balanced without one, especially with such a large
expanse of sail? He remembered watching a *vaka* that lost
its outrigger when worn lashings suddenly parted. The
wind's force had laid the craft right over.

''Only the gods could hold such a *vaka* upright.'' Paruru
glanced to the adjacent tree and saw that the lookout's lips
were trembling.

''We must run,'' said the youth, ''and summon the high
priest. The *marae* must be cleansed, the offerings chosen.
Aue! Aue! The gods are coming!''

Paruru ordered the young man to be silent, but his own
thoughts were in turmoil. Could this indeed be a vessel
bringing divine ones to the atoll? Was this the event that the
ringoringo had foretold?

Paruru knew how fickle the gods could be, benevolent
and savage by turns. He recalled a tale about Oro that he had
recently heard in Tahiti. When the god first visited that high

island, he came in a rage, wasting the land and forcing its people into hiding.

But another thought kept returning to the warrior's mind as he watched the ungainly craft. Would gods disgrace themselves by sailing so poorly?

He could not answer this question and he certainly could not remain up this tree, like a bewildered coconut picker, while the unknown canoe approached his island.

He descended so hurriedly that his warrior's girdle, a narrow, plaited belt around his waist, snagged and tore on the rough trunk. This insult to his badge of office was a bad omen, and blackened his mood as he strode out to find his warriors.

The men emerged from shade when he called them, hurriedly laying their spears into the bottoms of outrigger canoes that were kept on the seaward shore. A gap in the breakers here allowed canoes to be launched directly into the sea.

With shouts and the scraping of wood against stone, the canoes were hoisted up and run into the pounding surf. Spray glistening on their sun-blackened bodies, the men scrambled into the slender hulls and paddled frantically to get out. Paruru joined the melee, leaping into the bow of the largest *vaka*. He felt his canoe leap forward as the paddlers bent to their strokes.

To either side he saw the prows of the other canoes following in a tight formation behind his. Bucking on the rollers, his flotilla arrowed swiftly toward the invader. Now he could see how truly strange the craft was.

Its hull, painted dull red, was as wide as a man is tall and five times longer. The vessel bore no outrigger float, nor any trace of ever having had one. The huge sails flying from the single mast were not made of the stiff plaited mats used by all islanders. They appeared smooth and flexible, billowing out in the wind like enormous pieces of Tahitian bark-cloth. Yet no type of bark-cloth that Paruru knew could hold up to gusts and water without shredding.

Sails hung where he had never seen them—great three-sided sheets fastened to a pole that stuck forward from the prow. The wind made these sails bulge like a pregnant woman's belly.

He heard a cry of disbelief from Two-eels, the warrior behind him. Two-eels was a sturdy young man, a fierce fighter and an able leader of his own *kaito* group. "An outriggerless *vaka* that does not capsize! Cloth sails that do not tear! What kind of vessel is this?" he asked Paruru.

The *kaito-nui* stared ahead, his eyes narrowing. Such signs spoke of magic. Yet, as he watched, the boat lurched and wallowed in the swell, losing the wind. Gruffly he answered, "Gods may have made that vessel, but it is not a god who sails it."

Two-eels agreed, and then Paruru remembered something he had heard while traveling among the northern atolls. Now and again, strange moving islands had been sighted, islands fitted with huge billowing wings. Canoe-masters thought that these might be great *pahi* from afar. The moving islands were said to be as high as the tallest coconut palms, yet able to remain upright in the water.

Such miraculous things seemed scarcely to belong within the world of man, yet Paruru had heard that they were surprisingly flawed. Sometimes these winged visions met with accidents at sea. They fell prey to underwater coral banks, hazards that every seafarer knew to avoid.

Recalling the tales, Paruru scrutinized the oncoming vessel. Though far smaller, it fit descriptions he had heard, and it, too, shared the flaw. It was not heading for the pass, as he had assumed earlier, but on a collision course with the reef!

Paruru shouted at his men to paddle faster, then cupped his hands to his mouth and called a warning to whatever fool might be steering the strange boat. For answer he heard only the washing of the sea and the cries of gulls. The craft held its course.

Spray soaked Paruru's back, and a gust of wind chilled him. Behind him, Two-eels muttered about ghosts. Paruru stiffened as he considered grim possibilities. If the canoe carried corpses, then their angry spirits might still be close by, ready to attack anyone who approached. He would be better letting the reef have such a vessel. . . .

"*Aue!*" came Two-eels's cry.

Paruru, too, had seen it—something moving beneath the other boat's sail. A crouching figure. A head, shoulders, arms, hands. He heard the paddlers arguing among themselves.

"What is that?"

"Shaped like a man . . ."

"A man with blue arms?"

"The blue part is clothing," said one of the older paddlers. The others laughed in scorn.

Paruru sided with the scoffers. What were all those wrinkles, wattles, strips, and flaps hanging off the body? The figure looked more like a kelp-plastered sea creature than a man.

The face had two eyes and a mouth, but the nose stuck out like a bird's bill. The skin was darkened unevenly. The eyes stared wildly from within deep hollows. Hair the color of sun-bleached grass stood up in spikes and tangles about the head.

The figure's motions did not seem human. It lurched, stumbled, groped. When the mouth opened, only a croaking groan came forth.

A figure out of nightmares, thought Paruru, and raised his arm to give the signal to veer away. At that moment the apparition leaned over the boat's hull, extending both blue arms in a beseeching gesture. A hand went to an open mouth, jabbing a finger frantically inward in a sign of desperate thirst.

Paruru sat frozen, his arm still raised. Gods and demons might suffer on their journeys, but never were they reduced to such begging wrecks as this. Despite the odd coverings, this creature before him had to be a man!

Even as the stranger made his appeal, his craft was taking

him toward the frothing waters that pounded the reef. Paruru watched fear spread across the strange sailor's face as he finally realized his danger. Weakness made him clumsy as he struggled with the shaft of his steering oar. Paruru caught a glimpse of other men sprawled beneath the thwarts, but none rose to help.

Now Paruru's thoughts turned in a new direction. The crew seemed incapable of defending their *vaka,* and it seemed a prize well worth taking. Its remarkable sails alone would astonish everyone who saw them. He could not imagine what other wonders the craft held. Yet all would be lost if it struck the reef.

With a yell the *kaito-nui* ordered an intercept course and urged his paddlers to stroke harder. "Steer away!" he shouted at the foreign boat while he gestured at the breakers.

At last the stranger shoved on his oar handle and his craft swung around, heeling so far over that it nearly capsized. The mainsail swung to the wrong side and began to flap and then backfill. The boat slowed, drifting broadside to the wind.

At their leader's command, men at the bows of their canoes tossed loops of sennit cord over the invading vessel's stem post. Bending to their paddles, the islanders struggled to tow the doomed boat off before it could hit the reef. But the backfilling wind in the huge sheets made the task impossible.

"Cut down your sails!" Paruru's shout was hoarse. He knew the order was extreme, for much time and effort went into lashing sails to masts and booms. But unless the stranger sacrificed his rigging, he would lose the boat.

Paruru was not sure if the foreign sailor grasped his meaning. The warrior slapped the side of his canoe with impatience while he watched the other's slow movements, his hands manipulating something at the bottom of his mast. Suddenly the mainsail slid down in a tumble of cloth. More fumbling at a line freed the two foresails, which flapped out to the side like banners.

Paruru gasped in surprise. These strangers had a way of dropping sail that he had never seen before. He had no time to puzzle over this wonder, for he was busy giving orders to his men.

At last the paddlers began to make headway, towing the ungainly craft away from the churning breakers. With voices lifted in a paddling chant, the men drove their blades deep.

The tide was starting to turn now, Paruru noticed as he looked toward the pass. Soon a strong current would be flowing out from the lagoon, a current that his men could not fight. The strange craft must be brought home now or abandoned.

"What is your wish, *kaito-nui*?" called the masters of the other canoes.

Paruru had not forgotten that unseen dangers might lurk on the foreign craft. His task was to protect his people. If he towed the vessel far to sea, and set it adrift, he would be taking the safest course.

But he recalled what he knew of the moving islands that had been seen elsewhere. A few had stopped, sending out men who offered trade—astonishing gifts in exchange for coconuts and vegetable greens. If this craft came from the same place, there might be similar treasure within its hull. What a prize to bring his new chief!

He gazed once more at the remarkable vessel. Perhaps the gods had sent it for his benefit so that Tepua would recognize that her *kaito-nui* was a man of courage. If he let the strange craft slip away, then he would have only words to bring her. . . .

Paruru could delay no longer. He shouted the order to tow the boat into the lagoon. The paddles began again, closing the short distance to the pass.

The lead canoes halted just at the entrance to the channel. Backing water, they waited for a powerful wave to gather. Paruru heard a hoarse cry and looked at the foreigner in the boat. The outsider's face showed alarm as he gestured with

one finger at the surging water. Paruru laughed. Had this
man never before entered a pass?

"The wave comes," he bellowed to the towing canoes.
"Ahead!"

Stroking powerfully, the men drove through the channel
on the wave crest, dragging their load behind them. Paruru
ordered his own canoe to follow. The rush of boiling surf
just beneath the bow, and the jagged coral on the sides of the
pass, made his heart beat faster. He might mock the
foreigner's fear, but a part of him understood it.

There was always a risk of the unexpected here—a canoe
upset or dragged against the reef, a paddler washed overboard, his head smashed or his limbs broken against the
rocks. Perhaps, as Tepua had told him, there *was* an evil
spirit dwelling in the channel. . . .

But this time the ocean's surge carried all the vessels
safely through, into the calm of the lagoon. Once out of
danger, the outsider craned his head about, his expression as
rapt as a child's. The warrior had seen this before—visitors,
particularly high-islanders, gaping at the azure waters and
the graceful sweep of coconut palms against the sky.

The foreign boat now glided easily behind the canoes.
Paruru noticed that the arrival of his odd flotilla was already
attracting attention. Several *vaka* were approaching from
the far side of the lagoon. On shore he saw children running,
and heard their shrill shouts as they tried to keep pace with
the canoes.

Paruru's boat took the lead, and he headed for an
anchorage that lay close to the residence of the chief. Now
he stood downwind of the foreign craft. Cautiously he
inhaled its scents.

At sea, the briny wind had overwhelmed all else. Here,
the smells wafting from the boat were strong—urine,
excrement, and the rotting-pork stink of sick and unwashed
bodies. He caught fainter scents that reminded him of tree
sap. The familiar odors of a *pahi* were lacking—the dry tang

of sennit, the fishy odor of nets and tackle, the aroma of sweet coconut oil from the bodies of one's canoe mates.

He noticed the boat starting to drift, blown by the onshore breeze toward the shallows. "Throw out your anchor stone," Paruru called to the sailor, miming the action of lifting something and tossing it overboard.

Evidently the foreigner understood, but the stone was too heavy for him. Grunting and sweating as he knelt in the bottom of the boat, he finally managed to haul up a huge black fishhook with four prongs. It was attached to a strange line made of many interlinked little pieces. With a clank and rattle that sounded like a cascade of pebbles falling, the anchor descended to the bottom.

The clattering rope grew tight and the boat ceased its shoreward drift. Some of Paruru's men pounded their thighs with approval and amusement. The foreigner was not a total fool. He knew how to drop an anchor stone.

"Drinking nuts!" Paruru demanded, remembering the stranger's signs of thirst. He took a *viavia* that was passed to him from the supply carried beneath the thwarts. Ordering his canoe closer, he tossed the partly husked nut to the eager hands. The stranger brought out a bright blade that flashed sun into Paruru's eyes. Instead of peeling away the bit of green husk that covered the nut's mouth, he began hacking and stabbing at the middle, as if trying to wound an enemy.

Paruru heard whispers from the men behind him.

"He does not know how to drink from the *viavia*."

"He must come from far away. Even our infants know how."

It took several shouts to turn the foreigner's attention from his futile efforts. Finally the ravaged face looked up. The *kaito-nui* held aloft a second drinking nut and showed how to poke open the small mouth at its end. Paruru lifted the nut and drank.

Clumsily the stranger followed suit, making too large an opening and dribbling half the contents down his chin.

Astounded at the man's ineptitude, Paruru tossed him several more coconuts. On his second try, the outsider did better, but began to gulp with a frenzy that alarmed the *kaito-nui*. Paruru had seen starved men kill themselves by swallowing more than their shriveled stomachs could bear. He shouted a warning.

To his surprise, the sailor did not drain the second nut but instead bent to the bottom of the boat. Beneath the tumbled sail lay another man, like himself in appearance except for the dark color of his hair. Cradling the head of his companion in his arm, the stranger poured coconut water on the dry and cracked lips. Paruru watched as a man who seemed dead gradually regained life.

At once he felt a mixture of approval and concern. This stranger was not as stupid as he had first seemed. He knew enough not to sicken himself after his privation. And he was generous enough to help his weaker comrade.

But the presence of a second recovering foreigner, and possibly a third, worried Paruru. How would he deal with these men?

As he pondered the question he grew aware of voices in the distance and the splash of approaching paddles. He turned and saw canoes coming from every direction. On shore, men and women were gathering in a large crowd.

"Stay back!" he ordered, and told his warriors to pass the word along. "No one may board!" He glanced at the onlookers in the shallows—men with sweaty faces, women holding naked babies, girls decked out in sunshades of coconut fronds. He was not sure he could control their curiosity.

"Summon the high priest," he bellowed toward one of his men ashore. Then he called a swift canoe and gave another order—to find Tepua, who had gone to visit Paruru's sister Heka, and bring her back at once.

Tepua would be pleased with this prize, he thought. No other chief had ever captured such a vessel. Yet Paruru felt uneasy as he watched the bright-haired man reviving his third companion. He wished, not for the first time, that Kohekapu had kept his strength awhile longer.

His daughter, lovely as she was, did not possess the wisdom of a chief. Worst of all, she had spent too much time in Tahiti, where men were soft and women lazy. A strong will was needed now. A great chief would know how to use this gift that the gods had sent.

FOUR

As the sun rose toward noon Tepua sat with Heka, Paruru's sister and chief of Piho Clan. The women relaxed on mats laid out under a stand of palms by the lagoon. Within calling distance servants stood ready to bring food or drink. For now, the women were content just to talk.

Heka and most of her clan lived on their own long, slender islet far from the reef's pass. After the frenzy of activities surrounding her assumption of the chiefhood, Tepua had come to this quieter part of the atoll for a few days of rest. Her decorated *pahi* now stood high on the beach, while her paddlers lolled in the shade.

Tepua felt no hurry to return to her own clan. She had come to relax, but also to ask advice. "I am just starting to learn what people expect of me now," Tepua said. "Sometimes I am surprised."

Heka smiled. She was a tall and well-made woman, with broad cheekbones and sparkling eyes. Her sizable figure and deep voice commanded respect, yet Tepua knew that she had a gentle side as well. "Perhaps I can help you, Tepua-ariki," Heka replied.

Tepua sighed as she recalled how a clan chief called White-stick had brought her a problem immediately after she had assumed her duties. "White-stick wanted to discuss his disagreement with Varoa Clan," she explained. "He took me to walk over his lands so I could see where the boundary was disputed. But then I started to ask questions

42

and his mood changed. He turned from worrying about who owns which *fara* tree to complaining about fishing. He seemed to forget about the boundary.''

''That is an old argument he troubled you with. His father could not settle it with Varoa. White-stick will leave it to his son.''

''Then I think he does not truly want an end to it.''

''Now you are showing the wisdom of a chief, Tepua,'' answered Heka. ''If White-stick settles the argument, then what will he have to grumble about?''

Tepua smiled, then picked up the pierced coconut beside her and took a long drink. Gazing out over the placid water, she saw an oncoming canoe in the distance. The men were paddling hard. She wondered vaguely if this was a race, with one boat far ahead of the others.

As she watched with mild interest Tepua tried to imagine what was happening at home. The people of her clan had promised to build her a house near Kohekapu's; by now it should be done. When she went back, she would have to resume the role they had forced on her. But it still seemed impossible.

Tepua squeezed her eyes shut for a moment. She missed the friends she had left behind in Tahiti. How long would it be until the priests and elders consented to let her go? What would it take to convince them that Umia should assume the chiefhood? She knew she could not ask Heka for advice on these questions. Heka had been in the forefront of those urging Tepua to take the office.

Now, in this quiet spot, Tepua heard voices sounding faintly across the water. She opened her eyes and glanced out at the oncoming canoe, a sleek and speedy *vaka*. The bodies of the paddlers glistened with sweat. If they were racing, she wondered, where were their opponents?

Suddenly Heka stood up. ''I think there is trouble,'' she warned. A young man leaped from the boat, swam a few strokes, then stood up and splashed his way ashore.

''*Maeva ariki!*'' the young man managed, though he was

still short of breath from his paddling. Tepua recognized him, Sea-snake, one of Paruru's ablest warriors.

"What is wrong?" she asked uneasily. Sea-snake's words came out in a rush. Tepua held up her hand to stop him, then turned to Heka.

"You go with them," advised Piho's chief. "I will send your *pahi* to follow." Waving the servants aside, Tepua waded into the shallow water.

The paddlers brought the narrow canoe close to shore and held it steady while she climbed in. Then they began stroking, resuming their rapid pace. Sea-snake sat just behind her, and she listened to him gasping out the details between breaths. His words brought only confusing images.

The *vaka* moved swiftly. Soon she saw on the horizon a tall and unfamiliar mast rising out of the lagoon. Up to that moment she had not paid much heed to Sea-snake's babbling about a demon vessel.

Islanders sometimes came from afar, she knew, sailing strange craft. But the sight of this foreign mast gave her a chill. As the paddlers continued, she peered ahead, waiting with curiosity as well as fear to glimpse the hull that Sea-snake had described.

She saw first only a dense cluster of local canoes and could not tell what lay at the center of attention. Then, as she came closer, someone had the sense to blow a conch trumpet and announce her presence. The canoes began to clear from her path.

Tepua drew in her breath when, at last, she had a clear view of the wide hull and the oddly clothed people within. Sea-snake had said that the craft possessed no outrigger float, but only now did she believe him. The hull rocked even in quiet water. She could not imagine what would keep it from tipping in a heavy sea.

Suddenly she recalled a troubling tale from Tahiti, of a prophecy that old people remembered. An oracle had said that one day a huge vessel with no outrigger would appear, and that its arrival would bring sweeping changes. She had heard that priests made offerings to the gods in hope of forestalling that day.

She narrowed her eyes. Here was a *vaka* that floated with no outrigger, but it was not huge. And the crew seemed in no condition to harm anyone. With rising interest, she ordered her canoe closer and studied the strange figures aboard the vessel.

Sea-snake had talked of oddly colored sea demons, but the face peering at her over the washboard resembled that of a frightened man. She saw black hair and eyes like those of her own people, a protruding nose, and a mouth with thin lips. The dark-haired stranger crouched, cradling something in his lap, but she could not see what he held.

Stretched out in the boat's bilges lay a second sailor. The shade of this one's hair made her raise her eyebrows, for it was red, a color rarely seen among islanders. He appeared younger than the others, almost a youth. His face showed a pained expression as he lay amid a tangle of ropes and sails. Only a slight twitch of his mouth indicated that he remained alive.

When her gaze moved to the third outsider, she gasped in astonishment, wondering if Sea-snake had been right after all. This one truly appeared to be more demon than man. His hair was impossibly bright—the tawny gold of sand beneath the afternoon sun.

He seemed in better condition than the others, though his face was bristly, his skin a peeling and mottled reddish brown. He sat straddling a thwart near the center of the boat, scooping soft meat from a coconut and stuffing it into his mouth. As he watched her draw closer, he stopped eating, put aside the coconut, and stared back at her.

Tepua blinked twice, unwilling to believe what she saw. Were his eyes really that intense blue-green or was it a reflection off the lagoon? Even at a distance she was startled by the aquamarine lightness against the bronze of his face.

She felt the drumming of her pulse as she remembered legends of evil spirits from the sea. *"Aue!"* she cried, looking away from him to the comforting black and brown eyes and hair of the islanders.

But spirits did not need boats to carry them, nor did they suffer from hunger or thirst. Their skin did not blister and peel beneath the sun. This was a man, she concluded, not an apparition. If she drew closer, she was certain that she could touch the rough bristles on his face.

Her fingers prickled as she imagined how it might feel. A shiver ran up her back, and she ordered her paddlers to hold their place. Even if these outsiders were men, invisible dangers might be lurking aboard their vessel. Until she summoned the high priest, she dared not touch anything.

The blue-eyed sailor stared at her as if expecting her to speak. Still uncomfortable with her new role, she felt her words catch in her throat. "I am . . . the high chief," she managed. "Tell me where you came from."

He answered only gibberish. She questioned him again, but could not grasp his speech. Yet she knew, from watching other visitors, how people could talk using signs. Hoping to learn his place of origin, she gestured with an open hand toward one horizon, then back to the foreign boat. When he did not respond she gestured in another direction. At last he seemed to understand, for he pointed with his forefinger toward where the sun rose.

As he did so the coverings on his arms fell back, revealing tanned forearms and wrists that lacked any tattoos. Tepua frowned, trying to remember what she had heard of eastern islands. These men certainly had not come from the atolls that her people knew. Perhaps they had crossed the vast seas that lay farther east.

"How many days' sail?" she asked. She moved her hand across the sky following the sun's path, then mimicked sleep by laying her head down on her hands.

The sailor answered by holding up his fingers. He kept holding them up and taking them down until Tepua laughed. No one could sail for that many days!

The bright-haired stranger spoke again as if trying to

explain. Despite his unfamiliar features, Tepua saw an earnestness in his expression and sensed that he was not joking. He pointed at his *vaka* and held his hands up with a short gap between the palms. Again he pointed to the *vaka,* this time spreading his hands far apart.

For a moment Tepua was confused. Among her people, one showed the length of something like a fish by holding the edge of one hand across the other arm.

"A larger boat?" Tepua asked. The man kept making signs and gradually she understood. He had sailed for many days in a far larger vessel. In this *vaka,* he had spent only fifteen nights. She could not understand what had happened to the other vessel, only that it was gone.

How he had run out of food and water remained unclear. Perhaps some of his supplies had washed overboard, or he had expected to find land long ago. The frustrating task of communicating had worn down her patience. In silence, she studied the sailor, hoping for answers to questions she could not ask.

Though clothing covered him, she could see that his limbs were nicely shaped, his shoulders broad, his arms well muscled. Despite his exhaustion and privation, he carried himself proudly, showing no fear of the warriors in the boats that faced him. His features were far more angular and hard-edged than those of her people. The contour of his nose was straight rather than curved softly inward.

The planes of his cheeks seemed to echo the determined line of his nose, for they slanted back and to the side. In this way he seemed very different from her people. His entire face had more forward thrust, as if it contained a restless spirit fighting to get free.

And those mesmerizing eyes! It was as if a god had taken a handful of water from the lagoon depths, preserved the magic of its color, and poured it into them.

At last, with some reluctance, she ordered her paddlers to take her ashore. Canoes filled with warriors stayed behind to keep any curious fishermen from getting too close. She

glanced back, watching the strange sight of the foreign craft
ringed loosely by outrigger canoes.

On the beach she found the high priest waiting. Faka-ora,
his eyes sunk deeply in the wrinkles above his cheeks,
shuffled forward to speak with her. The vast crowd of
onlookers stood back at a respectful distance. Even the
children kept silent.

"Do you know the famous prophecy?" Tepua asked the
priest in a low voice.

"I do," he answered.

"But this is not Tahiti," she said. "Nor is it the first time
a strange craft has been seen among the atolls."

"So I have heard."

"Then tell me, Faka-ora. What do you make of this
strange arrival? Are the men dangerous?" In her mind she
thought she knew how he would answer, yet she held a faint
hope.

Faka-ora pursed his lips. "We have listened to the
ringoringo crying. Now we are visited by people unlike any
we have seen before."

She replied in a tone of disappointment. "Then this is
what the voice was warning us about?"

"I am sure of it."

Tepua frowned, recalling the sorry condition of the men.
They had come from afar, enduring hardships she knew
well.

Not long past, after days of suffering at sea, Tepua herself
had been washed up on a foreign shore. She understood
what these men had undergone. "In Tahiti, I learned
something else," she told the priest. "The people there help
a stranger who is in need. A simple fisherman took care of
me once, though he knew nothing of my family and had no
hope of reward."

"Then give these strangers food and drink," said the
priest. "Enough to stock their canoe so they can sail on. I
see little harm in that. But I advise you strongly—do not
allow those men ashore."

"If we send them off, they will not get far," Tepua said. "Their vessel will tip over in the first squall. And if it does not, I am afraid that some hungry Pu-tahi will catch up with them."

"Then the man-eaters deserve whatever ills the strangers afflict on them," Faka-ora said scornfully. He glanced aside as footsteps approached. Tepua saw that Paruru had just arrived.

The *kaito-nui* had discovered the foreign vessel and brought it in. She asked him if he had a plan for dealing with the outsiders.

"I see no weapons in their boat," Paruru answered. "But they carry other things that I would like to examine."

"Then you do not think the foreigners dangerous?"

Paruru laughed. "Three weak men against all of us? How can they be?" Yet Tepua noticed a worried look in his eyes.

"Once when I was traveling to the north," Paruru continued, "I met a chief whose wife wore a necklace like none I had ever seen. It was made of shiny blue stones, each round as a pearl but much bigger. The necklace came from strangers like these—men who clothed their legs. That is the kind of gift I would like for you, Tepua-ariki."

Tepua stiffened, wondering at his motives. "The outsiders have not offered to trade us anything," she answered cautiously. "Even if they did, would Faka-ora allow us to touch the foreign things?"

"The chief's wife I saw was in good health," Paruru answered. "After many years of wearing her necklace."

"But *our* visitors have the evil of sickness about them," the priest objected. "Perhaps the traders who brought that necklace were not so out of favor with their gods as are these men."

"I have also seen an adze made of a stone we do not know," Paruru continued in a tone of longing. "It was far better than any high-island adze. The edge was hard and very sharp. You should have seen it cut!"

Tepua recalled the discussion she had had with Heka,

about men who argue endlessly and do not settle. "I have heard enough," she said suddenly. "I, too, am curious about what these strangers carry, and what they can tell us of the world that lies toward the dawn."

When she saw Paruru and Faka-ora staring at her, her mouth grew dry. So far she had been chief in name only. She had given orders, but only to servants. People had come to her with problems, but had not really wanted to hear her advice.

Now, for the first time, she was about to assert her authority . . . and see if these important men were willing to listen.

She began cautiously. "I do not wish to turn these foreigners away. I will help them, but without allowing them ashore." The priest's bushy eyebrows rose, but he said nothing to contradict her.

"Faka-ora," she continued. "I ask you to find a *tahunga* who will try to heal the sailors. If they recover, then we will know that their gods have been appeased, and that we need not send the men away."

The high priest did not reply at once, and she tried to find an answer in his glittering eyes. In the silence she heard her pulse drumming in her ears, beating faster. . . . "It will be done, *ariki*," he said. "I will bring a *tahunga* who is so powerful that he is safe from foreign evils. He alone can risk boarding the vessel."

She glanced at Paruru. Did he, too, accept her decision? He was the one most eager to examine the foreign craft, but perhaps he was not willing to wait. He merely gazed at her, in mute agreement with her plan.

Tepua lifted her chin. "Then I will go and tell the strangers my decision."

Paruru ran on ahead. Passing one of his guards on the beach, he took the man's spear, lifting it high as he went. He made an impressive figure as he strode through the shallows, sunlight brightening his tattooed back and thighs. Yet something about the warrior troubled her. He seemed to be trying to please her—trying too hard.

She watched him a moment longer as he joined a canoe filled with his men. Tepua climbed into a small *vaka* and led the way toward the visitors' craft, hearing the splashing of many paddles behind her. Glancing to the side, she saw Paruru gaining on her, while several double-hulled war canoes followed closely. The men standing on deck held their long spears at ready, the sharp bone tips pointing out over the water.

On their vessel, the outsiders stirred, looking up with alarm. "Do not frighten the foreigners," Tepua called back. "Go slower," she ordered her paddlers. "Everyone, slower!"

Ahead, she saw the black-haired man staring at the oncoming canoes. A sudden look of fear crossed his face. "We come to offer you help," she shouted to him across the water. Now she wished she had brought a young palm branch as a sign of her peaceful intentions.

The dark-haired stranger, crouching near the bow, glanced down at the thing he was holding. His hands moved, but his actions remained hidden. Then he lifted something resembling a straight shaft the length of a man's arm; he pointed it toward the sky above Tepua's head. From the stern, his light-haired companion shouted what seemed a warning, but the other man took no notice. The light-haired man shouted again, lunged forward, clambering over the thwarts. . . .

A sudden dread gripped Tepua. "Is that a weapon?" she cried. Then a noise shook her, a sound louder than thunder. Gray smoke billowed. Men screamed, some diving into the water. On shore, the crowds fled the beach.

Tepua felt fear pounding inside her chest, but she forced herself not to move. She smelled the harsh smoke, unlike any she knew. Then she saw Paruru, whose paddlers had never halted. His arm was raised, his spear tip aimed at the man who held the terrifying thing. She called out, trying to stop him, but the warrior did not seem to hear.

The dark-haired sailor tried to dodge. He could not move quickly enough. Paruru's long spear thrust forward. . . .

The foreigner gave a cry as the slender bone point plunged into his gut. Then his hands flew up and the weapon tumbled from his grip, dropping with a splash into the lagoon. The bright-haired sailor tried to help his companion, but Tepua saw there was no hope for the man.

"Everyone move back!" she shouted. At last, Paruru's men complied. Warily, she ordered her canoe to approach the foreign craft alone. Her paddlers were trembling and she understood their fear. What if the strangers possessed another of those weapons?

"We do not wish to harm you," she called. "We want only peace."

The bright-haired man paid no heed to her. He bent over his companion, his face contorted by grief. Tepua felt a flood of sympathy.

She called to the few people left on shore, and to those brave ones who were creeping back from the shadows. "Bring gifts of friendship—mats, baskets. Light a fire and bake food for the strangers." Then she turned once more toward the mourning sailor.

She knew only one way to express her feelings, her *aroha*. She let out a mourning wail, as if one of her own people had died. The women on shore understood at once; they also began to wail. Some picked up sharp pieces of coral and gashed their foreheads. Then others came out from hiding, a long line of women. They waded a few steps into the water and faced the strange *vaka*. The din of their cries, Tepua hoped, would be heard even by the gods of these foreigners.

At last the grieving sailor looked up and made signs toward Tepua. He wanted to come ashore, she realized. He pantomimed digging a hole, burying the body.

"We cannot allow that," Tepua called back sadly.

The man made more signs and beat his fist angrily against the side of the boat.

"No. That is not our custom." Tepua was relieved to see the high priest coming in a canoe to speak with her.

"Tell him," said Faka-ora shortly, "that the corpse must be given to the sea. The great waters will make it clean."

"You must go out," she called to the sailor as she pointed to the pass. "Out to the ocean again. We will help you, and then we will bring you back here. We are your friends."

The stranger stared at her in silence. She could not tell if he believed her. Those eyes spoke of thoughts that she feared she might never understand.

Sometime later, after the tide had nearly ceased to ebb, Paruru stood on shore while he watched the dead man's journey begin. Taking advantage of the slight outward current, a *pahi* began towing the foreign craft toward the pass. Paruru observed this operation with relief. He knew the importance of sending the dead man's soul on its way. The spirit could cause grave harm if allowed to linger here.

Earlier, Paruru had watched the stranger with water eyes wrap a piece of sailcloth around his fallen friend, weighting the contents with blocks of coral sent from shore. Now the outsider sat staring at the bundle he had placed in the bow of the boat. The other surviving sailor, the one with red hair, had recovered somewhat, and sat close by his grieving companion. But the younger man kept looking about nervously, as if afraid that another spear might come.

All along the shore, people stood gazing at the odd procession. Many continued their mourning, men as well as women. For now, all attention was directed toward the boats.

Paruru glanced around and was glad to see that no one was watching him. What he had to do now would not please Faka-ora. But Paruru had spoken with another priest, and believed that he could carry through his plan safely.

As he waded out toward where the foreign vessel had been anchored, Paruru recalled with satisfaction the bold moment of his attack. Even the weapon's roar had not shaken him. How many other warriors could boast of facing such a danger? Soon, travelers would carry songs of his deed throughout the atolls. People would speak of the weapon he had overcome, calling it the thunder-club or the spewer-of-smoke.

It troubled him that Tepua seemed far more angry with him than impressed by his courage. In time, he hoped, she would understand what had happened, realizing that he had saved her life from another blast of that terrible weapon. And greater things might come of this incident. . . .

Paruru waded deeper, feeling warm water swirl about his thighs. At the edge of the sloping reef flat, he dove into the clear depths. He swam a short way out, and then down. The dropped weapon lay just below him, resting among the dark sea cucumbers. The thing lay in plain view, where anyone could find it. He did not want to lose this prize.

As a boy, seeking pearl shells, he had often gone far deeper. He remembered holding on to ledges, pulling himself along the bottom, staying under longer than any of his friends. But now, as he kicked his way into the chillier depths, he felt an unexpected need for air. He stretched his arm downward, but the bottom still lay out of reach.

Angry with himself, he came up gasping for breath. What a fool—to dive without preparing himself! Swimming toward a submerged coral head, he found a place to stand. With waves lapping at his shoulders, he whispered a brief prayer to his guardian spirit.

Next he began his exercise, pulling in deep breaths and blowing them out quickly. Again and again he did this, until he felt almost dizzy. This time he carried a chunk of coral, to make the descent easier. He dove once more, using feet and his free hand to help pull himself under. The water pressed against his ears and eyes with a force stronger than any he remembered.

This was not right. Some evil force was trying to keep him from the weapon. He refused to give in to it, though the pain in his ears grew fierce. Kicking with a frenzy, he fought his way down to the stony floor. Then his hand touched the hard shaft of the weapon and he closed his fingers around it.

Releasing his stone, he rose in a cloud of bubbles, his body upright, his hands raised over his head. As he neared the surface he remembered to pull the weapon out of sight. His head and shoulders broke the surface, and then he felt acute pain shooting through his body. He could scarcely see and barely had strength to keep his head afloat.

For a time he knew only the pain that filled him. At first he feared this was his punishment for touching the foreign thing. Then he recognized the diver's agony, though it had never afflicted him so severely. The suffering would end soon, he knew, and then all would be well.

Slowly, his senses returned. At last he could look toward shore, and was relieved to see that his dive had attracted no attention. He began to swim at a moderate pace, preserving his strength. His destination lay a good way down the beach.

When he staggered out of the water, Paruru felt weak in all his limbs. Exhausted as he was, he remembered to be careful with the thunder-club. It had erupted when the man pointed it skyward. Paruru held it low, pointed toward the ground.

His swim had brought him to an isolated and rocky shore, a place he had chosen for privacy. A dense stand of *mikimiki* bushes reached almost to the water and screened the interior from view. He crawled under the low-hanging branches and emerged in a shadowy forest. As arranged, the priest named Lost-the-wind stood waiting for him.

Lost-the-wind was younger and stouter than his superior, Faka-ora. Paruru had found him far easier to deal with than the older priest. Lost-the-wind had agreed to dispel whatever evil might adhere to the weapon, and to the *kaito-nui* for touching it. Now, as Paruru stood before him, the priest lifted a coconut shell filled with seawater. He sprinkled its contents, first onto the warrior and then onto the object he held.

After Lost-the-wind recited a long prayer, he led Paruru to a crude shelter, a thatched roof on four poles that was screened by bushes and young trees. Around the shelter, *tapu* signs made of coconut fronds had been tied to branches, to warn off anyone who came by.

"Stay here," the priest said, signaling for Paruru to go in under the roof. "I have left food and drink. Do not come out for three days. If all is well after that, you are safe."

Paruru went meekly into the shelter. He gently placed the weapon on a mat and seated himself beside it. Drinking nuts lay waiting for him, but he did not want anything just yet. "The arrangements are pleasing," he said in acknowledgment of the priest's efforts. He would make return gifts later, of course.

"Then I go," said the priest.

Paruru sighed, resigning himself to three days of solitude. His curiosity about the rest of the outsiders' goods would have to wait. But he had what might prove to be the most important item.

For a time he did nothing but stare at the mysterious weapon. Much of it was made of polished wood, broad at the back, long and slender in front. The part that resembled hollow bamboo was made of something he did not recognize. Its color was gray as a stormy sea, its surface smooth and cool.

If this was not wood, then he assumed it must be a kind of foreign stone. Paruru bent his head down so that he could look in through the hollow end, which flared slightly. What a marvel! He wondered how long the carver had worked on it.

More important was learning how to use the weapon. He had thought, at first, that merely pointing the hollow end in a certain way would make the noise. Now, with sudden bravado, he seized the thunder-club and pointed it above the trees.

No blast!

Only faintly disappointed, he turned his attention to the strange parts near the center of the weapon. Perspiration ran down his chest as he imagined the noise erupting again. Yet it had not seemed to hurt the black-haired sailor. It was Paruru's spear that had brought the man down!

Slowly he let his fingers explore the puzzling mechanism. One part resembled a bird's head on a long and sinuous neck. Below this hung a long, narrow tooth. He poked and prodded, discovering eventually that the bird's head could move. He had to exert some force to pull it back a short way, and suddenly it slipped from his fingers. The beak sprang down and struck a tiny bowl. Sparks flew . . .

He yelped in surprise. The weapon sailed across the floor of his shelter. But still there was no blast of thunder.

He began to laugh at himself for his fear. Retrieving the thing, he held it once more on his lap. There was a secret here, one that would take patience to discover. This time he forced himself to watch carefully as he pulled back the head and let the beak strike. Once more, sparks jumped in the bowl.

Despite his surprise, he managed to hold on to the weapon. He produced sparks several times, but that was all he could achieve. Something was lacking, and only the foreigners could tell him what it was.

He lay back and wondered how he could get the answer.

FIVE

The next morning Tepua stirred at dawn. This was a quiet time, when the only sound was the distant roar of waves pounding the reef. She sat up in the gloom, waking in the house that had just been built for her. Using material brought from every part of the atoll—rafters, cord, sheets of thatching—the structure had been hastily erected. Compared with the open, airy Tahitian houses, it felt low and cramped. But the furnishings were the best her people could offer—mats, fine baskets, stools of polished wood. In the air Tepua smelled the tang of drying leaves and the subtler scents of the building's lashed, wooden framework.

Her attendants still lay sleeping in a row, one stretched out beside the other. Tepua could sleep no longer, not on this morning. Her thoughts turned to the welcome news brought last night by the *tahunga*. Under his treatment the foreigners showed signs of improving. She had hope now that their gods would relent and take away their sickness.

Eager to see how the strangers were faring, Tepua rushed outside before her yawning servants could rouse themselves. On the expanse of coral sand in front of her doorway, her paddlers also lay asleep. They jumped up from their mats when they heard her approaching and raced to launch her *pahi*.

The first rays of sunlight touched the beach. She stopped a moment to gaze out at the foreign vessel, anchored beyond the underwater reef flat. With its wide, red-painted hull, the boat seemed utterly out of place there. Lagoon water lapped quietly, disturbing the reflection of the bare mast and its stays. She could see nothing of the sailors and assumed that they were sleeping beneath the thwarts.

Tepua glanced about her, noting that the shore was almost deserted. What a change from yesterday's commotion! Yet she knew how fast word of the remarkable arrival could spread. Soon the waters would be teeming with canoes. If she wanted a quiet visit with the strangers, then she must go to them now.

Guards stood waiting to join her on her *pahi*. They held their spears upright, the ends resting lightly on the ground. "Stay here," she told the men.

"The *kaito-nui* said we must remain with you," the leader of the guards insisted.

"Then where is he? I will have him change your orders."

The guard looked first at his companions and then down at his feet. "Paruru's hand touched the foreign vessel," he said in a low voice. "A priest sent him away—to make sure that he took no taint."

Tepua scowled. She had not heard anything about this from Faka-ora. "I admire the priest for his caution, but with Paruru gone you must take orders directly from me. No warriors. I do not want the strangers frightened again." She turned, signaled to a brawny paddler, and was carried through the shallows onto the waiting craft.

"*Ariki!*" the warrior captain cried from shore. "We do not know what weapons these foreigners have. Let us follow you in our own canoe. We will not approach unless you need us."

Tepua sighed. The strangers had shown no signs of hostility since yesterday's unfortunate event, yet she knew that the man's advice was sensible. "Launch your canoe," she told him, "but stay near shore. I will signal if I want you nearer." Then she stood on the deck while the *pahi* was quietly paddled toward the outsiders' vessel.

She came far closer than she had on the previous day,

almost close enough to climb aboard. In the bottom of the
boat, between the thwarts, lay slender paddles, coils of rope,
and other gear. In the stern, a long seat held uneaten
coconuts and leaf-wrapped packets of food. She saw round,
drumlike constructions of wood, but none seemed large
enough for a man to crawl into. Where were the sailors?

Then the faint sound of snoring made her look again.

"They sleep hanging!" exclaimed a paddler.

When Tepua saw what he meant, she began to laugh. A
long bundle of cloth hung just above the thwarts, one end
tied to the mast, the other to a pole that was lashed upright.
A sailor's arm dangled from the bundle. From a second,
similar sling she saw a foot protruding, but neither man
stirred.

"All you paddlers—out of the way," she ordered,
motioning them toward the stern of her own boat. She did
not want the waking sailors to see a crowd peering at them.

While the outsiders continued dozing, her attention returned to the drumlike containers. Most lay turned on their
sides, reminding her of the hollowed logs used in Tahiti for
holding valuables. The walls of these foreign boxes were of
thin planks, tightly joined, but with no sennit binding. What
kept them from falling apart?

One container stood on end in the stern. The top was open
and she caught a tantalizing glimpse of bright colors within.
She leaned closer. While the men slept, she thought, she
might easily step aboard and look inside. . . .

No. She remembered what had happened to Paruru. She
would have to wait for Faka-ora to tell her when she could
safely go aboard.

Then she noticed another thing that made her cautious.
Near the suspended bed lay a pole with a blade lashed to one
end. The tip was made of some lustrous material—perhaps
a kind of shell—that she had never seen before.

This was surely a weapon, though it appeared to be
something that the men had hastily put together. The handle

was short for a spear and lacked a proper grip, but the blade looked extremely sharp. Each of the men had one.

Her concern grew as she searched the boat for anything else that might be dangerous. The strangers might have lost one weapon, but they knew how to improvise others. Her first impulse was to command her warriors to go aboard and confiscate the crude spears, but Faka-ora had forbidden any contact. Uneasily, she gave an order to the paddlers, widening the gap between herself and the foreign craft.

"Life to you!" she shouted from a safe distance, hoping to wake the two sleepers. A hand stirred. The light-haired sailor swung his legs out and got down from his hanging bed. His appearance was less shocking now than when she had first seen him, certainly less bristly. Evidently he had scraped the whiskers from his face. The ointments of the *tahunga* had helped his skin.

She pointed to the sailor's spear, trying to make clear her displeasure. Then she pointed to her own vessel, showing that her men had put aside their weapons. This seemed to relieve the sailor, for he set his implement behind him, its blade facing away from her. He did this hastily, as though something else was on his mind.

The sailor made signs, first pointing his finger at Tepua, then making a motion with his arms. When she did not respond, he put his hands over his eyes, then pointed once more at her. Was this a game? she wondered. Or an insult? Among her people, pointing with the forefinger was considered rude.

The foreigner seemed in distress, making odd grimaces and shifting his weight from side to side in an impatient dance. Shaking his head and frowning, he finally turned his back to her and urinated noisily over the side. When he returned, his face was even redder than before.

Tepua wished that she could grasp his thoughts. She suspected that a custom or *tapu* of his people had been broken, though she was not sure how. For a moment she stared at him in frustration.

She had thought about the problem of communicating with the strangers. Signs would not be enough. She would have to teach them her language, or there could be no hope of making them feel at ease, or of learning anything about them.

She began with a simple first step, placing her hand on her chest and speaking her name.

The sailor looked up at her, and he seemed to regain his composure. Again she took in his alien yet compelling features. Compared with the faces she knew, his nose appeared narrow, even pinched. Yet an ordinary nose, she thought, would ruin the strange beauty.

He opened his mouth, and she realized that he was trying to repeat what she had said. "Mua-ariki . . ."

She spoke it again, and this time he managed the whole name.

"Tepua-mua-ariki."

"Well done!" she praised, then gestured toward him, hoping he might speak his own name in reply. He did make a sound, while poking a thumb at his chest. When she heard his strange noise, her mouth fell open. "Again," she urged. Once more he made sounds that she had never heard before.

Suddenly she felt foolish. Some time ago she had come to grips with differences in speech, discovering that the people of Tahiti could not pronounce the "k" and the "ng" of her atoll language. Now here was a stranger who made sounds that even she could not manage.

She tried to repeat what the sailor had said, but one part eluded her. "Kiore!" she said at last, coming as close to his name as she could manage. "You are Kiore. Tell me what you call your friend." She turned in the direction of the other hanging bed. The ruddy-haired stranger was looking out through half-closed eyes. At her insistence he emerged, warily, and sat on his own thwart at a distance from her. He put his spear across his lap.

This second outsider seemed much younger than his companion. His eyes were gray-green, his face sunburned and peeling; a few wisps of reddish beard decorated his chin. She asked again for his name, and Kiore answered, "Nika."

"Nika." This name came more easily to her tongue. "Nika, you do not need that weapon," she told him. Kiore said something in his own language, and his companion finally put the spear aside. But she could not induce Nika to come closer, so she turned her attention back to Kiore.

She gestured at the sky and spoke. When he mastered that word, she taught him "paddle" and "mast," then started on parts of the body—the lips, the eyes. *Eyes*. She paused and cocked her head as she studied his. "Brown eyes," she said, pointing to her own. "Lagoon-water eyes!" she said, pointing to his face.

He laughed and repeated what she had told him. What a pleasant expression he showed at times! He seemed willing to continue, though she sensed that he was still weary from his ordeal at sea. What could she teach him next? She could not help staring at the garments that fully covered his arms and legs and feet. If only she could reach across, touch the strange cloth, and feel what lay beneath.

"Foot," she said, bending to touch her own, which was bare. She rose and waited to see how he would respond. He hesitated, finally sat on a thwart, and began to adjust his stiff foot covering. Tepua watched with curiosity as he pulled it free. . . .

"Foot," he repeated, but there remained a tube of cloth that started at his toes and ran up his leg. Why so many layers? In frustration, Tepua bit her lip as she thought of more questions she wished to ask him. What were the women of his people like? Did they also wear so much clothing? How long did it take to unwrap themselves? She stamped her heel, wishing she could find some quick way to make herself understood.

Kiore began to take the initiative, sometimes speaking his own words as well. He pointed to his knee, gave his name for it, and then repeated hers. His hand slapped against his thigh and he made another foreign sound. Tepua lifted her mat skirt to point to her own thigh, and noticed his face redden again. From the side, Nika shouted something, and Tepua realized that the other sailor was finally taking an interest in the lesson.

They continued awhile longer, until Kiore grew tired. He moved to a seat under a length of sailcloth rigged as a shade. Tepua watched him with regret. The lesson had been like a child's game, yet more fun than any she had played in a long while. "I will send fresh food," she promised, miming as she spoke to make herself clear. "The *tahunga* will look after you. Tomorrow we will talk again."

Arriving on shore, Tepua ordered the guards to keep all her people away from the foreigners. As she glanced across the lagoon she saw canoes coming even as she spoke. A fleet of outriggers had arrived, all so packed with people that they were barely afloat. She sent the warriors out to hold them back.

Then she went to see how Kohekapu was faring. Lately he had been too weak to say anything to her. Today, when she entered his house, she was pleased to hear him speaking.

Natunatu sat at his side. Tepua made no attempt to greet the woman, for she knew she would get no response. "Daughter," said Kohekapu in a fragile voice when Tepua knelt close to him. "Tell me what you think of these outsiders. Yesterday, I heard whispers that they might be demons."

"No, Father. They are just men from some far-off island. It is true that they wear strange garments and talk in a gabble. But they eat and drink and void water just as we do."

"Are their bodies not covered with hair?"

She realized that he was just repeating tales heard from travelers. Perhaps those travelers had never actually seen foreign men. "I do not know about their bodies," she confessed. "It is not easy for them to take off their clothing."

"But the outsiders must bathe."

"That is true. The *tahunga* insisted on it last night. But the men waited until moonset, so the *tahunga* saw nothing."

"That is puzzling, daughter. Perhaps they have something to conceal."

Tepua sighed. "These men follow customs we do not understand. Perhaps that is why they keep their bodies covered."

He looked up at her with a skeptical frown.

"Father, I wish you could see these sailors! After a short while you would not think them strange at all."

"I am curious," he admitted. "If I had the strength, I would go to their boat."

"Then I will tell you all about them—every new thing I learn."

"That will be enough." He paused, still frowning. "Daughter, I ask you to be cautious about approaching these . . . men. Take Faka-ora's advice."

"I am doing that."

"Good. Then all will be well." He closed his eyes wearily.

"Yes, all will be well," she agreed. As she watched her father slip into a doze, she hoped that his confidence was not misplaced.

Several days passed. Each morning, Tepua went out early to see the sailors. Nika seemed unwilling to make much effort, however. He often sat alone in the bow and occupied himself shaping bits of wood with his gray-bladed knife. Kiore welcomed her visits, and when he grew stronger, she began going twice a day, despite the crowds that watched from shore.

Whenever Kiore saw her coming, he took out a strange assembly and held it on his lap. The thing looked like many small squares of cloth, all cut to one size and stacked neatly together. He would turn aside the first sheets, then make marks on a fresh one with a sharpened quill. Every time he learned a new word, he made more marks in this thing he called his "puk." She understood that the marks helped him remember.

Tepua's enjoyment of the visits was marred, however, by Nika's refusal to participate. The younger sailor merely sat and glared at her while she continued the lessons with his companion. Once in a while Kiore would turn his head and say something in his own language. It pleased her to hear Nika's few attempts at repeating her words. He spoke well, when he tried.

On the fourth morning after the stranger's arrival, Tepua was greeted by an unexpected sight. When she walked out onto the beach, she saw another *pahi* floating beside the foreign vessel. She had given orders; now she turned angrily to her guards. "Who is out there?" she demanded.

"It is Paruru. He is well."

Paruru! Tepua scowled and called for her own *pahi*. How would the sailors react, she wondered, to a visit from the warrior who had killed their friend? And now that they had made spears . . .

As her boat drew near, Tepua's apprehension eased. No weapons were in view on either side. Using signs and a few words, the *kaito-nui* appeared to be carrying on an amicable discussion—with Nika. Kiore, who had been the dead man's friend, sat to one side but watched intently.

When Paruru saw her coming, he broke off. *"Maeva ariki,"* he called to her.

"Life to you," she responded coolly. She could not bring herself to say that she was pleased to see him back.

Glancing again at the sailor, she noticed that Nika's expression of interest had faded. The conversation with Paruru appeared over.

"Do you know what he asked me, Tepua-ariki?" the warrior said to her with a laugh. "He wanted to know if we are man-eaters—Pu-tahi."

"Did he think we were preparing him to be baked? Maybe that explains his unfriendliness."

"He wants to go ashore, my chief. That is all. He has been in this boat too many days."

Tepua lifted her chin. "He will go ashore only when Faka-ora tells me it is safe."

"I told him that, but he doesn't like the answer. Is there nothing we can do to make these men more comfortable?"

"Send them delicacies, then. The best food we have. I can promise nothing else, but I am hoping. I, too, would like to have the sailors ashore." She stared at Paruru, trying to fathom his attempt to intervene. Did he wish to make amends for the third man's death?

He seemed changed somehow. The recent events had left a mark on his face. He bore a haunted look, the expression of a man who desired something that was far beyond his grasp.

That night Tepua had vague, unsettling dreams. Faint voices seemed to drift to her from across the lagoon. She half-woke, thinking the sounds real, then fell back into sleep.

In the morning, when she went out for her visit to Kiore, she had servants carry several baskets to the *pahi*. To aid her lessons she had been using articles of various sorts—tools, plants, fishing gear. For today, the servants had collected coconuts—the very young, the drinking nut, the aged nut that was already sprouting. Each had a name that Kiore needed to learn, if only to be able to request the food that he wanted.

Small waves rolled toward shore as the boatmen took her out. Above the foreign vessel, the high mast swayed slowly against a sky of unspoiled blue. She heard soft creaking of ropes and timbers as she approached.

She was glad that Paruru had not put in an appearance this morning. Yesterday the sailors had seemed restless after his visit. Kiore had yawned often and cut the lesson short, making Tepua stamp her foot in irritation. There was so much to teach him!

"Kiore!" she called as her *pahi* neared the foreign *vaka*.
"Kiore, wake up." She watched his hanging bed for a sign
of stirring. An arm came out, then drew back.

"Why are you so slow this morning?" she demanded.

At last, after repeated calls, she got him to come out. His
hair was an unruly mess, poking like straw from beneath his
cloth headdress. With a great show of weariness he leaned
over his round water carrier and splashed his face. Then he
sat on a thwart and gazed at her drowsily. *"Maeva ariki,"*
he said with no enthusiasm. His head tilted slightly to the
side and his eyes fell half-closed.

"Why are you so sleepy today?" Tepua asked. Then she
remembered the sounds during the night. Perhaps the two
men had sat up late swapping tales.

She looked toward the stern and noticed some changes
since yesterday. Containers had been moved around. Behind
one that was open, a handful of glittering stones and a length
of red-striped cloth lay on a thwart.

Kiore rubbed his eyes. "Talk . . . later," he said with a
grimace. He mimed going back to sleep.

"Sleep," she said, and made the same signs. Only after
he repeated the word several times, proving that he had
learned it, was she content to leave him alone. With a
feeling of annoyance she headed back to shore.

As Tepua walked up the beach a thought struck her.
Many days had passed since she and Maukiri had slipped
away to Ata-ruru. With the sailors sleeping late, she had no
other plans for this morning. The sky was clear, the air
pleasantly cool. What better time for an excursion?

Forgetting the dignity of the chiefhood, Tepua ran toward
her house. "Maukiri!" she called, expecting to find her
cousin inside. Maukiri had joined Tepua's household. When
the servants reported her cousin gone, Tepua sent them to
find her.

Maukiri soon appeared. When she came inside, Tepua
noticed a petulant expression on her cousin's face. Maukiri
held something in her hand, but kept her fist closed.

"I spent the night with my mother," Maukiri said in a hurt tone. "I told you I was going there. Why did you send servants rushing all over looking for me?"

"One came back from your mother's house and said you were not there."

"Because I went clam digging!"

"Ah. Then you must have found something interesting." Tepua suddenly grabbed her cousin's wrist and tried to force open her fingers. As children they had often wrestled over small prizes, and Tepua had generally won. Now Maukiri fought harder than usual. Mats went flying, feet kicked thatched walls. It did not matter that Tepua was chief and Maukiri her attendant. They were sisters squabbling.

"What is this, and where did you get it?" Tepua was breathing hard as she held up the trophy. It was rich yellow in hue and shaped like a large pearl. From the tiny hole that pierced it, she knew this was meant to be strung—as part of an earring or necklace.

"I found it in a pearl shell," said Maukiri sullenly. She would not meet Tepua's gaze.

"Or maybe in a foreigner's *vaka*!"

"I did not go near the strangers."

"Then who did go there? This pearl came from no shell." Tepua cupped the bead in her hand and brought it to where a tiny shaft of sunlight pierced the wall. The bead lit up with a glow that made her gasp.

"It is very pretty," said Maukiri sourly. "Now I give it to you, *ariki*."

Tepua tried to keep her voice firm. "I want to know how this precious thing came ashore."

Maukiri did not answer, and Tepua repeated her question in a harsher tone. At last Maukiri blurted her reply. "The sailors were lonely! They were tired of being caged like pigs!"

"So you did go."

Now Maukiri raised her head and looked at Tepua slyly. "Do you know how long they had been without a woman?"

She held up her fingers in the manner that the strangers used for counting. "That many days!" she said triumphantly after waggling her fingers up and down, up and down, up and down. Then, with a wicked grin, Maukiri threw herself back onto the rumpled mat behind her, spreading her legs as she tumbled.

Tepua could not understand why tears came to her eyes. Never in her life had she been so angry with her cousin. "Faka-ora will have something to say about this," she said spitefully as she ducked out through the low doorway. The foreign bead felt hot in her hand, as if it were going to burn through her flesh.

She was halfway to the priest's house before she realized that she could have sent someone after him. But it felt good to walk the path, crunching the gravel underfoot. The exercise helped ease her fury.

Faka-ora was sitting beneath a tall *pukatea* tree outside his modest thatched house. He was plaiting coconut fronds in a manner that only priests knew, shaping them into small bundles for use in ceremonies. "Tepua-ariki!" he said with surprise. "Let me bring you a seat."

She declined his offer, and perched on a fallen log instead. She thrust out her hand to show him the bead. "All our caution was for nothing," she complained. "Women have been out to the foreign *vaka*. They have taken away gifts."

"But how? Were there no guards?"

Tepua paused. She had almost forgotten that she had ordered sentries to stand on the beach during the night as well as the daytime. By their firelight, the guards should have seen any intruders. "Paruru must have an answer. . . ."

"Ah, Tepua," said the priest in a conciliatory tone. "Do not be too harsh on your people. Men sometimes fall asleep on a long night watch."

"But what can we do now? Are we not still at risk?"

"The strangers have recovered well," said the priest. "I no longer think their gods' ill favor clings to them. I am far more concerned about the goods their boat carries."

Again, Tepua showed him the bead.

"Yes, but that is a small thing," he said, "and I see no harm in it. I have heard reports of strange tools and weapons and cloth. We must be far more careful in how we deal with those."

"Then is it safe to let the men ashore?"

"It will be difficult to keep them out there much longer . . . now that they have found some friends." Faka-ora gave her a knowing glance. "Unless, of course, you wish to do away with the strangers."

Tepua drew in her breath.

"No, I did not think that was your intention." A look of concern crossed his wrinkled face. "We will have to watch the men carefully. Since there are only two of them, that should be easy. But they have brought many things, and some may prove dangerous. It is important to control what happens to the foreign goods."

"Yes, I see that now."

"Remain cautious. I advise you to touch nothing on their vessel until I have been there."

"I will send for you," she promised. They spoke awhile longer before she headed back to the lagoon.

As soon as she got past the trees that blocked her view of the water, Tepua knew that something unexpected had happened. She heard shouts, and saw a seething mass of canoes surrounding the foreign *vaka*. "*Aue!*" she cried as she raced toward the commotion.

The onlookers had abandoned all caution. Evidently word of last night's foray had spread. She saw people actually boarding the strangers' vessel. Faka-ora's warnings had been in vain!

And what of the guards? As Tepua glanced about furiously, the captain rushed up to her. "Forgive me, *ariki*," he said. "There were so many canoes, all filled with women. We could not stop them all. . . ."

Sounds came across the water—the splashing of paddles, the banging of canoe hulls, the chatter of people who had found a new amusement. Close to the outsiders' boat she saw bright patches of color and shiny objects held high. *More foreign gifts?* She heard shrieks and splashes as children dove from the strangers' bow and came up to clamber aboard again.

In the center of it all stood Nika beside a tall drumlike container. With one hand he reached out for pearl shells that were thrust at him for inspection. With the other he tried to keep the lid on his treasures. Kiore appeared to want an end to the commotion, signing and shouting at the people surrounding him, trying to get them to leave the boat. Yet his companion kept inspecting the pearl shells, returning most of them, keeping a few, dipping into his drum for gifts in exchange.

What a change had come over Nika. Clearly he had lost his fear of islanders—at least of those who carried no weapons. But she could not tolerate what he was doing.

Tepua called orders to her men. She sent someone for the priest, others to her *pahi.* Her herald blew the conch trumpet, sending a long blast in the direction of the crowd. The revelers froze at the sound, then turned and scrambled to get away.

Tepua boarded her *pahi,* which moved swiftly forward, chasing the smaller canoes from its path. A few holdouts remained by the foreign boat, and Tepua saw the glitter of pearl shells in their hands as they clamored for Nika's attention. A second blast on the conch shell finally put them to flight.

As she neared the strangers' vessel Tepua saw that the small canoes were not going far. The paddlers halted, evidently waiting for a chance to return to the fray. The people in the canoes looked sullen and resentful, like youngsters who had been refused a favorite food.

When Tepua's craft came alongside the other vessel, Nika reached down into his drum again. He drew out something new and dangled it before her face. It was a necklace of many stones, transparent, yet infused with a shade of blue that was deeper than the color of the sky. The beads sparkled when sunlight hit them, as if tiny fires lay within. They made Maukiri's trinket look like a worthless pebble.

Tepua glanced up at Nika's gray eyes and saw an expression of contempt on his youthful face. He knew that she wanted his treasure. And he viewed her as a child, she realized with a shock. A child, to be soothed by the promise of a pretty toy.

She held out her hand and let Nika drape the necklace over her fingers. Then she held the gift high, turning so that everyone could admire the glittering stones. "Do you see this lovely thing?" she shouted to the people in the canoes. "Is it not suited to a chief? Is it not a marvel that I can boast of all my days?" She watched the wide-eyed stares of the women, the gaping mouths of the men. "In return for this fine gift, what will the strangers ask? I do not know. I cannot ask." Then, in a gesture she found difficult, she gave back the necklace to the astonished sailor.

She glared at Nika, motioning for him to close up his drum. She had an impulse to scold him, but knew that he would not understand. "I wish you to come ashore," she said to both men, gesturing from them to the beach. "You have stayed long enough on your *vaka*."

Nika and Kiore glanced at each other, their expressions brightening as they grasped her meaning. Kiore pointed to the drums and sacks and other belongings that surrounded him. "Shore?" he asked.

"No," said Tepua. "Not now. We will take care of your goods." She mimed her meaning.

It did not surprise her to see the men's expressions darken. They argued with each other, their voices rising.

Abruptly Nika stooped and grabbed his crude spear. With seeming reluctance, Kiore also took up his weapon.

"Stop!" she cried. Then she turned to her own men and ordered them to stand back.

She looked again at Kiore, sympathizing with his distress. In a mysterious way, she felt drawn to him. It was not his fault that people had defied her orders and gone to his vessel. The thought of Maukiri coming here at night even gave her a pang of envy. . . .

"You must leave your boat now," she told him firmly. She showed the sailors a canoe that she had called for them. When Nika took a defiant step backward, Tepua's warriors picked up their own spears from the deck. She wanted to order the weapons put down again, but how could she make the strangers obey?

The bristling of so many lances, all much longer than his own, seemed to unnerve the red-haired sailor. He voiced a few more complaints, then silently dropped his weapon into the bottom of the boat. Cautiously he turned toward the canoe that lay alongside. After taking one more glance back at his small pile of pearl shells, Nika swung a leg out. He grimaced as the smaller boat shifted under his weight. With a grunt he was over the side and into the outrigger canoe.

She thought Kiore would need no persuasion, since he, too, had been chafing to come ashore. Instead of boarding behind Nika, however, he retreated to the stern, taking his weapon with him.

When she beckoned him again using the palm-down gesture, he gave several quick shakes of his head. Frowning, she ordered her paddlers to bring her closer. She wanted to see what he was doing, but Faka-ora had warned her not to touch the boat.

At first she thought that Kiore had thrust his hands through a square hole in the vessel's hull, but she realized that the hole was a storage place. He brought out a small wooden chest.

"This. Shore," he said. He opened the lid of the box

briefly, showing her that it held his "puk" and the black dye that allowed him to make marks with pointed quills.

There was something else as well inside. She caught a glint of yellow, of hard edges and corners. "What else do you have there?" she asked as he shut the lid all too quickly.

He scowled defiantly, putting the box on a thwart. He tried to pretend that he did not understand her, but at last she prevailed on him to open the lid again. This time he pulled out what looked like a toy made of flat sticks. Two sticks were straight, meeting at a sharp angle. These ends were crossed by a third one that curved like the edge of a crescent moon.

Never had she seen edges that looked so hard and straight. The yellow sticks were fashioned of a material that did not seem to be wood or stone or shell. As she leaned closer she saw small, tiny marks spaced evenly along the edges.

A prickle of fear touched her nape. "What is it for?"

He seemed at a loss for words. He held the contrivance to one eye, pointed from it to the eastern horizon and then higher up. "Watch . . . star. Find . . . home . . . land."

Tepua's brow wrinkled as she tried to make sense of his words. Of course seafarers needed stars as guides, but she had never heard of using sticks to follow them.

"And what is that other thing inside the box?" she demanded. Kiore hesitated, meeting her gaze. Then, with a sigh, he brought out the last of his precious belongings. This was a smaller box that held something shiny and round. Looking into it, Tepua saw a design that resembled the petals of flowers pointing neatly outward from the center of a circle. As she watched, her eyes widened, for the design began to move!

The pattern turned, but then swung back again. Kiore pointed to the tip of the most prominent petal. "North," he said, using the word she had taught him as he gestured toward the horizon. He indicated the other markings around the pattern, calling out the directions of the winds.

"A wonder of the gods!" Tepua whispered. She felt dizzy and short of breath as she studied the strange object in his hands. She barely heard the sound of paddles stroking and quiet voices approaching. When she saw that Faka-ora had arrived, she almost cried out with relief.

Kiore glared suspiciously at the priest and seemed reluctant to display his treasures again. "I have heard of such a thing," said Faka-ora, when at last he saw the swinging petals. "The tales of winged boats mention this. But no one knows what lies behind it. Perhaps some sorcerous trick . . ."

"Then it must not come ashore," said Tepua quietly.

"Leave it here," agreed the priest. Tepua relayed the message to Kiore.

The sailor reacted angrily, closing the things back inside the box and moving to the stern of his boat. Once more the warriors raised their spears, but Kiore held his ground.

Again she ordered him to leave his belongings and board the canoe. Again he refused, this time picking up his weapon.

She glared at him, feeling the intensity of those blue-green eyes. Beside her, she heard Faka-ora mutter that there was a quick way to end this contest of wills. Perhaps, she thought, another *ariki* would already have done so.

Yet, as she watched Kiore defiantly holding the box under one arm and brandishing the spear with the other, her irritation gave way to a mixture of astonishment and then reluctant respect. Did these implements mean more to him that his life? Perhaps they did if he could not find his way home without them.

"Store them in a safe place," she suggested to the sailor, adopting a soothing tone. "Here. On the boat."

"Here?" She thought that he understood her, for he began to glance around him. Under the seat in the stern lay a storage place that was covered by a wooden board. The board swung up under the touch of his foot, and then fell with a clap. At last, to her relief, he put his weapon aside.

He found a length of cloth and used it to wrap up his yellow sticks and his magical petals. These wonders he placed behind the swinging board. Then he picked up a tool that resembled a food pounder mounted on a shaft. With his other hand he held a thin sliver—she did not know if it was made of wood or bone.

He pressed the sliver's pointed end to the board and then he pounded its flat end with the head of the tool. The noise startled her and she took a step backward. He took another sliver, and then another, making loud blows as he banged each into the wood until only its flat end showed.

At last he stopped pounding and put his hand on the board. He shook it and pulled it, but now it would not swing open. "Good," he said. As a final test, he kicked at the storage place and then grunted his satisfaction.

"Will you come now, in peace?"

When he indicated his agreement, walking away from his own spear, Tepua ordered the guards to put down their weapons. Then, for a moment, Kiore turned his aquamarine gaze on her and she felt an odd tingle go up her spine. His eyes were deep-set and shadowed, but that only made their glow more intense. His eyebrows were straight, paralleling the top line of each eye before angling down to the inner corner, adding a certain stubbornness to his face.

"It is good that we can be friends," she said, relieved that the disagreement had been settled. Yet Kiore still held on to the small box that contained his "lok-puk".

She turned to the priest, explaining the nature of the "puk" as well as she understood it. Faka-ora signed for the sailor to open it again, and remained silent as he leafed through the sheets. Some marks looked like bird tracks, others like tiny finger signs. "Cloth with marks," said Faka-ora. "I see no harm in it." He made a brief incantation and allowed Kiore to carry this last of his belongings into the canoe that stood waiting.

"We will take care of you. You will be greeted well," Tepua assured Kiore. Then she gave orders to men in another canoe. "Have a guesthouse readied. Make these strangers welcome." On the beach, she saw that a large crowd had gathered in anticipation of the sailors' arrival. Women were braiding wreaths of vines and blossoms to drape over the visitors' necks. Others carried coconuts and *fara* fruit. She watched with satisfaction as the foreigners headed to their welcome.

Then she turned to Faka-ora, waiting for him to chant the words and complete the rituals over the goods remaining in the boat. Everywhere she looked she saw something that piqued her interest—glints of color, tangles of cord and cloth, shapes she had never seen before. She could scarcely contain her eagerness to rush aboard.

SIX

By late afternoon, the clan chiefs and their advisers had gathered in the clearing outside Tepua's house. As was her right, Tepua sat on the carved four-legged stool that raised her above the rest of the meeting. This seat, which so long had been her father's, felt wrong beneath her. How she wished he could be here to take it.

She had no illusions that the task before her would be easy. Everyone knew about the foreigners' goods, now unloaded and in Faka-ora's keeping. The chiefs had come to demand a share.

Paruru sat at her right hand, here because of his position and not because she wanted his company. When she had asked him to explain how women had visited the foreign vessel at night, he had answered that his guards saw nothing. Where had they been looking?

To her left sat an elder from her own Ahiku Clan. Rongo Clan's people came next, providing a slight buffer between Ahiku and its longtime rival, Varoa Clan. Rongo's chief was beardless as a boy and fat as an overfed Tahitian, Tepua thought. He had come here despite the fact that he did not acknowledge her leadership.

Beside him sat Cone-shell, Varoa's chief, and close kin to Natunatu. Cone-shell, who had long ago taken on the role of Umia's protector, also refused to acknowledge Tepua's authority. Yet he was here, and made an impressive sight. He was heavily built, a man of solid strength, though aging.

Beneath his thick black brows glittered eyes that missed nothing. He wore a string of dolphin teeth braided into his short, dark beard, and another string around his neck.

Among the others, Tepua thought that only Heka of Piho Clan might be counted as her ally. She felt out of place here. It was Kohekapu who should be sitting regally on this seat, she thought, his calm but powerful gaze keeping order.

Varoa's chief eyed Tepua with unconcealed distaste as he spoke. "We of Varoa do not accept Tepua-mua's claim that the foreign *vaka* and its spoils fall under her control." He leaned forward as he spoke, making the teeth in his necklace rattle against each other.

"Varoa is forgetting the traditional right of the high chief," Tepua answered.

Cone-shell glowered at her. "Traditional right! This daughter of Ahiku Clan dares to invoke such tradition when everyone knows that she is but a pretender. If the rightful heir of Kohekapu were on that seat—"

"He would still need his mother to wipe his nose," interposed Heka, evoking a few laughs from the others. "Cone-shell," she added, "will you stop dragging that stinking fish around the beach? Regardless of what may come later, Tepua rules us now. And it was to her clan's shores that the foreign vessel came."

"Respected Heka," growled Cone-shell. "You have not seen Umia lately or you would be choking on your jest. It is only because of your ignorance that I let the insult pass." He gave another fierce rattle of his necklace. "As for the right we dispute, let me remind you that the foreign *vaka* was not wrecked on the reef. It was captured by your brother Paruru and brought into the lagoon. If any clan has rights to the spoils, it is your own."

"The *kaito-nui* can have no loyalty to any clan," Tepua objected, feeling an edge creep into her voice. "Paruru was serving his high chief. He renounces any claim Piho Clan may have. Is that not so?"

"It is, *ariki*," Paruru replied, but Tepua sensed his

reluctance. And why not? From what she had seen, the *vaka* and its contents were a great prize.

She turned to the circle of faces before her. "Paruru acted for the benefit of us all, not just for one clan. It is my duty to say what will happen now."

"I know what your decision must be," said Cone-shell. "To share the goods among the chiefs."

At this a hubbub rose, but Tepua quelled it with a sharp gesture. "These foreigners are now my guests," she said. "We do not take the belongings of a guest. And even if the outsiders offer us gifts, I am not ready to accept them."

"And why is that?" Cone-shell demanded.

"Think of the dangers! Ask yourself what we know of these foreign things! Perhaps they are offensive to the gods, or have been tainted by evil spirits. Would you endanger your people because of greed?"

This touched off another round of furious discussion, which Tepua again had to silence.

"The priest has conducted purification rituals," said Cone-shell.

"But how do you know that his power is strong enough to cleanse an unknown evil?" asked Heka. "I support Tepua's caution." The arguments raged back and forth until one of Faka-ora's assistants appeared and asked to speak. His master, he said, had completed his examination of the strangers' goods. He was ready to receive the chiefs in the large storehouse where everything had been taken.

Tepua rose from her seat. "Those of you who wish to inspect the things, come with me. Then you will have a better idea what we are arguing about."

When she stood, she was not surprised to see the others hesitate. The talk of danger had dampened everyone's spirit. Even Cone-shell was slow to rise.

Drawing her feather-trimmed plaited cloak about her shoulders, Tepua followed Faka-ora's man into the store-house while the clan chiefs trailed behind. The building was long, airy, and lit by sunlight streaming in through the loosely thatched sides. Despite the ventilation, strange scents pervaded the air. She sniffed deeply but could not sort them out.

Once she was inside, she noted that the goods had been separated into four distinct piles. The high priest, looking weary after his task, stood by as Tepua and the chiefs gathered about the closest heap. On top she noticed a long-handled wooden blade that resembled a canoe paddle. It lay amid other vaguely familiar articles—items that appeared to be a sea anchor, a bailer, and other equipment needed in an oceangoing craft.

"These are things we understand," said Faka-ora, gesturing at the first heap. "They are of the sea, of fishing and the sailing arts. Any magic in them is magic that I know, and I have taken measures to make it harmless. You may handle anything in this first pile without fear."

Tepua reached for the foreign paddle, ran her hand along the smooth shaft. The wood was close-grained and heavy, the crafting excellent, but the proportions wrong. The shaft was far too long to be of use in an outrigger and lacked the usual flared handgrip at the end.

Faka-ora was moving on to the next collection of goods. "These," he said, "are things that resemble those we know and use, but are made from materials we have not seen before. I urge caution in handling them."

Tepua bent over this second heap. In a band of sunlight lay a strangely shaped knife, its edge gleaming brighter than pearl shell. She squinted in puzzlement, trying to fathom how the blade was lashed to its hilt of bone. The edge looked sharp; she decided not to pick it up.

Her attention turned to a long roll of cloth, resembling the material in the foreign sails. Looking closely, she saw the appearance of a weave, but the threads were so thin and uniform that she couldn't imagine human fingers doing the plaiting. Taking a length, she yanked it taut between her fists. *Tapa* would tear under such treatment but this cloth held. She hoped that Kiore could explain what made it so strong.

Here also stood the drum that held small gifts—the items that Nika had been trading for pearl shells. As she peered into the container Tepua recalled the blue necklace she had been offered. Now she saw other tantalizing glimpses— bright beads, and ribbons of cloth in astonishing colors. Perhaps, in the strangers' land, such wonders were as common as pretty shells on the beach. . . .

Faka-ora moved on to the third pile, cautioning that he was far less certain about the uses or hazards of these objects. "If you must touch them, protect your hands," he advised.

Cone-shell, who had been leaning close to the third heap, gave a triumphant cry. With his hand wrapped in part of his plaited cape, he snatched up a hafted tool. The thing was evidently used for chopping. Its head had a dull sheen like that of the knife blade and a shape like that of an adze—an adze whose blade was in line with the handle instead of being properly lashed crosswise. "This might prove useful," said Cone-shell, "if we could turn the blade around."

As he was examining the piece his hand slipped. The blade sliced through the fine matting to meet flesh. "*Aue!* It bites," he cried, dropping the tool at his feet. He frowned, sucking at the wound while Faka-ora chanted over him, asking the gods to dispel the evil.

Tepua put her own hands behind her as she bent over to look at a similar tool. "If the blade could be taken off the shaft, it might be used to chop food."

Heka eyed the tool. "It has a keener edge than our stone or shell adzes. Perhaps it would be valuable to our canoe builders."

Tepua disagreed. "A canoe-maker swinging this would risk cutting off his toes, or his thumbs."

"You are right," said Heka, turning away in disgust. "I think these foreigners are fools to make such a useless thing."

Attention shifted to other items. One was a small drum-like container that appeared to be completely sealed. Though she did not intend to touch it, Tepua's foot accidentally bumped a protruding stick near the bottom. A thin stream of liquid began to flow, its pungent odor rising. "*Aue!* What is that?" she cried.

"It is only something the strangers drink," explained Paruru, who had been unusually silent up to this point. With no hesitation, he bent down and adjusted the stick so that the flow of liquid stopped. "I have seen the strangers draw it into cups. It seems to make them joyful, then sleepy. Perhaps it is like your Tahitian *ava*."

"It surprises me, Paruru," Tepua said coldly, "that you know so much about the foreigners' customs."

"We should be pleased that our *kaito-nui* is so obser-vant," said Cone-shell. "Surely, you will not keep us from tasting the strangers' drink. At least that is something we can get some use out of. And they will not even notice that some is gone."

Tepua remembered the time in Tahiti when she had tried the intoxicant that chiefs and nobles enjoyed. Its effect had been mild, numbing her lips and making her drowsy. The strangers' drink neither looked nor smelled like *ava*.

She paused, realizing that all eyes were watching her. So far, she had managed to keep control of the meeting, but she understood the resentment of the other chiefs. If she did not allow them a small victory now, they would soon demand a larger one. She looked toward Faka-ora for guidance but could read only a hint of curiosity in his expression. After all, the outsiders drank this with no harm to themselves. . . .

"Bring cups!" she ordered. When hollow coconut halves had been handed out, she asked Paruru to pour some of the drink into hers. As chief, it was essential that she go first. No one must doubt her strength of will.

She tipped the cup. Her mouth began to sting as if she had licked fire coral. The liquid caught at the back of her throat, making her cough. Harsh fumes flooded her eyes with tears.

Instinctively she spat the stuff back into the cup. Sputtering and blinking, she wiped her mouth on her hand. Then she hurried outside, leaving the others to do as they wished. A servant brought her a *viavia*. She drank its soothing water to cool her mouth.

Through the wall of the storehouse she heard the sounds of others trying the stinging brew. "It is too vile even for fish poison," proclaimed Heka. She heard Cone-shell's yelp of pain as he, too, fell victim to the drink. Tepua could not help smiling; perhaps Cone-shell would now be less eager to meddle with the foreigners' goods.

She went back inside, wrinkling her nose at the odor that filled the air. Evidently some of the stinging brew had been sprayed onto garments. Cone-shell's cape reeked of it. She bit her lip to keep from laughing aloud.

But serious matters still lay at hand. The examination was not finished. Faka-ora had moved to the fourth and final heap.

"I have not been able to learn the purpose of any of these things," he said. "For that reason, I urge the greatest caution here. Do not touch anything, but allow my assistant to help you." A young underpriest came forward. The man appeared uneasy, though he had evidently dealt with these objects before. With a nervous motion, he lifted the first implement and let it dangle.

For a moment Tepua thought that he was holding two knives, each with a strange open ring for its handle. The blades were crossed, and held together by a pin. When the underpriest slipped his thumb and fingers through the rings, the blades opened and closed like the jaws of a barracuda.

Puzzled, Tepua ordered the assistant to take up something else, a yellowish kind of cup with a ring beneath its base and a swinging pendant inside.

Faka-ora's assistant held the ring so that the mouth of the cup hung downward. When he moved his hand back and forth a noise sounded that made everyone step back in alarm. "It speaks!" said the shaken chief of Rongo Clan.

"Only when it is moved," said Faka-ora. He nodded to his assistant. The young man closed his eyes, tightened his lips, and shook the cup vigorously again. It clanged more loudly than before.

"A noisemaker," said Heka, laughing. "A drum that beats itself."

"I would not want such a drum," said Cone-shell. "It hurts the ears to hear it." He gestured impatiently. "Put the useless thing back."

The underpriest did as he was asked, next opening a dirty cloth bag that sagged with the weight of its contents. Tepua glanced in and saw what appeared to be small round stones, all the same size.

Cone-shell snorted in disgust. "A well-made bag, and what do these foreigners put into it? Worthless stones."

"Perhaps they are weapons," someone else suggested.

"Too small," said Paruru, frowning. "But what is in there?" He gestured at a strange kind of bottle that curved like a boar's tusk and tapered to a point at one end. The underpriest picked it up, removed the cap from the wide end, allowing the chiefs to peer at the contents.

"Worse yet," said Cone-shell, grimacing. "Black sand. I can imagine putting many things in such a finely made bottle, but never that."

As Tepua squinted inside she caught a sharp odor. Tahiti had plenty of black sand, but none carried a scent like this powder. The smell was faintly familiar. . . .

Then she remembered, and her hand knotted in a fist of anger. *The thunder-club's smoke. The gray cloud over the lagoon.* Of the people here, only she and Paruru had been present at that terrifying scene.

She narrowed her eyes when Paruru asked for a closer look. He, too, sniffed and then grimaced. He turned away from her, but she had already caught his look of recognition. *Why does he say nothing?*

The smell lingered unpleasantly in her nose. It spoke of harshness and impatience. "I have seen enough," she said to Faka-ora. "But now I remember that one thing is missing. The foreign weapon. It fell into the lagoon."

"I would not like to leave it there," said Faka-ora. "It might affect the fishing."

Tepua turned to Paruru, whose face now bore a troubled look. "Something must be done," she said. "Why not send divers to bring the weapon up?"

Paruru's frown deepened. "They may not find it. You know how currents move things around. Sand shifts . . . And even if someone does locate the foreign weapon, he will not want to touch it."

She drew in a breath and stared at the warrior for a moment. Surely the problem was not as difficult as he made it seem. "Let us announce a competition," she said. "To see which diver can locate the thing. Then we will let the priests find a way to safely bring it up." She saw Paruru glance once at Faka-ora, who had fixed him with a curious stare. The words seemed to catch in the warrior's throat, but he agreed to carry out her plan.

"Then I am finished here," Tepua said, gesturing for the clan chiefs to follow her out. "Come. We have all had too much of this foul air."

Cone-shell was just behind her as she stepped out into the open. She breathed deeply, trying to rid herself of the black powder's stink. "We have not settled anything," Cone-shell said angrily as he came up beside her.

She answered, knowing that she could not satisfy him, "I have told you that the goods belong to the men who brought them."

"If those men are your guests, then they must be allowed their freedom. If they choose to dispose of their belongings, then you cannot stop them."

"And what would you want from their stores?" She glanced down at his cut hand. "I saw nothing there that pleased you."

''That is for me to decide,'' he answered harshly. ''And not only me. The strangers have goods that would please my women. In the deep drum . . .''

''Ah. We must not forget the pretty things.'' Tepua turned back toward the storehouse, where Faka-ora and his assistants were posting *tapu* signs of braided coconut leaves. Now the goods would be protected by the spirits; woe to anyone who dared trespass.

She tried to soothe Cone-shell. ''I am learning to speak with the outsiders. Soon I will be able to ask what these things are and how they were made and how they can be used safely. When I can explain these marvels to the priests, they may allow us to keep some. But only if the men are willing to part with them.''

Cone-shell seemed unimpressed by her promise. ''This is no way to win my allegiance, Tepua-mua,'' he said, pointedly omitting her title. ''The people of Varoa have no use for weak hands at the steering oar. We need a chief who has allegiance only to this land.''

Tepua stared at him, trying to fathom his meaning. Was he hinting that her time in Tahiti had made her disloyal to her own people. Or did he think that she unduly favored the outsiders?

His other concern remained unspoken, but she understood. He was impatient, along with the others of his clan, to see Umia become high chief. And now Cone-shell had another reason to want to push her from office. With Umia as chief he could do what he pleased with the foreigners and their goods.

Umia must take the office, she agreed, but not if he remained under Cone-shell's troublesome influence. She needed to woo her brother from his uncle. Somehow Umia must learn to stand on his own.

SEVEN

Early the next morning Tepua stood in the shade of the *fara* palms beyond her doorway and gave orders to her growing retinue of young attendants. Later in the day she would present a feast and entertainment, to help the outsiders feel at ease among her people.

She hoped Umia would join the celebration. If he accepted her invitation to attend, then perhaps she could begin to make peace with him. But she feared that Coneshell would refuse to let Umia come. Then she would have to find another way to speak with her brother.

When the tasks had been assigned, and the attendants had gone off to make their arrangements, Tepua at last found herself free. Kiore was still in the guesthouse. She was eager to continue the lessons and thought that they might move quickly now that he was ashore. Perhaps he would soon be able to tell her about life in his own land.

When she met him at the guesthouse, Kiore looked well rested. His expression brightened as he approached her. "Walk?" he asked eagerly, waving his hand in one direction and then another.

"Yes. We can do that. What about Nika?"

"With . . . Paruru."

Tepua was not entirely surprised. She had seen the warrior conversing with Nika on the boat. It puzzled her that Paruru would take such an interest in the young sailor, but she was glad to be alone with Kiore. She wished to show

89

him many things—trees, shrubs, the long pits where taro plants were cultivated. She hoped to find things that Kiore would enjoy seeing.

As they began to walk a shady inland path, the sailor took a glance behind him. "Men watch," he said with a grimace. Tepua turned and signaled the guards to stay back. This was no way to make a stranger welcome!

Only at Paruru's insistence had she agreed to let a contingent of armed men shadow her. Paruru had warned that she could not safely be alone with the foreigner. Tepua sensed something else—jealousy—in the words of her *kaito-nui*.

It was because she remained cool to Paruru, she thought, that the warrior believed her interest had turned to the sailor. But the attention she paid Kiore was mostly a matter of curiosity. Everyone on the atoll wanted to know more about the outsiders.

Tepua admitted to herself that she found Kiore's company a refreshing change. Now that she was chief, Paruru and the other men often seemed uncomfortable in her presence. Though Kiore understood that she was ruler here, he appeared to enjoy being with her.

"Look!" she said, pointing to a lofty *pukatea* tree. The sailor threw back his head as he studied the upward-pointing branches and the high clusters of leaves. "A fine tree, very useful," she tried to explain. "For houses." She gestured at a branch, then stepped to a small, thatched dwelling that lay just off the path. She touched one of the poles that framed the doorway. "*Pukatea*," she repeated. "Strong." For emphasis she mimed trying to break the pole, without success.

This performance made Kiore laugh, and do his own imitation of straining to break a tough stick. "Strong wood," he agreed.

She explained more about the house. The thatching was of slender *fara* leaves folded over a stick, one leaf overlapping the next, and held in place by a long wooden pin. She made motions with an imaginary needle to show how the pinning rod was inserted.

"What are your houses like?" she asked, pointing to Kiore and then the dwelling.

He paused, seemingly bewildered. Then he knelt and began to heap up fist-sized pieces of coral beside the path. He showed with his hands that the pile should be taller and thicker than the one he was making. He stood and raised his arms above his head, indicating that he needed to go higher still.

Tepua laughed, and wondered if she had misunderstood. "Come, let me show you something," she told him. As she headed down the path she noticed, to her annoyance, that a crowd of youngsters had gathered to see the foreigner. Their expressions, as they watched him approach, showed both curiosity and fright.

"Go away, all of you," Tepua commanded. The children scattered into the bush, but she knew they had not gone far.

"Children," said Kiore, speaking the word almost perfectly.

"Do you have sons?" she asked him.

He seemed taken aback by the query, first frowning then smiling. "No," he finally answered. "Maybe."

Unable to make sense of that reply, she returned to the question of houses. After a short walk she led him toward one of the island's lesser *marae,* an open-air sanctuary. Carefully she circled the sacred site, repeating the word *"tapu"* and raising her outstretched arm in front of his chest to show that he must not approach closer. At the narrow end of the courtyard stood a low platform of coral blocks. She showed it to him, asking, "Is that how you build the walls of your houses?"

"Wall," he repeated, pointing to the blocks, then miming building a much taller structure.

Tepua tried to imagine the house he was trying to describe to her. Thick walls of coral all around . . . She frowned, for it seemed more like a place where the bones of the dead might be stored. In such a house, how would one feel the cool night air, or see the morning sunlight?

As they continued their walk Kiore began to frame clumsy questions. He was interested in fresh water and seemed to be looking for a stream or spring. "To drink?" she asked. "To wash in?" She tried to explain that fresh water was scarce. Her islet had a few pools that caught rainwater and a well for drinking. Most people preferred to drink coconut milk.

"My water . . . gone," he told her. He made her understand that his boat carried water in a large drum, which he had been able to fill only partially before setting out from the larger vessel. When he spoke of that time, his brow furrowed and a look of despair filled his eyes.

"We will fill your drum," she said. "But you have only just arrived. Are you already planning to depart?" He did not understand her until she framed the question another way.

He wetted his finger, raised it to the breeze. "Winds not good." In his small vessel he hoped eventually to travel north and then west. That way he could reach a port used by his own people, and find a larger boat to take him on the long journey home.

"Then you will stay with us awhile." Favorable winds were not all he required, Tepua realized. He would need to learn his way through the swarm of atolls and underwater reefs. He would also have to replace the dead crewman. . . . The thought that Kiore could not leave soon made her mood brighten.

They walked a bit more, and Tepua had to chase off the persistent gawkers again. After a stroll over a sunlit stretch of coral sand, she noticed that Kiore's face was damp with sweat. "Too many clothes," she said, pointing to his outermost wrap. She fingered the blue cloth at his wrist and playfully gave it a tug. "They make you hot." She fanned her face with her hand.

"Clothing hot." Kiore looked down at the garment,

which was slit open in front and decorated on one edge by a row of round, flat bits of shell. He made a shrugging motion with his shoulders, pulled one arm free, then the other. Tepua felt a moment of anticipation, followed at once by disappointment. Underneath he was covered from neck to waist in a cloth even finer than the one he had removed; not even his arms had been bared.

She indicated that she wanted his discarded wrap, and he handed it to her. With a cry of delight she thrust her arms through the round openings. Then Kiore began to laugh, wiping tears of mirth from his eyes.

"What is so funny?" she demanded. Of course, her arms were too short. They did not reach all the way through, and the ends of the garment flapped as she moved.

Kiore evidently saw something else amiss. He tugged at the closed part of the garment in front of her, then went around to her back where the cloth lay open. She felt his warm touch on her skin, his fingers softly moving, as he tried to explain. *Wearing it the wrong way.* When she understood her mistake, Tepua also began to laugh.

Now that she had it on, however, she paraded around awhile, admiring the blue cloth as she waved her covered hands. She was glad that the guards were far behind and that no children were spying. People must not say that their chief put clothing on backward!

When she finally tried to pull her arms free, they caught, and she needed Kiore's aid to untangle herself. He tugged gently at the cloth, easing it over her hands. Then, standing behind her, he helped her don the garment properly. The sensations—the foreign cloth against her skin, his firm hand encircling her waist as he guided her—were so odd that Tepua found herself giggling like a girl.

She discovered that her arms were still too short, but he rolled up the end parts that covered her hands. For a moment he stood before her, gazing with a look of admiration. Then he began a surprising feat. Moving his fingers down the front of the open garment, he slipped each round little shell through a matching hole so that the two cloth edges gradually closed up.

She was not sure which was more amusing—the cleverness of the fastening or the gentle tickling of his fingers as he worked. Then he lifted his fingers to her neck. One fastening had been left open. He started to do it, then paused.

His fingertips lingered on her skin, then slowly glided up the sides of her neck. Little shivers ran down to her shoulders. As she looked in his face the color of his eyes seemed to change. They had been light and playful, but now the color shifted, like the azure hue of the lagoon, growing more intense as one gazed into greater depths. . . .

In Kiore's face she saw a kind of beauty unlike any she had ever known. She wanted to tell him so in all the liquid poetry of her language. But she held back, knowing that he would hear only wordless babbling.

There was another way to speak, the language of hands. As she looked into his eyes she put her palms to his cheeks. Gently she drew them together across his face. She felt the brush of his blond lashes and the soft skin beneath his eyes. At last her thumbs rested together on his upper lip, her fingers meeting across the bridge of his nose.

Then she took her hands away, showing how they met at an angle, hoping he would understand. *Your face is like the edge of a great rock that fronts the sea. It looks as if it can withstand anything.*

She felt her stomach give a jump when she realized that he was pleased. A warmth like a sunbeam shone in the blue-green depths of his eyes.

Then he put his hands gently to her face, but instead of starting at the sides, as she had done, he laid his fingers together where the bridge of her nose dished in slightly. His fingers were rough with calluses, yet he moved them with care and tenderness. He paused to stroke her eyelashes and he did not have to speak to make her feel that they were as long and black as tropic bird feathers. He traced the arch of her brow, then let his fingertips travel over the flare of her nostrils.

Speech might lie, but touch could not. He, too, had found beauty in a face that was new to him. She trembled inside at the way he paused for a moment on the plane of her cheekbones.

Finally, he slid his hands behind her neck and began to draw her face toward his. She leaned toward him, eager to feel the warm silkiness of his nose sliding against his. But he hesitated, as if afraid that the gesture was not permitted.

Tepua had seen every woman on the beach vie to give him an embrace. "It is not *tapu,*" she said. Kiore smiled and seemed to forget his caution. He bent closer . . . but something went wrong. Instead of pressing nose against nose, he touched lip against lip!

So strange was the sensation that Tepua gave a muffled cry, pulling away from him. He let her go just as the guards came running, their long spears ready to strike. "It is nothing," she shouted to the men while she struggled to regain her composure. She waved the guards back, then touched her finger to her mouth, remembering the hot, moist pressure that had startled her. What an odd way of showing affection!

"Not good?" Kiore asked her, raising pale, bushy brows. If the guards' appearance had frightened him, he seemed only mildly frustrated now. In the glitter of his eyes she thought she even detected a certain amusement.

"You surprised me," she answered. She felt her face warming under his stare. In truth, the touching of lips had not been unpleasant. "Come," she said, "let us keep walking."

The garment remained on her shoulders, and she made no attempt to take it off. In fact, she was unsure how to unfasten it. The cloth pressed softly against her breasts, producing a faint tingle as she led him farther inland. Kiore strode beside her, but his earlier playful mood seemed dampened.

"Do you see that clump of trees ahead?" she asked in a mischievous tone. "When we get there, the guards will not be able to see us." She did not know if he understood. But when they reached the shadows and she felt well hidden, she turned and faced him, putting her hand lightly against his arm.

A momentary doubt stopped her. Then she remembered her resolve—to learn his customs as well as teach him her own. A smile played on his lips. "Tepua-mua," he whispered. "Tepua-mua-ariki." Then he spoke in his own language, words she could not grasp. Yet they made her want to step closer still. She brought her mouth to his and tried to repeat the foreign kiss.

Now it was Kiore's turn to act surprised. He threw his head back and shouted with delight. Then he put his arms about her, lifted her off the ground, and whirled her once around. "The guards!" she warned.

A moment later she and Kiore were standing chastely apart. "Now I will show you the taro pits," she said in a controlled voice as she glanced toward Paruru's oncoming men. "It is not easy to make vegetables grow on these islands. Coconuts and *fara* take care of themselves, but taro needs hard work. I want you to remember that when you enjoy the good food from our ovens."

When they returned to her house, Tepua was still wearing Kiore's garment. "I will give you another," she told him as they stood outside. She sent a servant to bring the best *tiputa* from her stores. Proudly she held out the rectangle of finely plaited matting, and showed Kiore how to put his head through the hole in the center. The matting hung down in front and back and over his shoulders, though his arms, with their fine cloth covering, made an odd contrast sticking out.

Kiore seemed pleased with the gift, turning around so that everyone could see it. A large crowd of children had gathered; they began capering with their arms stuck out to imitate his. Tepua watched with a sense of happiness she had not felt for many days.

It was with reluctance that she sent her visitor back to his guesthouse. She knew he could not learn any more this day. He had to go back to make marks in his "puk" so that he could remember what she had taught him.

Maukiri, who had been watching with great amusement, came forward and studied Tepua's new garb. "I am glad to see this," her cousin said with a sly grin as she stroked the cloth on Tepua's arm. "Now you will not chide me about spending my time with foreigners."

"Chide you?" Tepua had almost forgotten her earlier displeasure with Maukiri, but now her anger threatened to flare again. "I think you are mistaken about my interest. I am teaching Kiore our customs and he is teaching me his. Do not make too much of that."

Maukiri's grin grew wider. "Good. Then you will not mind showing me how to wear this." Her fingers ran past the round bits of shell that held the garment closed.

Tepua laughed at her cousin's boldness. It was impossible to stay angry at her for long. "Come with me, away from here," Tepua offered, "and then I will show you."

"Away?"

She turned, gazing at the crowd of onlookers. "I am tired of being a spectacle!" Tepua lowered her voice. "Let us go to Ata-ruru."

"But you are chief now. Do you think we two can still go off by ourselves, in that leaky *vaka*?"

"I am chief, and that is what I wish." She bent to whisper in Maukiri's ear. "I will even open my own coconuts when we get there."

Maukiri's eyes sparkled. "If that is your wish, *ariki*, then I will go with you."

Tepua had some difficulty persuading the guards to stay home. Finally they seemed to relent, but while she was paddling, Tepua glanced back and saw war canoes following far behind. She scowled, hoping that they would not come closer.

"You are slowing down, cousin," said Maukiri, who dropped all pretense of servility when they were alone.

Tepua tried to paddle harder. She did not wish to admit that the sun beating down on Kiore's garment made her feel like a pig baking in an *umu*. When Maukiri paused for a rest, Tepua tried to open the fastenings, but the holes had closed up and the shells would no longer fit through.

"You want to take it off?" asked Maukiri from behind. "Turn around so I can help you."

"There is no need, cousin."

They paddled awhile longer, until Tepua's back ran with sweat. Still she refused Maukiri's aid. At last they made their way past the coral heads and landed on the beach of Ata-ruru.

Tepua's throat was dry and her tongue parched. She found a pair of drinking nuts and handed one to Maukiri. When their thirst was satisfied, Maukiri offered once more to help with the fastenings. Seated before Tepua, she twisted and pulled, but quickly lost patience.

Then Maukiri picked up the shell-bladed knife that was used for puncturing coconuts. "I know an easy way to do this," she said. "Remember the tale of Maui-the-elder and the string figures?"

Tepua, in her discomfort, recalled the tale of that wandering hero. He was once challenged by an expert in the string art to name the figures as they were made. Maui succeeded time and again, until he saw a design that he could not recognize. The sly Maui avoided defeat by slicing through the cords with his knife, destroying the pattern.

Now Maukiri cut away the topmost shell and let it drop to the ground. She cut away the second, allowing a hint of breeze to reach Tepua's throat. "I think you are enjoying this, cousin," Tepua said in an accusing tone. "You want to destroy this fine thing that Kiore gave me."

Maukiri stopped her work and stood back. "Do you have another way?"

Tepua looked down and noticed that the third hole had opened slightly. "I think there is a trick here, and a simple one at that." She took the disk between her fingers, twisted it one way and then another until she found she could slide its edge through the hole. The motion did not come easily to her fingers, but now she knew it could be done.

When the garment finally came off, Maukiri immediately snatched it up and thrust her arms through—the wrong way, of course. Now Tepua knew how ridiculous she had looked on her first try. She sat beneath a coconut tree and laughed until her eyes were wet.

"Enough play, cousin," Maukiri said finally, tossing the garment onto a bush while she joined Tepua in the shade. "Now you can tell me about this Kiore."

Tepua glanced at Maukiri. "Perhaps you know him better than I do. At least, in one way."

"Cousin, I was with the red-haired foreigner, Nika. We could not speak a word to each other. I want to know what land these men come from, what their women are like—"

"Tell me first who was with Kiore." At once Tepua wished she had not let out the question. Maukiri would draw the wrong conclusion.

"In the darkness I could not see. But since you won't tell me about your sailor, I will tell you about mine."

Tepua feigned a lack of interest. "I think we are misled by the strange clothing of these outsiders. They are not so different from other men."

Maukiri's eyes brightened and she leaned back, gazing into the distance. "Ah, Tepua. I am sure that Kiore will be glad to teach you otherwise. These outsiders do something that no man of our island has ever thought of. They press their lips here and there, very gently. . . ." She gave her hips a little wriggle of delight.

Tepua felt a breath of hot air across her skin, but thought it must be the wind. She tried to force the memory from her mind—the memory of Kiore's mouth against hers—but she could not get rid of it. Her imagination filled in what Maukiri was hinting at, lips moving softly to her neck, her shoulders, her breasts. . . .

"Enough talk of *hanihani*," Tepua protested. "You asked where the outsiders come from, and now I will tell you. Their island is called Piritania, and it is even larger than Tahiti. In a day and a night you cannot sail from one end of it to the other." Maukiri turned to stare at her in disbelief. "Yes, that is what he told me. And his high chief is named Kinga Kiore."

"How can that be?" asked Maukiri. "How can your foreigner bear the name of his chief?"

Tepua scowled. In all the lands she knew, the high chief's name was reserved for his own use. "Let us view this as a warning," she said. "These men do in their land what is forbidden in ours. They take what names they wish. Who knows what else is permitted them? I must teach Kiore our customs quickly and hope that he passes them on to Nika. Or perhaps I should let you teach Nika."

"If he will listen," Maukiri answered.

"He is young," said Tepua, "and wary of places that are strange to him. Kiore told me that this was Nika's first sea voyage, and that he did not find it to his liking."

"Now that he is on land again, perhaps he will be happy."

"I would like him to be," said Tepua thoughtfully. "It is my duty to keep these men out of trouble.

Maukiri's eyebrows raised. "Perhaps I can help."

"If you wish to spend time with Nika, you may."

"Noble chief, I did not expect you to give me such pleasant orders. Of course, I will obey." Maukiri lay back once more and looked dreamily up at the palm trees.

EIGHT

When Tepua returned with Maukiri, she found the preparations for the feast almost completed. The sun was still high, but a breeze offered some relief from the midday heat. Tepua hurried to her screened bathing area, where servants poured well water over her to rinse off the salt of the lagoon, then rubbed her with scented oil. While the young woman helped her don festive clothing, Tepua heard drums start to patter.

She moved her feet impatiently, in time to the rhythm, while attendants wrapped a mat skirt around her waist and tied it with the red sash that only chiefs wore. Quickly her women brought the rest of her attire—the fringed cape, the ornaments, and the headpiece.

Her necklace was of pearl-shell disks, the gift from Kohekapu. Her headdress was a circlet of soft black feathers woven into a *fara* leaf band. At the front of the circlet, fiery red tropic bird feathers stood up, forming a high crown.

At last she was ready. A servant held out a shell, blackened inside and filled with water, so that Tepua could see her reflection. "Well done!" she said. "*Maitaki!*"

The regal headdress had also come from her father, and was too large for her, but she kept her head steady and hoped that the circlet would not slide down over her eyes. What a sight that would be for the crowd!

She walked slowly toward the gathering at the assembly ground, acknowledging the many cries of "*Maeva ariki.*"

101

When she reached the place of honor, she saw Kiore and Nika making their way toward her.

Kiore wore the *tiputa* she had given him. He looked freshly washed, his hair still damp, his face free of whiskers. He made a strange yet pleasing appearance as he approached.

Nika, on the other hand, offered little to please her eye. She found his coarse features and ruddy coloring unappealing. And worse, he made no effort to adapt to his surroundings. He still wore his foreign garb, including his round, battered headpiece. His one concession to local custom was the single large pearl shell that dangled across his chest. The shell was magnificent, an ornament fit for a chief. She could not guess what marvel he had given in exchange for it.

Kiore and Nika were seated on low stools beside Tepua, and then she took her higher stool. Nearby sat her closest kin and all the important men and women of Ahiku Clan—all but Kohekapu, who remained in the care of healers. Tepua nodded at Ehi, Maukiri, and several others. She regretted, however, the absence of Umia. She had sent a messenger to his uncle's islet far down the lagoon, but Umia had refused her invitation. If she wished to make peace with him, she knew now, she would have to visit Varoa Clan.

Tepua tried to direct her thoughts to the entertainment ahead of her. The crowd almost completely surrounded a large clearing, leaving only a small gap for the performers. Everyone grew quiet as the drumming announced the start of festivities. Beyond the clearing she saw fiercely dressed men gathering, hefting their double-ended spears.

Kiore seemed uneasy at the sight of the armed warriors. Quickly she tried to explain. "What you will see now is not real fighting. It is a display—to show the skill of our warriors. Do not fear." She mimed a demonstration of a man being felled and then rising.

"Those men?" He gestured in his foreign way, aiming an

extended forefinger. She had been trying to teach him the
proper way to point, with all fingers extended, but she did
not correct him this time.

"Yes," she said. "First we show spear fighting. After
that we eat, and then we dance."

"Dancing. Ah." Kiore spoke to Nika, who replied with a
smile.

"What does your friend say?" asked Tepua.

"He asks—do women dance?"

"Certainly."

Nika seemed pleased by that answer. Then she heard
footsteps. Holding their spears high so that everyone could
see the sharp points at both ends, eight men ran into the
clearing. Their skins gleamed with sweat and coconut oil;
their shadows were dark against the sandy ground.

The men split into two parties, each group taking the
opposite end of the field. They were garbed in the warrior's
maro, a loincloth of finely plaited matting that was tied with
a cord winding six times around the waist. In addition each
man wore half a split palm frond wrapped about his hips to
form a fierce-looking kilt. Another split frond tied about the
head made a spiked headdress. The crowd grew so quiet that
Tepua could hear the stiff leaves of the costumes rattle.

She glanced at her guests for their reactions. Nika was
staring with rapt attention while Kiore shifted restlessly on
his seat. She hoped that the men had understood her
explanation.

With a guttural yell, the attackers rushed the defenders.
Feet pounded, coconut fronds shook. On one side, the
squatting men waited until almost too late as the enemy
advanced. Only when the attacking spear points came
within an arm's length of their chests did the defenders leap
up and cross spears with their opponents. The crack of wood
striking wood resounded across the assembly ground.

The conflict rolled back and forth as each side shouted
the traditional taunts and replies. The battle kilts fanned in
a spread of sharply tipped leaves as the warriors jumped and

whirled. Pieces of war dress broke off and were trampled underfoot.

At last the battle ended when the attackers fell, groaning as if mortally wounded. *That is how we should deal with the Pu-tahi,* Tepua thought while the onlookers pounded their thighs in approval. Alas, there was a vast difference between drills and real fighting. The Pu-tahi had proved that they could defeat her warriors, but Kiore and Nika need not learn that now. The display had clearly impressed them—especially Nika—and she did not wish to ruin the effect. The younger sailor was moving his arms as if he were thrusting a spear of his own.

"You wish to learn?" she asked the younger sailor. His eyebrows rose with interest. "I will ask Paruru to teach you," she promised, glad that she had found a way to please him.

When the applause died down, soot-smeared cooks appeared at the edge of the assembly ground. "Let us feast!" shouted Tepua, rising. At her signal the crowd dispersed, boys and men heading to one side, girls and women to the other. Paruru came forward to guide the visitors to their places of honor among the men.

Paruru noted how Kiore's gaze lingered on Tepua as she left to join the women's feast. He did not blame the foreigner. In her cape and feathered crown she was a lovely sight. But Paruru knit his brows when he recalled the reports he had heard from her guards. There was too much friendliness between this pair.

Paruru refused to believe what some people whispered—that Tepua might take the outsider as her lover. If she took any man, it should be the one who had brought her back from Tahiti and had protected her ever since.

"Come this way," the *kaito-nui* said, guiding the visitors through the throng. The two seemed puzzled by the arrangements. "Men eat with men, women with women," Paruru told them. "Is it not that way in your land?"

He and Nika had been learning to communicate, with words of each man's language and with signs. But Nika's reply so shocked Paruru that he believed he had misunderstood. *Men and women sharing the same food!* No, that defied all good sense, and mocked the teachings of the gods.

He led the guests to their places, each well separated from the next. Bowls of seawater and coconut sauce lay beside little mats that had been quickly woven from *fara* leaves. The servers began to distribute the portions—leaf-wrapped parrot fish and cod, baked taro and greens, and large helpings of the atoll's mainstay—meat of the *pahua* or giant clam.

Paruru had watched with dismay how the foreigners dealt with the food brought to their *vaka*. Now he endeavored to give them a quick lesson in manners. "First we wash," he said, ordering a server to pour well water over each man's hands. "Now watch how I use my fingers. Before eating, I offer a morsel to the spirits. . . ."

Kiore made an attempt to follow Paruru's lead while Nika grabbed carelessly at the food, dropping pieces in his lap. The *kaito-nui* had expected no more. Nika was like one of the wild birds that some men tried to tame. He was strong and arrogant, unwilling to submit to rules made by others.

Yet Paruru sensed that the younger man might ultimately provide him the knowledge he sought. Of the two sailors, Nika took a stronger interest in weapons and fighting, and he seemed to enjoy Paruru's company. With patience, the warrior thought he might bring Nika under his influence. When Nika finally understood the need to protect the atoll against raiders, Paruru would ask him for the secret of the weapon.

With these hopes, the *kaito-nui* unleashed his own hearty appetite. From time to time he glanced at the two sailors, who were seizing whole small fish, digging their fingers into chunks of bonito, eating steamed oysters from their shells. The only dish they left untouched was the raw meat of *pahua*.

Paruru urged the foreigners to try it. He showed them how to dip the meat in seawater, then in fermented coconut sauce to enhance the delicate flavor. He was pleased to see that Nika made the first attempt to follow his lead, warily taking a bite, pausing to savor the taste, then licking his lips. When Nika reached for his second piece, Kiore seemed to view this as a challenge. Slowly, and with determination, the light-haired sailor began to chew. A few people around him exchanged approving looks. "The food of our land is good," they murmured.

After the leavings of the feast had been cleaned up, and everyone had rested, the drums started up again. Hastily the audience assembled around the clearing. Paruru led the guests back to their places by Tepua and took a seat beside them. "The dancing begins," he announced with pleasure.

Both guests leaned forward to watch a group of lithe young women, arms outstretched, chins held high, race onto the assembly ground. Wearing skirts of swaying fiber strands and necklaces of flowers, they began to roll their hips to a slow drumbeat. Paruru was less interested in the dancers than in how the foreigners would react to them. He noticed that Nika's attention remained fixed on the performers, but Kiore's kept straying to Tepua. And worse—she kept glancing back at him!

In disgust, Paruru turned away. How was it possible that she preferred this overdressed buffoon to her own *kaito-nui*? The drummers picked up their pace, but he scarcely noticed the change. He paid little heed as one group of dancers departed and another came on.

Then a hand on his shoulder jolted him from his daze. He looked up at his warrior Two-eels and suddenly remembered about his own performance. Hastily he made his way through the crowd to the place where he had left his costume.

Two-eels helped him, settling the coconut-frond headdress into place, then rubbing Paruru's chest and back with oil. Finally Two-eels tied on the warrior's kilt, stiff, narrow leaves fanning out from Paruru's waist. As he hurried back to the clearing Paruru heard the drumming take up a fiercer rhythm.

He felt his pride and confidence returning as he strutted to the center of the open area, flourishing a spear in each hand, rolling his eyes, showing his teeth in a snarling grimace. Not only was Paruru the *kaito-nui*. He was the best male dancer on the atoll.

With a stamp, he halted and began to chant in a strong, clear voice. A chorus of warriors answered him back.

"What wood, O gods, is the best for a spear?" he sang out. "Is it the wood of the coconut?"

"No, a spear made from coconut will split," answered the chorus.

"Is it the white wood of the *fara*?"

"No, a spear made from white *fara* will rot."

Paruru drew himself up and raised his arms high for the final refrain. "Then here is the hard red heartwood of the *fara*. From this I will make my spear. A spear to thrust with delight!"

Everyone joined in on the last chorus. "A spear straight and strong. A double-pointed spear. A weapon to thrust with delight!"

A roar of approval came from the onlookers as the drumbeat switched to the pace of the warrior's dance, the *hipa*. Paruru now stood directly in front of Tepua, and he saw from her widened eyes that he had gained her attention. He took up his difficult dancing position, his arms extended to balance the two spears that lay across them. His palms were down, his hands opening and closing with the same rhythm as his step.

Paruru kicked out with his right foot as his left came down flat with a heavy thump. He repeated the step, moving to his right in a slow circle, all the while keeping the spears in place across his forearms.

At last, as he completed his circuit, his gaze met Tepua's. He watched her lips part and the look of understanding

come in her eyes. Now Paruru did not care if the whole
crowd saw it. He was dancing only for her. Just as the tropic
bird wooed its mate, he was showing off his strength and
agility. He was strutting for the eyes of the *ariki,* for the
eyes of the woman he wanted to please.

The intensity of Paruru's performance surrounded Tepua,
making her breathless. His body gleamed like the polished
red wood of his weapons. Every move was controlled,
perfect, as he went around several times in one direction,
then in the other. His black eyes kept seeking her. She
understood their message. Her body and spirit cried out to
respond.

But she caught herself. She had told the elders that there
would be no man for her here. Not Paruru. Not anyone else.
She pressed her lips together and tried not to meet his
gaze. . . .

At the end of his performance, the *kaito-nui* wiped sweat
from his brow as he received the adulation of the crowd.
Then, as was customary, he issued a challenge. "Who will
try it?" he called. Several young men came forward to show
their own renditions of the dance. The crowd cheered each
in turn, but no one could match Paruru's grace and power.

Tepua noticed Kiore eyeing the contest with growing
interest. Soon her guest turned to her and said, "I try." She
was startled by his offer.

"Sailors dance," he insisted. "I show."

She glanced uncertainly at the people around her, wondering how they would react to the foreigner's offer. "Send
him out," called Ehi, who was seated close enough to have
heard Kiore's request.

"Yes, let him dance," came other voices.

"No drums," Kiore said. This puzzled Tepua further, but
she ordered the drummers silent. Then Nika reached into his
garments and drew out a little tube that was the thickness of
his finger.

Tepua leaned closer and saw what resembled a smaller

version of the nose flutes played in Tahiti. Instead of blowing from a nostril, Nika placed the instrument at his lips, producing notes that were surprisingly loud and shrill. Then he paused, waiting for his companion to step to the fore.

Kiore stood up and began to remove his *tiputa,* pulling it over his head. Underneath, Tepua suddenly realized, he was bare-chested! From every quarter came a hissing of indrawn breath.

Kiore seemed to grasp that people were curious about the body that he usually kept covered. Tepua glimpsed his flush of embarrassment as he threw the *tiputa* aside. Glancing once at the curious faces, Kiore squared his well-muscled shoulders and strode forward to stand before the crowd.

Tepua recalled tales that were repeated about foreigners. It was true, she saw, that his skin was pale where screened from sun by clothing. His arms were thick and corded, his waist surprisingly slender.

As for thick pelts, the reports were obviously false. On his broad chest she saw only wispy swirls. He bore no tattoos, but the curling patterns of light-colored hair down his chest almost made up the lack.

Now Paruru came forward carrying the spears, and made a sign for Kiore to hold out his arms. But the sailor waved him away. "Different dance," he said. He called to his companion, who began playing his flute again.

The melody was lively, but totally unlike anything Tepua had heard before. Kiore launched into a step that left everyone breathless. He folded his arms across his chest, then crouched and began to kick his legs out from that difficult position.

Seeing such an outlandish display, the onlookers grinned. Meanwhile Paruru glanced about in bewilderment. He had issued a challenge, but the foreigner had cheated him by starting his own performance. Tepua felt a momentary sympathy for the warrior as she watched him retreat from the center of the clearing. Poor Paruru! In an instant he had been forgotten.

From behind her, she heard cries of people who wanted to try the sailor's step. A few came forward, then more, children and even elders joining in behind Kiore. They quickly discovered that the foreign dance was not easy. People tripped over their own ankles and went sprawling. They accidentally kicked each other, backed into each other, and fell down.

Tepua watched Ehi, mat skirt flying, breasts and rump bouncing, necklace threatening to fly off. She laughed until her sides ached. Then Kiore left the field and came before her. "You try?" he asked. "Different one."

His suggestion, she realized, had not gone unnoticed. Many faces turned to watch as Tepua hesitated. But she was *ariki,* one who must excel in all things. As a girl, she had won renown for dancing. How could she refuse him?

She put aside her cape and headdress, and heard a murmur of approval from the onlookers. She let Kiore take her left hand in his right, and they walked into a clear space that the crowd made for them. The new step was far easier, involving a heel-and-toe movement, but no deep bending of the knees. Soon they were bouncing together to Nika's piping. Kiore called "Come dance," to the onlookers, holding out his free hand, and Maukiri eagerly clasped it. Then a bold little girl took Maukiri's free hand and the line began to grow.

What a strange and exciting rhythm the little flute produced! Nika, usually so dour, beamed with pleasure as he played. But Kiore was the one who held her attention—his fingers warm against hers, the musky scent of his body, the glow in his eyes when the late rays of afternoon sunlight caught them. The dance went on and on, the line growing, then spiraling inward so that others could find places. At last almost everyone in the crowd joined the merriment.

Breathless from exertion and laughter, Kiore finally stopped. He bent over, resting his hands on his thighs while he gulped air. The others quit soon, breaking up into small groups and drifting away. Night was coming on. Some revelers headed home while others lingered, talking and joking.

Tepua watched as a group of stout and matronly women—grandmothers every one—crowded toward Kiore. She stepped aside to leave him with his admirers. "Look at those thick arms," shouted one. "How the muscles show beneath the skin!"

"Feel that thigh!"

"His shoulder!"

She saw Kiore straighten up, startled. He began to look alarmed as more women grabbed at him, putting their hands on his calves and feeling the corded muscles of his forearms. He yelped when someone evidently poked at a sensitive place.

Tepua stepped closer. With a sharp clap she ordered the women to let him go. They dispersed, grumbling among themselves, complaining of weakling husbands and lazy sons at home. Kiore, with an odd grin, turned to face Tepua. "The big ladies . . ." he began, but then seemed lost for words.

"They are old," Tepua said with a laugh. "Sometimes we let them do as they please. It is not much fun for them looking after grandchildren all day. Do the grandmothers of your land enjoy seeing strong, young men?"

"Strong?" He seemed to ponder her question. Then he puffed out his chest and strutted around a bit. "Yes. Crowds go. To watch . . ."

"Then that is a way our people are like yours." When a look of amusement showed in his eyes, she had an urge to embrace him, but with so many people watching she did not dare. Worse yet, she noticed Paruru gazing toward her unhappily. Going up to her *kaito-nui,* she spoke a few friendly words, trying to ease his glum expression.

How strangely things had turned out. Both Kiore and Paruru were competing for her favor—and with everyone watching! She resolved to discourage both men without making them angry. She wanted Paruru and Kiore to be friends. Somehow she must end this foolish rivalry.

"Come," she called to the attendants who stood behind her. These young women, too, had been dancing; their faces gleamed with perspiration. "I am ready to go home."

The attendants followed her with evident reluctance. Later, Tepua knew, they would slip away to meet their lovers and dance again on the moonlit shore.

With a twinge of regret she recalled the nights of her own youth—when she had been forced to remain inside with her chaperon while the sounds of music and laughter drifted to her from the beach. Now it must be the same again. She had made her decision. If she took a lover, it would mean one more entanglement here, one more reason to stay.

She followed the path along the shore, hearing the drumbeat begin again. Tightening her fist, she tried not to envy the others.

NINE

In the days that followed, Tepua was gratified to see how well people took to the foreigners. All the important families wanted them as guests; each day the sailors received new invitations.

Sometimes Tepua attended these small gatherings, watching with keen attention whenever the newcomers offered to entertain their hosts. In their early visits, the men showed only the chants and dance steps of their fellow sailors. Later they began to act out scenes from life in their own land.

In one instance, Kiore played the part of an animal that was big enough for a man to ride on. Nika, straddling his back, wielded an imaginary stick. Kiore made sounds through his nostrils, shook his head wildly, and finally tossed Nika to the ground. This performance proved so popular that every child on the island wanted to try it.

Almost every day, Tepua spent time with Kiore, gradually teaching him her language, and learning words of his. She also kept up her visits to Kohekapu, whose condition seemed little changed despite all the effort of healers.

Suddenly her routine was interrupted by a message from Cone-shell. He invited Tepua to visit him, promising a grand welcome. She talked to the priests and elders to ask their opinions.

"Kohekapu will be the same when you get back," said one. "He will not complain if you leave for a few days."

"The foreigners are no trouble," said another. "Paruru's men can look after them."

Tepua was less than eager to see Cone-shell, expecting him to renew his demands for the foreign goods. Nor did she care to give up Kiore's engaging company. But the prospect of seeing Umia again drew her to accept Cone-shell's offer. She decided to visit Heka first, to see what advice Piho's chiefess might give.

"Come," said Heka to Tepua as they stood on the lagoon side of Heka's islet and gazed at the calm, blue-gray water. "The tide is out and the air is cool. A good morning for walking on the reef."

"It is a good time for walking," Tepua agreed, wishing she could put aside her worries about the chiefhood. She glanced up at white clouds hiding the sun and patches of sky showing through. The faint breeze was refreshing. Some exercise might help clear her thoughts.

Heka's servants brought sandals made of the white inner bark of hibiscus. Tepua generally had no use for such comforts; the soles of her feet had been toughened by years of walking over rough terrain. But she knew how a chief must act. She stepped into the ropy, thick-soled sandals and strode down toward the water.

"Where we are going," said Heka in a low voice, "there will be no chance for anyone to overhear." Heka's well-fleshed legs did not seem to slow her down as she splashed through the shallows, following the shoreline. Tepua walked beside her, enjoying the feel of cool water. The air smelled moist and briny.

Followed by servants, the two women rounded a point of land. Here woody *mikimiki* grew almost to the water's edge; the shore was covered with white, fist-size chunks of smoothed coral. Tepua felt the breeze stiffen as she came around the bend.

They had reached the extremity of the islet, and now Tepua had a clear view seaward. As the wind ruffled her hair she watched breakers crashing against the distant reef, rising in columns of foam. Above the wave tops, birds swooped and cried.

Within the lagoon and close to shore a long coral bench stood almost exposed, its covering of kelp showing above the water. One could walk far out on such a reef and find many good things to eat along the way. Tepua glanced back and saw that Heka's servants had prepared themselves. Several men held fishing spears; women carried *fara* leaf baskets.

A good meal would come from this walk, Tepua thought. But more important was the advice that Heka had for her. Tepua stepped up onto the kelp-covered shelf. The surface was uneven, cratered with many small pools. A starfish of velvety blue lay in one. A sea urchin's black spines bristled from another. The reef also had occasional deep holes, which might be home to an octopus or a fierce moray eel.

"Your chiefhood is like this path," said Heka when they had gone a short way out. "There is firm footing if you are careful. But you cannot afford a misstep." She pointed to a stonefish that lay close by, its mottled body and venomous spines nearly invisible.

"I will have even firmer footing," Tepua answered, "if I can settle my differences with Cone-shell."

"If they can be settled."

Cone-shell's invitation had said nothing about acknowledging her rule as high chief. "I think I know what is on his mind," said Tepua. "Cone-shell was hoping that the foreigners would prove my undoing. But the visitors have charmed everyone and made themselves welcome."

"Yes," said Heka. "Cone-shell sees that you are only growing stronger. If he had thoughts of toppling you from office, he knows now that he will have to wait."

"Then perhaps that is why he offers friendship."

"It is possible," said Heka. "If he shows his pretty colors, you may overlook the sting he is saving for you."

"Even so, I have accepted his gesture of friendship. The

people of Varoa support me. I saw crowds of them hailing me on the day of my investiture.''

''The people of Varoa are wiser than their chief. But what about Umia? You say nothing about him.''

Tepua paused. Far behind her she heard splashing and a quiet cry as one of the servants made a catch. ''I am hoping to speak with Umia. That is one reason I accepted the invitation.''

''Then I wish you a pleasant stay with Cone-shell.'' Heka quickened her pace, stepping over a pool where tiny hermit crabs crept in their borrowed shells. In earlier days Tepua would have stopped to pick one up and watch it pull in its claws, but that was no game for a chief.

''There is something else I wish to say, Tepua-ariki, and I hope you will hear my advice.'' Heka came to a sudden halt. In front of her the walkway ended where the reef was cut by a deep channel. ''It is something you have heard before.''

''That I should take a husband . . .''

''Ah, Tepua. You are so stubborn. You keep saying no, when you mean yes. Everyone has heard about you and the bright-haired foreigner—''

''It is nothing—''

''That is not what people tell me. This man may be popular, but only as a novelty. Nobody will accept him as the husband of our chief.''

Tepua stepped back in surprise, and almost lost her footing. ''He will not be.''

''Then you must end the rumors. If you take a proper consort, those voices will be stilled.''

Tepua frowned. Evidently Heka had not forgotten her own stake in this. ''Do you suggest Paruru?''

''And what is wrong with my brother?'' Heka asked indignantly.

''He is a good warrior,'' Tepua managed, though she heard the lack of conviction in her own voice. Recent events had changed Paruru; sometimes he no longer seemed the man she had looked up to as a girl. That was not the only reason for turning away from him. Tepua did not wish to encourage *any* suitor.

"Tell me this," said Heka. "Have you thought of what will happen to these outsiders? Will they remain with us?"

For a moment Tepua considered how to explain the situation simply. What she understood of the sailors' misfortune came from Kiore. He and his companions had set out from home on a huge three-masted vessel. After many days at sea, discontented crewmen had turned against their master, though he was an able leader, and had thrown him into the sea to drown. Soon afterward Kiore and two friends had escaped the dire troubles aboard and gone off in the smaller boat.

"The foreigners cannot reach home in their *vaka*," Tepua said. "Kiore wants to head for a closer port and search for his countrymen, but Nika is not in a hurry to leave. I think the sailors will be with us awhile."

"Then I offer you this advice. Find a wife for each of the men and get them settled. Otherwise the outsiders will always be causing trouble."

"Wife?" Tepua felt a gnawing in the pit of her stomach as she gazed down at the surging water in the channel.

Heka put her hand on Tepua's arm and began to talk excitedly. "Yes. That is your answer. Marry him to Maukiri."

"Maukiri will be happy enough. If Nika is willing, why not?"

"No. Not Nika. *Your* outsider. Marry Kiore to Maukiri."

Tepua stared at Heka's sly expression as the implications began to sink in. It was customary that a woman could share the husband of her sister, so long as she did not make a habit of it. In these islands, cousins were the same as sisters—they were free to share their men. If Maukiri married Kiore, then sometimes he could be Tepua's. . . .

"This is foolish talk," said Tepua angrily. "Kiore and

Maukiri have no interest in each other. I will not force my cousin to quit the man she cares for and take another.''

''Ah, Tepua. I am sure there is little difference between one outsider and another. Tell Maukiri to try them both in the dark and see if I am right.''

Tepua felt heat rush to her face. Looking down at Heka's meaty hand clamping her arm, she felt a strong urge to topple Piho's chief into the water. Harshly, she retorted, ''I do not agree that men are like so many coconuts.''

''There are plenty of both,'' answered Heka, undeterred. ''And for that, I am always praising the ancestors.''

''I will settle this in my own way,'' said Tepua. ''I'm sorry to disappoint your brother, but my home is now in Tahiti. In the end, I will return, and I do not intend to leave a child behind. Umia will rule next—when he is ready. The priests decided that long ago.''

Heka sighed and released her grip. ''Tepua-ariki, that is just how I thought you would answer.''

Tepua squeezed Heka's hand. ''I will not be leaving soon. Faka-ora refuses to let me go. At least you and I will have more time together.'' Both women turned around to retrace their steps toward shore.

Now Tepua saw that the servants' baskets swung heavily from their hands. The walk had yielded a good harvest and it was not over. A short distance ahead, a man was still at work. He had poked a stick into a deep hole; now a spotted tentacle was wrapped around the stick. The man knelt, lunging his hand down until his entire arm was underwater. Then, with a cry, he brought up a squirming, white mass.

''Octopus . . . good!'' Heka called with delight. ''We will bake that one with taro leaves. A delicacy for the high chief.''

Tepua agreed, licking her lips. But even anticipating this treat could not keep her thoughts from Kiore.

The day after her visit with Heka, Tepua arrived at the nearby *motu* where Varoa Clan held sway. Cone-shell put on the show of welcome she had expected—women dancing on the beach, warriors strutting. But he did not speak the words of acknowledgment she wished to hear: *maeva ariki*.

Looking elegant in his tall headdress of feathers and his necklaces of dolphin teeth, Cone-shell escorted her toward his assembly ground above the beach. Along the way, Tepua saw a horde of servants preparing a feast. Her gaze passed over the brightly colored fish and heaps of vegetables, then paused at a pile of knobby roots attached to jointed stems—dried roots of *ava,* known here as *kava.* Cone-shell must have had recent dealings with other islands, she thought. The intoxicating *kava* plants grew poorly in atoll soil; he could not have obtained them locally.

Custom required Cone-shell to provide a feast. In serving her *kava,* however, he would bestow on her a special honor. She wondered if he was trying to make amends for his coarse behavior when the foreign goods were examined.

She put the question aside as she walked with him to his sitting place in the shade of a huge *fara* tree. "I am pleased by your welcome," Tepua said, recalling the crowded beach at her arrival. "But someone is missing. I hoped to see Umia here."

A faint frown showed on Cone-shell's face. "Umia is with me, but I speak for him. I see no need for my nephew to join us."

"What would people think," she countered, "if they knew that I came here and ignored my young brother? After my long absence, we have only spoken a few words in passing."

When she persisted, reminding Cone-shell that Kohekapu was eager to hear from his son, Varoa's chief relented. Umia arrived, but looked ill at ease, glancing at his uncle before stepping forward to greet Tepua. He quickly pressed his nose to her cheek, giving the briefest of embraces.

Tepua invited Umia to walk with her alone. She glared at Cone-shell, whose mouth was already open to deny her request. "I will walk with my brother," she said firmly. Grudgingly, Cone-shell gestured his assent.

Umia followed her to a deserted stretch of shoreline. Here strands of beach morning glory, blearing flowers of pale violet, crept over the sand and halfway down to the water. Tepua turned to her brother.

Today, for the first time, she noticed Kohekapu's features in his face—the high-boned cheeks, the flared nostrils, the large, dark eyes and bushy brows. He was certainly no longer a boy. His arms and legs bore the tattoo marks of a young warrior. His long, black hair was bound back by a warrior's knot.

"Why is that you were gone so long, sister?" asked Umia in a clear voice when he finally raised his eyes to hers. "When you came back, I barely remembered you."

"For me, it was not that long. But while I was away you changed from a child into a man."

"Then why am I not chief? Why did Faka-ora push me aside?"

"That is what I want to talk to you about." Tepua sighed. "Do you understand that I came home only because of our father's illness? I did not want the chiefhood. It was forced on me."

"I have heard otherwise." He eyed her warily.

"From your mother and Cone-shell?"

"They say you tricked the high priest . . . with Tahitian sorcery."

"Tricked?" Tepua caught herself before she could fling back the accusation. Natunatu, of all people, blaming someone for using sorcery! "What of the chiefs and elders? Did they also succumb to my spells?"

Umia gave a faint smile. "Perhaps."

"Then you are not certain."

"Of that, no," he replied. "But everyone agrees—even you—that signs appeared at my birth, and the gods showed that I must be chief."

"The signs did not tell *when*."

He hesitated.

"There is your answer, Umia. You will rule after me. And soon, I hope."

"Cone-shell talks of a different outcome. He says you will stay here and lead us into disaster. He says you will adopt foreign ways and scorn the teachings of our ancestors."

Tepua stamped her foot. "Your uncle is full of bad wind!"

Her brother sighed. "I have listened to him all my life."

"That is too long. Tell me your own thoughts. If you were in my place, what would *you* do with the foreign sailors?"

"I think . . . I would be careful."

"You would not send them out to drown?"

"They have skills and goods that may help us. I would like to have those, so long as we do not offend the spirits."

"Good. Then you and I agree on something."

"Perhaps not, Tepua. I am told that these men show no reverence for the gods, unless they are constantly reminded. They set a poor example."

"Paruru is teaching them. Soon they will learn all our ways."

"If they do not?"

Tepua felt a chill on her shoulders as she studied Umia's troubled face. "Then I will send them away," she answered hoarsely. "Does that satisfy you?"

"I will be happy when they are gone."

"But you have not even seen these men! You spurned my invitation to their welcome, so let me make another. Leave your uncle. Come live with the clan of your father."

Umia looked at her in astonishment. "How can you ask that? My home is here."

"Someday, my brother, you will have to stand up to Cone-shell. You will have to show him that you can make your own way. Until then, you cannot be high chief."

For a moment she saw a new expression in Umia's face,

a hint that she had gotten through to him. Then his features hardened again. "We must go," he said brusquely. "My uncle is waiting."

When she returned to the others, she saw that Cone-shell had assembled nearly all the important men of his clan. Umia was not included in the gathering, nor did Cone-shell explain the omission. Tepua also noticed that a heap of *kava* roots had been placed nearby on a mat of palm leaves. A large wooden bowl lay on the mat, along with polished coconut-shell cups. Was Umia considered too young to drink *kava?* she wondered.

And why was Cone-shell making this unusual offer of hospitality? She recalled tales of legendary heroes who were tricked into imbibing too much *kava.* But the stories exaggerated the effect of the drink. When she had tried it in Tahiti, she had felt mildly invigorated, then drowsy, but had not fallen into a stupor.

She glanced about until she found Two-eels, the leader of the escort that Paruru had sent with her. Two-eels could be trusted to look after her safety, she thought, but found herself wishing he had brought along more warriors.

Cone-shell offered her the squat, four-legged stool beside his own. It was the same height as his, not the proper seat to be offered the high chief. "I will stand," Tepua told him, unwilling to let her head be lower than his.

She glanced about at the other men and saw frowns of disapproval. Had they hoped that she would give up her privileges? "My guest will not stand," said Cone-shell firmly.

"If I sit there, then you must bend over," Tepua answered Cone-shell. "That is a position I do not think you will enjoy."

The other men muttered among themselves. Tepua wondered if this meeting would end before it even got started. Cone-shell made an angry gesture, beckoned a servant, and gave an order.

Tepua felt no sense of triumph when she saw the servant returning. He did not carry the higher stool that she had expected, but only a handful of mats. The servant slipped these under the seat intended for her.

Again Cone-shell offered her the stool. Tepua sighed her acceptance and sat down, realizing as she did so how cleverly he had arranged things. The mats had merely raised her head to be even with his. He had acknowledged her as his equal but no better. She could do nothing about that now but clench her jaw.

At Cone-shell's signal three girls came forward to ready the drink. Tepua had performed this task for her father, and took little notice now of the preparations. Cone-shell began to speak while the maidens chewed the roots, spitting the infusion into the wooden bowl before them.

With forced joviality he said, "It is good that you visit us today, daughter of Kohekapu. We of Varoa Clan are happy to have you here. It is not often that one of such distinguished lineage comes for a visit." He went on in this manner, speaking of the history of Varoa Clan and of Ahiku Clan and of the atoll, but always avoiding the issue of her claim on the chieftainship. Meanwhile the maidens finished the first part of their task and began straining the root fibers from the cloudy liquid.

Tepua also made a speech, expressing her pleasure at being a guest of Varoa Clan. She, too, avoided the issue of her rank. It was a topic that would be discussed later, after the *kava* and the food.

She noticed the men leaning forward with eagerness as the preparations continued. Fresh coconut water was added to the *kava* brew, and the contents stirred until whipped to a froth. The first maiden filled a cup for Tepua. The second filled one for Cone-shell. Together the girls came forward and offered the drink.

Tepua dared not refuse it; in presenting *kava*, Cone-shell was paying her the highest respect. Fortunately, she knew the proper procedure for drinking. She took a deep breath and began to swallow, not stopping until she had drained the cup.

The peppery spice of the infusion was so strong that she barely tasted the mild coconut water that was mixed with it. She felt a numbing of her lips and noticed a sudden racing of her thoughts. The elders of Varoa Clan, partaking also, made brief speeches, but soon all talk ceased. Her legs felt heavy, suffused by the comforting lethargy that she had experienced before.

But an unexpected part of the ceremony began. Men sitting outside the central gathering were being offered the drink. Normally only people of high rank imbibed *kava*. Now one of the maidens invited Two-eels to come forward, and the young warrior was so flattered that he seemed to forget his station.

Tepua tried to speak, ordering him to refuse the drink. She found that her tongue had grown as heavy as her limbs. Helpless, in anguish, she watched Two-eels take a full cup.

He gulped his portion, made a brief speech, then stepped back to accept the adulation of his warriors. For the moment he seemed unaffected, and Tepua began to think that her suspicions were misplaced. Perhaps only she was so strongly touched by the drink. . . .

In the excited state induced by *kava*, she found visions flashing in her mind almost too quickly to be followed. She imagined Kiore married to this woman or that, saw their children born and growing up, the hair of their youngsters colored in patches, dark in places and sandy in others. Then she saw Nika and Maukiri producing boys with black eyebrows and red beards. The sight made her want to laugh, but her lips did not move.

Then another vision came, and this one frightened her. A huge vessel, bearing many outsiders, arrived at the atoll. The men carried thunder-clubs—dozens of the loud weapons.

The strangers demanded food. To appease them, every coconut palm was stripped. When the invaders asked for more, and none could be found, they filled the sky with the smoke and noise of their weapons. Women screamed; children fled to the forest.

She had a sense that this would actually happen, if not on her own atoll then on some other, if not to her people then to their children or grandchildren. Greedy foreigners in large numbers would come; not even the gods could stop them.

Somehow the island people must survive the onslaught. She did not know how, only that she must play some part in helping them prepare. This was the thought she clung to as her visions became more and more tangled, and the weight of her head ever greater. Her arms grew as heavy as ironwood logs. Her eyes fell shut and she knew that she was falling. . . .

Tepua woke, and sniffed for the scents from Cone-shell's ovens. The *kava* had overcome her, but now she felt ready to rejoin the festivities. She rubbed her eyes as her memory of the unsettling dreams began to fade.

Gloom surrounded her, and she thought for a moment that dusk had come. Had she dozed that long? And why was she sprawled on old leaves instead of on a comfortable mat? Around her, thick stands of trees screened out all but a few glimmers of sunlight.

She jumped up in fright, suddenly realizing what Cone-shell had done. Someone had taken her to the forested interior of his islet. There was not even a sign of habitation here.

She drew in her breath when she saw shapes standing beyond the nearest trees. Yes, there was a sign of human presence in this deserted place. While blood began to pound in her ears she crept closer, until she could clearly see the arrangement of coral blocks and the majestic *pukatea* trees shading them. The site was overgrown, but the ruins of a *marae* still stood here.

A small pile of skulls in the shadows made her stagger back. This was a place of spirits, a place where ancient ghosts of Varoa Clan lingered. It did not matter how she had come here; she wanted only to find the brightness and open air of the shore.

Behind her, through the forest, she heard the faint pounding of waves on the outer reef. She turned in the opposite direction, heading for the lagoon, but met small uprooted trees blocking the way. Twisted roots and sharp broken branches made every step treacherous. In her haste, she stumbled, scoring her ankle painfully. Another stick snapped against her skin, cutting her calf.

Nothing here looked familiar. She had never seen so dense an atoll forest. Where people lived, fallen wood did not remain in heaps, but was gathered for heating the ovens. This area looked as if no one had walked on it for many seasons.

The thought made her blood pound even harder. Had she somehow wandered onto forbidden land? She plunged on through the damp, steamy undergrowth until swampy ground stopped her. Insects swarmed about her face and arms as she hastily retreated. None of this made sense. She wondered if she could still be on Varoa's main islet.

Where were the friendly waters of the lagoon? Around her she saw shadowed trunks blocking her way, entangling vines, stray chunks of coral that shifted underfoot. She ducked low, crawling beneath the angling bare branches of old hibiscus trees.

She reached a dense stand of *fara,* where aerial roots descending from each tree formed a barrier she could not cross. She bypassed the *fara,* to enter a pleasant corridor under piney ironwood trees where nothing grew from the needle-covered ground. But the corridor took her in the wrong direction and she had to turn back.

Arms and legs scratched and bleeding, she stumbled through another swamp, then past young coconut trees that barely reached her waist. She tore her way through another wall of vines, and then, with a cry of joy, glimpsed bright, calm water. In another moment she was down the slope and out onto the glittering beach. She turned around, shouting to anyone who might hear her, but nobody came.

Gooseflesh rose on her arms as she surveyed the unfamiliar scene. She was surely no longer on Cone-shell's *motu*. Where were the houses, the canoes, the people? Looking across the lagoon, she could not even see the other islets that were visible from Cone-shell's shore.

Refusing to believe her senses, she ran along the beach, shouting, expecting to hear an answering call or to reach a settlement. Then the beach ended in a tangle of *mikimiki*, and she was forced to splash through the shallows.

She turned back to run in the opposite direction. All too quickly she reached the other end of the *motu*. From here she could just make out, in the far distance, a few tops of palm trees marking another islet of the coral ring. But that other *motu* was hopelessly out of reach for someone without a canoe. Even if she had the strength to swim that far, she dared not try with so many scratches on her body. The sharks would catch up with her long before she got across.

She fell down on the damp beach and buried her face in her hands. Now she understood where she had been taken. This was an isolated *motu*, a haunted place once inhabited by Varoa Clan, but long abandoned. It sat alone in a corner of the atoll that people rarely visited.

How had Cone-shell managed this? Two-eels had undoubtedly succumbed to the *kava* as well, leaving her guards with no leader. She pictured her confused men still waiting outside a guesthouse, believing that she lay within under a *tahunga's* care.

She had badly misjudged Varoa's chief. He was not planning to wait until she made an obvious misstep. He would try to seize the chiefhood for Umia *now*, while her brother could still be controlled. Perhaps, in trying to woo Umia, she had even strengthened Cone-shell's resolve.

Tepua groaned softly. She was trapped where no one would find her. Cone-shell could leave her here as long as he wished.

TEN

From the *motu* beach, Tepua glanced at the sun, already far down the sky. Her throat felt dry, her stomach empty, but her first thoughts were not of drink or food. She dreaded the oncoming night. She would be alone here, with only the light of the waning moon for company. This would be a night when spirits walked the land.

The ghosts were already alive in her imagination—vengeful phantoms who ripped apart and devoured anyone they caught. She needed a shelter; even a crude one might offer some protection. Better still would be a fire.

Tepua closed her eyes and recalled all the times she had seen fire kindled. It was a duty usually performed by men. Even in her unhappy days as a servant, long ago, she had never carried out this demanding task, although she knew how.

She needed to make a rubbing stick or "fire plow" and a grooved bed of dry wood, and she had do this without proper tools. Looking about her at broken shells, she tossed aside many that had been worn smooth by water and sand. At last she cracked a clamshell between two pieces of coral and obtained a sharp, if ragged, edge.

To find wood meant going inland, but the thought of returning to the dimly lit forest made her tremble. Instead she ran along the beach until she finally spotted a *kahaia* close to shore, its branches sweeping the ground. After a brief prayer she bent underneath, catching a faint perfume

129

from the clusters of white flowers. She snapped off a stick for the fire plow and put it aside. That was the easy part.

Searching beneath the leaves, she found a branch that had partially broken from the tree and died. This was just what she needed for the bed. All she had to do was extend the split until the branch broke in half lengthwise.

She wedged the sharp shell into the gap and hammered it with another piece of wood, slowly splitting the rest of the branch. Twigs rattled above, dropping small green berries down on her head. At last, with a snap, a section of her branch broke free. The split portion was short, but she thought it would serve.

Returning to the beach, she used a sharp piece of coral to cut away the exposed pith, leaving a lengthwise groove. To finish the plow itself she sharpened the thinner stick. Now all she needed was dry kindling and firewood.

Looking around at the dampness of the forest, she immediately felt disheartened. The old coconut husks on the ground were soaked from recent rains and would prove useless for tinder. On an exposed part of the beach she collected dry ironwood needles and hoped they would do.

Finally she gathered fuel for her fire, fallen coconuts for food, and palm fronds to use in a shelter. By now the sunlight was almost gone. Standing on the beach, she took up the fire plow and began a chant she had heard many times.

Hika, hika tau ahi!

She put the end of the bed-stick under her foot and rubbed the plow's point along the groove. Again and again she stroked, repeating the chant, until she could smell the scent of heated wood. A few specks of smoldering wood dust collected at the end of the groove; quickly she dumped these onto the tinder, which she had spread on a leaf.

Mau tutu, mau rangaranga!

She fell to the ground, blowing gently, expecting to hear the welcome crackle of flames. She waited, then began shaking the tinder impatiently. No fire!

With a sigh, she stood again, resuming the work and the song. Her back ached from the unaccustomed posture, but she kept at it, until the air was filled with the scent of smoldering wood. Once more, she attempted to set the tinder alight. . . .

No matter how often she tried, however, she could not produce the tiniest glimmer of flame. "The spirits of this place are against me!" she cried as she angrily tossed the sticks aside. The short twilight had already begun. She barely had time left for building a shelter.

She jammed a forked stick into the ground and dropped another stick in the fork to serve as a simple ridgepole. Against this pole she leaned several mature coconut fronds, as she had seen fishermen do; producing a thin wall that fluttered in the gathering breeze. She threw a few other fronds over them, tied everything in place with lengths of beach vine, and crawled inside.

Her mouth was dry, her throat parched. In her haste to finish the other tasks, she had not stopped to open the coconuts. Now, in darkness and without tools, she could do nothing to help herself. Within the tiny space of the shelter she curled up in a ball and tried not to think about ghosts or thirst.

In time the moon rose, but Tepua did not care to look out at it. She saw glimmers of light against the palm-frond walls and wished she could sleep. She wanted to believe that no harm could come to her within the shelter.

But the forest refused to be silent. Every gust of wind made the leaves rattle. She heard other sounds that she could not explain. Creaking branches? Birdcalls? Hermit crabs scuttling over twigs?

There were chants for warding off spirits, and she recited every one she knew. Unwillingly she recalled the *marae* in the woods, its coral slabs blackened by age. Restless spirits of the dead dwelled among the bones that lay hidden there.

She felt perspiration forming on her face and back. When

the wind picked up, seeping through the walls, the moisture grew cold and made her shiver. Cone-shell had even taken her cloak, leaving her only the mat skirt for clothing.

All she had was this flimsy shelter for protection. How the ghosts would shriek their laughter when they came to swoop down on her! She imagined wild tangles of hair streaming behind their blue-black faces, and long teeth gleaming in the moonlight.

"Tapahi-roro-ariki!" she cried, calling on the ancestress who had protected her for so long. "What am I to do?"

She listened for an answer. The wind dropped suddenly and all she could hear was the soft lapping of waves nearby and the distant thundering of the reef. A voice seemed to speak to her, but at first she was not sure that she understood.

"Be defiant, daughter," she thought the voice said. Tepua squirmed in the narrow confines and tried to listen again.

Then she saw Tapahi-roro-ariki as her ancestress must have looked when she ruled long ago. She was a tall fierce woman, her loins bound with the *maro kura,* her head adorned by the high headdress of tropic bird feathers. One hand clenched the shaft of her double-ended spear; the other gripped the handle of a polished ironwood club.

Tapahi-roro-ariki, Head-cleaving Chief, was the name she had taken. She had been the first to unite the atoll's quarreling clans. Many skulls were broken by her war club, but in the end she brought peace and ruled wisely.

Tapahi-roro-ariki would not have tolerated a sea slug like Cone-shell. As for the ghosts of Varoa—she would have laughed in their long-toothed faces.

Now the voice that Tepua had heard seemed to speak again. "You are Kohekapu's daughter," whispered the waves lapping in the lagoon. "You are *ariki.* Have no fear," boomed the breakers on the reef. She thought of the coconuts she had gathered, the sweet milk, the soft meat within.

With a cry of defiance against Cone-shell and all his clan, Tepua pushed her way out of the shelter and stood on the beach. Raising herself to her full height, she turned toward the center of the island. "Here I am, ghosts of Varoa Clan," she shouted, watching the shadows in the moonlight. "Here I stand—Tepua-mua-ariki. Come to me if you dare."

From the woods she heard an answering flurry of creaking and flapping, and her heart almost burst from fright. But it was only the wind that had risen again, bringing the scent of the sea. She was hearing the natural sounds of the forest.

With a sudden fury, she picked up a coconut and battered it against a splintered log. A sharp stub of branch sticking out served as her husking stick. When the end of the nut was exposed, she cut open the "mouth" with a sliver of coral, put the cool, soothing liquid to her lips, and began to drink. . . .

In the morning, Tepua saw two canoes approaching the island. Unsurprised, she did not stand and call to the boats. Instead, she finished eating the meat of the clams she had gathered, then hastily buried the leavings. She perched herself high on a log, sat erect with her chin held high, and waited to be found.

When the first *vaka* came close, she did not even blink. From the bow, Cone-shell gazed at her, his smug expression rapidly fading. Her calm exterior, she thought, was already unnerving him. If he had come to find her crazed by fright, he was surely disappointed.

She said nothing as he strode ashore. Behind him, the second canoe come in; with a quick glance she surveyed the men aboard. *Priests!* Suddenly she felt her courage faltering. She had expected Cone-shell to appear, intending to bully her into some concessions. But what did he need with priests? Was there some bizarre ceremony he wished performed on the ancient *marae*?

"Life to you," said Cone-shell as he stepped briskly from the canoe and strode up the beach.

Tepua stared at him and did not respond.

"I regret that the *kava* was so strong," he continued. "I have warned the girls to be more careful next time."

Still she refused to speak.

"I am glad we found you safe."

Glad? As if he had not ordered her put here. Was he trying to make her believe that spirits had carried her away? She tried to hold still as the priests came up behind him.

The only one she knew was Raha, Cone-shell's brother, high priest for Varoa Clan. Raha was uncommonly thin, a head shorter than his brother. His bulbous knees made a strange contrast to his slender legs. In his hand he carried the feather-tipped staff of his office.

"We have serious matters to discuss," said Raha, coming to a halt beside his brother. "I am concerned, Tepua-mua, that you are not qualified for the high office you have taken. Faka-ora has chosen to ignore the obvious difficulty, but I cannot." He stepped closer, raising his staff high as he spoke. "I know all that has happened. You left these islands as a maiden, and never reached your destination. The marriage planned for you did not take place. Your obligation to remain chaste never ended."

Tepua glared at him. Behind her, against the log, she had propped a sharp stick of ironwood. It was a crude spear, but one that might cut deeply. Perhaps she could defend herself, if only for a short time.

"If you have been defiled," continued Raha, "then the gods will not tolerate your presence among us. We will be forced to get rid of your evil. You and everything you have touched must be destroyed."

"The great crimson cloth was wound around my loins," she answered indignantly. "The *maro kura* is the pride of all our people, worn by a long line of chiefs. Will you destroy *that*?" She felt blood rush to her face as she waited for an answer. Too many times she had heard men claim that some sacred object would be ruined by a woman's touch. They made exceptions for female chiefs, but always seemed eager to put those exceptions aside.

"If the question arises, I will pray to the ancestors," he replied firmly. "They will give me guidance."

"And if *you* touch me, will you have to destroy your own flesh?" She thrust her hand toward him.

Raha stepped back hastily, his lips curling with distaste. Was he really afraid, she wondered, or putting on an act for his companions? The high priest called another man, older, but heavily built, whose tattoos marked him as a *tahunga*. "You will be examined," Raha told her, "by one who can do so and not be harmed. He will tell us what is to be your fate."

Examined? Tepua felt an instinct to draw her skirt more tightly around her, but forced her hands to remain still. She glanced from one grim face to the other. Behind the priests she saw the paddlers and the warriors who had also come in the canoes. She began to tremble, and hoped that no one would notice. "Where is Umia?" she shouted so that everyone could hear. "If you challenge my claim to the chiefhood in his name, why is he not with you?"

"He ate too much at yesterday's feast," Cone-shell said, trying to make light of it as he patted his belly. "He needs to rest."

"Then come back with him tomorrow. He must be part of this. I want to hear the challenge from his own lips."

"I told you, Tepua-mua, that I speak for Umia," Cone-shell answered impatiently.

"Do you also *act* for him? Will you wield the sacred power in his place until he is ready to rule?"

Cone-shell gave no reply, but signaled the *tahunga* to advance. Tepua drew in her breath and fixed the man with a stare. "Cone-shell's silence is answer enough," she said harshly. "He plans to seize what can only be conferred by the gods." The *tahunga* seemed taken aback by her accusation, and for the moment he held his place.

"I am not the only one who must be tested," she continued loudly, wanting everyone to hear. "You, Cone-shell, must prove yourself worthy of assuming this power you crave."

"I need no test," said Varoa's chief.

Tepua looked away from him and addressed the others. The loyalty of Cone-shell's priests and warriors, she thought, would not easily be shaken. But the canoe paddlers might listen. . . . "Will you follow this man without a sign?" she asked. "A fisherman wants to know everything about the steersman of his boat. Are you ready to trust Cone-shell to steer our clans?"

Several paddlers frowned. One warrior wiped sweat from his brow. Whatever happened here, Tepua thought, these men would remember her biting words. "Are you sure that Cone-shell carries no sin?" she asked them. "What of his wives? Have they been questioned?"

"I can vouch for my family," declared Raha. "I have no such assurance in your case."

The worried looks eased. "Enough talk," said Cone-shell. "We will settle this now. Agree to our examination, Tepua, or give up your office."

Cone-shell's man stepped forward; Tepua reached behind her for the ironwood branch. She swung it around; the *tahunga* halted before its jagged point. "My own sins have been cleansed," she insisted, her voice beginning to crack. "Test me if you doubt, but let it be against Cone-shell."

She had a way to prove her worthiness—or learn, at the cost of her life, that she was wrong. For an instant she looked toward the end of the islet at the dark water running in from the sea. Everyone knew that the outer reef was broken there by a narrow channel. Boats never risked this pass, but sharks swam through freely.

"Is it possible that Cone-shell has no trust in his gods?" she taunted. "If he holds divine favor, let him take up my challenge. We will go to the sharks and ask which of us should rule."

A warrior muttered to his companion. Priests exchanged whispers. "There is no doubt clinging to me," answered Cone-shell. He signaled his men to advance on Tepua, but they seemed rooted in place.

"Then refuse my offer," she went on, hoping that no one would notice her trembling. "Do what you wish to me. Then try to make your way home, and see how the wind and waves deal with your canoes. In the end the sharks will prove me right."

She saw a few paddlers in the rear ranks arguing among themselves. Several others had apparently made their decision and were slowly moving toward their canoes. Suddenly there was a flurry of action. Three men dragged a boat into the water. Others hurried after them, some trying to hinder the launching, the rest joining it. Fighting broke out between those who wanted to abandon Varoa's chief and those who wished to stay.

Cone-shell sent warriors splashing after the *vaka,* but they were too slow to catch up. The men stood thigh-deep in water, shouting and waving their spears at the departing craft.

"My canoe!" screeched Raha, seeing that his *vaka* also had been launched by paddlers.

Tepua felt jubilant as she watched Cone-shell's dismay. "We are marooned together now," she called to him. "We can spend a pleasant night here. I will show you how to keep the ghosts away."

Some of Cone-shell's men flung themselves into the water and tried to catch the departing boats, but the paddlers only stroked faster. The men ashore cast worried looks toward the inland forest. Priests began chanting.

"Wait!" shouted Cone-shell to the men who were deserting him. "You misunderstood. I need no test, but I am not afraid to prove myself. Bring the canoes back and I will show you. I will swim the sharks' channel."

The paddlers returned and nervously faced their chief.

Cone-shell gazed at them with seeming indifference, waiting for the priests to agree how this test was to be carried out. First they insisted that Tepua sit in the stern, on a piece of matting, so that she would not touch the boat. Then the paddlers took the canoe into the fast-moving current beyond the islet. Trying to control her fears, she stared down into the clear water, dreading what she might see.

As they crossed the depths Tepua glimpsed a gray shape prowling below. Farther out she saw another shark surface, and the sight of black edging on its tail fin made her freeze. She had hoped to find blue sharks, for the great blues protected high chiefs of the islands.

These were not blues. The black-edged tail told her that they were gray reef sharks, small but swift killers that attacked *ariki* and commoner alike.

Cone-shell, seated in the bow, showed no fear. Was this a bluff, she wondered, an attempt to regain the confidence of his men? Or was he convinced that his gods would protect him? Tepua did not feel the same confidence. Although she had been ritually purified in Tahiti, she might have transgressed afterward in some way she did not know. If punishment came now, it would be swift.

As Cone-shell's canoe went on across the channel the priests' *vaka* remained behind. She and Cone-shell were to swim from their canoe back to the other. The gap between the boats kept widening, but the paddlers continued their strokes.

"I am ready," said Cone-shell at last, and raised a hand to signal the priests' *vaka*. Ahead lay a broad expanse of choppy dark blue water. Tepua wished she could make herself forget what lay below.

The other *vaka* looked tiny against the sky as the lagoonward current made it drift away from the *motu*. A sea wind began to blow stiffly, bringing a briny scent. Tepua's *vaka* rocked as Cone-shell stood up in the bow and tossed aside his cape. Hastily she offered a prayer to her guardian spirit. When Cone-shell dove, she forced herself to follow.

The chill of inrushing ocean water shocked her into a new awareness of her danger, but she did not pause to look about for sharks. Reaching ahead, she pulled herself forward, trying to swim quickly yet smoothly. So long as she avoided making sounds like a struggling fish, the sharks might keep away.

But she could not ignore the stinging from the cuts and scrapes she had suffered on the *motu*. This morning she had washed herself in the sea, cleaning off streaks of dried blood, but taking care not to disturb the fresh scabs. Even so, some seepage from the wounds might give her away. Cone-shell, so far as she knew, had no such handicap.

The current from the sea was even stronger than she had expected, pushing her so hard that she would miss her target. In order to meet the swimmers, the men on the *vaka* began paddling again. Tepua glanced over her shoulder and saw that Cone-shell had fallen behind. He was swimming slowly, just fast enough to stay afloat.

And for good reason. Just ahead, Tepua saw the upper lobe of a reef shark's tail break the surface. A splash made her look sharply behind as a swift gray form cut between her and Varoa's chief. Cone-shell might be able to back off. For her it was too late. *Tapahi-roro-ariki,* she called silently as she slowed, trying to control her rising panic.

She tried to keep her movements slow and even, doing nothing to draw attention, but the reef grays were already aroused. Despite her stinging eyes, she watched the sharks underwater. The nearest one lowered its black-tipped front fins and swam slowly with a stiff body motion. The gold eyes with their vertical-slit pupils seemed to fix on her.

Changing course to avoid the shark, she found two others coming on. Tepua submerged, knowing that she would be safer deep underwater. As she kicked her way down she caught a blurred view of gray forms zigzagging back and forth above. She tried to put some distance between herself and the sharks, but a need for air forced her to surface. She could not dive again; she was still gasping, and her terror made her breathing worse.

She choked back her cries and kept swimming, trying for an even, gentle motion, though her limbs quivered in fright. The briny taste seeping into her mouth took on a bitter tang. The burn on her tongue went to the back of her throat. Again she sent a silent plea to the spirit of her ancestress.

Ahead Tepua saw open water and no sign of the second canoe. Far to the side lay the *motu* where she had spent the night. How long ago that seemed now!

She swam on, with no clear sense of direction. The tangled greenery of the *motu* grew closer, though her course was taking her far past the islet. And the sharks would not leave her alone. They were constantly about her, sometimes deep, sometimes right at the surface. She heard shouts from behind, possibly Cone-shell's voice, but did not look back.

In the sound of the blood thrumming and keening in her ears, Tepua thought she heard someone speaking—a woman's voice, indistinct, but growing closer and clearer. It echoed the words that Tepua herself had shouted long ago:

You are the daughter of the reef, mothered by coral, fathered by coral. You are the sister of the shark, mothered by sharks, fathered by sharks.

"But these reef sharks do not listen to the gods!" she cried silently.

They listen to fear. They can taste weakness. To one who faces and overcomes both, they are no more than angelfish dancing past the coral.

Tepua's spirit sank. Was her ancestress mocking her, abandoning her to death?

The sharks drew closer, dorsal fins and tails rising up from the water. They slid so near that she could feel the underwater pull of their wake and see how water ran down the grain of their skin.

Something brushed past her feet. She felt another touch, by her hip, and she no longer thought she could control her scream. She had once seen the remains of a fisherman after reef sharks had attacked him, one leg bitten through to the bone, the other completely gone. The face of the dead man grew vivid in her mind. . . .

She had heard that there was no pain when a shark struck, only numbness. Some people claimed that the victim did not recognize the loss until he saw blood blossoming up through the water. Tepua could not believe that. Surely she would feel the shock, the pulling sensation as flesh parted. . . .

No. Such thoughts were only sharpening the grays' hunger.

You are the sister of the shark. The words quieted Tepua's shuddering. She remembered great blues that she had seen long ago, how they swam with easy sweeps of their tails. They were powerful, but held that power inside, not needing to churn the water with it.

I can be like them. In Tepua's imagination, she clothed herself in the skin of a shark and swam the same way, with powerful strokes and long glides. She was not a reef shark, but a great blue, swimming through a pack of grays as if they were a school of mullet. In her mind, the sea swept through her open jaws, through her gill slits and out again. She watched what lay ahead through the slitted eyes of a shark.

At that moment a gray appeared, the largest she had ever seen. It swam toward her, then suddenly adopted a threatening pose. Its back humped, its snout lifted, its forefins dropped. Then it stopped swimming and began to sink.

Tepua had been warned of this dreaded sign. In a moment, she knew, it would shoot forward to make its slashing attack. Yet she did not waver or change course. She felt no fear in her intestines, for they were the intestines of a shark.

The gray's tail trembled as it saw her coming on. It made a short rush, but instead of attacking, it turned before her and fled. Triumphantly she swept through the remaining grays. She no longer needed to evade them. The sharks knew her, sensed her power, and gave way.

* * *

Gradually Tepua came out of the trancelike state she had gone into. She found herself moving, not with a powerful tail, but with strokes of human arms and legs. Soon she realized that something else had changed. The channel's current had stopped pulling her. Now the islet lay between her and the sea, blocking the flow.

Here the lagoon was calm, its color verging from pale green to yellow. *Shallows!* With her last reserves of strength she headed toward shore. One moment she was in deep water, the next she found herself skimming over a sandy bottom that was close enough to touch. She looked back and saw the reef sharks—possibly as many as a dozen—remaining far behind. They seemed in a turmoil, swarming about, tails thrashing.

Exhausted, Tepua stopped swimming and began to walk over the soft bottom, pushing through water that barely reached her knees. Her body felt heavy, as if loaded down with stones.

At last she came out onto a shaded portion of the beach, not far from where she had made her camp. A few coconuts lay on the ground, but she did not have strength to satisfy the thirst that clawed at her throat. She threw herself down beneath a *fara* tree and slept.

When she woke, Raha and his fellow priests were crouching beside her. At once she stood, grabbing at the tree for support. When the priests stood also, she noticed that they bent forward so that their heads remained lower than hers. "Cone-shell?" she asked in a dry whisper.

"He lives," answered Raha.

She swung around and saw Varoa's chief seated in his canoe. He was wrapped in his cloak, his face pale, his wet hair in a tangle. Had he been attacked? Fear and curiosity drove her a few steps closer. She saw no blood pooling in the bottom of the boat. But she recalled how the second canoe had moved out of sight, heading toward Cone-shell. She wondered how far he had swum before his men pulled him from the water.

One of the paddlers humbly walked up to her and offered an open *viavia*. Tepua drank deeply before she spoke. "Cone-shell, the gods have given you your answer," she said in the firmest tone she could summon.

His eyes looked red and his face incredibly weary. When he spoke, his voice was faint. "The priests will take you back to my land," he said. "You will have the welcome you were promised."

"I want no welcome from you." She turned away, hesitated, then faced him once more. "When you are ready to acknowledge my authority, I will see you again." She stalked away from him and paused to speak with the cowering knot of priests. "Send my *pahi* here to take me home," she told them. "I will not ride with the men of Varoa Clan."

Then she walked on, toward the high log she had used as her perch. She sat rigidly, staring straight ahead while she chanted her praises to the gods, until both canoes were gone. Only then did she permit herself the tears, the rush of relief, the taste of the sea that had spared her.

ELEVEN

As Tepua approached her home shore, all appeared quiet. A few fishermen in canoes looked up to call a greeting. Children glanced at her and then returned to their pebble games. Clearly, the news of Cone-shell's treachery had not yet arrived. Tepua dreaded the stir this news would bring.

Two-eels, in his shame, had barely spoken to her during the journey home. His men had performed woefully on Varoa's territory, and now they tried to make a gallant show of escorting her to the beach. Tepua refused to be carried. She stalked away from them and headed to the one place where she might find solace—to Ehi's house.

The rhythmic pounding Tepua heard as she approached brought back the days of her childhood. How often she had watched Ehi and other women using stone mallets to break open keys of *fara* fruit for the edible seeds.

"Tepua-ariki," cried Ehi, rising from her work. "It is my daughter, coming back to me."

"Ah, Ehi," Tepua answered, eager for the embrace. She was glad that her foster mother had no company today. Tepua's tears started again. "I do not want to be chief. But the gods will not let me go."

"Daughter, come and sit. Refresh yourself. Then we will talk."

Tepua accepted a cool drink and slowly began to describe what had happened. "Cone-shell will suffer for this," Ehi said bitterly when Tepua was done. "The men of Ahiku will not sit on their heels when they learn of his outrage. They will pick up their spears and avenge the insult to our clan."

"No battle," Tepua protested as she recalled the frightening visions caused by the *kava*. "We must not fight among ourselves. Not when there are enemies ready to swoop down on us."

"Enemies?" Ehi's tone of outrage changed to one of alarm. "Pu-tahi?"

Tepua hesitated, uncertain whether to describe the fears that troubled her now. She realized that she was not ready to tell Ehi, or anyone else, about the vision that had been brought on by *kava*. She had seen invaders arrive in huge boats, but perhaps they were a different breed of men from Kiore and Nika. Why raise alarms based on something so uncertain? "Pu-tahi," Tepua said finally. "Yes. They have been seen in nearby waters. Heka has heard this from traders."

"I know you do not come to me for advice," Ehi answered. "But I can guess what the men will tell you. If we are to be strong against the Pu-tahi, then we cannot tolerate Cone-shell's impudence. Varoa must acknowledge your rule."

"We may be rid of Cone-shell soon."

"And how is that, daughter?"

"He offered himself to the sharks, but he did not stay in the water long. Some men who watched will tell what they saw. If they saw weakness, soon everyone will know. I wish to do nothing now but wait. Let the people of Varoa take care of their own problem."

Ehi's eyebrows raised. "Our warriors will not want to wait."

"Let us see if I can convince them." Tepua finished her drink, and for a time they spoke of lesser matters.

"Why is it, daughter," Ehi said at last, "that you ask me nothing about the foreign sailors?"

Tepua wished she could explain the vision that worried her. Whenever she thought of Kiore now, she remembered the smoke-belching weapon. "When I left here, the visitors were doing well. . . ."

"It is true that they have learned to speak better," Ehi admitted. "But that has not kept them from mischief."

Tepua's eyes opened wide as she remembered Umia's warning. "What sort of mischief?" she asked nervously.

"The blue-eyed one talks much of continuing his journey. He needs a sailor to replace the one who died. A man named Pinga agreed to go with him, but his wife is complaining loudly about it."

"That will not do," said Tepua. "I must tell the sailors to find someone else."

"And they are gathering provisions for their journey—dried fish, clams, octopus. This is where most of the trouble lies. The foreign goods remain under *tapu,* so the sailors can give nothing in return for what people bring them. Instead, the outsiders offer lengths of dried *fara* leaf inscribed with black marks."

"Marks?" Tepua recalled Kiore's quills and bottle of dye.

"Yes. Designs I have never seen before. The foreigners say that before they depart, they will exchange these marked leaves—for beads or choppers or colored cloth."

Tepua tried to picture what Ehi was describing. "What a strange way to do things. I have never heard of using marks to make promises."

"That is why people are starting to shun the sailors. They are afraid that the dried leaves are all they will ever get."

"That is sensible," said Tepua. "I see no reason the sailors cannot collect their own fish. From what I have seen, they are two strong and healthy men."

"There is more, Tepua. They built a platform for all these provisions and surrounded it with a high fence. They allow no one inside but themselves."

"Fence!" she answered in angry astonishment. The men were behaving like savages. Her people did not hoard food. If a friend or kinsman asked for something, it was cheerfully offered, with the understanding that its like would be returned. "They still do not know our ways," Tepua said, "but they have not been here long. I must continue teaching them."

"I am sure you will enjoy doing that," Ehi said, giving her a sly look. "If the sailors gather their own supplies, and share with their neighbors, then they will need more time to prepare for their journey."

"That is not my reason—"

"Tepua," she chided. "I have seen how you look at Kiore. Why do you hold yourself back? You can have fun, if you do it discreetly. In Tahiti, you had a man. Now you are unhappy without one."

Tepua beat her fist against the side of her stool. "Other things are at stake here," she said hotly. "You and Heka make two of a kind. I will decide for myself if I need a man, and which one. I want no advice on that score."

"Good," said Ehi. "At least you have not closed your mind on the matter. I'm tired of seeing so many scowls on your face."

At last Tepua summoned the sailors. She was happy to see Kiore again—more than happy. She began to forget the doubts raised by her vision.

"I have . . . much to tell," Kiore said.

Studying his glistening eyes and the warm expression on his lips, she wished Nika gone. "I have much to tell you also," she said to Kiore. "But first I must speak with the elders, and deal with questions that do not concern you." He knew nothing about Cone-shell's challenge, and she saw no reason to tell him now.

"There is a problem about this man Pinga," she said.

"Yes," Kiore agreed reluctantly when she explained her wishes. "Pinga is not for us. But who?"

She told him to try recruiting among the unmarried fishermen who lived at the end of the islet. Some were from distant islands, with no ties here.

Finally she suggested that the sailors gather their own provisions and share them, as was the custom. They could easily learn to collect and dry the meat of clams. Even a child could teach them.

Kiore told her that he would try, then stared at her, as if expecting more pleasant conversation. His eyes spoke of other times, of quiet walks on the white coral sand or through the forest.

"I will show you where we gather tern eggs," she offered lamely. "Tomorrow, perhaps. Or the day after." She wished to say other things, but the words did not come.

And then she found that she had no time for Kiore. The news of her encounter with Cone-shell spread quickly. Clan chiefs came from all parts of the atoll to discuss what should be done. Over the next two days, Tepua heard much unwelcome talk of war against Varoa.

Paruru said little, however. Tepua knew how chagrined he was over the poor performance of his men. Perhaps, because he blamed himself, he did not condemn Cone-shell.

Kohekapu, weak as he was, managed to make his views known. When the arguments became heated, he surprised everyone by sitting up to speak. "I am tired of listening," Kohekapu said in a whispery voice, "so let us . . . settle this." Unwilling to miss a word, Tepua tried not to breathe.

"A good chief knows . . . how to judge the wind and water." He paused, looking first at his daughter and then at the others. "There are times when we eagerly launch our canoes, and times when we are wise enough to keep them ashore." His head slowly slumped forward, as if the effort of his speech was exhausting him. The *tahunga* rushed to his side, but Kohekapu motioned him away.

"Listen to what . . . your chief has told you," Kohekapu continued. "The priests of Varoa Clan admit that she is the *ariki*. Even Cone-shell's maggot of a brother, who calls himself high priest, has shown his deference. Cone-shell cannot deny her now."

The men who had been urging war glanced about

uncomfortably. Earlier they had argued loudly, but now no one seemed willing to speak against Kohekapu. An elder of Piho Clan said, "Cone-shell is a maggot who must be squashed—before he becomes a fly and can bite."

Kohekapu turned his head slowly, his dignified expression showing no anger. "I will not dirty my heel on him. But there are other ways to deal with this. Do not forget Rongo Clan. It is time to woo them away from their vile ally. If the chief of Rongo is made welcome here, then Cone-shell will know for certain he is alone."

With that last bit of advice, Kohekapu had seemingly exhausted his strength. He slid back down onto his mat and said nothing more as the *tahunga* began to fuss over him. Tepua let the arguments go on, paying them little heed, while she knelt at her father's side. "Stay with us awhile longer," she begged him. "I will need your help again."

The last of these meetings ended, the chiefs agreeing reluctantly to follow Kohekapu's advice. Tepua went out into the bright afternoon to watch her important visitors depart. She was free of her duties—at least for a short while. She remembered her promise to Kiore.

The day was warm, the shadows just starting to lengthen. With light steps, she made her way toward the guesthouse where the foreign sailors were quartered. As she approached she heard both men shouting, the voices coming from behind the dwelling.

Hurrying around the thatched house, she saw the enclosure that Ehi had told her about. The sailors had used woody mid-ribs of old palm fronds, burying the ends to make a crude fence that bellied outward as it rose. Cords held these staves against each other, and poles reinforced the structure. She gazed in dismay at the ugly piece of work.

"I have you now, thief!" she heard a voice say angrily, but she could not see anyone. She ran to the narrow opening in the fence and peered through. There she saw Nika confronting a young boy who was clutching a handful of dried octopus. The sailor had a hold on one ear and was cuffing the boy about the other. Behind him, Kiore was struggling with a second youngster.

"What are you doing?" she cried, rushing toward Nika. "We do not strike our children! And to touch the head— anyone's head—is *tapu*!"

"He is a thief," said Nika, relaxing his grip and pushing the youngster away from him. Still holding his prize, the boy turned to the open gate. Tepua made a subtle movement with her hand. The boy saw the gesture and took a dash for freedom.

"Release the other child," Tepua demanded, turning to Kiore.

The sailor's face was flushed with anger. "Not the first time for this one," he said, shaking the boy by his thin shoulders. "I teach him!"

"You two are the ones who must be taught," she answered, stamping her foot.

The second boy squirmed and managed to kick Kiore in the shins. The sailor shouted angrily as the youngster slipped from his grasp. "Forgive me, *ariki*," the boy cried as he raced past her and out of the enclosure.

"Soon they come back!" Kiore complained, brushing his hands against each other, then wiping his dusty brow. Behind him stood his platform, where dried fish and octopus were piled on a shelf of tied sticks. Beneath the platform, coconuts lay in an untidy heap of browns and greens.

"This is folly," Tepua shouted. "We do not hide food like this. How long do you plan to keep those coconuts? Until they start sprouting?"

Kiore answered her indignantly. "We do honest trade. All this is ours now."

"I have heard more than enough about your trading," she answered. "And you see it has made you no friends. The boys were not stealing, they were borrowing."

The sailor stared at her, shaking his head.

"I do not know how people live in your country," she

said. "Anyone can see that you have plenty of food. That is why the boys came to you. They will bring something back when you are in need. That is our way."

She heard footsteps behind her. "What—is this commotion?" asked Paruru, arriving out of breath. "Someone said—the *ariki* was arguing with the foreigners."

"It is this—" Tepua, speechless for a moment, made a sweep of her hand.

"I did not know the fence would offend you, *ariki*," the warrior replied. "I saw no harm in letting them gather provisions."

And perhaps you wanted to hurry them on their way. "These men will be with us awhile longer," she said. "We must do a better job of teaching them our ways."

"As you wish, *ariki*. I have befriended the one with red hair. Perhaps—"

"It is Nika I blame for this," Tepua replied.

"I do not wish to disagree, but Kiore did most of the work. Nika is not eager to leave our island. And I have been able to teach him many things. Did you hear how well he speaks?"

She did not answer, for she suddenly noticed something out of place. On the ground behind the platform stood a foreign chopper, its blade half-buried in a log, its handle sticking up at an angle. "Did you also teach him to break the *tapu* on the goods?"

"I would not allow that," Paruru answered indignantly.

"Yet he has that chopper."

"So he does, *ariki*. It came ashore before the *tapu* was imposed. Nika traded it for a large pearl shell, but the new owner traded it back."

Tepua was about to answer angrily, but she recalled the remarkable shell that Nika had worn to the welcoming feast. Paruru's tale was plausible. "That tool is a dangerous thing."

"Then I will take charge of it," said Paruru. "As well as

any others I may come across. And I will continue to watch over Nika, if that pleases you. But what about Kiore?''

Tepua saw a coldness in the warrior's eyes that made her draw in her breath. Everyone knew that Paruru saw Kiore as his rival. If she gave him a chance, he would be happy to get rid of the blue-eyed sailor. "Let the other sailor stay with me awhile," she answered. "I have made some progress with him."

"Yes, I am aware of that." Paruru's voice was edged with bitterness. "If you wish to continue, then I beg you not to run off by yourself. Allow my men to protect you."

"Your warriors are always at my heels!" Except when I truly need them, she thought.

"Then I will order my men to stay back when they follow you. But they must always be within earshot. To do otherwise would be foolish. We still do not understand these strangers." He spoke briefly with Nika, who gave Tepua a hard glance before pulling the chopper from its log and handing it to Paruru. Then Nika followed him from the enclosure.

Kiore had folded his arms across his chest, in a gesture now familiar to her, and stood watching her with narrowed eyes and a faint smile.

"Ah, Kiore," she cried. "I am afraid for you." She stepped closer and allowed him a brief embrace. "You must not get Paruru angry."

"Paruru is no trouble," he answered.

"You say that of the man who killed your friend."

"He is no enemy," Kiore repeated. "He talks . . . he learns from us."

"Yes?" Paruru had said that he spent time with Nika, but she did not know what drew him to the young sailor.

"We talk of battles . . . on sea and land. Nika knows much that interests Paruru."

"Nika . . . a warrior?"

"No. But his father makes weapons. From his father he knows many tales of war."

Tepua stiffened. "And you?"

"I care for sailing, not battle."

"Then Paruru has no need of you. What is to keep him from shoving a spear into your belly?"

She looked up to see Kiore break into a grin. "Paruru thinks I keep secrets. He waits for me to tell him."

Tepua studied the confident set of his shoulders, the determined lines of his mouth. Perhaps he *was* clever enough to keep her *kaito-nui* guessing. "It is good that you keep learning our language and our ways," she told him. "But not from Paruru. I will find teachers."

"Not you?"

"I cannot teach you everything. You should learn fishing, gathering coconuts—"

"Maybe I surprise you," he said. "Watch me!" He reached beneath his platform and took a brown nut from his hoard. Tepua could see that it was old and waterlogged, evidently something that had washed up on the beach. She did not stop him when he carried it to a pointed stake that was set in the ground behind his platform.

He rammed the husk onto the point, then tried breaking it free of the shell within. A spurt of foul-smelling liquid poured out, and Kiore shouted an angry word of his own tongue. With a look of embarrassment he peered into the smashed side of the rotten nut.

"If you want good coconuts," she said, "you will have to climb after them."

He tossed aside the useless husk and gazed at her with new interest, his blond eyebrows raised.

"I have many trees," she said, "and I give you permission to harvest from them."

"It is good, *ariki*. I wish to learn climbing."

Tepua reflected a moment. Why not start now? If she could find a teacher . . . "Come." She motioned for him to follow. As she expected, Paruru had left two guards outside to keep an eye on her.

Spies. No, she would not ask one of them to help Kiore. Then she noticed the boys who had been chased from the enclosure peeking at her from behind a bush. With the *ariki* here to defend them, they seemed to have regained their courage. ''You, come,'' she said to the older of the pair. ''Give the sailor a climbing lesson and then he will not be angry with you.''

She began to walk inland with Kiore, toward a grove that was a bit secluded. It would not do to have a crowd watching this first attempt. She stopped in a well-shaded place and explained what she wanted to the boy.

At first the youngster stepped back from her in dismay. ''Do not scold me, *ariki*,'' he said in a high-pitched voice. ''But what you ask is forbidden. If I climb, my head will soon be above yours.''

She sighed. *So many rules!* No wonder the strangers were having difficulties. ''I give you permission,'' she told the boy. ''This one time. And I will stand far from the tree.'' This seemed to overcome his reluctance. The youngster peeled some bark strips from a fallen hibiscus branch and began plaiting a strap for his feet. Tepua set the other boy to plaiting a larger strap for Kiore.

''At home,'' said Kiore, ''trees have branches all the way up. It is easy to climb high.''

''We need no branches,'' she explained, running her fingers down the ridged trunk. ''You can hold on with your hands and feet. The little belt makes it easier.''

His face lit up with understanding as he studied the task before him. For a moment his expression became that of a child at play. Tepua thought then that her frightening vision could not possibly be warning her against *this* foreigner.

''Watch how it is done,'' she said. The boy hesitated, seemingly still in doubt. Impatiently she gestured for him to go, and at last he began to bound up the trunk. "Slowly!" Tepua insisted. "Let the sailor see what you are doing."

Kiore, barefoot now, crouched by the adjacent tree and stretched the plaited loop between his feet. He reached up, feeling for a grip, then pulled himself off the ground. "Use the strap to brace yourself," Tepua advised.

The blond-haired sailor laughed and pulled himself higher. In the other tree, the boy was already halfway to the top! Tepua tried to signal that he should slow down, but the youngster failed to get her message.

"Not hard," said Kiore. She heard the scraping of cloth and the heaving of his breath as he went higher. Then the trunk began to sway and he gave a short cry of alarm.

"It will not fall," she assured him. But what if Kiore lost his grip? Why send a man so high on his first attempt . . . ?

He was past the halfway point. "That is enough for this lesson," she called to him. "Tomorrow you can try again." But Kiore kept climbing, bending and then straightening his body, taking a rest between each advance. The higher he went, the more the trunk swayed under his weight. Meanwhile the boy reached the top of his own tree, twisted off a drinking nut, and sent it spinning to the ground.

The thud of the coconut's landing made Tepua imagine a stronger blow—of Kiore himself striking the ground. She looked away from the sight of his body swinging against the sky. She felt dizzy; her brow was wet. Faintly she heard the rattling of fronds overhead. The rattling grew fiercer and the ground seemed to sway beneath her feet. Suddenly there came a louder thud.

Her heart was hammering like Ehi's food pounder as she spun around. On the coarse sand she saw only another coconut! From above, Kiore was shouting in triumph. "Come down," she called again, but he did not seem to hear. At last he began his slow descent. She caught herself gnawing at her fingers as she watched.

"Not hard," said Kiore when he finally reached bottom.

"On the big boat I climb high every day. Up the tall masts."

Tepua suddenly found herself in his embrace, her cheek pressed to the smooth damp cloth of his shirt. She could hear the thudding of his heart and feel the rise and fall of his breathing. His broad hands pressed the bare skin of her back, holding her tightly against him.

Then she heard muffled giggling. *The boys!*

Tepua pulled away. She turned and saw grins on both youngsters' faces. "Go now," she told him. "Come back to my house at dusk and I will reward you." The first boy picked up his *viavia*. The second, with a sly glance at Kiore, hefted the nut that the foreigner had sent down.

"Good," said Kiore. "You take." The pair scampered off with cries of delight. "Now they talk," said Kiore, his brow slightly furrowed. "Tell about us. It is not good?"

"Nothing has happened."

He seemed briefly relieved, but then his brows knitted again. "Much is forbidden here," he said. "Touching someone's head . . . walking in the *marae*." His eyes caught hers. "This too is forbidden? *Ariki* with a man? Me?"

Tepua let out a long breath. She did not know how to answer. Perhaps he would not understand the obligations of her rank. A liaison with this foreigner, a man admittedly of low birth, would please no one—except, perhaps, herself.

"It is not forbidden," she answered. "Only unwise. I have enemies, people who say I should not be chief. I must prove them wrong, if only for a short while. That is what the gods expect of me." She paused, knowing that she had not satisfied him. "It would be better for you to find some other woman. I know many—"

He shook his head. "Others are not the same. Only the *ariki* pleases me." The color of his eyes seemed to shift and she stepped closer, drawn by their curious hue. He reached for her and she took another step. Then she lifted her face, offering him the foreign kiss as she had days before.

It was different this time, warmer, like the taste of ripe

fruit just plucked from a sunny bough. The tip of his tongue darted between her lips, but she did not pull back from that strange sensation. Her breath quickened. She put her hands around behind him and playfully slipped them up under his shirt.

Now she could feel the surprising smoothness of his back, and the quiet strength of the muscles beneath the skin. She leaned into him, wishing only to be closer, but there was an obstacle. . . .

Pulling her mouth away, she stood back and began to laugh. "Too many clothes," she said, tugging his shirt upward. Obligingly, he tugged it over his head and tossed it aside. "You need tattoos," she told him as she stretched her fingers over the swirling hairs on his chest. "But these will do for now." The curls grew more densely in the center, thickening at his belly, arrowing downward. And below?

She stopped asking herself questions as Kiore began pressing his lips to her cheek, to her shoulders, to the tops of her breasts. His gentle hands made her shiver with delight. Each place he touched felt warmer, until she was aglow from the soft skin of her cheeks all the way to her belly. His hand was at her sash, undoing the fastening about her skirt, when a noise came that made her cry out in surprise.

She turned toward the shore and saw a bush quaking, though there was no wind. Furiously she raced toward the disturbance while clutching her loosened garment to keep it from falling. A knot of children erupted from the shadows. "I will feed you to the eels!" she shouted after them as they ran squealing down the beach. "Bait for eels, all of you."

Kiore's face and neck had reddened all over. He retrieved his own garment and pulled it back on while she retied her wrap. "Many children," he said with a shake of his head. "They tell about us."

"Nothing has happened," she said again, as if she could deny the feelings that still clung to her. The glow had spread downward, to her vulnerable place, and outward to her fingertips as well. What she wanted now was to run to him, to feel the pleasure of his touch and the strength of his embrace. But she did not go.

How will I control these strangers if one is my lover? she asked herself. She closed her eyes for a moment, recalling the plans she had made. Tahiti seemed so far off now; she could no longer convince herself that she would ever return there.

"We must leave this grove," she said sadly, "and stand where everyone can see us." She began to walk back along the shore and he came with her, carrying his foot coverings, his bare feet scuffing the sand. She glanced at his sober face and wished she did not have to say the rest.

"Do not think me cruel, Kiore, but I have been thinking about your friend Nika. I do not wish him to stay with you any longer. He will only cause you trouble."

"Take Nika away?" He flung the foreign sandals to the ground and glared at her.

"For a time. It will be better if Paruru takes him to live somewhere else."

"Not better!" He stood with his legs spread wide apart and his hands on his hips.

"I am sorry, Kiore. Later, when you two know our customs better, you can be together again."

He refused to listen. She glanced at his petulant mouth and saw the child in him again, this time a stubborn child.

She had not wanted to provoke a quarrel, and now she saw no way to undo the hurt she had caused. Perhaps Kiore would choose to leave her now rather than bear the separation from his friend. But if the two sailors remained together, she felt certain that they would soon be forced to leave her atoll.

Tepua felt a stinging in her eyes as she turned away and headed back alone. Behind her, she heard Kiore angrily pitching chunks of coral into the lagoon.

TWELVE

Paruru took Nika to visit Piho Clan, with hope that the sailor might find life agreeable on another islet. His sister Heka welcomed them both eagerly, arranged a feast, invited all the prominent people of the clan.

While fires were heating the oven stones, Paruru and Nika sat with the warrior's uncles and brothers in the shade above the beach. Nika had recently told a fine tale of a sea battle. Paruru urged him to repeat it in this distinguished company. He wished everyone to hear how well the outsider spoke.

"It is better," said the sailor, "if I make little boats." He took a brown bit of palm leaf and folded it into the crude shape of a boat, then pressed it into the sand. He enlisted the aid of the other men in making more, some from dried leaves and some from fresh.

"These brown ones are of our enemy," Nika said, placing the "boats" in formation. "They are heavy and slow. The green ones are of my land. Light and quick." He spoke of the weapons aboard, which flung stones a great distance. He explained how the vessels had to maneuver to point the huge weapons at their targets.

Paruru watched the looks of amazement on his kinsmen's faces as Nika revealed the foreign methods of battle. Finally Nika reached the part where burning ships were sent at night to set fire to the enemy fleet. To demonstrate, the sailor made a crude palm leaf torch, igniting it at a nearby cook

159

fire. With the torch, he set alight one brown vessel after another.

"*Aue!*" cried Crabs-sleeping. "That is a quick way to get rid of them."

"But those craft ride high out of the water," argued an uncle. "With so many masts and so much rigging, they catch fire too easily." He turned to Nika. "It is good that your enemy did not use *our* kind of war canoe!"

Nika laughed and said this might be so. The men kept raising new points over the tactics he had described, sometimes arguing heatedly among themselves. By the time servers brought the meal, Paruru was satisfied that his sailor had made a strong impression.

The next day, the *kaito-nui* found Heka with a group of women, seated on mats in a grove of coconut palms. When he asked to speak with her in private, she sent the women away. "Everyone is glad to see you again," she said pleasantly, brushing back long hair that glistened beneath a braided headdress of vines and lavender morning glory. "And I hear that Nika has found many friends."

"I am happy to be your guest, sister. And so is Nika. He is with Crabs-sleeping now, searching for the black-lipped oysters."

"I heard that he is fond of pearl shells," she replied thoughtfully. "And we have the best. Is that what you wish to talk about?"

Paruru did not answer directly, but began praising Nika's skills. "He is talented at working wood. The foreign tool does wonders in his hands. I would like to see him learn to build canoes."

Heka looked skeptical. "I thought that Tepua gave all the tools to Faka-ora for safekeeping."

"Yes. But a knife and chopper came ashore separately from the rest. Tepua put these in my charge."

"I did not know that, brother. You must be careful. Remember how Cone-shell cut himself."

"Nika knows how to use these tools. You should see how fast he can work with them."

"Perhaps Nika can cut faster than our men," she answered, "but skill is not enough. He must speak the proper chants at every stage or the work will fail."

"He will learn the chants."

"Perhaps he will." She paused, then spoke in a chiding tone. "Paruru, is this all you came to talk about? Should I call the master canoe-builder and offer him a new pupil?"

"There is more, sister." He realized that he must reach his point quickly as she was already losing her good humor. "I have thought long about Nika. Listen carefully before you answer. He has no real home on this atoll and I wish to give him one. I wish to have him adopted into Piho Clan—as my brother."

"*Aue!*"

"Do you find it so strange?"

"I know that you and he are good friends. But think what you ask!"

"I have good reasons, sister."

"Yes, I can see one. Half the treasures from the foreign *vaka* are his. Eventually Tepua must release those things. If Nika is part of our family, then the treasures will be ours as well."

Paruru felt his anger rising. He cared nothing for cloth and colored beads. The one foreign thing he wanted he already had, and Nika was the one who would teach him how to use it. "There is a more important reason," he insisted. "People are starting to question Tepua's wisdom in keeping these outsiders with us. And the sailors are growing restless. If Nika causes trouble, there will be more talk against her."

"So you think you can help Tepua by bringing Nika to us?"

"I cannot have him near me and watch him constantly. My duties for the high chief keep me too busy. But if Nika stays here, he can become part of our family. He will learn the proper ways to do everything. My brothers and nephews will teach him.''

''I have heard them talking about your sailor.''

''He has made himself welcome.''

Heka looked at Paruru sharply. ''Many of our men will support you. They will say that the sailor can bring renown to our family. But we must not forget the risk—that the outsider can also bring disgrace.''

''Have I asked too much?''

Heka paused. ''If this were for your sake alone, I would not take the chance. But I, too, wish to support Tepua. It will help her if this man joins our family and makes himself useful.''

''Then you agree!''

Heka folded her hands. ''I will speak to the elders in favor of your proposal. I may have to remind them about that strong foreign cloth!''

''Then I will wait for your answer.'' He stared at his sister a moment, wondering which of his arguments had been most persuasive. Surely she had not guessed the fate of the thunder-club. She could not know that the weapon meant as much to him as regaining Tepua's esteem.

Nika stayed on for several days, enjoying feasts, entertainment, and fishing expeditions. He amassed a collection of fine shells and a few small pearls.

Also, Nika had a chance to look over the young women of Piho Clan. At Paruru's urging they visited the sailor, encouraging his interest with shy, yet flirtatious glances. Following Paruru's instructions, however, they did not linger.

It was on the third morning of his guest's stay that Paruru decided to bring up the question of adoption. By now the elders had consented to Heka's request. Only Nika's agreement was needed.

Paruru found the foreigner sitting in the shade with his pile of treasures, tossing away those shells that had even tiny defects. Good pearl shells were prized here, of course, but they did not consume anyone's interest. And pearls, so difficult to pierce, were rarely used in adornment.

Nika had astonished him by saying that these things could make him wealthy when he returned home. Indeed, it seemed that the wealth of distant Piritania was not measured in mats and coconut trees, or even in pigs and cloth. Nika prized riches of another sort, of which he could only display a small handful—disks of bright foreign stone, carved with strange designs.

Seeing him absorbed in his work, the warrior approached and squatted on his heels. "I am glad," Paruru said, "that you find so much to please you here."

Nika smiled and looked up from his shells. "This is a good island. Better than the other."

"Would you like to stay?" asked Paruru.

Nika's eyes searched Paruru's. "What are you offering?"

"I want to help you find a place for yourself—as part of a family. Then you can remain here as long as you like."

"Right here?" He gestured toward the house where he was staying.

Paruru raised his eyebrows in assent. "And my family is among the best. We hold good lands and fishing sites and many coconut trees. We have excellent nets and swift canoes. All of these will be yours to share."

The sailor grinned. "I think I understand."

"I am offering you a high honor," Paruru said. "I have watched you, and I believe that you are worthy. I would like you for my brother."

A wary look crossed the sailor's face. "Tell me how it is done—the joining of brothers."

"By a short ceremony. You will see."

"And after that, the girls . . ."

"Will no longer treat you as a stranger."

"That is what I am waiting for. Too many girls are running off. I think they are a little bit afraid."

"It will be different when you are my brother. But

remember this. My cousin is your cousin, and cousins are *tapu*."

Nika grimaced. "Rules and more rules. How many cousins do you have?" When Paruru gave no reply, Nika did not press him. Instead, the sailor asked, "Will you send a message to Maukiri? Tell her I am not coming back soon."

"I will," Paruru answered. "Now come, and meet a few more of your new family."

On the day of the adoption ceremony, the weather was clear with a mild breeze. Wearing feathers and ferns in his hair, Paruru went to the *marae* to join his elderly father, his sister Heka, and other relatives. Since Nika had no kin here, he walked apart, accompanied only by a woman called Karipea who had been borrowed from Varoa Clan for the occasion. She was to serve the role of Nika's "mother" and was already devoting herself enthusiastically to the part, much to Nika's evident distress. Paruru wondered if Heka had indulged her capricious sense of humor by selecting Karipea.

He could see that the sailor's discomfort was worsened by the plaited cape and loincloth that he wore. Nika had complained the night before that mat garments itched, but Paruru had insisted that he give up his foreign clothing for the ceremony. Now the sailor was constantly scratching, undeterred by scolding and slaps from Karipea.

Outside the low coral-block walls of the *marae,* a priest met the party. Several men brought an enormous rolled mat of plaited *fara,* spreading it on the ground while the priest handed out leaves of *pukatea.* Paruru took his seat at the mat's center. Prompted by Karipea, Nika joined him, sitting in the proper place on his left.

"Stop scratching," Paruru hissed.

"If you let me wear my shirt . . ." Nika began, but Paruru silenced him with a sharp motion of the hand. The ceremony had begun. It must not be profaned by idle talk or argument.

Paruru watched as his relatives, led by Heka, gathered at one end of the mat. On the other end sat Karipea, as Nika's representative. It bothered Paruru to see the two sides so unbalanced, but there was no way to produce Nika's true family.

Shark-tooth flails appeared in the hands of Paruru's kin. Heka was the first to strike her forehead with the shark's tooth, causing blood to trickle onto her face. Others followed her example, with impassioned prayers and outcries to the gods that the heritage of two families would be well mingled.

Across the mat, Karipea replied in kind. Perhaps, thought Paruru, Nika's family was fairly represented after all, for the loudness of Karipea's outbursts and the amount of blood she shed make up for the lack in numbers.

Nika seemed to pale at the sight of crimson running down so many foreheads. What was wrong with the man? Paruru wondered. Had he never seen an adoption or a marriage before?

Paruru's elderly father stepped forward, carrying the juice of a young coconut leaf in a shell. He poured the libation onto a leaf of sacred *pukatea,* set the leaf briefly on Paruru's head and then on Nika's.

Now that the leaf's contents were imbued with the spirits of both men, it was brought before the other celebrants. The priest chanted prayers while the token was sealed by drips of red. At last the leaf was carried by the priest into the *marae,* to rest on a sacred stone.

Heka took her place beside the priest and chanted, "This man we take as a brother. I give to him the name that Paruru bore as a youth. His name is now Kero, and he shall be known as a member of this family and of Piho Clan." She paused. "And in turn he gives a name to Paruru. The name is Tama, one that is old and honored among his people." With a wave of her arms, she bade both men to stand.

"Paruru-tama, here is your brother, Nika-kero. Nika-kero, here is your brother, Paruru-tama. Each one shall chant the genealogy of his family so that it may be known to the other.''

Paruru was first. The names flowed easily from his tongue, for he had learned them as a child and repeated them to himself every night before sleeping. This was essential knowledge, the sole means to prove one's claim to land or fishing rights.

''Here is my descent,'' he began. ''The god Atea fathered the god Tu-makino who fathered the great god Tangaroa. Tangaroa fathered Tapai'aha . . .'' Paruru continued, watching his audience as they listened attentively. He glanced at Nika, whose uncomprehending stare reminded him that his venerated forebears were but a jumble of names to this man.

That would soon change. As a member of the family, Nika would be expected to become as fluent in genealogical recitation as anyone in the clan.

The warrior finished his narration, ''. . . who fathered a son, Paruru.'' He turned toward Nika, noting how unsettled the foreigner appeared as he prepared to take his turn. On the previous evening, Nika had been inconsistent in his repetitions. Paruru had been forced to drill him so that he would not embarrass himself by making a mistake in public.

With a nervous glance at the priest, the sailor began. ''The first man of my tribe was Atama and he took Eva to wife. Their firstborn was . . . uh . . . Kaina, and he had Noha . . .''

Paruru listened critically. He wondered if anyone would notice that Noha, whoever he was, had not been mentioned in the earlier versions. It worried him that Nika's memory was so poor. Paruru did not wish to consider the possibility that all these names had been fabricated.

Suddenly the recitation was over, and Heka was speaking. ''Nika-kero, enter your place of judgment and take your stand among us,'' she said.

Cautiously Nika stepped forward. Heka embraced the sailor and pressed her face to his. Paruru, remembering the strength of his sister's arms, hoped that Nika would not gasp aloud under the onslaught. But he proved himself a man in that respect, stifling any outcry and only staggering a little as Heka released him. Then, one by one, the rest of the family greeted their new kinsman.

It is done, thought Paruru. *May it please the gods.*

The next few days passed quietly, and Paruru decided that he could soon return to Tepua's service. On a sunlit morning he went looking for his new brother to tell him his plans. Crabs-sleeping had said that Nika was hunting octopus just offshore.

The tide was out and the lagoon had drawn down, exposing dark patches of reef. Women were busy gathering clams in the shallows. Paruru saw no sign of Nika as he walked along the beach.

He shaded his eyes, gazing over the water. Nika had been warned of the local dangers—the stonefish, the shifting currents, the sharp-edged coral—but perhaps he had been careless. Paruru felt uneasy as he began a long circuit of the islet, facing a stiff breeze as he turned toward the seaward side.

The shore had no covering of sand here, only heaps of smoothed coral chunks that clinked against each other as he crossed them. Suddenly he heard a cry and the splashing of feet in shallow water. He saw Nika pelting toward him, his arms flung wide. The sailor shouted something, but his words were lost in the wind. The *kaito-nui* was alarmed until he saw a grin of delight on Nika's ruddy face.

"I caught one!" Nika yelled. The sailor slid to a stop in front of Paruru, breathless, red hair tangled by wind and spray. He was wearing his own garment again. The rags of his shirt bore a dark stain. Paruru was close enough to smell the blood of a sea creature, a scent disturbingly familiar.

"What is it?"

Nika did not seem to know the word in Paruru's tongue.

He used his own language and made signs. "A big one!" he said proudly. "I speared him."

Paruru felt a chill as he stared at Nika, for he thought it possible that the man had caught a sea turtle. *"Honu?"* he asked Nika, dreading the answer. When the sailor did not respond, the warrior realized that he had never taught Nika that word. Having no turtle at hand, Paruru had carelessly neglected to tell him about the animal—or the *tapu* surrounding it.

"Show me," the warrior demanded. Nika sprinted off and he followed, trying to make himself believe that Nika had caught a ray or some other bottom-dwelling flatfish. Nika led him to a stretch of sand, and Paruru was relieved to find the area deserted. At least he would be the first to see what his new brother had done.

Strutting like a cock fowl, Nika led Paruru toward the scrubby trees above the beach. A moment later the warrior knew that Nika had done his worst. He glanced with horror at the gray-green shell, the pointed tail. . . .

Paruru wanted to squeeze his eyes shut, hoping that the gods would relent and take the scene away. But he could not hide from the smell, the terrible, dank smell from the sea's depths.

Sennit cord was wrapped about the turtle's two rear legs, tethering the creature to a coconut stump. It lay, churning sand with its winglike front flippers, straining its neck back, opening and shutting its powerful beak. A fish spear was jammed deep into a gap in the shell, piercing the soft wrinkled flesh between the turtle's neck and the left foreleg. Blood welled up around the spear shaft every time the turtle heaved at its bindings.

Paruru felt engulfed by a feeling of despair. How had he neglected to explain the importance of the turtle?

"You are speechless." The sailor's voice startled him. "What a big one!"

It was all Paruru could do to keep from seizing the fish spear, jerking it from the turtle, and burying it deep into human flesh. If this man had not been made his brother . . .

Paruru watched the turtle trying to escape, snapping at the cords that tethered it. Nika picked up a shell-bladed knife and bent to cut the beast's throat. For a moment Paruru could only gaze numbly at the sight of the blade moving closer. Then he reacted, shooting out his hand to catch Nika's arm.

"No!" Paruru shouted. While the turtle still lived he might find a way to salvage the situation. If the foreigner slaughtered the animal, all would be lost.

"What is the matter?" Nika's voice sounded petulant as he dropped the knife. "Why is this not pleasing? Here is my gift to you and the rest of the family."

Paruru listened sadly as he began to grasp Nika's reasoning. The foreigner was not truly to blame. He had wanted to prove that he was worthy of adoption, a man who could provide meat for his new family. Now Paruru looked at Nika's expression and saw feelings of puzzlement, anger, and pride. The warrior found himself groping for words.

"You were adopted as a younger brother," he said at last, "so I will speak as your elder. This act is *tapu*."

Nika shook his head as if unwilling to hear.

"It is forbidden," Paruru continued, biting off each word. "The turtle is sacred food. There must be ceremonies before the hunt and after, or the gods will be offended. Only important men, such as chiefs and priests, may eat the flesh."

Nika's face reddened and the veins in his temples were swelling. "There is no meat for me all the time I am here," he answered angrily. "All I get is fish and coconuts." He gestured impatiently with the knife. "You are an important man, so you can eat it. Now I am your brother, so why cannot I eat it, too?"

Paruru wanted to laugh at Nika's ignorance. Only after sacred rituals was a man allowed to share the feast. For Nika's act there could be no reward, only punishment.

The warrior tried to explain again, telling how turtles

were descended from the god Tu-who-dwells-in-the-sea. The god would be angered by Nika's affront. No one could say what the result might be—famine, storms, sickness.

"And do not forget the ghosts of our ancestors," Paruru continued. "They, too, will avenge this insult. They will come for you at night, with their long sharp fingernails and teeth." Paruru saw Nika pale beneath the red bronze of his face. His hands began to clench and unclench nervously.

"All just for *honu*?"

"If I had not adopted you into my family," Paruru said, "the punishment would fall on you alone. Now it may fall on me as well, and on all of Piho Clan."

At last the sailor put his knife aside and slumped down onto the sand. "It is nearly dead now. Why keep talking about it?" he asked angrily.

"Because I am still looking for a way to save us!" Paruru crouched beside the wounded turtle. If its injuries were not severe, then perhaps it could be released into the sea and the incident forgotten. But the turtle's smell, damp with seawater and heavy with approaching death, ended that hope. From the length of shaft remaining, Paruru knew that the spear had gone deep. Removing it would only hasten the animal's end.

If he cut off the protruding shaft, turned the turtle loose, and it died at sea, no one else would know. But the gods would see, and their wrath would be swift. The entire atoll might suffer for the crime.

Paruru watched the movement of the flippers growing weaker. The turtle was dying. . . .

He had one hope. He could take the creature to a chief while it still lived. If the chief accepted it, then the required rituals would be followed and the gods might relent, despite the improper hunt.

But which chief? Tepua was too far away, even if he were willing to tell her what had happened. And Heka? He had urged her to accept the outsider in hope of keeping him out of trouble. Now she would see how her brother had failed.

No, it would have to be someone else, someone unlikely to question too deeply. Then he thought of Cone-shell, whose own clan's islet lay just across the channel. After his recent troubles Cone-shell might welcome such an offering. A turtle feast on his *marae* could help him regain prestige among his wavering followers.

Paruru wondered how to explain such a gift from Tepua's *kaito-nui,* after Cone-shell had treated her so harshly. Suddenly he saw how to explain it. But everything depended on his delivering the turtle alive. Quickly he told Nika the first part of his plan. "You must help me bring the creature across the channel."

Nika stared at him, his hostile mood returning. "You say I cannot keep my turtle. Now you want help to give it away."

"It is not yours. It is stolen from the gods," Paruru reminded him. "What do you think will happen if Tepua learns about this? She will put you back in your *vaka* and set you adrift." He pinched the flesh of Nika's thigh. "The Pu-tahi will catch you and have a good meal."

Sweat beaded on the sailor's upper lip and forehead. He glanced once more at the dying turtle. "Then do it. Get rid of this thing."

Shortly Paruru brought a small *vaka* around the point and anchored it in shallow water. He carried a roll of strong cordage ashore and looped it around the turtle's shell. Then Nika cut the bonds on the creature's legs. Despite its wounds and weakness, the turtle began to thrash its way toward the water, the new cord trailing behind.

Once afloat, the heavy creature was far easier to handle than on land. Paruru tied his end of the cord to the stern of the canoe. With Nika's help paddling they headed into the lagoon, towing the struggling animal across the current.

By now the sun was high, beating down fiercely on Paruru's face and hair. He had lost his plaited sunshade and had no choice but to endure his discomfort. The distance was short, yet the journey seemed endless. Each time the turtle's head stopped waving or its flippers sagged, he feared that death had stolen his chance to make amends. He prayed to his guardian spirit, and somehow the beast always began moving again.

At last he saw Cone-shell's beach, with tall palms and a cluster of thatched houses above the shore. The men paddled in; Paruru felt the *vaka* ground on sand. Cone-shell's attendants came to greet him and ask the purpose of his visit. When they saw what he was towing, some ran to tell their chief, others to get help in dragging the prize onto the beach.

"You must be silent while I speak to him," Paruru told Nika in a low voice. "He must believe that I was the one who captured the turtle. Otherwise he will guess that it was not done properly." Grudgingly the sailor agreed.

Soon Varoa's chief appeared, wearing a simple hip wrap and his tall headdress. "What is this?" Cone-shell asked, his expression a mixture of puzzlement and delight. "Why does the eminent Paruru bring me such a gift? Surely Tepua is not behind this."

Paruru had already planned his response. "Let this be a token from Tepua-ariki. To show that she is not angry with you for testing her. Let this turtle help keep peace between the clans."

"That is a . . . generous offer on her part." Cone-shell fell silent, as if trying to explain this surprising development to himself. "She will expect something in return," he said in a hard voice.

"A token of your friendship will be enough," answered the warrior.

Cone-shell grunted. "Several large albacore, perhaps?"

Paruru knew what he was thinking. Even such prized fish as albacore would not make an adequate return gift. "Perhaps something more," said the *kaito-nui*.

When Cone-shell scowled, Paruru hastily made a suggestion. "I heard that you have some high-island trees growing here."

"Carefully tended!"

"Tepua longs for the food of Tahiti. If you send her a few breadfruit—"

"It will be done," replied Cone-shell, seemingly relieved that this would suffice. He drew himself up. "You may convey to Tepua that I am pleased to accept her gift," he declared loudly. Then his keen gaze turned to Nika. "But what of this outsider with hair like fire? Tell me his role in this."

"He is now my brother," Paruru said casually.

"Brother!" Cone-shell contemplated the news and his eyes narrowed again. "Yes, that was a clever move for you." He scowled and fingered the necklace of dolphin teeth about his throat. Paruru could guess that he was thinking about the sailors' goods, aware that now half might be claimed by Piho Clan.

"Tepua approves of this?" Cone-shell asked angrily. When Paruru raised his eyebrows in assent, he ground his heel into the sand, then turned to where the turtle lay. "Then perhaps that explains this gift. She hopes to keep me from voicing my discontent."

Paruru did not know how to answer him, and was afraid of wasting any more time. The turtle was nearly dead. "You must begin the ceremonies—"

"Yes," said Cone-shell. "I have accepted the gift and now everything must be done quickly. But do not think I will forget this other matter. I should have been told about Nika." He clapped his hands, summoning servants. Some went to inform the priests. Others brought refreshments for the guests. "Paruru, it is your right as hunter to join us at the feast," said Cone-shell. "And since this man Nika is your brother . . ." He paused, biting the words off in distaste. "I invite him to come as well."

Nika leaned forward eagerly, but Paruru jerked him back. He answered, "Your offer is well-spoken, chief, but in this case I give up my rights to the meat. Let my share go to men of your clan.''

Cone-shell stared in astonishment at this refusal. It was now, Paruru knew, that his whole plan might run aground. ''It is because of a dream,'' the warrior improvised. ''I saw myself bringing a turtle to a great chief, but I did not eat of the flesh. The dream puzzles me, but I think I must follow it.''

''That is a strange dream,'' Cone-shell replied with a frown. Paruru could see, however, that he had not missed the flattering phrase. ''Rare is the hunter who gives up his portion,'' Cone-shell added, ''but I will not press you to go against your dream. You may stay here. My servants will look after your needs. I leave now to prepare myself for the rituals.'' As Cone-shell strode out of sight Paruru mouthed silent praises to his guardian spirit.

When the chief was gone, Nika began to complain again. ''I am not entitled to a share,'' Paruru hissed. ''And neither are you. Be glad that Cone-shell accepted my story.''

Nika fell silent. The servants brought a meal of fish, coconut, and taro, but he ate little. He toyed with the placemats of plaited leaves. ''What are all these ceremonies that you keep talking about?'' the sailor asked at last.

''If you wish,'' Paruru answered when he was done with his meal, ''we can sit outside the *marae* and listen. Maybe you will learn something that way. Maybe you will understand how careful we must be with the turtle.''

When he heard the sound of chanting, Paruru followed the path to the sacred place by the shore. The two men sat nearby, their backs against coconut trees. The priests' chants made the warrior think of days long before, when he had sung and danced in the rituals for catching turtles. Now the remembered words filled his thoughts.

> Come! Come to the shore, great turtle.
> Rise up to the white waves of the sea
> Ride the waves to the shore.

> May you come here, come straight here
> To where your navel cord is buried
> To where your *marae* stone is set up. . . .

Beside him, Nika shifted restlessly. "I wish to see what they are doing."

"We must stay here, but I will tell you," Paruru said. "I have watched many times." He explained each step, the invocations, the offerings, the preparation for the first oven.

"The first? How many times is the turtle cooked?"

"Twice. First to melt the turtle's fat and make the flesh easier to divide. The portions are then baked in a second oven, dug nearby."

Nika grinned. "I know why you cook it twice. Because your knives are not sharp enough to cut it up. You should try one of my knives."

Stolidly, Paruru answered, "We cook it twice because that is the way the ceremony is done."

"I do not like your answer," Nika replied. And soon he was complaining again as the aromas of the first cooking wafted to him from the *marae*. Paruru heard the sailor's belly growl and saw how his mouth watered at the smell.

"The men of Varoa will eat heartily," Paruru said.

Nika buried his head in his arms and groaned. "Enough of ceremonies. Let us go home."

"No. I want you to listen to the rest of the ceremony."

"I am suffering!"

"Then let it be your punishment." Paruru sat back against the coconut tree and wondered if he was safe now. Cone-shell's priests had accepted the offering without question. Perhaps there would be no reprisal from the gods if the wrongdoers got no benefit from their acts.

But what other mistakes might this outsider commit? Paruru remained quiet for a long time as he contemplated what had happened. The smell of roasting meat filled his nostrils. Nika's soft moans sounded in his ears, but the suffering brought Paruru no pleasure.

His thoughts returned to that bright afternoon when the foreign vessel had appeared on the sea. Now he wondered gloomily if he had made the wrong decision. Perhaps he should have kept his men back and let the sailors crash into the reef.

THIRTEEN

After her last encounter with Kiore, Tepua decided that someone else must take over instructing him—at least until his temper cooled. She charged a young man named White-sea with the task, and for days she did not see her sailor. Paruru came back from his visit to Piho Clan, leaving Nika behind, and still Tepua avoided Kiore. One morning, however, she saw White-sea when she was returning from her freshwater bathing place, a small inland pool filled with rainwater.

"*Maeva ariki!*" called the young teacher. He was carrying a hooped flying-fish net, its long pole handle dragging behind him.

"I will talk to his man alone," she told her attendants, sending them on ahead.

This was not a good time to be lingering, she knew. Kohekapu was once more close to death, and now she doubted that the deep-voiced drum in the *marae* or the prayers of the priests would induce the gods to relent. Yet her thoughts were constantly on Kiore. She stopped for a moment to ask about his progress.

"He is doing well, *ariki,*" answered White-sea, a slender sinewy young man, with crisp curly hair and bright black eyes that looked large in his triangular face. Tepua saw a glitter of excitement in those eyes, a sign of his pride in being chosen as the teacher. "I have borrowed this net from my cousin," he said. "Kiore will study it, and then we will make one for ourselves."

"Good work," said Tepua, wishing she could watch. It would give her pleasure, she thought, to see Kiore's hands holding an implement, or his intent expression as he worked.

"And the outsider is also finding new things to eat, *ariki*. Yesterday he tried the slate-spined sea urchin, fresh from the lagoon."

Tepua recalled hearing how Kiore had once hesitated to eat raw clams. This, too, had changed for the better. As Kiore came to appreciate the foods of the land, she thought, he would be happier here, perhaps less eager to depart. "You are doing well, White-sea."

"There is more, *ariki*. He wished to learn how to sail a *vaka*. Now he can handle a small one on his own—so long as the wind is steady."

Tepua felt disheartened by this news, but tried not to show it. "Where will he go? To some other islet?"

"He wants to speak with canoe-masters of other clans. He needs their knowledge of reefs and currents. Otherwise he will not be able to sail his foreign boat away from here."

"Yes, he needs that knowledge," she agreed coldly. "What else have you taught him?"

White-sea seemed taken aback by her change in mood. Cautiously he spoke of other activities that Kiore was trying. He had improved his spearfishing. The fire plow frustrated him, but at least he could get the wood to smolder. When he broke the handle of a stone adze, he was able to lash the head onto a new handle.

"And his speech?" she asked. "He must make himself clear if he wishes to talk to canoe-masters."

"He surprises me sometimes," said White-sea. "He is beginning to compose chants. . . ." The young man's voice trailed off, as if he felt embarrassed to continue.

"Tell me."

"Do not be angry, *ariki*. He uses the words of a poet. He

calls you his rainbow fish or his high-winging tropic bird."

She felt heat rush to her face. "Does he ask why I do not see him?"

"He does not ask, but I feel his unhappiness. He told me that he was angry because you sent away his companion. Now that he has neither you nor his friend, I see that he is doubly sad."

"Tell him that I will bring Nika back soon," she answered. "And try to make him understand why I am preoccupied now. Explain to him, if he does not know, why the priests are beating their drums."

I have shared the grief of his loss, she thought, and soon he must share mine. She remembered Kiore's sorrow over his dead comrade. It was then that she first saw Kiore as a man, and not as a demon from afar. . . .

Her thoughts were interrupted when she heard hurried footsteps coming toward her and frenzied shouting. From farther off, in the direction of Kohekapu's house, came a piercing wail. Had it already happened?

Her heartbeat quickened. Tears stung her eyes and a sob rose in her throat. Leaving the astonished White-sea, she turned and rushed down the path.

Just before the cries sounded, Paruru was drilling his warriors on the training field. These men included Two-eels and the other guards who had succumbed to Cone-shell's trickery. Stripped of his rank and ornaments, Two-eels wore only a coarse, frayed *maro*. He lunged and grunted and sweated with the common warriors.

Today the exercise was combat with clubs, and the sharp sounds of parried blows made a frantic rhythm. Paruru had paired Two-eels with a large and enthusiastic youth who often forgot that he was training and not on the battlefield. Paruru watched the punishment that Two-eels was suffering, seeing that he bore it without complaint. Two-eels was fortunate to still have his life. Another chief might have been far less lenient than Tepua.

Now Paruru felt the burden of his own failings and was glad that he had not urged stronger punishment for the young warrior. In the eyes of the gods, he believed that his own deception of Cone-shell was a far more serious offense. Paruru could not forget the turtle. He saw it in dreams. Even in the daytime it sometimes floated, ghostlike, before his eyes. He knew every patch of color on its shell, and the ugly, red wound in its neck.

Had the gods accepted the offering? He could not know. And to conceal what had happened, he had been forced to fabricate one story after another.

He had created his lies for Nika's sake, but also to protect Tepua. If news of Nika's transgression got out, her enemies would have what they wanted—proof that she was unfit for high office. The misdeeds of the foreigners would be blamed on the chief who had taken them in.

Despite all the strength Tepua had shown, Paruru believed that people might still turn against her. Lately there had been troubling signs. A two-headed fish had been caught in a net. At night, strange howls were heard in the forest. Recalling these events made him cold and hot by turns, until sweat streamed from his forehead. . . .

So deep was he in thought that at first he did not recognize the outcry that broke from a cluster of nearby huts. As the shrieks and wails grew louder one pair of men after another stopped fighting, tossed clubs to the ground, and turned to listen.

Paruru filled his lungs to order the warriors back to their drill, but he halted, finally understanding what the cries meant. *Kohekapu was gone.* Was this yet another sign of the gods' displeasure? As his men broke ranks and ran off, howling and wailing in mourning for the old chief, Paruru heard a different cry from his own lips. It was a moan of despair.

The outcries were spreading from house to house as Tepua hurried by. The tear-streaked faces that looked at her seemed filled not only with grief, but with reproach as well. *Reproach for what?* To Tepua's ears the laments carried a new concern—that Kohekapu's successor might not be capable of replacing him.

When she neared her father's house, she saw a crowd of mourners gathering by the doorway. A group of women led by Natunatu were screaming in frenzied grief and gashing their foreheads with shark-tooth flails.

As Tepua approached, a cold hand seemed to reach into her bowels. She tried to make a path through the rocking, wailing mass of women, but Natunatu leaped up and fixed Tepua with hate-filled eyes.

"There goes the daughter of Kohekapu—without a mark on her forehead. Look at her!"

"Let me pass," said Tepua weakly.

"So that you can assure yourself that he is gone?" Natunatu thrust her trembling cheeks so close that Tepua smelled her sweat mixed with trickling blood. "You are the one who made him die," Natunatu accused. "Your black arts brought him down. Helped by that pale-skinned pig you call a sailor." With a scream of rage Natunatu flung herself at Tepua. "False *ariki*! I will make the gashes on your forehead, if you will not!"

Tepua grappled with the older woman, trying to dodge the wild swings of the tooth-edged flail. But a vicious strike hit the side of her cheek and another scored her forearm. She barely felt the sting, or the warm trickles of blood.

Tepua could not hold back her rage at the accusations. "False wife," she retorted. "You cared nothing for my father. All you wanted was to make your son chief."

Natunatu shrieked her denial and struck again, but others entered the fight. Suddenly Natunatu was pinioned and pulled back. Tepua, flinging tangled hair from her face, saw that Ehi had a grip on her attacker.

"Let me go!" shouted Natunatu, but Ehi shook the smaller woman as she would a recalcitrant child. There was no anger, only regret and sorrow on her broad face as she struggled to hold Kohekapu's widow.

"She is maddened by grief, daughter," said Ehi. "Pay no heed to her."

Tepua glanced once more at Natunatu's tormented features. Then she straightened her shoulders and walked forward. At the low doorway she paused a moment, whispering a prayer before she slipped inside.

The priests moved away, letting her approach the body of her father. She recalled the Kohekapu of long ago—a magnificent man, tall, clear-eyed, broad of shoulders. Since coming home, she had preserved that memory, never really noticing what he had become. Now she tried not to see the shape of the shrunken body beneath its cover of mats. Even at the end his face had not lost the majesty and dignity of one who was a true *ariki*.

The enormity of her loss burst upon her. She wailed aloud, bending to strike her forehead against a heavy beam of the house. Then someone handed her a flail, and she began to gash her face with repeated strikes, letting the mixture of tears and blood fall onto Kohekapu's chest.

She heard the women outside take up her cry, then men as well, until the air resounded with howls of grief. She used the flail in self-reproach as well as mourning, for Natunatu's words had struck a note of truth. Tepua and Kiore had done nothing to harm her father. Yet her attention to the foreigner had often taken her from Kohekapu's side. Even at the old chief's final moment she had been talking about Kiore when she should have been sitting here.

"Father, I did not mean to neglect you," she whispered. Then she moved aside so that others could enter the house. It would be Natunatu's privilege to remain by the body and accept the offerings of sympathy. People would bring her mats and ornaments and even red feathers. These would be Natunatu's keepsake—to forever show how her husband had been esteemed.

And Tepua would have—only her memories. She gripped the shark-tooth flail and began to moan. . . .

Through the night she grieved for her father, until her forehead was covered with gashes and her throat raw from wailing. It was then that gentle hands lifted her and guided her away. Numbly she followed Ehi out into the light of early morning.

With kindness that made Tepua weep all the more, Ehi put her to bed in her own house, and stayed by her, dressing her cuts and speaking softly to her.

"Do not blame yourself," Ehi said. "It was time for Kohekapu to join the others of our line, and that is all." She took the flail from Tepua's clenched hand and laid it aside. "Do not let Natunatu's words make you strike deeper than grief demands."

"Natunatu cares only for Umia," Tepua answered bitterly. "My father served her purpose. Now she is glad he is gone. Maybe she even used sorcery to get rid of him."

Ehi soothed her again with soft hands. "The gods have taken your father for reasons we will never know. Flinging accusations does no good. Sleep, and gather the strength you will need for tomorrow."

"Sleep? With that woman's foul words still in my ears?" But gradually she allowed Ehi's comforting words to soothe her and at last she drifted off.

When Tepua opened her eyes in Ehi's house, she thought for a moment that she was still a young girl in her adoptive mother's household. About her were all the things she remembered from childhood, the arrangement of the mats, the rough wooden bowls, the many bundles hanging from the roof beams. In the twilight between sleep and awareness she could almost persuade herself that the recent events were only nightmares. But full wakefulness stole the illusion. She remembered the night of wailing, and how Ehi had finally brought her here. Now she felt the ache of the cuts on her skin and the knowledge that her father was dead.

Many times I have been without him, Tepua thought. *This will only be another.* Tears spilled from her eyes and she reached once more for the shark-tooth flail. A heavy but gentle hand on her arm stopped her. She looked up into Ehi's face.

"There will be plenty of days to bleed for your father," she said. "You must rest awhile longer. Besides, you have a visitor. Umia has just arrived to join the mourners, and he wishes to see you."

Groggily Tepua made her way outside and found her brother standing under a *fara* tree. Salt from the canoe journey still crusted his hair, and she saw traces of tears on his face. Haggard as he looked, she knew her own appearance was even more disheveled. He could not reproach her for lack of feeling.

She recalled her last meeting with him, when Cone-shell's influence had seemed to control his every word. Now she sensed a change, though she could not see it in any one place. Perhaps he held himself with a new dignity, as if some of the grace that had fled from Kohekapu had come into him. As she looked at her brother Tepua longed to lift the burden of rulership and let it fall onto his younger, broader shoulders.

"I have not had a chance to tell you this," said Umia after they had greeted each other. "It is important you hear it first from me. I had nothing to do with Cone-shell's act of deceit. He arranged it all secretly. He kept me away from the *kava* drinking so that I could not interfere."

"You need say no more, brother. I did not believe that you had any part in that."

"I will say something else. You have suffered abuse not only from Cone-shell, but also from my mother. I heard what happened yesterday." He picked up Tepua's hand, touched her arm where Natunatu's flail had cut. "Is this where she struck you?"

"It did no true harm," Tepua managed to say.

"And here?" Umia drew his fingertips along the sides of

her face. "She tried to blind you? *Aue!* I am greatly shamed!"

She caught his wrist. "Umia, I do not wish to speak of Natunatu. Tell me about Cone-shell. When you left, did he try to hinder you?"

"His priests advised him not to interfere with my coming here. A son must be permitted to mourn his father."

"But Cone-shell will not mourn him," she replied angrily. "Though he honored Kohekapu as high chief during his lifetime."

"Cone-shell is not ready to be seen here," he explained. "He is preparing a grand arrival and does not want it overshadowed by the great chief's death."

"Then when will he come?"

"When he has finished gathering the gifts. He means to acknowledge your rule and pay you homage."

"That is good news," said Tepua. "I would like to hear only one more thing from you."

Umia wrinkled his brow. "I know what you want."

"Listen to my offer. I have a house for you here. You can fill it with your own attendants. I will call you to the meetings of the chiefs and you will sit by my side. That is the proper way to ready yourself for high office."

"Tepua, I cannot agree."

"Because you still doubt my leadership?"

"I am sorry to say it, but that is one reason. I worry about the sailor you sent to Piho Clan. Cone-shell was wrong for what he did to you, but he may be right about the foreigner."

"I thought that Nika was doing well."

"My uncle calls him a troublemaker."

"Does he say why?"

"He doesn't always confide in me. But I have spent enough time with my uncle to know when he is serious."

"Then I will find out for myself. But that should not be the reason that keeps you away."

"Tepua, you know that I have always lived with Varoa Clan. My friends and my foster parents are there."

"Yet you must leave if you ever want to be free of Cone-shell's power. How can you aspire to the chiefhood if you aren't willing to stand on your own? Your father was of Ahiku Clan. Your place is here."

He let out a long breath. "I cannot answer you now, sister. Perhaps you are right. But the mourning for our father has begun again. We must join the others."

By late afternoon a high bier had been erected near the family *marae* of Kohekapu. Paruru stood with many others, looking up at the remains of his chief. About the annointed body lay sweet-smelling ferns and fruits of *fara* to scent the air.

The wailing of the death chants continued, each mourner adding new praises to the account of Kohekapu's deeds. Paruru would not say so aloud, but Natunatu had shown herself to be gifted with words. Her dirge had been the longest by far, and the most touching. Now the day's mourning was coming to an end.

With dusk approaching, no one wished to linger in this place of spirits. The last speaker finished. After a final chant by the priests, almost everyone headed home. But for Paruru and a few others there remained one more duty.

By the time he reached Kohekapu's house, priests and a few people of high rank had gathered outside for the cleansing rite. The sleeping mats and other things that Kohekapu had touched during his illness would be burned. Paruru had seen many such ceremonies. He realized quickly that something was wrong here. The mats and other goods had not been carried out into the yard.

An elder turned to him, and Paruru saw the troubled look on his deeply lined face. "The priests say they must burn everything. The house, too."

"*Aue!*" Paruru realized what this meant. As was always done, diviners had sought the cause of the old chief's death.

Sometimes they blamed sorcery, sometimes a punishment by the gods. Paruru did not know what signs the priests had discovered, only that they were ominous. He knew one reason why the gods might be angry. . . .

The sun had just set, and the waning daylight did little to dispel the gloom beneath the trees. No one spoke. In the quiet air, the beating of waves against the reef seemed to grow louder. All attention focused on the uncovered doorway of Kohekapu's house.

The deep voice of a *tahunga* sounded from within. Then a flame sprang up and the *tahunga* rushed outside. Paruru heard the crackling of dry brush that had been used as kindling. He saw flames licking at the thatch above the doorway, then spreading higher.

The *tahunga* faced the house, continuing his chant as smoke streamed through the narrow openings in the walls and fire raced along the roof. The women began wailing again. How Paruru had come to despise that sound!

As the fire consumed the belongings of the chief, the sounds of mourning eased. Paruru saw, in the glow of the flames, expressions of relief on the onlookers' faces. They felt safe now, he thought. The evil had been cleansed. Kohekapu was gone, but no further harm could come to them.

Paruru felt no relief.

: FOURTEEN

One evening, days after the cries of mourning had finally ceased, Tepua was sitting in her house listening to stories told by her newest attendant. The girl, a distant relation, had been raised on another atoll to the north and brought here recently by her father.

The new girl was a good storyteller. Everyone in the house had clustered around her to listen. Even Tepua was entranced, and had moved her stool so that she could see and hear as the tales unfolded. Wedges of burning copra provided a dim illumination, enough so that the storyteller's expressive hands could be seen. She finished one legend and began another. "Now I will tell our version of Maui's search for the sea slug," she began.

The sound of drumming interrupted, however, before Maui even started his adventure. All heads turned to listen to the beat. Even the storyteller could not compete against the insistent voice of the slit-log drum.

"The dancing begins," Tepua heard the servants whispering to each other. To the new girl, they said, "You will come with us tonight. If the *ariki* permits."

Tepua quickly gave her agreement. The phase of the moon, she knew, marked this as a special night. Ghosts would not walk; it was a safe time to be outside, a time for young men and women to enjoy each other's company.

The attendants ran off, leaving Tepua alone. As she sat, watching the lights burn low, she remembered similar

188

evenings during her youth. Then, too, the servants had
bubbled with excitement as they went out, leaving Tepua
with her chaperon. How she had argued and complained,
making her guardian groan with despair! Tepua had known
well what the other girls were doing while she remained a
prisoner. Had she not been the high chief's daughter, she
would have been with the others—dancing, making love.

And now, here she was again, isolated by her high rank
while others were free to celebrate under the lovers' moon.
But this time there was a difference. She had no chaperon.
No old woman was sitting here, telling her what to do. . . .

The drumming grew louder. The hard *tok, tok* of the
slit-log drum sounded a frenzied rhythm. The deeper boom
of the skinhead-drum beat with the pulsing of her blood. Her
feet were already moving to the music.

She knotted her fist. How could she stay inside while
everyone else was dancing? She untied her red sash and
flung off her fine skirt. Then she went to the servants' end
of the house, where she found a coarsely made garment
and wrapped it about her hips. Someone had discarded a
wreath of beach vines. That would be good enough for her
hair.

There was little she could do to disguise her face, or her
height. She would have to keep to the shadows if she did not
wish to be recognized. The air inside her house suddenly
seemed heavy with fumes from the burning copra. She
could not wait to get into the fresh air under the stars.

"I am going for a walk," she told the guards outside. The
men were so busy gazing longingly down the beach that
they merely grunted their assent. She hurried past them,
hearing the drums grow louder, feeling her feet picking up
the steps of the dance.

She did not seek a partner, but kept to the edge of the
crowd, stopping under the shadow of an overhanging
ironwood tree. The drummers were so close now that she
could feel each beat as if her own skin were being struck.

Her hips began swaying of their own accord, keeping

time to the wild beat, while her arms and hands made graceful figures in the air. She breathed deeply, catching scents of flowers and perfumed oil from the other dancers. And behind the sweetness lay other scents—musky hints of growing desire.

Tepua watched the other dancers, many close to her own age. In the light of the low crescent moon she saw faces aglow with excitement. Perspiration gleamed on backs and thighs and chests. Now and again an exhausted dancer would stagger to a halt, then extend a hand to his or her partner. Then the couple would hurry off to find a quiet nest for themselves.

Tepua was content, for now, just to abandon herself to the music. In Tahiti she had grown used to dancing every day, practicing her skills for the Arioi performances. Long before that she had danced among her own people—but never with a partner, and never out of sight of her chaperons.

She knew that she might find Kiore here. The sailor was back from the islet he had visited during the time of mourning. On his return yesterday she had greeted him coolly and sent him off with White-sea. She had not cared to hear him talk excitedly of canoe-masters' lore.

Now she kept looking here and there among the dancers, expecting to see him. The words he had said once—that he wanted no woman but Tepua—meant nothing now. She could not blame him for seeking other company.

The drumming continued as Tepua advanced slowly along the beach. The dancers were fewer here, all moving with the grace of long practice. Even from a distance she thought she would recognize Kiore. Perhaps he had already found his companion for the night.

At last she was alone, far from the crowd, dancing on wet sand by the water's edge. Alone? No. Someone was watching her from the shadows! She stopped, picked up a clamshell, and tossed it at the figure that leaned motionless against a palm tree.

"*Aue!*" came the cry. "You have good aim."

Recognizing Kiore's voice, she laughed and picked up another shell. "On my island," she said, "we dance under the lovers' moon. We do not stand and watch."

"Then I will dance," he said, coming out into the pale light.

Tepua felt a new pitch of excitement as she started again. Before this, she had not really felt part of the festivities. She had been like Kiore, watching, envying the others. Now, with the sailor so close to her, her body seemed to be moving only for him. Her limbs felt weightless. Her hips swung as easily as leaves in the wind.

Kiore began in his own strange way, yet she found his steps appealing. She saw grace in his movements, foreign though they were. His chest glistened with sweat as he kept up his pace.

Out in the open, she knew she was far too conspicuous. Yet, for a time, she kept on. Her breathing came faster. Kiore's steps grew wilder. The drumbeat possessed her and would not let go.

At last, panting for breath, she halted and reached for his hand as she had seen other girls do. She tugged at him to follow, leading him away from the music. "Do not mistake me for the chief," she told him quietly. "Tepua is asleep in her house."

He turned to study her, lifting his hand to gently brush her cheek. "Then what do I call you? You must have a name."

She thought of the vines running down toward the water. "Beach-pea."

He laughed and pressed his nose to hers. The feeling was delicious, but she pulled away. "We must go somewhere else." She had not thought ahead this far. Under the trees lay many outrigger canoes; there was no reason she could not borrow one. With Kiore's eager help, she dragged a *vaka* over the sand.

The wind had dropped. The surface of the lagoon was perfectly still, moonlight reaching the shallow bottom. She could scarcely see where air ended and water began.

Leaving shore, Tepua glimpsed fish that did not stir as the canoe floated over them. The undersea gardens of coral seemed close enough to touch. Behind her she heard the rhythmic dip and stroke of Kiore's paddle.

She hesitated before telling him which way she was heading. Never had Tepua gone to Ata-ruru with anyone but Maukiri. She had an unspoken agreement with her cousin that this special islet was theirs alone. But what better place to take Kiore? Tepua thought of soft sand beneath the palms, of shrubs that offered shelter from the breeze.

They crossed the lagoon slowly, as if in a dream. She fell silent awhile, hearing only the sound of paddles stroking and water parting before the bow. She watched the glimmer of tiny ripples, then turned her gaze upward.

Overhead, star clusters glittered. Tepua called out their names, and sometimes Kiore told her the names his own people used. For a while Tepua put aside her paddle and moved back in the canoe until she could lean against the warmth of Kiore's chest. They whispered stories to each other, tales heard long ago.

The night was vast and timeless. Tepua felt no need to hurry. The sky and water belonged only to her and Kiore. The islet ahead was also theirs; it would wait as long as they wanted.

Dipping and stroking and resting as they chose, they crossed the placid water. At last, under the setting moon, she found the secret channels that led to the islet's beach. The canoe came in to shore, and suddenly Tepua emerged from her reverie. She felt awake now and filled with desire. As soon as the canoe was beached, she raced off, heading for the trees. "This way!" she called to him.

She picked up several large palm fronds and made a simple bed on the sand. Then she flung her skirt aside, lay down, and waited for him to join her. He seemed startled by her sudden directness, and for a moment he hesitated. Then he tumbled down beside her.

"How many layers?" she asked him playfully, tugging at the garment that covered him from his waist to his legs.

"Only one," he promised. And finally, there were none.

For a time it was enough just to hold each other. "We are alike," she said softly, "in a way I did not see until I found you tonight. We are both strangers here. This is not your home, nor is it mine any longer."

He sighed, and pressed her face against the heat of his chest. "Home," he replied. "It is very far."

Tepua recalled some wonders of his land that he had talked about. Water that turned to stone when the weather was cold. Ovens that burned inside a house but did not fill the room with smoke. "Do you long most for the strange things and foods of your country?" she asked. "Or for the company of your kin?"

"So many things. But you make me forget." He held her to him, gently caressing her shoulders and back. He brought her face up to his. His lips touched her forehead, her cheek, her mouth. His darting tongue began to trace a path down her neck, eventually circling her breasts. Then the circles grew smaller, ever smaller, until Tepua was wriggling with delight.

"Let me try that!" she said, rolling out from under him. He seemed surprised when she fell on him and began to apply her tongue. She started at his neck, tasting the salty tang of his skin. Slowly she worked her way down. When she reached a nipple, he cried out, a soft moan of pleasure.

He reached up and gently, softly, massaged her breasts with his fingertips until she could not stay still for the sweetness that coursed through her. She pulled away for a moment, catching her breath. Then she lowered her mouth to his and they began to explore the foreign way of kissing.

Now Tepua felt like a newly launched canoe, traveling a heated sea. She pitched and rolled on top of him, reveling in the warmth and power that buoyed her. A strong current pulled her onward as she bounded from crest to crest, heedless of where she was heading. But so far—so long a journey. She was ready to cry out from need, when at last she felt his tip thrust inside her. *Aue!* she cried as the canoe sped forward into unknown waters.

The waves lifted her and set her down, lifted her and set her down. Slowly and shallowly and gently it began, a small pleasure whispering to her at every surge. Then the waves grew higher, the troughs deeper, until she knew nothing but the music of the ocean, the singing of the deep. . . .

She realized that she was shouting, crying, shuddering with great spasms. Kiore began writhing so beneath her that she thought she would surely fall off. And then he cried out, too, his head tossing, his hands gripping her fiercely.

Still in the throes of her own release, she reached out and began rubbing his chest and arms with the palm of her hand, making him jerk and sigh and moan until he lay still. He relaxed, breathing with great contented heaves as she nestled her head against his chest.

"Tell me," she said later as they lay curled together, his chest pressing warmly against her back. "What is it like with your women. What are their ways of making love?"

"The women are not like you," he answered. "I think they know little of love. Maybe someday you will come teach them."

She answered playfully, "If I come to your country, how many layers of clothing will I have to wear?"

"I have not counted them," he replied with a laugh. "In the cold season, we need every one. But even in the hot season we cover ourselves."

"Why is that?" She remembered how uncomfortable she had been on a hot day wearing the one garment he had given her. Yet there were reasons for enduring worse discomforts. "I have heard of high-islanders," she said, "who wrap themselves around and around in bark-cloth, to show off their wealth."

"It is not so different with us," he answered. "But there is also another reason. Do you remember Atama and Eva?" Some time ago Kiore had told her the names of the first man

and woman that his god had made. Now he spoke of their
early life in a place of fruit trees and flowers. From his
description she thought their land had been much like
Tahiti. But unlike the Tahitians, this couple knew nothing of
love.

"Because of an evil spirit in the garden," he said, "the
two learned unhappiness." The demon had tricked the
young people into breaking a *tapu*. As part of their
punishment, they had come to feel shame at exposing their
bodies.

But this was not the worst part of their punishment. Kiore
said that his god, the creator of his race, made strict rules
about *hanihani*. Tepua was astonished when she heard
them.

"How can you tell the young men and women not to
enjoy themselves after dancing on the beach?" she asked.
"And how can the trees bear and the earth flower if we do
not freely show affection for each other?"

Kiore confessed that sometimes he thought the priests of
his god might be mistaken. "I was taught," he whispered,
"that my one god is everywhere, and that yours are not
anywhere at all. It is a sin that I say this, but I wish to
believe that here your gods do rule."

"Without them we would have no life, so they must be
here. Tell me. Does this single god of yours take charge of
everything—the wind, the seas, the crops? It seems too
much for one."

"The one god knows if a tiny bird falls from its perch."

Tepua frowned. "We have high gods, like Tangaroa, who
would not notice if a *flock* of birds fell into the sea.
Tangaroa is too great to care about our ordinary problems.
We depend on the spirits of our ancestors. They have the
most to lose if they do not help us—they will be forgotten!"

Kiore laughed when she said that. "You are wise, Tepua.
You do not think as I do, but you are very wise."

After a time they got up and strolled along the small,
sandy beach. The moon had set and the stars shone

brilliantly against an inky black. Maui's great fishhook gleamed overhead. "See how the fish go for his bait," Tepua said, pointing to the long, milky streamers that crossed the sky.

Some stars she recognized as guides used by canoe-masters in sailing between islands. Perhaps Kiore already knew the ones that could lead him home. She did not ask what he had learned on his recent travels or how he would use that knowledge. Tonight she wanted to think that there was no world beyond Ata-ruru.

Under starlight Tepua could just make out the tiny white crabs that prowled the beach. As she approached one it scuttled away across the sand. "Here is a game we can play," she suggested. "I chase a crab, and you have to catch it before it reaches its hole. If you win, we change places."

It was a game that young children played, but it suited their mood. Kiore tumbled happily onto the sand, never quite catching his prey. At last they changed places, Kiore startling a crab so that she could run after it. The little thing led her on a zigzag chase, down to the water and back up to the trees, until finally she lost it.

Tepua fell down, breathless from laughing, and lay with her face to the glowing sky. "It would be fine if there were no other place than this," she said when Kiore kneeled close to her. "Only this tiny *motu*. Only the two of us. The first man and woman."

"Atama and Eva," he said. "But with no demon to misguide us." He came closer, pressing his lips to her cheeks and then to her mouth. Hungrily she pulled him on top of her. *This is how I please my gods,* she thought as she wrapped her legs around the small of his back. *And if Kiore's god is not happy with him* . . . But the pleasure was beginning again and she could think no longer.

The night had seemed endless to Tepua, but finally dawn approached. She and Kiore paddled back hurriedly, aided by a gentle wind at their backs. There were no words to be spoken at parting. She touched his hand gently, laid her cheek against it, and ran off.

Slipping past her dozing guards, she dropped on her mat and pulled a cape over her. She could tell by the quiet sounds of breathing that everyone else remained asleep, but Tepua had no desire for slumber. She lay in the darkness, her eyes open, gazing at her memories.

The pounding of waves on the reef grew louder. She tried to lose herself in the sound. At this time of day, she thought, the voice of the *ringoringo* was sometimes heard. Long ago, her father had promised to send her a message when he reached the world of night. She wondered if the voice would come now, when she might hear it.

Her skin seemed warm, still flushed from Kiore's touch. She felt herself drifting as she listened. Her body seemed to grow light. And then she did hear a whisper, but it was Kiore's voice, speaking of the beauty that he found in her, the blackness of her hair and the whiteness of her teeth, the taste of her lips and softness of her skin.

The crashing of the surf took her back to Ata-ruru, lifted her as he had done, made her want to cry out his name. As she lay, engulfed by the sound of the sea, she imagined him beside her. The memory of his warmth made her forget the troubles that had come and would come again. . . .

FIFTEEN

Tepua was still adrift on tumbling seas when Maukiri woke her. The high chief rubbed her eyes and sat up, wondering hazily why her sleep had been disturbed. Normally, it was her right to doze as late as she wished. . . .

"A messenger from Cone-shell just arrived," said Maukiri, slightly out of breath. "Varoa's chief is coming. Today. With gifts for the *ariki*."

"Today! Then Umia was right. . . . But why did Cone-shell have to choose *this* day?" After the dancing the servants had been up late, and Tepua even later.

"Cousin, I see how weary you are," said Maukiri, speaking in the familiar manner she used when no one could overhear. Maukiri seemed to be waiting for an explanation, but Tepua offered none.

Surely it was no secret by now that the chief had vanished during the evening and had not been seen until dawn. Tepua hoped that no one knew more than that. "You must help me, Maukiri. Order preparations for the feast. Find some dancers who did not exhaust themselves last night."

Her cousin stared at her, a slight smile forming on her lips. "Dancers . . . Yes, there were many on the beach." Her eyes asked a question.

Tepua tried to hold back her irritation at Maukiri's prying. "I am aware of that, but we have to entertain Cone-shell—" She stopped speaking as Maukiri's look of amusement grew. *"Aue!"* cried Tepua. "Cousin, will you give me no peace? The drumming was loud last night, and the air inside very warm. I went out to walk on the beach and watch the stars."

"And nothing more?"

"If there was more, you will not hear it now. Go. Start the work."

Tepua watched her cousin leave, then rubbed her eyes again. Poor Maukiri had been unhappy since Paruru took Nika away. She claimed that she was consoling herself with someone else, but Tepua guessed that this was more pretense than fact.

Separating the two men had been helpful, forcing Kiore to speak only in the island language and to immerse himself in the way of life. But Tepua sympathized with Maukiri's plight and had recently insisted that Paruru bring Nika back.

Tepua was keeping this news as a surprise. Perhaps it was time to tell Maukiri.

When Cone-shell's *pahi* arrived, in early afternoon, the earth ovens had already been lit. Pleasant aromas drifted toward Tepua as she stood above the shore waiting for him. She was dressed in royal finery—her best mat skirt and a cape trimmed with cowrie shells. A new headdress of stiff, shiny tropic bird tail plumes encircled her head.

Varoa's chief, too, wore a tall feather headdress. Holding the staff of his office high, he stood on the deck of his large *pahi* as it came in. His necklaces of dolphin teeth glittered. The feather trimming of his cape shimmered under the hot sun.

Behind him on the deck Tepua saw bundles, rolled mats, baskets—the gifts that Umia had said that Cone-shell would bring. But how sincere was this gesture? she wondered. Her feelings of elation were tinged with doubt as she watched Varoa's ruler being carried ashore.

The bearers set him down and he halted deferentially before her, remaining close to the water while she stood at the top of the gentle rise. Then he spoke the words that he had withheld for so long. "*Maeva ariki!* May you have life!"

"May you have life," she answered. He seemed a changed man since the time she had seen him shivering in the canoe, his face pale from his encounter with the sharks. Now he looked robust and full of confidence. Tepua was puzzled. Not long ago there had been talk that his people might topple him from office. Now, with his large retinue around him, he seemed secure as chief of Varoa Clan.

Unable to explain this, she watched curiously as he ordered his gifts brought ashore. These included prized tools and utensils—adzes, food pounders, bowls—made of heavy, black stone only found on high islands. One gift was extraordinary—a cape trimmed with a fringe of white dog's hair. Cone-shell's servants carried it triumphantly from place to place so that everyone could inspect the remarkable fringe.

At last the ritual greetings and gift giving were done. Tepua escorted Cone-shell to the assembly ground for the entertainment. Earlier she had sent out messengers and had gathered important guests from several clans to welcome Cone-shell. It was clear that everyone present, especially Varoa's chief, acknowledged her superior rank. Yet she still felt ill at ease with him.

Once again, Umia was absent from a gathering where Tepua wanted his company. He had gone home to his uncle and had not returned. Now that Cone-shell had declared his allegiance, she hoped that Umia might find her invitation easier to accept.

As she tried to interest herself in the dancers, Tepua kept asking herself what lay behind Cone-shell's smug expression. Her thoughts began to wander, her eyelids feeling dry and heavy. The brief sleep at dawn was all she had gotten this day. Now she wondered how she would keep her wits keen for the discussions that would come later. Cone-shell had presented his gifts. He would ask for something in return.

The afternoon passed slowly as she watched the performers. Several times Tepua's head slumped forward and she woke with a start from momentary sleep. Then the food arrived from the ovens and Cone-shell demonstrated his prodigious appetite.

At last the moment came for the other guests to disperse, leaving Tepua and Varoa's chief alone in the place of honor at the edge of the assembly ground. She sat on her high stool, and he, facing her, on his lesser seat. Under the long shadows, guards looked on, but they stood well out of earshot.

"It is good," Cone-shell began, "that we have found a way to resolve our differences."

She agreed, watching him closely, trying to read his thoughts. He had exhausted all light conversation. Soon he would reveal his desires.

"I have heard nothing from you about the foreign goods," he said in a casual tone.

"That is because nothing has changed."

His tone hardened. "You said you needed time to learn to speak with the outsiders. By now, you certainly must know enough about them and their things."

"I do not know enough yet. The tools are sharp, as you have seen. With a foreign chopper, a man can cut down a tree far too easily. Think what that would mean in war." Tepua thought she had reason for concern. In fighting between islands, a common tactic was to destroy food trees of the enemy. Such attacks would prove even more cruel and wasteful if warriors had the new implements.

"Yet," Cone-shell countered, "Paruru encourages his new brother to use foreign tools. I hear that the red-haired one is building a canoe. The work moves quickly."

Tepua tried to conceal her surprise at that news. She had let Paruru keep the chopper, but had not guessed how he would put it to use. "Nika can handle that tool without getting hurt. And I am certain that he is well supervised in his work."

"I, too, could have the benefit of such tools, if I had someone like Nika to use them. . . ." Cone-shell's voice trailed off, and Tepua felt as if someone had aimed a blow at her stomach. It was all too clear now where Cone-shell was heading. With her wits dulled from lack of sleep, she had given him the opening he needed.

"Cone-shell, are you short of canoes?" she replied. "I always thought that Varoa had more craftsmen than any other clan."

"Think about trade! Do you know how much those lazy Tahitians will give for a *pahi,* even a leaky one? Think about pork! And rolls of bleached bark-cloth."

Tepua knew that canoes were sometimes sent to Tahiti in exchange for high-island goods. Cone-shell certainly had a weakness for such things. "It is possible that Faka-ora will release a chopper to you," she offered. "But do not blame me if your craftsman slices off his fingers."

"Would Kiore slice off his fingers? Do you mean that the outsider cannot handle his own chopper?" As she stared at Cone-shell he leaned forward and laughed.

It was not his joke that so amused him, she thought. Her expression had given her away. "What are you saying about Kiore?"

"Tepua, let us not circle each other forever. What I ask of you is no more than you have given Paruru, who is not even a chief. He has adopted Nika into his clan. Let me take Kiore. What could be more reasonable?"

I am not ready to give him up! She held herself back from shouting those words. "Nika went willingly. Paruru was already his friend. Kiore knows nothing of Varoa Clan. He would be a stranger there."

"We will make him welcome."

"What are you thinking? Kiore is not a child, and he is surely no kin to me. I do not have the right to give him away."

"You are the high chief. You will find a way." He stretched out his legs and paused, a derisive smile forming at the edge of his mouth. "You will do this because you need something from me."

Tepua answered coldly. "You have already given me all I want. Ask for whatever foreign goods you wish, and I will try to oblige you in return."

"I want more than goods, Tepua-ariki. Listen to what I tell you now. Soon after Paruru made Nika his brother the two of them brought me a turtle."

"Paruru gave you a peace offering in my name. Why should that worry me?"

He seemed taken aback when she answered so easily. Had he thought that she knew nothing of this? Tepua did not reveal that Paruru's explanation had struck her as odd.

Cone-shell drew in his legs and sat upright, glaring at her from beneath his heavy brows. His jovial mood was gone. Now she saw the fierce fighter who had long ago won renown in battle. "Since the day of that turtle feast," he said, "the waters off Varoa's shore have been troubled. When the tide is changing, the current suddenly becomes wild and unpredictable. Two canoes have been wrecked on patch reefs, and several others have come close."

She felt Cone-shell eyeing her, measuring her reaction. He continued, "My priests blame these incidents on the turtle offering. The spirits were angered by it. Fortunately, only one priest knows the reason for this anger."

"Fortunately?"

"Yes. I have told only Raha, and he knows how to keep a secret."

Raha! She wanted nothing to do with Cone-shell's unpleasant brother. She felt an urge to flee, to refuse to listen to what Cone-shell was about to say. Umia had warned her about Nika. . . .

"I know the cause of our problems," said Varoa's chief harshly. "After the turtle feast, a frightened fisherman came to me. His teeth were chattering so that he could barely speak." Cone-shell paused as if savoring the words he was about to say. "The fisherman had seen Nika attacking a turtle with a long spear. Nika alone. Paruru's story of the capture was full of lies.''

''Fisherman . . .''

''If you doubt me, I will bring the one who saw this, and let you question him.''

Tepua was too stunned to reply. Paruru's explanation had seemed contorted; his mood had been uneasy, his words evasive. Since telling her of the gift to Cone-shell, Paruru had taken pains to avoid her.

Now she could not help believing that Cone-shell's version was true. Why else would Paruru be acting as if he had committed a misdeed? The outsider had erred and his new brother had tried to hide the mistake. . . .

''So you see how I can assist you,'' Cone-shell continued. ''The offense to the gods must be wiped clean. Raha is willing to take care of that, at a private ceremony. No one else need know. But if I let the news out, then what do you think will happen to your foreign guests? Every priest on the atoll will demand an end to them before they do even more damage.''

''No!'' She felt weak, dizzy, exhausted by his onslaught.

''Then you agree.''

''What will happen,'' she asked hoarsely, ''if your own people find out about that turtle? You were the one who accepted it. Your priests made the offerings. If the gods are offended, then you must share the blame.''

''Yes,'' said Cone-shell, ''I will suffer for a time. It will cost us both if we do not settle this.''

''Then maybe you are bluffing, like the strutting warrior who hopes to spare himself a fight.''

''Do you wish to try me?''

She closed her eyes for a moment, gathering her strength. At last she understood why Cone-shell had come. He could take anything he wanted from her now, even Kiore. ''It is easy to frighten people with words,'' she answered. ''How do I know that Raha can appease the gods? Let him try. If he succeeds, then you and I will have something to discuss."

Cone-shell's mouth formed an ugly grin. "If he succeeds, then you will give me what I want."

She thought of a parrot fish thrashing inside a trap. There was an escape, but the fish could never find it. "Tell Raha to get ready," she answered hoarsely.

Tepua knew that she must sleep before confronting Paruru. If she spoke to him now, tired and angry as she was, she might open a rift between them that could never be closed.

She went to her mat and lay down, but sleep seemed far off. Her stomach felt hot and tight, still full from the feast. She wished that she had eaten less. She also wished that she had somehow foreseen what would happen with the chief of Varoa.

How foolish she had been to let herself care for the foreigner. How foolish to take the comfort and happiness that Kiore gave—only to lose him to Cone-shell.

In the morning she walked across the island, coming out of the forest above the windy seaward beach. It was here that Paruru could usually be found with his lookouts.

"*Maeva ariki!*" he called to her from his spot beneath the palms. His face appeared haggard, his eyes without luster. "The sea is empty this morning," he reported. "No sign of raiders."

She paused and frowned. "You sound as if you expect an attack."

"Another trader has seen Pu-tahi canoes . . . within one day's sail."

"I keep hearing such reports," she answered impatiently. "If Pu-tahi are planning to attack us, they seem in no hurry."

"I cannot explain that, *ariki*. But I promise you they will not creep up on us this time."

"Then I must tell you something else." She glanced up

at the swaying palms to make sure that the sentries were out of earshot. "Cone-shell has talked to me," she whispered harshly. "He knows the truth about the turtle you gave him—how Nika killed it. He found out too late, after it was eaten!"

Paruru paled as he took in her words. He gripped his spear and sagged against it the way an old man leaned on a walking stick. "*Ariki,* forgive me," he whispered. "I was afraid of what might happen. The turtle had to be properly offered at a *marae.* I saw no other way." His face contorted as he struggled to express himself. "I do not know if the gods are angry. There have been signs—"

"The priests have not said what the signs mean," she answered hotly. "But we dare not leave this unfinished. Cone-shell's brother will make amends for us, and the cost will be high. Cone-shell is demanding Kiore."

Paruru's eyes widened.

"Cone-shell wants to take him away. Perhaps you will welcome that news."

"*Ariki,* I was trying to protect the foreigners—"

"But there have been too many mistakes. From that first night, when women went to their boat—"

Suddenly Paruru threw down his spear. "Then choose another *kaito-nui.* I served your father, but he is gone and my obligation is done. I tried to please you, but I have failed."

Tepua had not expected this response. How easy it would be to take him at his word.

But no. It was not possible to deprive him of his rank. Not now, when questions would be asked on every side. "Paruru, pick up your spear," she said firmly. "You are still my *kaito-nui.*"

"But I am in disgrace."

"Then you must redeem yourself. Put Sea-snake in charge here for a short while."

"He is able. But—"

"Then take Nika to Varoa's priest. Let Raha make

amends for the sins you both committed. I will try to forget what has happened."

Paruru paused, narrowing his eyes. "You are too forgiving, *ariki,*" he answered at last. "You have given me a way to save my brother as well as myself. I do not know how to repay this kindness."

Her throat felt tight. She swallowed, trying to hold back her anguish. "When you go to Varoa Clan, try to persuade Umia to visit me again."

"I will try."

"And one more request. Think about this. Cone-shell expects to get a share of the foreign goods through Kiore. If the goods disappear, then Kiore won't do him any good."

"Disappear? How?" The warrior raised his eyebrows. "Ah, I see. Perhaps the priests can help. I will speak with Faka-ora when I come back."

"With aid from your men, I'm sure the priests can arrange it." As she turned away from her *kaito-nui* she wondered why she still trusted him. Perhaps because they had one wish in common—to keep Cone-shell from seizing her chiefhood. If that threat ended, she could not say what Paruru would do.

A short time later Tepua walked with Maukiri to a sandy point of land, a preserve of the chief of Ahiku Clan. Tepua stopped where she could sit beneath the dangling needles of an ironwood tree. Maukiri sprawled on her stomach and toyed listlessly with a pile of clamshells.

Tepua knew the cause of her cousin's sullen mood. "I have happy news for you," Tepua said. "Paruru is going back to Piho Clan. When he returns here, he will bring his new brother."

Maukiri glanced up warily, as if afraid that Tepua might retract her words.

"He told me that Nika is eager to see you," Tepua added.

"Eager? Why, when he has Piho women wherever he turns?"

"Not so many as you think. Most of the pretty ones are close kin to Paruru. Nika can only rub noses with them."

Maukiri began to smile. "I had not thought of that, cousin. He must be wishing now that he had not accepted Paruru's offer!" She tossed the clamshells aside and rolled over onto her back. "I'll find ways to keep Nika from wanting to go back to Piho Clan."

"Then practice diving for pearl shells. Nika enjoys collecting them."

"I know a good place for that," Maukiri answered. "And perhaps you can teach me a few other things that will help keep him here. I am waiting to learn about that long walk you took on the beach—when you stayed out until dawn."

"Maukiri!" Tepua could not help the single tear that slid from her eye.

"So my guess was right," said her cousin. "I do not blame you for whatever you did that night. But you had your man. You should be happy!"

"Cousin, you do not realize the trouble these sailors face. If they go on breaking *tapu,* I do not know how much longer I can keep them safe. Worst of all, Cone-shell wants to adopt Kiore."

"Don't let him!"

"I can hold him off awhile. In the end, Cone-shell may win."

"But Kiore will want nothing to do with Varoa Clan."

Tepua sighed. "If he does not like the idea, then he can sail away. But you will also lose Nika."

Maukiri groaned. "How can we stop this?"

"I do not know yet. For now, say nothing to the sailors. If we find a way out of the trap, then we will not have to tell them."

"How long can you delay?" asked Maukiri.

"Perhaps a month."

"Then we must take advantage of that time. We must make plans for both of us. How soon is Nika coming?"

SIXTEEN

The next morning Tepua rose early and sat outside her house, listening to the palms rustling gently. All seemed quiet today. After Cone-shell's visit, she welcomed the respite. Yet she felt a prickle of anticipation, a hint that the peaceful moment would not last.

In the distance she heard gulls calling, then footsteps, then a faint cry. Alarmed, she hastened toward the path just as a sentry came running. She recognized him as one of Pararu's sharp-eyed lookouts, coming from his post on the outer shore. Tepua's guards clustered about to hear his news.

Panting heavily, the sentry fell to his knees. "Sails sighted!" he managed to gasp. "Pu-tahi!" The warriors howled in anguish. "Not attacking!" the sentry added.

Tepua felt a rush of the old fear. "How many? What are they doing?" She remembered too many raids, when she had been hustled into a canoe and forced to flee. She could still hear the wails of the women whose men were lost in battle.

"Just one *pahi*," the sentry said. "The men aboard carry . . . a sign of peace."

"*Peace?*" Tepua stared at him, her hands itching to hold a weapon. She wished she had not scoffed at Pararu's warning.

"They shouted a message. Their chief wants to heal old wounds, come here and talk of friendship."

"Friendship? How is it possible?" she asked. She recalled the recent reports from traders, including one that claimed the Pu-tahi had given up their old ways. Paruru had insisted that this was another of their tricks.

"The *pahi* carries gifts. For you, *ariki*."

She scowled. No Pu-tahi had ever made an overture to her people. "And if I accept these gifts, I must agree to their chief's visit."

The warrior raised his eyebrows in assent. Recovered now from his run, he stood up and brushed sand from his knees.

Tepua took a deep breath. Her fingers were trembling and she wished she had some way to steady them. The men stared at her, waiting for orders.

Paruru was gone, but she knew what his opinion would be. She had no time to gather other advisers, no time to discuss the question in the usual leisurely manner. A decision was needed quickly. The Pu-tahi vessel must be sent off, or allowed to land.

"Wait here, and I will give an answer," she said, and then went alone to sit inside her house. She remembered what the elders had told her when she doubted her ability to assume the high office. *The sacred power will enter you and you will become wise.* Yet the wisdom did not always come when she needed it. Her hospitality to the sailors had already caused harm to her people. A mistake now could be far more serious.

For a few moments she sat quietly in the comforting shade of her house. It would be easy to send the Pu-tahi away. But nothing like this had ever happened before. She began to nourish a hope that the offer of friendship was sincere. If she could only have a sign . . .

She reached for the loop of cord that hung on a peg behind her mat. The last time she had looked at string figures they had shown her nothing. If the gods meant her to rule wisely, they would have to help her now.

She uttered her prayer and began to make the first figure.

As she brought her hands together and apart, picking up strings or letting them fall, she soon made the shape of a double-hulled canoe. She wondered if this was the canoe of the Pu-tahi chief. Staring into the strings, she recalled occasions when the figures had sparked a vision, bringing images of another place or time.

But the pattern before her was only an interweaving of cord. She could not see what lay hidden aboard the vessel, or what sort of men rode it. Disappointed, she let the string slip from her hands.

It was better if she did not try to choose a specific figure, but let her fingers weave in and out until a shape emerged. She closed her eyes, working by feel. When she opened them, a simple pattern had formed in the crossing strings, so simple that she thought at first she had made nothing. Then she saw the young coconut frond, a symbol of peace between enemies or strangers.

This time the vision grew vivid. Instead of strings, she saw pale green leaflets, and blue-black tattoos on the hand that held the frond. This was a Pu-tahi vessel, she realized, and the man who lifted the frond was the chief of their tribe. But was his offer a cover for deceit?

She studied the canoe, wishing she could see what lay within its thatched cabin. Gifts? Hidden weapons? She groaned in frustration, but found no answer.

Then the vision shifted and she was looking at the scene from far above. She recognized the shore, that of her own lagoon. Where were her people? The lone Pu-tahi vessel was surrounded not by Tepua's war canoes but by a host of sharks.

The water was so clear that she could see the tail fins waving smoothing. As she watched the graceful movements she realized that these sharks were the kind that protected her—great blues. She thought they would attack her long-time enemies. Instead, they led the Pu-tahi canoe toward her beach, then moved aside while the visitors landed.

Spirits of my ancestors . . . leading the Pu-tahi ashore!

When the vision ended, Tepua rested for a moment, trying to grasp what she had seen. Then she emerged, feeling disoriented as she looked at the crowd that had gathered about her house. Warriors edged in on all sides; she faced them uneasily.

"The Pu-tahi remain outside the reef, *ariki*," said Sea-snake, who had been left in charge of the warriors. "Their paddlers are fighting the current."

"I will not let them land," said Tepua firmly. The men turned to each other with expressions of relief. "Launch a canoe," she added. "Take some drinking nuts out to them for their journey."

"You are generous, *ariki*," said Sea-snake. "We will toss those eels the drinking nuts and send them on their way." He turned to shout an order.

"There is more," said Tepua. "Tell the Pu-tahi that I will accept nothing from them now. When their chief comes to me, let him present the gifts with his own hands. Then I will see how sincere his offer is."

The warriors seemed stunned by her answer. The captain opened his mouth to protest, but fell silent under Tepua's glare. "Tell their chief to come after the moon is new, no sooner," she added sharply. "Go now. Before the Pu-tahi boatmen grow impatient and try to paddle into our lagoon!"

For several days no one spoke of anything but the impending Pu-tahi visit. As the news reached other clans, chiefs and elders came to confer with Tepua. One day, her brother appeared in her yard.

"Umia!" She embraced him eagerly. "Are you also here to discuss the Pu-tahi?"

"Yes, Tepua," he answered in a somber voice. "And for another reason."

"Then you know about your uncle's scheming."

"I only know that he is hiding something. A ceremony was held at the *marae*. Nika and Paruru went there, but everyone else had to keep away."

"I will explain. But first, tell me if the priest is satisfied with the outcome."

"Raha and my uncle both seem cheerful. Nika and Paruru also seem relieved . . . about something."

"Good," said Tepua. "Let us walk, and I will clear up a few mysteries." As they followed the beach she told him about the turtle incident and Cone-shell's attempt to use it against her.

"My uncle was right about one thing," Umia said sadly when she was done. "He warned that these foreigners would upset our ways, and they have. But to my thinking, Cone-shell's offense is worse than Nika's."

"Explain."

Umia's brow wrinkled as he stopped to prod a piece of coral with his toes. "Tepua, my uncle put us all at risk. When he learned the truth about the turtle, he should have sent his priests at once to beg the gods' forgiveness. What disaster might have struck us?" He raised his eyes, gazing sharply into hers.

Tepua drew in her breath. "Now you see clearly, my brother. Cone-shell put his ambitions ahead of the best interests of his people."

"Yes." Umia clenched his fist. "I have seen him do such things before, but I said nothing. Even after what he did to you, I stayed at his side. Ah, Tepua, I have let him bully me too long."

"There is something you can do." She paused, waiting, hoping.

His eyebrows rose. "Twice you asked me to leave my uncle, and twice I turned you down. You need not ask again, Tepua. I am here. This time, I am staying."

Tears streamed down her face as she embraced him, pressing her nose against the firmness of his cheek. "Ah, brother, you have come just when I need your help."

When Paruru returned with Nika, he wanted to know more about the Pu-tahi visit. He asked question after question of the men who had gone out to deliver the provisions—how many warriors, how had they been armed, what else did they carry. He could not accept the answer that no weapons had been seen at all.

Time and again his thoughts returned to his first encounter with the man-eaters. He was a young warrior then and new to the ranks. One moonless night, standing guard along the shore, he heard a blow and a groan. Then the cries of warning sounded, far too late. In the dim light it was nearly impossible to tell raider from friend. Paruru bashed in one Pu-tahi skull and wounded another man severely. Other defenders came, and soon the beach was wet with blood.

Paruru trembled with rage as he remembered the companions he had lost that night. Where had Tepua been? A child, safe with her guards, far from danger. Throughout her life she had been spared Pu-tahi terror. That was why she did not understand the raiders. That was why she had agreed to hear their lies.

Despite his lingering feeling of disgrace, Paruru went to speak with his chief.

"I am glad that all has gone well," she said coolly when she saw that he was back.

"*Ariki,* I beg you to listen. My problem with Nika is small compared with what is coming."

She offered him a seat in her shaded yard. "I understand your fears," she replied. "My family has suffered the raids as much as any other. But we have something new here. No Pu-tahi chief has ever asked for a meeting of peace."

"It is a ruse. So they can slip their warriors into our lagoon."

"Mine was no light decision, Paruru. It is true that I sent my answer in haste, but afterward I spoke with the priests. They tell me that the omens are good."

And priests are sometimes blind! "You are determined to let the man-eaters through the pass?"

Tepua stared at him in that stubborn way he had often seen, her back straight, her chin high.

"Then, *ariki,* I am obliged to prepare for the worst. I must make plans to defend my people. Otherwise—"

"Otherwise, you will ask again to be relieved of your duties." Her mouth twitched, and he thought for a moment that she might free him. What would he do then? he wondered. Would he dare to join the voices that opposed her? Would he even take up arms to force her out?

"Prepare your plans, *kaito-nui.* I will not stop you from performing your duty. I ask only this. There must be no open show of distrust. Keep your weapons out of sight."

"As you wish, *ariki.* My men will stand ready, but we will be discreet about it." When she dismissed him, he felt only a slight lifting of his burden. Whatever defense he mounted, he knew that many of his warriors would die. There was only one way to avert the disaster that the raiders would bring. He needed Nika's help. . . .

Paruru turned first to settling his adopted brother into a new way of life. The sailor was no longer a guest. Now he would stay with Paruru in a house of warriors, eating food the men gathered and prepared for themselves.

Paruru was not certain that Nika would fit in, but he had seen encouraging signs. Nika had finally given up his foreign garb. He bathed at reasonable intervals and often remembered to follow the little rituals that the gods required. Paruru knew now that he could never make an islander of this man, but he was willing to accept Nika's faults.

For the first two days of his return, Paruru asked nothing of the sailor, allowing him to enjoy Maukiri's company. But at last he could wait no longer. He had done much for his brother and it was time that Nika did something in return.

The next morning, Paruru led Nika to a place that few people knew about. It was the shelter where he had lived in isolation after diving for the thunder-club. "Sit," said Paruru. He had prepared the shelter, bringing fresh mats and coconuts. Now he opened a *viavia* and handed it to Nika.

"Sometimes it is good to be alone," said the warrior. "I often come here."

Seated cross-legged beneath the low roof, Nika gazed at him expectantly, but Paruru was not yet ready to explain the purpose of the meeting. "You understand our ways now," said the warrior. "When brother asks help of brother, he does not refuse."

"Yes?" the sailor seemed hesitant.

"I want to show you something. It is a secret that I have had for some time. I share it with you, but no one else must know." The warrior turned to his side and reached for a long bundle covered in matting. Holding it on his knees, he carefully opened it, revealing the club that had belched smoke and thunder, before falling into the lagoon.

Nika gasped in surprise. "Where did you get this?" he asked, his eyes both eager and wary. "Does the *ariki* know?"

"Tepua thinks it lost. She asked me to send divers, but they could not find it." He watched Nika's eyebrows rise. "This is not something a woman can appreciate," said Paruru. "She does not concern herself with battle, as we men do. She does not grasp how this can protect us from our enemies."

"Protect us?" Nika said scornfully. He was leaning over the weapon and making sounds of disgust. "Look!" he said, running his fingers over a red scaly crust that marred the small parts of the thing. He tugged at the piece that resembled a bird's head, and when it did not move, he made more ugly sounds. "Why show me this? The thing is useless now."

"The weapon is harmed?" Paruru did not remember seeing the crusts when he first brought the thunder-maker out of the lagoon. Had they somehow grown there? He glanced at the long tube, shaped like a hollow bamboo that flared slightly at the open end. This tube had been smooth and gray; now it bore an ugly coat of reddish brown.

"Seawater!" Nika said, uttering the word as if it were a

curse. Once more he tried to pull back the bird's head, then gave up in disgust. He threw the weapon to the ground.

"Sick?" asked Paruru. Was it possible, he wondered, that a bath had stolen the thing's power? Or had some spirit intervened? He remembered the force that had tried to keep him from reaching the bottom of the lagoon.

"Sick, yes. Very sick." Nika turned aside, drained his coconut, and tossed the shell carelessly into the brush.

"You can heal it," said Paruru. He recalled hearing Nika talk of his father, a craftsman who built weapons like this one. Nika had disliked the work, yet surely he had learned something of his father's art.

"Too late," said the sailor.

"It must be healed. Call on your gods!"

With a grimace of disgust, Nika picked up the weapon again. He tilted it, open end down, allowing a few grains of sand to fall out. Then he swung the end around and peered inside. "Bad!" he said, then began muttering in his own language as he turned his attention back to the middle of the weapon, to the toothlike piece and the parts above it. His fingernail scraped at scaly patches in the bowl beneath the beak. "With proper tools," he admitted, "maybe this can be fixed."

"We have many tools."

"Made of coral!" Nika shook his head.

Paruru studied the expression on Nika's face. Over the years he had learned to read the hidden thoughts of men, and now he clung to a shred of hope. "Nika, I have seen you working with wood. You have skills in your hands, and you are clever. You find new ways to do things."

Nika's eyes remained on the ground. "I could spend much time with this and still fail. I prefer to be doing something else."

Paruru thought of Maukiri and understood. "You need not go back to Piho Clan," he offered. "Not for many days." Still he saw no softening of Nika's attitude. The man wanted something else, Paruru thought, and was not willing to ask for it.

"Then I must get rid of this thing," the warrior said, reaching for the weapon. "Throw it into the lagoon again where no one can find it. It has caused me enough trouble. . . ."

"Wait!" said Nika, putting a hand on the thunder-maker. He gave Paruru a curious stare. "My goods from the boat. I have been too long without them. Some are harmless, yet your priests do not give them back."

"Yes, my brother. I understand." With a feeling of relief, Paruru paused to drink from his own coconut. At last Nika was hinting at his true desires, and there might be a way to satisfy them. "Tepua asked me to make new arrangements with the priests," the warrior said. "It is possible that I can recover a small part of your goods. Perhaps your tools—"

"The tools there are no help. I can use the knife you already have."

"Then what is it you want?"

"This is not easy to explain," said Nika. "It is for me, not the weapon. So that I can enjoy myself while I work." He described an object that had made little impression on Paruru while he was inspecting the goods. It was a carved tube that was held in the mouth, and its purpose eluded the warrior. Nika made sucking sounds, inhaling noisily through his lips, then breathing out in a similar way. "Smoke," Nika said, fanning his fingers through the exhaled breath.

"Smoke from a man's mouth?" Paruru stared wide-eyed, thinking that Nika was about to reveal a weapon even more terrifying than the one that lay before them. "And thunder also?"

Nika laughed. "No noise, only smoke. It tastes good and does no harm. Bring it to me and try it for yourself." He also described a pouch that held fragrant, crumbled leaves.

Paruru sat staring at Nika as he tried to make sense of what he had heard. He had expected to be asked for the black sand or the round stones, or for some other thing connected with the weapon. "Is there nothing else you need from the stores?"

"Not now," answered Nika quickly. "I want only the 'pipa' and 'tapako.'"

"I will ask a priest who is my friend. Together we will speak with Faka-ora. He is a reasonable man."

"Good," said Nika.

"And now," said Paruru, "tell me what you need to heal this weapon."

A day later the two men met again beneath the isolated shelter. At Nika's request, Paruru had built a small fire outside. Now Nika sat beside the basket of articles that Paruru had brought and prepared his long, wooden "pipa."

Obtaining this "pipa" had not proved easy. Paruru had tried to explain to the priests that the thing was harmless, but Faka-ora remained doubtful. Fortunately for Paruru, the *tahunga* who had healed the foreigners was present during this discussion. The *tahunga* recalled seeing the "pipa" in use, and confessed that he had tried it himself. "It helps the men relax," said the old healer. "Keeps them out of trouble. I see no harm in it." At last, Faka-ora agreed to Paruru's request.

And so Paruru now watched curiously as Nika tamped some of his crumbled "tapako" leaf into the open end of the "pipa," then leaned out toward the fire. He sucked a draft of air through the tube, and suddenly the "tapako" was alight. With a huge smile of contentment, Nika puffed, releasing small clouds of fragrant smoke into the air.

"You try," said Nika after a short while. "Take the smoke into your mouth, not your throat."

Paruru recalled the healer's words. The old man had suffered no ill from this. But of course the *tahunga* was protected by benevolent spirits. . . .

"Afraid?" asked Nika.

Paruru did not answer, but took the end of the "pipa" between his lips. He drew in a breath and felt the smoke swirl within his mouth. It was acrid and parching, stinging the back of his throat. Pulling the mouthpiece away, he bent over in spasms of coughing. He felt Nika snatch the smoking thing from his hands.

"Not so much!" cried Nika.

Paruru eyed the "pipa" coldly. He felt no great enthusiasm for a second try. Nika, watching him, began to smile. "I ate raw clams for you," he said jovially. "Now you try my 'pipa.'"

Paruru recalled the moment at Tepua's welcoming feast, not long after the men had first arrived. Nika had shown himself more willing than his friend to try the islanders' foods. With a sigh, the warrior put the mouthpiece again to his lips. Now he sucked very gently.

The smoke merely tickled his palate. Slowly he exhaled. "No coughing!" the warrior exclaimed. At Nika's urging he took a second puff. The sweet taste lingered in Paruru's mouth, yet he did not find it pleasant. He was relieved when the sailor took back the "pipa" for his own use.

"Now can we heal the thunder-maker?" Paruru asked. It had taken him several trips to gather the things that Nika wanted. He had brought a supply of fresh water in coconut bottles, the foreign knife that Nika used for woodworking, and many small tools made by island craftsmen.

One unexpected item was a half coconut that held a special balm used by healers. This liquid unguent was made by heating the fat from a coconut crab. Nika had come across it a long time earlier when the *tahunga* had rubbed it onto his sunburned skin. The greasy balm performed wonders when applied to people, but Paruru could not imagine how it would help the weapon.

Nika finally put aside his "pipa" and took the weapon across his lap. He flipped it over, with the bird's head down, then inserted the tip of his knife into a groove cut across a tiny disk. He tried to twist the knife, muttering and grimacing as he strained.

Paruru's jaw dropped in astonishment at the way the

foreigner had begun his work—without calling on the gods for aid. Nika knew better. "Where is your chant?" Paruru asked. "How can you hope to succeed without one?"

"A chant for this work?" Nika laughed, putting down the knife. "The spirits who watch over it live far from here. But if it pleases you . . ." His voice rose in a brief song, all in his native tongue. The rhythm was lively, and to Paruru seemed ill-suited to his purpose. Was it possible, Paruru asked himself, that the "pipa" provided the true way of invoking foreign spirits for this task? He recalled how the pale smoke had risen from Nika's mouth and floated skyward. . . .

Once more the sailor attacked the weapon with his knife. This time Paruru heard a creak and saw the grooved disk begin to turn slowly. Nika performed the same trick with another groove. Then, with a clang, a flat piece of the thunder-club fell away into his hand. Paruru leaped forward in alarm. *"Aue!"* cried the warrior. "Now it is certainly ruined."

"No," said Nika as he flipped over the weapon and looked at the opening he had made in its side. "This is how I heal it." He poked his knife within and began twisting again, until he broke out a collection of smaller pieces that were covered with scale.

Paruru cried out once more in protest. One did not heal a man by prying apart his bones. "An old sailor told me a way to clean this," Nika said. "I will let you do the hard work." He washed the assembly in fresh water, then dropped it into a bowl that held watery sand. He told Paruru to stir the parts around until the sand scoured the scale away.

Meanwhile Nika busied himself with the other pieces, the long tube, the bird's head, the bowl, cleaning these with coral rasps and with sharkskin. The work went slowly, requiring many repetitions. Paruru's hand grew weary from his own task, but he refused to quit.

Under the sailor's skillful fingers, the scale vanished and a shiny surface began to appear on the larger parts of the weapon. He washed the sand from the complex piece that Paruru had been scouring and spent some time filing away the last remnants of stain. His final step was to rub the healer's balm onto each cleaned item.

The afternoon was almost gone before Nika began to reassemble the weapon. One by one he fitted the pieces back into place. "The bones are knit together again!" Paruru said with admiration. But Nika was not done. He worked awhile longer with the thinnest rasps and drills.

Finally, he swung the weapon, aimed the tube skyward, and moved his hand toward the center. Paruru drew in his breath as he carefully watched the movement of Nika's fingers.

First Nika pulled back the bird's head on top, pulling it much farther back than Paruru had done. When he let go, it stayed where he had left it. Then he hooked his forefinger about the tooth below. Paruru braced himself for a blast. . . . The beak fell forward with a snap and sparks flared where it hit. There was no thunder.

"Good," said Nika. "Very good."

"But no noise!"

The sailor gave a laugh that seemed edged with scorn. "It is cleaned and rubbed with oil. That is enough for now."

"Then what else is needed . . . to make thunder?"

He noticed, to his dismay, that Nika's expression turned wary. "Are your enemies here? Is it time to defend the land?"

"They are not here yet," Paruru admitted. "But you have heard about their visit and their plans. I cannot trust them. If they come with their chief, I must be ready for treachery."

"If the weapon is to be used, I will do it," said Nika firmly. "To make it work takes skills you do not have. If not done properly . . ." He made a booming noise, spread out his hands, then fell over in mock death.

"I am glad that you will handle it, my brother," said Paruru, concealing his annoyance. "Even so, we must gather everything you will need. We must do it now. The priests have agreed to move the goods from the *ariki's* storehouse, to hide them so that Cone-shell cannot claim a share. For a short while there will be no *tapu* on touching those things. My men will carry them to their new place. I can arrange it so that certain things are diverted.''

"I do not like this plan of hiding things," said Nika. "I should know where the goods are kept."

Paruru frowned. "The moving must be done," he said. "I will know where the goods are stored, and a brother need not keep secrets from a brother. But we must make our plans now. There will be no better chance to take what you need. I can risk the anger of the priests, but not the wrath of the gods."

Nika sighed. With reluctance he began to describe what was required. "And keep those things dry," he added finally. "The container of black sand. The weapon. Everything. Water ruins them."

"I will keep them dry," Paruru promised. *And soon you will teach me the rest of what I want to know.* He wrapped the weapon in its mat again, then began collecting the supplies he had brought. "You go back now," he told Nika. "While I stay here awhile. It is better that we are not seen together after this work."

"I am going," said Nika. He snatched up the "pipa" and "tapako." "And taking these. Maybe Maukiri will enjoy them more than you do."

Paruru smiled. Then his thoughts grew serious again. "Nika. Remember this. Tell no one about the weapon. Not Kiore. Not Maukiri. If Tepua finds out, she will take it away from us. Then we will have nothing to protect ourselves against the man-eaters."

"I know when to keep quiet," said Nika. But Paruru puzzled over the look on the sailor's face long after the man was gone.

....
SEVENTEEN
....

Knowing that the Pu-tahi chief was not due for ten days, Tepua asked for a rest from her duties. Faka-ora agreed and sent her off on her *pahi*. With Umia's help, the priest assured her, the elders could handle all small matters while she was away.

The day was bright and the wind steady as Tepua's party neared Piho's islet. She sat beneath feather pennants and watched the approaching greenery of the palm-studded shore. When she landed, Heka came to meet her, head crowned in flowers, a sly sparkle in her eye. It was no secret to Tepua that Heka had conspired with Maukiri to arrange this outing.

Everyone had been told that there was to be a women's ceremony at a shrine in the center of the island. It was a place that no man wished to approach. Tepua's guards seemed relieved when she ordered them to remain at the lagoon-side beach. They would patrol the shore, keeping a lookout for troublemakers from Varoa Clan.

About the necks of Tepua and Maukiri, Heka put wreaths of morning glory interwoven with herbs. Then she embraced the women heartily. "This should be great fun," Heka proclaimed. "No priests, no men and no food *tapus*. We can eat and dance and sing all we like." Tepua nodded, feeling an unexpected regret. The gathering of women was to be as Heka described, but Tepua would not be part of it.

Soon she was marching inland with the others, over vines and fallen leaves, chanting the words that she knew well.

224

But as the trail forked in a sunlit clearing, Tepua and Heka stood aside while the others went on. "Follow this path to the seaward beach," Heka whispered as she gave Tepua a last motherly embrace. "I will ask the spirits to watch over you."

"You are good to me, Heka. You and Maukiri, the sly little fish."

Heka sent her off with flapping motions of her hands. "Go. Your man has the canoe. He knows where to take you."

Filled with anticipation, Tepua hurried over the sandy path. Shortly she came out above the seaward shore, on a slope covered by smoothed coral rubble. Hidden beneath *mikimiki* bushes sat the canoe Heka had promised. Tepua glanced inside the *vaka* and saw that it was stocked with paddles, a sail, baskets of food, drinking nuts, and even two pairs of hibiscus-rope sandals for reef walking.

"What are you doing—stealing my canoe?" growled a voice from behind the shrubbery. Tepua leaped up in surprise.

"With you in it!" she shouted back. As Kiore crawled out from his hiding place, his blond hair windblown and his face aglow with mirth, she clapped her hands in delight. Before he could stand up she leaped onto his back, and they mock-wrestled for a few moments.

"Ouch! The stones!" he cried.

"I am a *motu* woman," she answered. "A bed of stones feels good to me." As she pressed herself against his bare back a delicious warmth began to fill her. "But *you* need something softer!" Tepua pulled free and jumped up before he could stop her.

"You are right," he said. "And I know where to find it." He pointed seaward to the tiny islet that she knew was their destination. Then he asked her to help him carry the boat.

Taking a good look at Kiore, she realized that he had finally shed the last of his foreign garb. Now he wore a gray-white *maro* between his legs, with a long string that wound around his waist. The skin of his upper body and powerful legs, once pale, had turned a rich, dark color. He was an island man at last, she thought, except for his foreign eyes and hair and face. But she had grown fond of that face.

"Pull harder," he said as they struggled with the canoe. The beach here was steeper than on the lagoon side of the islet. The slope ended in a broad stretch of blackened and eroded coral, awash in places, bristling with jagged edges in others. Wearing the rope-soled sandals, Tepua and Kiore carried the outrigger canoe along a shallow depression in the reef.

The open sea lay beyond distant breakers; the water here was rougher than that of the inner lagoon. With the bow of the *vaka* pointed into the surf, they waited for a wave. As it broke and surged back out along the channel, Tepua shouted and helped Kiore launch the canoe into the ebbing water. With a last shove, the two scrambled aboard, took up paddles, and stroked hard to get out before another wave could cast them back against the shore.

Tepua paddled until she grew warm from the effort. "We are off!" she shouted in triumph, pleased that they had managed the difficult maneuver. Launching from the calm and sandy lagoon side would have been easier, but not possible today with her guards patrolling the beach.

She looked across the outermost waters of the atoll, where the water was deep blue and tipped with whitecaps. Near the line of breakers she saw a speck of land. As she stroked toward it she chanted: "Here is the canoe, dipping its nose into the sea. Here is the canoe, pointing high, pointing low, drinking deeply of the sea."

"What is that?" Kiore called from the stern.

"A song for our voyaging canoes," she explained. "It is called 'The Road of the Winds.'"

"Then let me hear more!"

Dipping her paddle, Tepua sang again. "Here is the canoe, driving through spray, cleaving the sea. Hold fast the sennit, hold fast the sennit. . . ."

"Let me hear one of your own sailing chants," she asked when she was done. She recalled hearing these long ago, when the words meant nothing to her. Now she understood some of his language. He changed a few words to help her understand the rest.

> "When I was a roving sailor,
> I searched the lands for rarest treasure.
> Ay, ay, pull on the lines!
> I would not leave my life at sea,
> Until that girl caught up with me.
> Ay, ay, pull on the lines!"

"She is a woman of your own country," Tepua said when he was done.

"Who?"

"The girl in the song."

"It is only a song," he answered. "Every sailor dreams of finding someone." Then he changed the words and sang again:

> "I would not leave my life at sea.
> Until Tepua caught up with me.
> Ay, ay, pull on the lines!"

He sang on, with a new verse each time, as they continued to paddle, leaving the island shore and approaching the outermost reef. Now she could see clearly the speck of land that she had been watching. It was a small *motu*, with a handful of palm trees showing against the white and blue of the sky.

The sun peeked out from behind a cloud, turning the water a clear aquamarine that grew more transparent as they neared the islet. The color shifted as they crossed a wide shoal, until at last it was the brilliant white gold of the sand beneath. With a soft scrape, the canoe grounded on the beach.

Kiore jumped out into ankle-deep water. "Now it is time to carry the *ariki* ashore," he announced, as if he were one of her servants. As soon as she slid her legs around, he gave a cry of mirth and lifted her roughly, then rushed with her onto the beach, bouncing at every step.

"That is how you carry a heavy fish!" she shouted merrily. "And meanwhile, my clever fisherman, your canoe is slipping away."

"Canoe?" He tumbled her into the sand, then splashed back into the shallows to catch the drifting boat. She watched him struggle for a moment before helping him drag the vessel ashore.

"And now you have work to do, my man of the sea." Beneath the trees she had spotted a thatched shelter. "Help me unload the supplies and take them to the hut."

He turned to the shelter, which stood in the shade of a stout *tamanu* tree. "I will carry only one thing now," he answered, lifting her again, this time more gently. As they approached the shelter, Tepua saw that the ground around it had been swept clean. Someone had left fresh mats inside.

A moment later Kiore put her down, lay beside her and took her into his arms. She quickly forgot about the mats and the shelter and the *motu*. This was a pleasant place that Heka had sent her to, but with Kiore she would have been happy anywhere. . . .

After a time Tepua stirred. She felt a soft breeze on her face as she looked up at the fluttering thatch roof. Kiore was dozing peacefully. The booming of the surf and a few cries of seabirds were the only sounds.

"I'm hungry," she said, slapping him on the chest. She went out to see what Heka had sent in the food baskets.

"This is yours," she told him, when she heard Kiore come up behind her. She handed him his basket then went to sit alone.

"You do not eat with me?" he asked in a hurt tone.

"You know our customs by now," she answered. She

found a place on a fallen log, then took out the first leaf-wrapped packet.

Kiore crouched in front of her. "In my land, a man and his woman sit together and eat."

"I am not in your land, and I am not your woman," she answered with a toss of her head.

"Then whose woman are you?"

"There is a man in Tahiti," she replied in a serious tone.

"You have forgotten him by now."

"Perhaps he has forgotten me!"

"Then he does not matter. Come. Sit beside me. We are here, alone. No one will see us."

"The gods will see."

He turned suddenly, as if expecting to find a ghost staring over his shoulder. "Ah, you are a strange people," he said, shaking his head. He took his basket and walked a few steps away.

"Since you sailors arrived, *tapu* has been broken too often," she chided.

"Then I eat alone," he answered, taking a seat on the sand and facing the water. "So long as *hanihani* is allowed, I will be content."

"What we do together is not *tapu*. It is only foolish. But sometimes it is good to be foolish and happy." She tore open the bundle of hibiscus leaves and found a juicy piece of steamed fish inside. Silently, and with relish, she began to eat.

The tide had dropped, leaving a margin of wet sand. The food baskets and supplies had been put away. Now Tepua sat with Kiore, her heels just touching the water.

He picked up a dried coconut frond, stripped the leaves from it until only the center rib remained. He dragged the point in the wet sand, making a line.

"What are you doing?" Tepua asked. "Making pictures in the sand?" He had played this game with her several times, confusing her with his tangles of lines. In Tahiti she had watched women paint patterns on their bark-cloth wraps, but Kiore's drawings did not resemble any she had ever seen.

Kiore leaned to one side and began a detailed figure. "What it this?" he asked her after he had worked awhile.

Tepua frowned and moved closer to the picture. "Scratches in the sand."

"Is that all?"

She stared hard. At the bottom was something that looked like the outline of a fish. Above that, she saw the shape of a man leaning out of a canoe. . . . "He is catching a parrot fish," she answered suddenly.

Kiore's mouth fell open and he bent to stare closer at his marks. "You know what kind of fish I drew? That is more than I know."

"Draw a pig," she asked. He had tried this once before, producing something that did not look at all like the animal. This time he did better, except for the tail. "Too thin and curly," she said, bending over to smooth away that part of his work.

He laughed when she pointed out his mistake. "You are right. Your pigs are different. I keep thinking of the ones from my own land." He let her add in the woolly, dangling tail.

"Try some other animal," she suggested. "One that we do not have here."

In response, he traced out the shape of something that looked like a dog, except that the ears were wrong. No dogs lived on her atoll now, but she had seen many in Tahiti.

"The ears should point up, not hang down. Young dogs have floppy ears, but later they stand up."

Kiore explained that in his country the people had many kinds of dogs, some with ears that stood up and some with ears that hung down throughout their lives.

"What odd beasts your country has! Pigs with curly tails and dogs with ears that hang down."

"No stranger than the two-legged beasts of your island,"
Kiore countered.

"Yes. The foreign sailors are certainly strange!" Tepua
caught his hand. Looking at his pictures, she had not noticed
the growing heat of the day. "And now one of those sailors
is going to get wet."

Together they raced to the water's edge, then splashed
across the sandy bottom. She untied the wrap from around
her waist, tossed it higher up on the beach, and plunged in.
She felt a pleasant chill as she dove under. Out here the
water came directly from the sea and was cooler than that of
the inner lagoon. She flung back her hair, enjoying the
wetness against her skin.

When she came up, she found Kiore floating on his back,
his arms and legs stretched out in the water, his eyes closed
in bliss. In the sun, the curls of hair on his chest gleamed
ruddy gold against the deep bronze of his skin. Tepua crept
up on him in the waist-deep water. With a mischievous
smile, she decided to find out if the soles of his feet were
ticklish.

With a splash and a flurry Kiore pulled away from her
teasing. "So you think this a game that only islanders
know?" he asked in mock ferocity. "Well, I will show
you." She squirmed in agonized delight as he found her
own vulnerable places and attacked unmercifully. She
wriggled free, flinging water at him. This started a splashing
war that soon turned the water into froth. At last, when he
seemed to be retreating, he suddenly lunged at her, heaved
her high into the air, and flung her farther out.

She bellyflopped, came up with a mouthful of water from
laughing. Ducking beneath, she swam underwater, seized
the cord that held his loincloth, and nearly tugged it loose
before he picked her up again, lifted her high over his head,
and sent her flying. "You want my eel to be bait for the
fishes?" he roared, chasing after her.

At last, when the sun was descending, they waded
happily ashore. They stopped to wash the salt from their

bodies at a small rainwater cistern that had been chipped into the coral. Tepua went to the supplies piled neatly inside the hut and found a coconut bottle that held fragrant oil. Heka had done a thorough job of stocking the canoe.

Kiore lay on the mat. He had rolled on his stomach, cradling his head on his folded arms. In the fading daylight Tepua gazed down at the twin mounds of his buttocks, separated by the narrow band of the *maro*.

Chanting quietly, she drew the plug from the bottle and poured a portion of its contents into her hands. What a firm rump he had! Some men were too skinny, or sagged at the bottom, but Kiore was perfectly shaped. She knelt beside him, gently rubbing in the oil.

He woke with a start at her touch. Tepua straddled his thighs, pressed her palms against his buttocks and let them slide up to the hollow of his back, enjoying the feel of his muscles beneath the heel of her hand.

"Ah, that is good," he sighed. "I did not want to fall asleep."

"And why not?" she asked playfully. "The day is over. There is nothing to stay awake for." She kept massaging, listening to his groans of pleasure. He began to rock from side to side, squirming every so often. "What is wrong?" she asked. "Is a piece of the mat poking you?"

"It is not the mat poking me. It is me poking the mat." He turned over and she could clearly see the source of his discomfort.

"Kiore's eel is getting bigger," she teased.

"You are the one who makes it grow."

She began to unwind the cord from around his waist, stopping once to brush the inside of his thighs with oiled fingertips. He writhed and arched his head back while the cloth of his *maro* strained over the growing fullness beneath.

"Would your eel like to be massaged?" she asked, leaning forward to press her face to his.

He shifted, straining up beneath her. She felt an answering tingle and a warmth growing between her own legs.

The *maro* came free and his hardness arched up against his belly. The curls about it were a slightly darker ruddy gold than the ones on his chest. She slid her oiled hand along the underside, feeling him pulsate beneath her.

"Oh gods, both yours and mine," he breathed, shivering.

When she had stroked him for a while, she oiled her breasts. Straddling his thighs, she began to rub herself against him, dragging one breast and then the other over the tops of his thighs. She worked her way upward, gently sliding back and forth until she had the "eel" rolling between her breasts. Her nipples were hardening. The wetness and heat between her legs were becoming a demanding ache.

"No more," he said hoarsely. "I can hardly bear it."

Gently he pushed her off, rolled her onto her back. His hard roundness pressed against her thighs, then her belly. His kiss was warm and exciting on her mouth. With a tenderness that reached deep within her, his hands caressed her face then slid down over her neck to brush the tips of her breasts.

She gasped as the sensation from her nipples intensified the glow between her legs. She felt herself opening, deep, ready, hungry for him.

But he did not plunge right in, as he had when they first reached the little island. Instead he teased her, putting his tip to her moistness and drawing it away again. He brought her to the edge of release, but backed off, letting the fire dampen a bit before stoking it once again.

It drove her wild with desire and she struggled to impale herself upon him, but he moved away, leaving her to pant and throb and swell, both inside and out. Once more, he came to her, this time plunging deeper.

Slowly he slid up inside, as if he knew how exquisitely sensitive his teasing had made her. She took great breaths as ripples of pleasure cascaded within her. And then he lay down atop her, cupping her face in his hands, pressing his mouth to hers in a kiss of sweetness while he buried the final length of himself within her body.

With a groan, he backed out and thrust in again. Tension grew within her, for her desire had only been whetted by the first little ripples. Again he thrust and again, until the fiery place at her center was white-hot and her muscles were straining as tightly as she could bear. It built and built until she thought she would explode.

Release burst on her in great spasms, sending flashes of black and purple across her vision. She felt him holding her tightly as the waves washed through her, making her twitch and tremble helplessly.

He gave a long moan, raised himself on his hands, and threw his head from side to side as climax swept over him. A deep languor filled Tepua. Dimly she felt him lie down beside her, his body pressed close, his warmth reassuring, as she drifted into sleep.

At dawn Tepua woke to the booming of the breakers on the outer reef. It was a sound she had known all her life, but on this morning she sensed a discordant note in the sea's music. She could tell that today would not be like the idyllic day before. The waves sounded rough, the wind fitful.

She glanced once at Kiore, who lay peacefully beside her. Patches of crusted sand still clung to his naked back and his broad shoulders, now rounded in sleep. Gently she brushed him off before crawling outside to look at the sky.

A mass of clouds banked the horizon, filtering the sun's light, turning the dawn an ominous color. The sky nearest the rising sun was the hue of an ember, broken open to reveal its fiery heart.

The color bled into the sea, the lagoon, even tinted the exposed shelves of coral until everything was red with flaming light. A flock of seabirds wheeled high overhead, the white of their bellies dyed pink, their screams plaintive.

She heard a strange hissing in the wind, as if some spirit were trying to whisper a message.

Tepua needed no advice from spirits to read the sky. Quickly she crawled back into the hut and shook Kiore awake.

"Storm coming," she said, trying to ignore the catch in her throat when he opened his blue-green eyes. She could swim in those eyes, or sail, as an outrigger skimmed the waters of the lagoon. . . . She shook herself. This was no time for such thoughts.

She crawled out, Kiore scrambling after. He brushed sand from his limbs and stared to sea, muttering in his own tongue. Then his gaze turned toward the canoe, drawn up on the beach. "If we hurry . . ."

"Not enough time." They could not hope to outrun the storm. When it caught them in the light canoe, it would smash them on the reef or drag them far out to sea.

Tepua suddenly saw the little islet for what it was—a sand-covered bump barely rising from the sea. A bad storm could strip such a *motu* down to bare coral or even obliterate it entirely.

She remembered a typhoon that had struck when she was young. To escape the waves that swept inland, Ehi had tied her into the fork of a *tamanu* tree. Sometimes in nightmares she still saw the lashing sea and heard the deafening shriek of the wind.

Afterward, the shorelines of the atoll had been changed. Some islets had been altered in shape and others had entirely disappeared. Now, as she stood next to Kiore, remembering, the first gust hit, making her stagger backward.

"The *vaka*!" she cried, and rushed to save the canoe. In a moment Kiore was running beside her. The lagoon was alive with whitecaps as they half carried, half dragged the canoe toward the *tamanu* that stood near the hut. Tepua took a quick look at the tree, so huge that it must have survived many storms in its lifetime. She tethered the prow to its massive trunk with a sennit line, then turned to the hut to see what supplies might be saved.

Wind gusted again, making the shelter sway. The hanging mats that served as walls flapped loudly against the framework. Tepua had just picked up a roll of sennit cord when Kiore grabbed her hand and yanked her outside. Then a horrendous crash came behind her. As she raced after him she looked back to see coconuts, fronds, and branches cascade onto the thatched roof, bringing the whole structure down.

"We have to get back to the *tamanu*," she shouted, but she did not think he heard her over the shriek of the wind. Then the first wave broke across the islet, knocking her off balance, sending her sprawling in the chilly brine. Somehow she held on to the cord that she was carrying.

The water subsided, but the fierce wind tore at her hair and face. Clasping Kiore's hand with her free one, she fought her way around the wreckage of the shelter. Another wave hit and she had to let go of him, digging into the wet sand to keep from being washed away.

Then they stood up and rushed for the protection of the tree. "Climb!" she shouted, putting her hands on the rough bark. "It is strong enough to hold us both." But Kiore insisted that she go first. He boosted her up until she could reach the sturdiest limb. Glossy leaves fluttered all about her as she wound cord around herself and tied a few strong knots. She cut the cord's end with a jagged stub of a branch, then handed the rest of the coil down to Kiore.

She heard the thunder of a huge wave striking the reef. "Hold on!" she shouted. A column of foam hit him, and for a moment she thought he was gone. She screamed a prayer to her guardian spirit. . . . Then the sea subsided and she saw him still clutching the trunk of the tree. He spat out a mouthful of water, looked up and grinned in triumph, then pulled himself after her.

Quickly he secured himself on the adjacent limb, so close that they could almost reach across and touch. Above her, she heard the lashing of smaller branches. In the force of the wind the *tamanu* groaned.

"Sometimes these storms are short," she shouted.

"Do you think I am frightened?" he replied. "In worse weather, I often climbed to the top of the mast!"

Suddenly the crown of a coconut palm broke loose and went pinwheeling into the lagoon, shedding nuts and fronds. A smaller *tamanu* was torn up by the roots and tumbled into frothing water that surged across the island. Tepua looked down and saw no land at all, just coconut trees bent almost horizontal, crowns tossing and swaying above the white-caps.

As the storm grew wilder she could do nothing but pray once more to her guardian spirit. Rain sheeted down, adding its sting. She looked at Kiore, wishing for the comfort of his arms about her.

Her skirt was torn and she had nothing around her shoulders for warmth. She shivered as she hung there listening to the wind's fury. The spirits were telling her something. Why could she not understand them?

At last, the rain stopped for a time and the air grew still. "The storm is not done," she warned Kiore. Below her the surf was boiling, driven by waves rolling over the reef. Huge tangles of debris floated by. The water level climbed higher.

Then the wind started again, its shriek fiercer than before. Kiore looked a sorry sight, his sodden hair matted to his face, his *maro* in tatters. The branches began to sway and she wondered if one might break. "Tapahi-roro-ariki," she cried. "We are both depending on you now." Her only answer was the steady fall of rain.

Somehow Tepua dozed for a time. When she opened her eyes, she realized that the storm was nearing its end. The rain became a drizzle, then ceased. The clouds began to lift. At last, she saw a broad patch of blue amid the thinning gray.

"It is over," Kiore said, untying himself from the branch.

Below, the water was receding, leaving land bare of undergrowth but covered with new heaps of sand and broken coral. When she joined him on the ground, she found him kneeling, offering a prayer to his god. Tepua chanted praises to Tapahi-roro-ariki until she could speak no more.

Under a heap of sodden palm leaves she discovered a drinking nut. Kiore managed to punch out the soft mouth and they both took turns gulping sweet milk that soothed their salt-parched throats. At last they turned to examine the islet.

Tepua was astonished at the changes. Of the palms, only a ragged few had survived intact. Most were sticks, their crowns torn off. Not only the undergrowth but the sand itself had been stripped from much of the island. The beach where they had landed was gouged away, leaving only a rocky shore.

Here and there lay chunks of pink and gray coral, drowned seabirds, stranded fish. And the canoe . . . Tepua saw that it had been battered by the storm. She wondered if it could get back to Heka's island.

Kiore stood beside her, studying the *vaka,* his hand about her waist. His face looked drained and tired and he swayed slightly, leaning against her.

"The storm was a sign," she said. "A warning from the gods. But I do not know why. We broke no *tapu.*"

He studied her with narrowed eyes.

"It is true, Kiore. I am sure this was meant to tell me something. I must go back." How it pained her to see the disappointment in his face.

"A sign," he said thoughtfully, turning to survey the devastation. "If that is so, then the message was to me as well. I also have a duty to go back—to my own land. I wish that I did not have to tell you this."

She felt a twinge in her stomach. "I don't understand. I know you are homesick—"

"It is not that, Tepua. I can forget my old life and stay

here happily. But I once made a promise that I cannot forget, to a man who is now dead.''

"To the sailor in your boat?"

He shook his head. "To the master of my vessel."

Tepua had heard him talk several times of his anguish over the fate of his sea voyage. The men who had seized control of the great sailing craft, forcing him to flee, would probably never return to their own country.

Now Kiore explained a bit more about the "lok-puk" that he had taken such pains to preserve. The topmost sheets contained marks that his friend, the master, had made as a record of his voyage. In it he told of his crewmen's discontent, though their woes were not his fault. The "lok-puk" would enable others to learn what had happened.

Kiore had pledged to bring this home so that the man's good name, and that of his family, could be preserved. "I wanted to tell you this sooner," Kiore said. "But at first I did not have the words. And then you made me want to forget my promise."

"Kiore!" She took his hand and clutched it tightly in her own. There was nothing more she could say to him. The world of sun and sky and water seemed to shrink around her.

And then she heard voices. Looking up in surprise, she saw six of Heka's canoes paddling in to shore, the women aboard calling joyfully, "*Maeva ariki!* All is well on shore. Come home with us."

Tepua felt startled, as if awakened from a dream. She climbed into one canoe and sent Kiore off in another. The women seemed so cheerful, and Tepua wanted only to weep.

But how did Kiore expect to make his journey? she wondered. Maukiri had told her that Nika was far from ready to leave; no one else wanted to sail in the foreign vessel. Perhaps her man was not going after all, at least not soon. Perhaps she had not lost him.

EIGHTEEN

Before nightfall, Tepua was home again. Seated in the yard beside her house, she listened to reports of everything that had happened in her absence. Her spirits were lifted a bit when she learned that the storm had done little harm to the atoll. After passing her tiny islet, it had veered off and run out to sea.

"The storm may have struck land elsewhere," said one of her advisers, an ancient nobleman. "Perhaps it even caught the Pu-tahi chief on his journey." His wrinkled face lit up as he contemplated that possibility.

Another man disagreed. "The Pu-tahi know how to ride out a storm. If they are set on coming, then nothing can stop them."

The arguments raged until Tepua lost patience. As she was about to send everyone home a warrior came running. "Pu-tahi sails, *ariki*! We have just sighted them offshore."

She jumped to her feet in alarm. The visitors had come too soon, ignoring her instructions. Perhaps that was why the storm had sent her home early. "Are they close?"

"Not close enough to enter the pass before dark. We think they will stay offshore until morning."

"Or attack us during the night!" suggested one of the skeptics.

"You are too eager for blood," she said testily to the old man. But she remembered a similar warning from Paruru. Though she wanted to believe in the good intentions of her arriving visitors, she gave the orders that the *kaito-nui* had suggested. "Light a bonfire by the pass. Patrol the shores by torchlight."

She gave other orders. At dawn, canoes would take word to all the clans so that the chiefs could gather for the meeting. In the early morning, preparations for the welcoming feast would begin.

Finally she sent everyone away, except Umia. In the yellow light of a fire, she studied the wide-eyed face of her brother. They had spent little time together, yet she knew already that Kohekapu's wisdom had passed to his youngest son.

"Umia, I am curious to hear what you think," she began. "We are all guessing why the Pu-tahi are so eager to visit us, and today I heard a suggestion that worries me. I hope it is wrong."

"About their interest in the foreigners?"

She sighed. "Yes. Nothing is secret very long on these islands. One trader tells another. The Pu-tahi may know about our sailors."

"And that is why their chief has come?"

"I would like to be wrong," said Tepua. "I would like to believe that the raiders have changed their ways. But this visit could be a ruse—to allow them to seize the foreign goods."

"If that is their purpose, then we should not permit them ashore."

"Umia, I believe the Pu-tahi have good intentions. I invited their chief and I won't back out. But I must be careful. If he is looking for foreigners, let him find no sign of them here."

Umia glanced toward the inland forest. She had told him about her secret arrangements. "The boat and the goods are well hidden," he said. "The two men—"

"I will tell them to stay out of sight. If the Pu-tahi ever ask about outsiders, we must say that they have left us."

"Yes," said Umia. "Everyone must agree they have

gone. Perhaps I can help you, sister. Let me take charge of greeting the clan chiefs and elders as they arrive. I will tell them your concern. I am sure that nobody wants to lose the foreign goods.''

"That will please me," she answered. "But remember that you must greet your uncle along with the others.''

A look of worry showed briefly, but then he squared his shoulders. "I can deal with Cone-shell. He does not frighten me any longer.''

His words filled her with hope. "That is what I have been waiting to hear, Umia.''

Early the next morning, the first Pu-tahi canoe entered the pass into the lagoon. From the deck of her own *pahi*, Tepua stood watching near the inner end of the channel. She felt a chill as the lead vessel approached, driven by the current and a following wind. From her early childhood, the sight of the inverted triangle shapes of Pu-tahi sails had stricken her with terror.

Now all was quiet aboard her double-hull and the smaller vessels that surrounded it. She could feel the tension as the lead Pu-tahi craft drew near. The red feather pennants and carved figures marked this as the canoe of the chief, Ata-katinga, whose name alone was enough to frighten children.

Sea-snake, in charge of Tepua's war canoes, narrowed his eyes as more vessels followed their leader into the lagoon. "Is this raider chief bringing all his people with him?" she heard him mutter. He turned to her. "You can still summon Paruru and his men from shore, *ariki*. We can turn these man-eaters back.''

"No. Paruru will stay where I have put him. I will give the visitors no excuse for war.''

"They do not need reasons," someone else in the *pahi* growled, but Tepua silenced the complainer with an icy look. Once more she turned to Ata-katinga's vessel, watched with quickening breath as lean, fierce-looking men scrambled to bring down the mast and sails. Others paddled to keep the great canoe on course.

A tall, straight figure rose from among the warriors. He wore an elaborate headdress with a tuft of black tropic bird feathers in front. His beard was grizzled, his hair long and tangled. His face was not merely lined with the creases of age, but marked heavily with a dark swirl of tattoos.

"*Aue!*" Tepua cried softly. She had never before seen tattoos on a man's face. Nor had she seen a Pu-tahi warrior at close range.

Like his men, Ata-katinga was bare to the waist, exposing a vast array of tattoos. A broad black line ran down from each shoulder to join in a spear point above his belly. A myriad of smaller designs filled in the weathered skin over his huge chest. Below these the red sash of his office was wrapped about his waist. Tepua had heard that the garment was colored, not with the usual dye, but with the blood of his numerous victims.

And she wished to believe that this man no longer wanted war! She had been guided by what the string figures had shown her. Safe in her house on shore, she had felt confident. Now she swallowed hard as she tried to steady herself.

The Pu-tahi chief lifted a long and slender coconut frond in his tattoo-blackened hand. "I, Ata-katinga-ariki, offer the sign of peace," he proclaimed with a harsh accent. Yet he spoke so powerfully that Tepua thought he could be understood even by the crowds watching from the beach. "I ask permission to come ashore."

She saw no weapons, no sign of hostile intent. The smaller canoes behind him appeared laden with gifts. But she could not know what lay hidden beneath the thatched cabin of the chief's vessel. Polished war clubs? Bone-tipped spears?

Tepua needed help now. To be certain of peace, she needed to invoke a great power.

Only one name sprang to her lips. In Tahiti she had

served a god stronger than any her own people dared call on. "Ata-katinga," she called back. "I must have more than mere promises. I invoke the protection of a great god, the one who presides when enemies sit down together. Break the peace, and you defy the will of Oro."

"I acknowledge Oro-of-the-laid-down-spear," replied Ata-katinga. "And by the will of our own gods as well, I pledge peace between us."

Tepua glanced around at the anxious faces of her warriors. Few seemed impressed by the chief's declarations. But she recalled once more her vision of blue sharks escorting the visitors to shore. The ancestors had shown her what they wanted.

"Land your canoes," she called loudly, then sent her flotilla to lead the way.

On the beach below the assembly ground, Tepua stood, flanked by warriors, watching Ata-katinga and his company disembark. Behind her, onlookers had lined up in long rows. Glancing back at the crowd, she saw expressions of wonder mixed with doubt and fear. The air carried a low undercurrent of muttering as well as cries of dismay. Older children wailed and ran; younger ones begged to be picked up and comforted.

The arriving men were as fierce looking as their leader, their foreheads and cheeks heavily tattooed, wild tangles of hair spilling down their shoulders and backs. They kept flexing their broad hands, as if uncomfortable when not holding weapons.

Now that she could see Ata-katinga's headdress at closer range, Tepua noticed a disturbing detail. In the back, whipped by the breeze, dangled a fringe of brilliant gold. It was hair, human hair, almost the same blond color as Kiore's.

Her suspicions moved at a dizzying pace. Had these raiders also come across foreign sailors, or even foreign women? The fringe of the headdress might be a trophy from one such encounter.

Tepua dared not ask. Unless the Pu-tahi mentioned outsiders, she was determined to say nothing about them. She tried to put aside her misgivings as she waited to greet Ata-katinga.

The heavy steps came closer. The great tattooed face bore down on her. The broad, flat nose pressed her cheek, and she heard the raspy hiss as he inhaled. In the grip of his ceremonial embrace, her pulse drummed in her ears and a voice within her cried from fright. . . .

At last he stood back. *I am alive,* she thought. *I have touched the Pu-tahi chief and I still live!*

The tattoos on Ata-katinga's cheeks and forehead made his face seem like a grotesque mask. Tepua wondered if she would be able to speak another word to this apparition. Then she peered at the eyes behind the mask and saw signs of frailty, of caution, of hope.

Ata-katinga gave a sharp order, sending men scurrying to unload gifts from their beached canoes. Wild-haired Pu-tahi brought lashed wooden cages containing pigs. The animals squealed as the cages were heaved off tattooed shoulders and swung down to thump on the sand. The pigs appeared as fierce as their owners, glaring out with red-rimmed eyes, slashing at the cages with their tusks.

"These are warriors," said Ata-katinga, slapping a protruding snout. With an outraged grunt, the pig jerked its head back. "We will eat them together, and we will all share in their strength."

The men carried other gifts—delicacies such as whole sun-dried coconuts that rattled inside when they were shaken. They also brought fine baskets and mats.

Though the gifts flattered her, Tepua deliberately turned away from them. "Before I accept these gifts," she said to Ata-katinga, "I wish to know your reason for coming here. Your request for this meeting surprised me. The Pu-tahi are known for many things, but desire for peace is not one."

Her words caused a buzz among the crowd. A momentary scowl darkened Ata-katinga's face, turning it once again into a threatening mask. "You are right to be suspicious. It is not by our own wish that we lay down our spears."

I did not think you would willingly abandon your raiding, or your taste for human flesh, Tepua thought grimly, but she kept silent.

At last Ata-katinga began to speak in a low and steady voice. "This is my reason, Tepua-ariki, and it is one that you may already know. A new enemy has come to our ocean, an enemy so strong and ruthless that even we, the Fierce People, cannot stand against it." He paused and Tepua felt a tremor in her fingers. She could guess what was coming next. "There are strangers who do not travel in *pahi,* but in huge islands that have wings," he continued. "These people have no need for spears or clubs. They possess sticks that belch smoke and make a great roar!"

Ata-katinga's voice rose to a shout as if he were trying to imitate the sound and then fell almost to a whisper that made the back of Tepua's neck prickle. "When these weapons speak, men fall and lie still, covered with their blood, yet no knife or spear has torn their skin. And the foul smoke drifts down, making those who survived the blast choke and cry and run."

Tepua struggled to hide her feelings. She had watched Kiore's companion use his thunder-maker. Her vision from the *kava* trance had shown far worse. . . .

As Ata-katinga stared at her, she held herself stiffly, refusing to give any sign that she knew about such things. The one she had seen had frightened people, but had not harmed anyone. Perhaps it was not the same kind that the Pu-tahi feared.

"You are quiet," said the visiting chief, narrowing his eyes. "Is it possible that you do not believe me? That you think this another trick by the rascally Pu-tahi?"

She tried to thrust away any feelings that might betray her. With cautious dignity she replied, "I do not doubt your word. I only wish to know more. Tell me what these enemies look like.''

''More like sea demons than men. Their bodies are patched with strange colors, as if covered by seaweed. Some have brown hands and faces as we do, but others are black or white, or even red.''

Tepua recalled the ruddy flush that often deepened the bronze of Kiore's face. Again emotion swept through her. These enemies who so terrified the Fierce People almost certainly were men from Kiore's land.

Her tongue felt wooden; she willed herself to speak. ''I have heard tales of such people,'' she admitted. ''But I still do not know the purpose for your visit. Do you seek our aid against these outsiders?''

''We cannot hope to survive if we do not unite,'' Ata-katinga answered. ''All my life, I have trusted in the hardness of my spears, but I fear they will prove useless against these many-colored men. That is why I come to you. I do not wish to make war against the foreigners—their weapons would destroy us. But we must stop fighting one another. We must join in friendship and together find other ways to deal with the outsiders.''

Again scenes fleeted across Tepua's memory, smoke and turbulence swirling before her eyes. If Ata-katinga had a way to prevent this, then she would eagerly embrace it. Yet she foresaw how difficult any such arrangement would be.

Glancing about, she noticed the mistrustful glares of her warriors and the anxious looks of her people. She knew of no one eager to trust the Pu-tahi. Worst of all, she had to fight a part of herself that would always crave revenge—the child who had been hustled into hiding, who had listened to grieving women, who had felt the gnawing pain of hunger while looking at ruined coconut trees.

Ata-katinga was speaking again. ''To show you that we are honest in our desire for peace, we brought you a special gift, *ariki*. I saved it for last.''

He gave a sharp handclap and a Pu-tahi warrior walked

forward, holding a white animal in his arms. Tepua glanced in astonishment at its upright ears, pointed snout, and lolling tongue. *A white dog!* This dog was unlike any she had seen before. Instead of the usual sparse coat and narrow ratlike tail, the animal had a thick coat and a bushy plumed tail.

The warrior set the dog on its feet and led it with a sennit cord tied about its neck. It trotted along willingly, lifting ears and muzzle as it appraised the assembled crowd. On every face Tepua saw astonishment and delight.

Dogs were rare in the atolls. In Tahiti they were common, raised for feasts to mark important occasions. But Tepua knew that no one would ever eat a dog that had such brilliant white fur. The long hairs of its tail were precious. Fringes of white dog hair were highly prized on ornaments and clothing. She recalled what a stir Cone-shell had made when he presented her with the fringed cape.

"We call the dog Te Kurevareva, the Atoll Cuckoo," said the Pu-tahi chief. He took the end of the sennit leash from the warrior and handed it to Tepua. "You should not be surprised that she has a name. She is as valuable to us as a great canoe."

Other Pu-tahi came forward, holding up a fringed gorget and a fan as additional offerings. "Our craftsmen have decorated these for you with the hair of Te Kurevareva so that you may see how long and beautiful it is and how well it can be worked," said Ata-katinga. One of his men knelt down and with a quick pat on the dog's side plucked several hairs from the plumed tail. He handed them to Tepua.

She rubbed the hairs between her fingers, noting how long and fine they were. This was a precious gift indeed. Not only was the dog's coat beautiful, the hairs fine and silky, but the animal herself seemed pleasant tempered and amiable.

Tepua had never taken much interest in dogs, but this one appealed to her at once. Atoll Cuckoo seemed to sense it and her plumed tail began to wag. Her large eyes glistened, and her pink tongue flopped out of her mouth.

"She has been taught to stand still so that gathering the hair is easy," said Ata-katinga, in a proud, almost fatherly tone. "You must be careful, of course, not to take too much."

His face had lost some of its severity and the tattoos no longer seemed as grotesque. As Tepua reached down to stroke the dog's head, receiving several wet licks in return, she felt a growing warmth toward the Pu-tahi chief. It was clear that his affection for Atoll Cuckoo went beyond his appreciation of her fur.

Tepua saw Ata-katinga staring at her expectantly as he waited to hear her response. For a moment she looked away, trying to free her thoughts from the dazzling array of gifts. The problems that he had spoken of were real. She believed that he had come in earnestness. "Yes," she said at last. "I am honored to receive your offerings. I will sit with you and discuss the question of the foreigners." This time she found it easier to accept the chief's embrace.

Then she turned, addressing the crowd, and announced her decision for all to hear. She recognized that many people disagreed with her, and wanted to see the Pu-tahi forced back into their canoes. But others clearly had been impressed by Ata-katinga's show of generosity. They leaned forward for a better view of the dog.

Tepua called Maukiri and gave her cousin charge of Te Kurevareva for the moment. Maukiri took the leash hesitantly. "The Atoll Cuckoo will not bite. She is gentle," said Ata-katinga. "Try scratching her behind the ears." Cautiously, Maukiri knelt and did as the Pu-tahi chief suggested. The dog wagged its long tail like a palm leaf moving in a stiff breeze.

"Hairs are flying off!" cried Maukiri, trying to catch the drifting fluff.

"Have some boys follow and pick them up," Tepua told her.

With a laugh, Maukiri called for assistance. The animal did a little dance step as she led it away.

Now it was time for Tepua to present gifts in return. She called for the offerings that had been readied at short notice—pearl-shell fishhooks, finely woven mats, and other handiwork. Nothing she had collected could match the Atoll Cuckoo, but Ata-katinga showed no sign of disappointment.

When the gift exchange was done, she led the Pu-tahi to the guest houses she had ordered prepared for them. She explained that her clan chiefs had not yet arrived, and that she would meet with them before both sides sat down together. "First I wish to talk with you alone," she told Ata-katinga.

Sitting in her yard, Tepua asked the visiting chief to tell what he knew about the many-colored men. "I have heard of great vessels," she said, "but I have not been told where they were sighted."

"They have been seen in open water," he answered. "Several times the foreigners have sent small boats ashore at a place we call Cloud Island. It is there that I saw the thunder weapons and the men falling dead."

"What was the reason for the battle?" she asked uneasily, though she believed she knew the answer. "Did the people of Cloud Island attack?"

"The islanders desired to trade peacefully. The strangers wanted food and drink, and offered their foreign goods in exchange. The islanders were happy to have those goods, but they found that they could not satisfy the foreigners. The many-colored men ordered them to strip the palm trees bare, and to bring every fowl and pig on the island. To obey would have meant starvation."

"Food and drink. Is that all these outsiders want of us?"

"They are curious about our ornaments, but toss most of them aside with contempt. They care nothing for feathers or fine craftsmanship. Pearls and pearl shell are the only valuables that interest them."

Pearl shell. All Tepua's hopes vanished. She could not doubt now that Nika and Kiore were of the same breed as the foreign marauders. Her two sailors had seemed peaceful, but perhaps that was only because their weapon had fallen into the lagoon!

No. She refused to believe that Kiore could carry out such acts of cruelty. Regardless of what evil she heard about foreigners, she would not change her feelings toward him. Yet it did not matter that one man was different.

The Pu-tahi's story rang true. It fit perfectly with her own vision of terror. Now she knew how she must answer Ata-katinga's request. The outsiders were a danger that she dared not ignore. She must persuade her people to accept an alliance with their ancient enemy.

By the next morning, the chiefs and elders of all the clans had arrived. Even Rongo's arrogant young leader, the only chief who had not formally acknowledged Tepua's rule, came to offer his advice. They gathered at the assembly ground, under gray and threatening skies.

Meanwhile the Pu-tahi had been left to amuse themselves beside the shore. From her seat, Tepua glanced toward the choppy lagoon and saw young men racing each other in their fleet canoes or diving into the water. A few brave Ahiku youngsters stood watching, but no one dared join the visitors' games.

She turned her attention to the assembly. Never before had she presided over such a large gathering. As she studied the glaring eyes and down-turned mouths, she felt a knot growing in her belly. There seemed to be little sympathy here for making peace with the raiders.

Her voice wavered as she began to relate Ata-katinga's message, adding details she had learned from him in their private discussions. She described a foreign weapon that was even more terrible than the thunder-club. It was thick as a tree and poked out from the sides of their vessels. It spat huge stones that could smash canoes or even houses along the shore.

When she had finished, she saw many wide eyes and

gaping mouths in the crowd. Several old men were trembling out of fear and rage.

"Do not accept these lies!" Cone-shell shouted in reply. "The Pu-tahi want to frighten us and make us weak so we will agree to whatever they ask."

"Are these reports lies?" asked Heka, turning angrily toward him. "I have heard some of them before—from different travelers at different times. Would so many men invent the same tales?"

"Everyone knows there are foreign vessels on the sea," Cone-shell answered. "But the power of their weapons grows with every telling of the tales."

The chief of Rongo clan turned and eyed him. "Not so, my friend Cone-shell. I am certain that the weapons are as dangerous as Ata-katinga tells us." He turned back to address Tepua. "Yet these foreign vessels are few. I think it unlikely that they would trouble us here."

"The Rongo *ariki* speaks well," said a Piho elder. "A stray boat might arrive by accident, but why would anyone seek us out? The foreigners possess lands of their own, where they build great wonders. We have nothing they want."

"Their vessels must be provisioned," Tepua interjected. "The crews are large and they are at sea for many months. One vessel could swallow up all the food we have."

"Then let us prepare to defend ourselves," said Cone-shell, "We can build weapons like theirs." He lowered his voice to a loud whisper. "We have men who can teach us."

No! The thought of more foreign weapons made Tepua shudder. "We cannot make these things," she said to Cone-shell. "We do not have the kind of stone they need."

"Does this stone fall from the sky?" asked Cone-shell, grimacing contemptuously. "Is it something that only the foreign gods give their people?" He looked from one face to the next, but no one answered him.

Finally a Rongo elder spoke. "If outsiders come to us for provisions, we must ask for this precious stone in return.

That is how we will get what we need to build the weapons.''

Tepua heard this suggestion with dismay, then thought of a new argument. The gods had forbidden her people to shoot arrows at each other. What would they say about using these thunder makers? ''Let me hear a priest's view.'' She turned to Faka-ora.

The high priest took a deep breath. ''We dare not use such weapons against our own people. The gods would punish us severely. But I see nothing wrong with turning these spewers-of-smoke against the foreigners who made them.''

Tepua felt stunned by his answer. The idea of these weapons in the hands of her own people repelled her, regardless of how they were used. ''What could we offer in trade for the stone?'' she asked, hoping to discourage this talk. ''We have nothing but food, and little enough of that.''

''Plant more coconut trees!'' said one of Varoa's men. The reply brought an uproar of agreement.

''That is no answer!'' Tepua protested. The meeting became so unruly that she was ready to call an end to it. But nothing had been decided. The others seemed content with blustering and making vague plans. ''Umia,'' she said, when the voices had finally quieted. ''Tell us your thoughts.''

She watched the young man turn to Cone-shell and meet his hostile gaze. ''I wish to remind you, Uncle, of how our lives used to be. In the past we were always fighting among ourselves. Now our clans support each other. Yet an atoll is still a small place.''

''Small!'' said Cone-shell. ''Everything a man needs is here. If we lack something, we find ways to get it.''

''Until the outsiders came, I believed so,'' answered Umia. ''Now I see that there are people and places we know nothing about. Out of malice or carelessness these foreigners may do us harm.'' He paused, and no voice rose against him. ''We are fortunate,'' continued Umia. ''The gods wisely spread our atolls in a wide swath across the sea. There are so many islands that the outsiders cannot descend on them all. That is where our hope lies. And why we must settle our differences with other islanders.''

"He speaks well," said Tepua. She looked about and saw that Umia's words had made an impression. People glanced at each other in surprise. Such wisdom from the young man they had once dismissed as unready for the chiefhood!

"Yes, he has made a good point," said Heka. "The foreigners may be dangerous, but I do not think they can destroy all the atoll people. With alliances we will have places of refuge, and food when ours is gone."

"Alliances, yes," Cone-shell shouted. "But not with Pu-tahi eels."

"They are the strongest friends anyone could have!" replied Umia.

Some voices joined Umia's. Others still argued against Ata-katinga. "How do we know the Pu-tahi will not betray us later?" shouted someone. "They will act like friends for a time, then turn on us."

Tepua kept silent awhile. Umia was doing well enough on his own. Cone-shell persisted with the opposing view, slowly losing supporters. Yet many people remained adamant against making an agreement with the old enemy.

One man had not spoken—Paruru. Knowing his true feelings toward the Pu-tahi, she had not objected to his silence. Now he began to speak, in a firm voice that made everyone turn to him. "I have listened to these arguments and I have not been swayed. Those of you who have faced the Pu-tahi in battle understand. We can never trust them. We can never feel comfortable with them around us. Get rid of the man-eaters, I say, before they take advantage of our hospitality. Do not allow them to stay another night."

Tepua rose to her feet. "We have a meeting of peace here, sanctioned by the gods," she answered hotly. "I will not have it ruined by talk of distrust." She waved her hand at the assembly. "Discuss this all you want. Light fires, and

stay up all night if you must. Then we will meet again and
see who still clings to Cone-shell and Paruru.''

The *kaito-nui* was not surprised when Cone-shell approached him a short time later. ''There is too much bad air
about,'' said Varoa's chief, making a fanning motion in
front of his face.

''I know a place where the air is fresh,'' answered Paruru,
''and where a man can speak freely.'' He led Cone-shell
onto a little-used path across the island.

The men walked in silence. There was no telling who
might be listening, hidden under the sweeping branches of
hibiscus or behind the aerial roots of *fara* palms. Paruru felt
an obligation toward Cone-shell now, and the thought made
him uncomfortable.

Varoa's chief had never spoken a word to Paruru about
the turtle incident. He had let his brother, the high priest,
handle the problem at his *marae*. After the ceremony was
done, and the spirits appeased, Cone-shell had treated the
offenders as honored guests.

Now Paruru found himself together with Cone-shell on
the same side. It was a partnership that he did not welcome,
yet he saw no alternative.

''This is the way down,'' said Paruru, descending a short
slope toward the seaward beach. A brisk sea wind was
blowing, spray from the breakers leaping high. The water
beyond was gray under the clouded sky.

The warrior looked around with satisfaction at the barren
shore, where only a few scrubby bushes grew amid exposed
and weather-blackened coral. There was no place here for
an eavesdropper to hide.

Cone-shell found a stone perch and motioned for Paruru
to take a lower seat in front of him. ''I admire your little
island,'' said Varoa's chief. ''Do you know that it once
belonged to my clan? That was before Ahiku people lived
on this atoll.''

"We did not come here to talk of ancient wars," said Paruru, annoyed.

"That is true. We came to talk of helping each other."

"I have heard your opinions and you have heard mine," said Paruru. "They are much the same, though for different reasons. It is my duty to protect Tepua. And I will not have stinking Pu-tahi on our shores."

"Then we two must work together."

The warrior studied Cone-shell's eager expression. He looked like a spear fisherman at the moment of his thrust, but Paruru was not ready to be his prey. "I do not think our goals are exactly the same," Paruru cautioned. "You wish to challenge Tepua's rule. It does not matter if the issue is Pu-tahi or spoils or an argument over a coconut tree."

"I wish what is best for all the clans," replied Cone-shell, slapping his chest. "This chief is not afraid of battles. I will fight Pu-tahi. I will fight foreigners."

"What if we win?" asked Paruru. "What if sentiment grows so strong that Tepua is forced to send Ata-katinga away? Then her power to rule will be weakened."

"Is that not for the best? Do you truly believe a woman should lead us?"

Paruru's mouth felt dry and he had difficulty bringing an answer to his lips. "My opinion means nothing. She will continue to do so—until the gods place the sacred power with someone else."

"That day is not far off."

"Perhaps." *But you will not be the chosen one.*

"We certainly have differences," said Cone-shell in a friendly tone. "Yet there is something we both want. Let us work together to prevent an agreement with the Pu-tahi."

"And Tepua? What will happen to her if we succeed?"

"She is no fool. She will not make this a test of her authority. When the wind blows, the palm tree bends."

NINETEEN

Soon after leaving Cone-shell, Paruru found the outsiders at their secluded forest campsite. They had been told to remain here, out of sight of the Pu-tahi. He hoped that they would not grow restless too quickly.

The day's shadows had lengthened. In the center of a clearing a fire burned above ground, and the cooking odors made Paruru widen his nostrils. *Meat.* But of what sort? None he had ever smelled before.

"Come. Join us." Nika shouted, waving a charred lump at the warrior. His words were oddly slurred; his usually dour face bore a wild grin.

Paruru felt a lurch in his stomach. What new form of mischief had the men discovered? On the ground he saw the battered bodies of two coconut rats. The bloodied skins of others lay in a heap beside them.

"Good meat!" Nika said, his food muffling his words. His chin was greasy. When he took another bite, dark juices dribbled from the corner of his mouth.

"We . . . do not eat . . . rats," Paruru said, fighting the nausea that began to rise.

"Another *tapu*? I will eat them anyway!"

"The rats are our friends," Paruru muttered, but he saw that the men were not listening. Some strangeness, perhaps an evil spirit, had entered them. Their faces were glazed with sweat and displayed a childish kind of happiness.

"Try one," said Kiore, removing a stick that had hung over the fire. He offered the charred end to the warrior.

Paruru nearly gagged. Fending it off with one hand, he said, "I cannot eat that. But you are outsiders. Perhaps no harm will come to you."

"If you do not eat, then drink with us," Nika bellowed. He clapped his hand on Paruru's shoulder. "You are my brother. I share everything with you."

"I came to tell you about the Pu-tahi," the warrior said, his voice rising with his frustration. He smelled the rank odor of the men and knew that they had not washed themselves recently. With dismay he realized that the sailors, left alone, were reverting to their old habits.

"We know about those sharp-toothed fellows," Kiore assured him in tones of slurred joviality. He, too, clapped his arm about Paruru. "We spied on them from the bushes."

"You might have been seen!" said Paruru with alarm. "Those men are dangerous!"

"Fierce!" said Kiore, moving his forefinger across his face as if tracing tattoos. "Very fierce. If they catch us, they will eat us. Like this." With his teeth, he tore off another mouthful of meat. "After they eat us, they will be sick. Fall down. Unh! Dead." He clutched at his stomach, toppled over, then lay still while Nika heaved with laughter.

"This is no time for joking," Paruru hissed. "The visitors are deceivers. They will talk quietly for a time and then they will start a fight."

"No, my brother," said Nika. "These visitors will not harm anyone. We will not let them." He stood up and spread his legs, imitating the stance of a warrior. He held an imaginary spear, as if ready to throw it. "I am too strong for them. They will not get past me."

Paruru stared with narrowed eyes. He had never seen the men like this, beyond reasoning. A feeling of helplessness came over him.

Kiore staggered to his feet and tried to embrace Paruru

again. "You are my friend's brother. Come and drink with us. We are lonely here."

"Bring us women," Nika suggested. "Then we can be happy." He pushed a coconut cup toward Paruru and the warrior reluctantly took it. If he kept refusing their hospitality, he thought, then the sailors would soon scorn him.

The sharp odor rising from the cup was familiar. Paruru's eyebrows rose as he remembered the foreign drink. Another whiff convinced him that this was the stinging potion that Cone-shell had tasted and spat out. But what was the drink doing here? He had last seen its container when the foreign goods were moved.

"Take some," said Kiore. "Why are you waiting?"

Paruru remembered Nika's insistence that he try the smoke of his "pipa." Now he realized that he would have to swallow this unpleasant brew, though it burned his mouth and throat. Eager to get the chore done, he took a quick swallow. . . .

"*Aue!*" Paruru forced himself to take another gulp. He had not asked how the men obtained this, for he knew the answer. One of them had flaunted the priests' sanctions. Someone had committed a new offense against the gods. And now Paruru felt the punishment falling swiftly on himself. His insides were afire, from his throat down to his belly. "*Aue!*"

As Paruru sat looking at the grease-smeared faces of the foreigners, he knew that he could only blame himself for this newest offense. He was the one who had disclosed the hiding place of the goods, in order to gain Nika's trust.

But somehow, as he sat there, Paruru began to feel less disturbed about his mistake. He glanced down at the cup in his hands and thought that the drink was actually better than he had expected. He tried another swallow.

In some ways it was like *kava,* and in other ways different. *Kava* made men quickly turn silent, but these sailors had been imbibing with no such effect. Now they began singing loudly, a foreign song. He felt an urge to join them. Kiore began to dance with his knees deeply bent, as he had at the feast. Paruru had been furious with him then, but now he found the antics amusing.

"We are making too much noise," Paruru said. His lips felt strange when he spoke, and he heard laughter from his own throat. The noise did not matter, he told himself. Tepua and her guests were sleeping off the big meal they had eaten.

But Paruru remembered that he had come here for a purpose. He needed the outsiders' help.

"Dance," said Kiore, waving his arms crazily. "Remember the spears?" He held out two sticks on his forearms and clumsily tried to perform the *hipa* step that Paruru had demonstrated at the welcoming feast. Paruru wondered if he was trying to make amends for his behavior that night.

"I will show you," said Paruru. He picked up another pair of sticks, greasy from the meat they had held, and balanced them on his own forearms. His legs felt curiously light. While Nika played a tune, he began his dance.

Before he could get one time around his circle, the sticks rolled off his arms and Paruru toppled to the ground. He lay sprawled on his back and felt his body spinning. Above him he saw a clouded sky, tinged with red from the approaching sunset.

"This is not good," the warrior said, fighting the dizziness as he sat up. "We need to talk. Seriously. About the Pu-tahi." His head seemed to float of its own accord, drawing his body after it.

"Pu-tahi! We can finish them like *that*!" said Nika. He picked up another long stick and swung it at one of the dead rats that lay on the ground. "And *that*!" He kept hitting the limp body, knocking it across the leaf-strewn ground.

Kiore got his own stick, and soon they were batting the dead creature back and forth between them.

"No," said Paruru. He staggered forward, tried to grab one stick in each hand and stop the buffoonery. For a moment he succeeded, but the sailors tried to pull away

from him. "Listen," he said in a slurred voice. "I need help
from both of you—to stand with me and protect Tepua.
Nika, I must talk with you alone."

"I am your brother," said Nika, leaning forward, his
breath reeking of drink. "But Kiore is my friend. We keep
no secrets from him."

"No secrets," said the second sailor, leaning in the
opposite direction.

Then all three men toppled in a heap. The foreigners were
laughing, but now Paruru did not join in.

"I will save Tepua from the man-eaters," said Kiore. "I
will not let them harm her." He lifted his arms in a strange
gesture, as if raising a weapon that jutted out from his
shoulder. Not a spear . . . Paruru cried out in alarm as he
realized what Kiore was doing—acting as if he held the
thunder-club. *"Pam!"* said the sailor. "No more Pu-tahi."

"Kiore knows about the weapon!" Paruru cried hoarsely.

"No secrets," said Nika. "We can trust him."

"But Tepua—"

"I care nothing for Tepua," said Nika. "But I will fight
for her. Because of Maukiri."

Paruru could not clear his thoughts. He wanted to get an
agreement about the weapon, and to warn the men not to tell
anyone else, but he could not bring the words to his lips.
Silently he untangled himself from the intoxicated sailors
and left them to their foolishness. Behind him, they began
another song.

The drink was the cause of all these troubles. Though he
could barely keep his eyes open, Paruru resolved to get rid
of the stuff. His legs wobbled as he began to search for the
container. He staggered from tree to tree, leaning on each to
support himself as he looked around. Then, in the shadows,
he saw the slatted drum half-hidden by a branch.

Nika and Kiore were too busy carousing to notice, he
hoped. He recalled that the drink could be made to flow out
through a hollow stick at the bottom of the drum. He
reached down and twisted something. His fingers felt

clumsy, but the piece turned in his hand. When he saw the liquid spilling onto the ground, he went back to the sailors.

"Teach me your song," Paruru said through numbed lips as he eased himself down to rest against a log. His head seemed to bounce gently against the bark. "Maybe I can learn it." But the foreigners were quiet now. He heard slow breathing and a snore. Paruru felt his own eyes closing again and this time he could not stop them.

The sound of raindrops woke Paruru near dawn. He heard a gentle patter that changed to a steady shower of water against the overhanging leaves. The throbbing pain in his head almost made him forget the rain and all else.

In the gloom he tried to find his way to a better shelter. The sailors, too, were stirring. He heard them muttering together in their own tongue.

"What have you done to me?" Paruru cried. "My head!"

He heard Nika's muffled laughter. "After a time, you will grow used to drinking."

The rain was soaking the ground now, falling through the branches in a steady stream. Paruru thought that he might feel better if he remained still awhile. He found his way under a dense canopy, lay down and drew up his knees, but the throbbing in his skull continued.

The foreigners kept gabbling to each other, and Paruru understood almost nothing. "We must talk about the weapon," he called to the sailors.

"I do not think the *ariki* wants it used," said Kiore. "It is not good for this place."

Paruru turned toward the sound of their voices, but still he could not see the men. "The Pu-tahi will respect nothing less. I must have it."

"Too dangerous!" said Kiore.

"You said you would stand with me," Paruru protested. Finally he spotted the sailors, two dark figures seated beneath a tree. Yesterday, the drink had made the men foolish, but also amiable. Now they only seemed stubborn.

"I will not tell Tepua," said Kiore. "I do not want her to take the weapon. But we have no reason to use it."

"Nika," Paruru called in desperation. "Tell your friend that you agreed to help me."

"If trouble appears, I will help," the other sailor answered. "I see none now."

"The Pu-tahi are waiting for us to drop our guard!" Paruru's stomach felt queasy. Sitting here arguing was only making his head feel worse. For now, he had no strength to vent his anger at Nika. Later he would deal with him, insist that he honor his obligations to his brother.

But first he needed to get rid of his pain. "You will see that I am right," Paruru said in parting. "I will bring news that will make you listen." He forced himself up, leaning for a moment against a young *fara*. The rain was still falling heavily, but he was used to being wet. Dawn had come, spreading a dim, gray light.

Paruru brushed away leaves and sticks that clung to his damp body. Then he headed for a place of refuge, the house of a *tahunga* who often cared for his warriors' ills and wounds. Shortly he reached one of the main paths across the island and turned toward the lagoon. He heard footsteps ahead.

"Paruru!" called an indignant voice. "Where are you going, you sea worm? Do you think you can hide from me?"

When the warrior recognized Cone-shell's harsh voice, he gave a quiet groan. The bulky figure, covered in a dripping rain cape, came quickly toward him. "I want answers," Cone-shell demanded as he drew closer. "I am tired of chasing after you in these woods."

The only weapon that the warrior saw was the club that Cone-shell pounded against the ground. Paruru realized with chagrin that he had no weapon of his own. "The storehouse is empty!" shouted Cone-shell. "Where are the foreigners' goods?"

"I do not have them," Paruru replied, wishing he could somehow get past Varoa's chief.

"You know where they are!"

"Do not make me angry, Cone-shell. Yesterday, we put aside our differences."

"That has nothing to do with this treachery. I asked Tepua to give me Kiore. Now you and she are trying to cheat me of the benefit."

"Benefit? A few trinkets. Cloth. Choppers."

"Worth much in the right hands!"

Paruru wiped rainwater from his face and sized up the man who stood before him. Cone-shell had been a warrior once, but now he was too heavy, too slow. Paruru felt an impulse to grab the club from his hand and strike him with it.

No, that would not do. He needed Cone-shell's help or everything would be lost. He needed to regain this man's trust, even if it meant giving up his secret. . . . "The foreign goods you saw mean nothing," Paruru hissed, "compared with what I have hidden."

"Tell me!" Cone-shell took a menacing step closer.

Paruru's head pounded as he spoke. "You were not here when the foreign *vaka* arrived at the lagoon. Surely you heard what happened."

"Yes . . ." The chief's eyes widened.

"Come. I will show you something you have never seen before. Then you will stop asking about the other goods."

In a deserted part of the inland forest, behind the ruins of an old *marae,* Paruru halted and pulled at a heap of coconut fronds. Underneath lay the upturned hull of a canoe that had long ago lost its outrigger.

He glanced back at Cone-shell. Now that the rain had stopped, the chief had taken off his plaited cape and stood bare-chested in the cool air. "Help me turn this over," Paruru asked as he gripped the bow of the old boat.

When Cone-shell squatted to assist, a piece of rotten

planking broke away in his hands. On Paruru's side, the lashings holding the boards together were frayed, ready to part. "Gently!" warned Paruru.

At last they managed to roll the hull over to an upright position and prop it against a log. Inside lay several bundles lashed to the thwarts. Cone-shell grabbed the largest and began to tear at the cords.

"Everything must stay dry!" Paruru shouted.

Cone-shell ignored the warning. In a moment he had the weapon unwrapped. He turned it, sniffed at it, applied his teeth to the gray flared tube. "*Aue!* This is the thing of war. The weapon the Pu-tahi warned about."

"It will do nothing as it is now," Paruru retorted. "It is just wood and stone. The thing has no power."

Cone-shell lay the weapon across the rotting hull and crouched to study it. He ran his fingers over the smooth contours of wood, then came to the bird's head. "Show me how it is held," he insisted.

Reluctantly Paruru lifted the piece. He had succeeded in silencing Cone-shell's demands for the other goods, but now he faced a new problem. There was only one weapon and two men wanted it!

Yet he had taken Cone-shell here for a reason. If Tepua learned of the thunder-club, she would forbid Paruru to use it. In that case, giving it to Cone-shell might be his only recourse. The thought of doing so brought back the pounding to his temples.

"Here is how the thing is held," Paruru answered, pointing the open tube at the trees. "The head is pulled back like this. . . ."

Paruru let the beak fall sharply into its little bowl. He could not help smiling when the sparks made Cone-shell jump. "This is a weapon of flame," the *kaito-nui* said. "The spark must be what starts it. In one of my bundles is a fine black sand that smells like the weapon's smoke. My guess is that this powder can be lit by the spark, as wood dust flares in the groove of a fire-stick."

"Guess? You do not know?"

Irritably Paruru replied. "The foreigners refuse to teach me. They say the weapon is too dangerous."

"We need no help from them," Cone-shell snorted. "It is simple enough. Show me the black sand."

"There is more than just the sand. A canoe paddler heard small stones falling after the weapon thundered. Two dropped into his *vaka*. They are the same kind as the ones in this bag."

"Leave the stones for later," growled Cone-shell.

Paruru opened a second bundle, removing a container curved like a boar's tusk. He opened the pointed end, then shook a few grains of black sand into his palm. "Sniff it," he said. He watched Cone-shell's nostrils widen and his eyelids fly up.

"It smells of bird droppings!" Cone-shell whispered. "And foul water!"

Paruru's hand began to tremble. "There may be evil spirits in this."

"Your priest Faka-ora got rid of them," Cone-shell rebuked. "This powder did come from the stores I examined, did it not?"

The warrior raised his eyebrows in assent.

"Then waste no more time talking." Cone-shell took the bottle and poured powder onto the place where the bird's beak struck. He put the bottle down. "Stand away from me," he warned Paruru. Cone-shell spoke a brief prayer before pulling back the beak.

Paruru took a deep breath. There came a shower of sparks and then a flare of light. "It does burn!" shouted Cone-shell in triumph. An acrid puff of smoke spread outward from where the fire had been.

"But no thunder," Paruru added moodily.

"We will come to that," said Cone-shell. "If stones are part of this, then I see only one place they can go." He turned the tube and looked once more inside. Then he held out his hand.

Paruru was pleased that they had managed this much so quickly. Now Cone-shell seemed about to unravel the last of the secrets. With growing excitement Paruru opened another bundle, taking out a handful of heavy round stones. With a rumble, Cone-shell let them fall into the tube.

"Sand!" Cone-shell ordered. Paruru sprinkled more powder around the bowl. This time he was willing to believe that the weapon might actually work. He stepped back and put his hands over his ears.

Again came the sparks, the flare . . . and nothing else. "*Aue!*" cried Cone-shell, flinging the weapon aside and slapping at his fingers. "It stings! It burns!" He sucked on his hand, then spat out the unpleasant taste. He grabbed a handful of wet leaves and wrapped them around the hurt.

Paruru paid no attention to Cone-shell's suffering. He crouched and saw that the stones had merely rolled out of the tube onto the damp ground. The weapon itself was smeared with soil.

"This is what Nika warned me against," he cried. "The thing is dangerous if you do not fully understand it." Picking up the thunder-club, he tried to brush off the debris that clung to it.

"Then call your foreigner," said Cone-shell, "and let him burn his own fingers on the useless thing."

"He is not ready to help us."

"Your brother refuses?" Cone-shell unwrapped his hand, scowled at the red marks, and wrapped it again.

"He says the Pu-tahi are not threatening us."

"What does that pale-bellied stranger know? He should see the Pu-tahi when they get stirred up. Like barracudas!"

"How can I make him understand?"

Varoa's chief stared at Paruru. "He must see the *real* Pu-tahi," Cone-shell said, his mouth twisting into an ugly grin. "I will find a way to show him. And you will help me."

....
: TWENTY
:
....

As sunset approached, Paruru slipped away from the assembly ground, taking with him a basket laden with food. The day's discussions had concluded with a feast. The Pu-tahi were still stuffing themselves with albacore, taro, and pork, but Paruru had no appetite.

Pu-tahi as honored guests! In his anger, Paruru almost forgot his way to the sailors' camp. Crossing a path through the thickest cover of the forest, he ducked under low-growing hibiscus limbs. A few steps beyond a stand of young coconut he finally spotted a glimmer of firelight.

He had promised to bring the foreigners something from the feast. As he approached the small fire he saw both men jump up, their eyes bright with greed and anticipation. Evidently aromas from the cooking ovens had preceded him down the trail.

At least the men had not gone after rats again. "I hope you enjoy the meal better than I did," he said as he handed the sailors their dinner.

The men clawed at his basket as if they were famished children. Paruru backed away in disgust and let them squabble over the food. With savage cries they opened the packets of roast pork. *Meat,* he thought. *They crave it above all else.*

He refused to watch them eat, but could not help hearing their chewing and smacking noises, mixed with sighs of satiation and delight. His own stomach felt hard and cold.

268

"Nobly done, Paruru," Nika said at last. The warrior turned back and saw his brother licking juices from his fingers.

Paruru watched moodily as the contented sailors nibbled the last bits from the bones. After a long discussion with Cone-shell he had planned what he would say now, yet he did not look forward to starting. To save Nika, he had become a master of lies. To save Tepua from her own folly, he would need subtler methods of deceit.

At last, with feigned indignation, he said, "It is not right that I should have to bring you this meal in secret, while our enemies take seats of honor at the assembly ground."

"I do not like it either," said Kiore. "But Tepua—"

"You should see her!" said Paruru, filled with genuine ire now. "Feeding delicacies to that white-haired dog, and to the other Pu-tahi curs. Whatever sense she had is gone."

"I thought she had good reason to send us here," Kiore argued.

"She was mistaken," Paruru replied. "She thought the Pu-tahi might want your goods, but that is not why they came. If the savages want shiny knives and foreign cloth, they can get them elsewhere." The *kaito-nui* watched with grim satisfaction when Kiore's eyebrows shot up. "It is so," Paruru continued, choosing his words carefully. "The Pu-tahi have dealt with other men like you."

"Others?" Kiore stepped closer. "Explain."

Paruru hesitated, perhaps longer than necessary. He had baited his hook. Now he readied himself for the big fish to strike. "The Pu-tahi tell us they have seen huge *pahi*, with wings. Foreign sailors have even come ashore."

Now Kiore stood directly in front of him, his eyes intense. "Ashore! I need to know where. And the banners they flew—what color?"

"You ask too much," said Paruru, refusing to say anything else even when Kiore pressed him.

Nika shouted a few angry words at Kiore. By now, Paruru had picked up some of their language, enough to make sense of what they were saying. They began to argue about the "lok-puk" that Kiore had been so zealous in protecting. Paruru knew how strongly he wanted to find a vessel from his own island. Nika did not care about the "lok-puk" or returning to his homeland. Losing patience with his companion, he threw insults at him.

At last Kiore addressed the warrior again, this time more politely, asking him to tell all he knew.

"There is a place called Cloud Island," Paruru answered quietly. "The Pu-tahi say that foreigners have taken on supplies there."

"Can you tell me how to find it?"

"Our canoe-masters should know. Ask any of them."

"And what of the flags that the foreign boats fly?" Kiore knelt in the dirt beside the fire and drew lines with a stick.

"The Pu-tahi said nothing about flags."

An impatient glint came into Kiore's eyes. "They have seen the vessels. They must know. Ask them."

"Ask? How can I get close enough to speak with them when I gag at their smell?" In truth, the odor of these unwashed sailors offended Paruru's nose far more than did the Pu-tahi. Ata-katinga's people might be cannibals, but at least they bathed frequently.

Kiore stamped around the fire. He argued with Nika awhile, until the other man finally turned to Paruru.

"You are my brother. Now I am asking a favor," the red-haired sailor wheedled. "Do not forget that you want something in return."

"I am willing to help you, but your friend needs to learn patience." Paruru told Kiore, "These Pu-tahi seek an alliance, and Tepua wishes to accommodate them. If that happens, you can be sure that many Pu-tahi traders will come here." He took a deep breath, trying to contain his disgust at such a possibility.

"How can—"

Paruru interrupted. "A trader will know the answers to

your questions. Offer him one of your foreign choppers and he will tell you everything.''

"That is too long to wait," Kiore complained.

"Maybe not. I heard Ata-katinga speak to the clan chiefs." Paruru hoped his resentment did not show through. "He convinced most of them that his people have changed their ways. He is close to the agreement he seeks."

"We cannot be sure when traders will come," said Kiore. "And these Pu-tahi will leave without telling us anything."

Paruru replied. "You will get no answers from our visitors. They are not the kind who pay attention to colored bits of cloth. They are warriors."

Kiore shook his head and groaned.

"I am sorry. That is the best advice I can offer. Tomorrow there will be another feast, and more pork. I will not forget my friends."

In the gathering darkness, Paruru took his leave, but he did not go far. He doubled back and crept silently into the bushes that flanked the clearing. He listened as the sailors argued, though he grasped few of their words. They were speaking of Cloud Island and of men in their own far-off land.

It was clear that Kiore refused to wait when the information he wanted might be available for the asking. He stormed about the campsite, slapping his fist into his hand.

Nika seemed afraid of the Pu-tahi, but Paruru was glad to see that Kiore's arguments were wearing him down. Paruru was puzzled, however, when Kiore pulled off his tattered foreign leg coverings and slapped his arms and legs as if to show Nika that his skin was as dark as an islander's. Unwillingly Paruru agreed. He had not anticipated this and wondered what Kiore was planning.

Beneath the garments, the light-haired sailor wore only a simple *maro*. With a laugh, Nika pulled aside the rear band of Kiore's loincloth and remarked that the skin beneath was still as white as a fish's belly. Kiore slapped his hand away and rearranged the garment.

Paruru then heard baffling arguments about the shapes of noses and the colors of eyes and hair. Kiore took a handful of old charcoal from beside the fire. First he darkened his cheeks, to divert attention from his nose. Then he smudged his fair hair until it appeared black. Finally he made designs on his skin, crudely imitating tattoo patterns.

Paruru frowned as he watched. Kiore was showing more cleverness than he had anticipated. Maybe he would succeed at disguising his foreign appearance—at least in the dimness of night. Pu-tahi were stupid. Perhaps they could be fooled.

As a final touch, Kiore plaited a headdress from palm fronds to help conceal his face. When he finished and stood by the fire, Paruru was astonished at the transformation. As long as no light caught the brilliant aquamarine of Kiore's eyes, he might actually get away with his deception. Finally the sailor picked up one of his discarded garments—the fine *tiputa* that he had received from the *ariki*—and folded it in a neat bundle.

To be used as a gift? With a mixture of anticipation and dismay, Paruru watched Kiore slip away from the campfire. The *kaito-nui* had alerted his men to be ready for trouble tonight. He was not sure what kind of trouble they would face.

A chorus of bellowing cries startled Tepua, making her jump up from her mat. After the feast, her attendants had all gone to sleep early, leaving the house in darkness. Trembling with apprehension over what might be happening, she found her way to the door and hurried outside. A sliver of moonlight lit the white coral sand.

As she emerged, a warrior ran up, shouting, "*Ariki!* There is fighting in the Pu-tahi compound!"

"Fighting over what?" Flanked by the warriors who guarded her household, she followed the messenger. As they approached the cluster of guesthouses she heard louder shouts, angry voices.

"Treachery!" came Ata-katinga's roar.

One of her warriors, holding a lit palm leaf torch, met Tepua at the entrance to the low wall that surrounded the compound. Paruru appeared next, a stormy look on his face. He held up a spear that resembled no weapon made by Tepua's people. In the flickering torchlight she saw a broad, leaflike blade and ornate carvings along the shaft.

"Those sons of eels tricked us," Paruru shouted. "They had weapons hidden."

Again Ata-katinga's bellow came from behind one of the houses. "Bring Tepua-ariki! She must explain this outrage!"

Tepua glanced angrily at her *kaito-nui,* wishing to ask how the uproar had started. But first she had to soothe Ata-katinga. She hurried toward the commotion, and when Paruru tried to accompany her, she said harshly, "I will go alone."

"*Ariki,* you need my protection. The men have spears."

"And if you come with me, they may be tempted to use them." She turned her back on him and stalked around the nearest guest house. There she saw other torches and shadowed figures. For a moment the scene confused her.

"Ata-katinga, what has happened?" she demanded. Then she saw a large man who wore only a *maro* struggling in the grip of two Pu-tahi warriors. The man looked familiar. . . . Her breath caught as she realized that the miscreant was Kiore, his hair blackened and his face smeared with soot!

One Pu-tahi clutched his jaw while another spat out broken teeth, held his ribs and moaned. Tepua guessed that these injuries had not been inflicted by weapons, but by the way of fighting with closed hands that only the outsiders used.

Tepua glared at Kiore, who looked back at her with an expression of arrogance mixed with embarrassment. Welts and bruises showed on his arms, proof that he had tried to defend himself from Pu-tahi clubs. Gashes bled on his chest and shoulder.

Not knowing whether she wanted to shout at him in anger or tend his wounds, she waited for Ata-katinga to speak.

Flanked by armed spearmen, the Pu-tahi chief stood angrily watching the sailor. "Do not feign ignorance, woman-chief," he hissed. "You deceived me once. I will not hear any more lies."

Tepua stared at him, stunned. "Lies?"

The Pu-tahi chief turned on her. "You took a great interest in what I told you about the foreigners. Now I know why."

Tepua glared again at Kiore. He tried to straighten up and face her. "*Ariki—*"

"Do not talk now," she ordered. His pained expression stabbed her with remorse as she turned away. As much as she wished to hear his account, she had to answer the Pu-tahi chief.

"Ata-katinga," she said, trying to force a soothing tone. "I intended no deceit."

"You did not send this man of the enemy here to cause trouble in my camp?"

"No."

"You did not know that he was living among your people?"

She let out a long breath. To lie now might salvage the moment, but the truth would surely emerge. And she could not abandon Kiore to Ata-katinga's wrath, whatever he had done.

Quietly she said, "It is true that two outsiders have been living among my people, but they did not come here as enemies. The sea cast them into my waters. They were almost dead when I found them."

"You gave aid to such men?" Ata-katinga turned from Kiore to glower at Tepua. He folded his arms, awaiting her explanation. She was startled to see a bleakness in his eyes along with the anger, as if he mourned the dying of his hopes for peace.

"The sailors I harbor are nothing like the foreigners you

warned us about," she persisted. "They live among us, following our ways, speaking our language." She gestured toward Kiore. "If this man caused any offense, it was through ignorance, not ill will."

The Pu-tahi chief stared at her a moment longer, then faced the captive Kiore. "Let me hear it from your own lips," he demanded. "I want to know why you invaded my compound and fought with my men."

Tepua stifled a protest. It would be better if she could learn the truth in private. But Ata-katinga would sense trickery if she tried to keep the sailor from answering now.

Kiore sent her a searching look, as if asking her advice, but she had none to give. She felt her pulse hammering as she waited for him to speak.

"I came here to consult one of your canoe-masters," Kiore said at last.

Ata-katinga frowned in puzzlement at Tepua. "Is it not true," he asked Kiore, "that the people here have many good navigators? Why would you seek help from one of mine?"

"I am told that your people are the best of all sailors," Kiore answered. "Your canoes are the swiftest and your journeys the longest of any atoll dwellers."

Ata-katinga's fierce expression softened as he said to Tepua, "This foreigner is not the fool I took him to be. Even if he does speak with a barbarous accent."

"It was my intention that the foreign guests not disturb you," Tepua answered. "This man disobeyed my orders."

The Pu-tahi stared at her long and hard before commanding his warriors to lower their weapons. He was a large man and an imposing leader, but behind his tough exterior Tepua sensed his desperate need for the alliance. How powerful must the foreign enemy be to make the Fierce People plead for friendship?

"I will turn this outsider over to you for punishment," said Ata-katinga, stroking his grizzled beard, "but I am not satisfied with his answers, despite his flattering words. I want to question him further. Perhaps he can enlighten us about certain things the you and I have discussed."

Tepua swallowed. "Yes, that is a good suggestion. But I can tell you that I have questioned the man myself. He knows nothing of trouble between foreign sailors and islanders."

"I must determine that for myself," said Ata-katinga. With a meaningful yawn, he added, "But not tonight." He gave a signal for Kiore to be released. Tepua ordered her warriors to take charge of him.

"Your men have spears. . . ." she pointed out to Ata-katinga, hoping that he had not forgotten his earlier pledge to remain unarmed.

"I came here seeking peace," the chief answered. "I have not given up that intention, but I am not a complete fool. Of course I have weapons to protect myself, as do you. I will keep them close at hand."

She knew she could ask for no more. At least Ata-katinga was not stalking off in outrage. "Then keep your spears," she answered. "I trust that you will not want to use them."

On the way out, she came on Paruru where she had left him. The warrior began to fume. "*Ariki,* you cannot let this pass. The weapons—"

She spun on him. "The Pu-tahi did not arm themselves until Kiore invaded their compound."

"And now that the spears are out, how many of us will they kill?"

"None—if you do your job of keeping order," she answered harshly.

When Tepua reached her house, she sent her entire household to other quarters for the night. She ordered lights—burning copra wedges that cast a ruddy illumination. Then she called Kiore inside and gestured for him to sit. For a long moment, she could not find anything to say to him.

"I wished no harm, *ariki,*" he said, breaking the silence.

"Did I warn you to stay away from my visitors?"

"Before they arrived—yes."

She stamped her foot in rage. "Did I send word to come back?"

He shifted his long legs, ill matched to the low stool she had offered him, but did not reply.

"Answer! Why did you disobey?"

His head snapped up. His eyes were a new color, an icy blue. "Did you ever think, *ariki,* that I would have obeyed more willingly if you had confided in me?"

"Confided what? I told you and Nika to hide for your own safety. And to keep the Pu-tahi from stealing the goods from your boat."

"Perhaps that was your reason at first—"

"Did you expect me to send a messenger to explain everything as it happened? I had new reasons to keep you hidden from the Pu-tahi. Everything was going well until you entered their compound and started a fight—"

"I did not start a fight. I showed the guard my gift for the canoe-master. He took the gift, then called his friends to attack. I only fought to save myself."

"The Pu-tahi attacked because they have seen men like you and think they are dangerous."

"I know that now." He shifted his feet. "I am sorry for the trouble I caused," he said grudgingly. "Is that enough?"

"I still want an answer. If you needed help from a Pu-tahi canoe-master, why did you not have me ask?" Kiore looked away, silent. "What were you so eager to find out?"

At last, with reluctance, he told her about Cloud Island, and the possibility of meeting some of his countrymen. He explained how to distinguish vessels of one land from those of another. "Yes," she said stiffly, interrupting him. "I do understand now. You thought I might not wish to help you, that I would prefer to keep you here against your will. But you have always been free to go."

"Tepua, let me finish! Cloud Island can change everything. If I meet a boat from my own land, I need not make the journey myself. I need only give my 'lok-puk' to the master of the vessel, who can take it home and hand it to the ones who must see it. My promise will be kept, and I will be free to come back here.''

She felt tears threatening. ''I would have tried to help you in any case,'' she said softly. Yet she knew that he was too hotheaded, too stubborn and proud to have asked. ''Kiore, how can I be angry with you now that I know what you were thinking?'' She wanted to embrace him but held herself back. ''This trouble you started is not over yet,'' she said, wiping her eyes. ''You will have to face Ata-katinga again.''

Kiore clenched his fists. ''So you want to parade me before that savage and have me recite like a child.''

''He is not a savage,'' Tepua retorted.

''He and his tribe have killed many of your people. And some of mine, too, judging by that tassel of gold hair in his headdress.''

Your kind began the attacks, but you make no mention of that. Aloud, she said, ''So that is what really angers you about Ata-katinga.''

''Maybe it does not bother you to see pieces of dead people used as ornaments.''

Her eyes widened in shock and hurt. Yes, her people wore fringes made from the hair and beards of old men, and from elders and chiefs who had died. ''We honor their ancestors by wearing their hair,'' she flung back. ''This is our custom.''

Kiore set his jaw. ''The hair on Ata-katinga's headdress came from no islander's head.''

''I do not know that. Black or brown hair can be sun-bleached.''

In answer Kiore seized a lock of his own hair and held it out. Tepua stared. In color and texture it bore a dismaying resemblance to the tassel in Ata-katinga's headdress.

''Yes, it could have been mine,'' he hissed. ''Perhaps a

foreign boat struck a reef, or sailors went ashore peacefully. I am told that Pu-tahi like to creep up on their victims.''

Then I would never have known you, she thought as breath caught in her throat and tears began brimming in her eyes. Now she realized how deeply entangled she had become with this outsider. Though foreigners seemed responsible for the conflicts, she was angry at the man who wore foreign hair as a battle trophy.

No, I dare not give in to anger. I must make peace with Ata-katinga. ''Kiore, I cannot ask the Pu-tahi chief about the headdress. There is already too much suspicion between us. Can you not put that aside for one day?''

Kiore leaned close to her. His expression was strange—a mixture of anger, sorrow, and extraordinary tenderness. She did not want to stop him when he touched her face with his fingers, his eyes never leaving hers.

''Sometimes I think there is *aroha* within you, my beautiful woman. Yet tonight you seem to feel nothing. No outrage, no grief over what this man has done.''

She wanted to cry out that yes, she did feel outrage, but too much was at stake here. Regardless of what she felt for Kiore, she dared not put him above the interests of her people.

''Kiore,'' she replied at last, ''it would be too easy for me to hate Ata-katinga. I do not like the hair either. He may have killed to get it.'' She paused. ''Yet now I have good reason to trust him.''

Kiore exhaled, a long deep sigh.

''I promised Ata-katinga to take you back to him,'' she said. ''If you do not go, then I will lose my hopes of peace. But perhaps I can make it easier for you. Perhaps I can get him to remove the headdress for a time.''

She waited, watching Kiore's face. ''That will help,'' he conceded. ''But if he questions me, he will not like some of my answers. He may decide that I am a threat to him.''

She closed her eyes. For a moment she remembered the storm that struck the *motu,* the lashing waves and shrieking winds. How glad she would be to face the gale again, rather than this.

"You know much more about the men of your own kind than the Pu-tahi do," she said at last, recalling some of what Kiore had told her. "Can you explain that foreigners come from different islands and that they war against each other just as we do?"

"Yes—"

"I think that will enlighten him. We do know where these dangerous foreigners came from. Perhaps the men who attacked the islanders are also your enemies."

"They may be."

"That should help him accept you as a friend. If you are clever, you can bring up the question you so dearly wish to know—about the colors of the flags."

Kiore's eyebrows rose and then his face showed his smile of delight. "I think you also want to know about those flags."

The next morning, when Tepua and Kiore went to the Pu-tahi compound, Umia walked with them, bringing a gift. Ata-katinga's dark eyes glittered when he saw what Umia carried. It was one of Kohekapu's best headdresses, magnificently feathered, with a high plumed crest and decorations of rare shell.

The Pu-tahi chief rose from his seat in the shade, emerging into the bright morning sunlight. Tepua stepped forward to address him. "Ata-katinga, my brother and I bring you this as a token of our goodwill. It is our wish that we continue the peaceful discussions that we have begun."

Tepua watched the Pu-tahi's mouth purse as he took the headdress into his big hands and carefully inspected it. She could see that he was dazzled by the rainbow shimmer of feathers. The best ones came from high-island birds never seen in the atolls. They had been a gift to her father from a wide-ranging trader.

Oh, Kohekapu, she thought. *Forgive what we do with*

*your treasure. You wanted to end the raiding and warfare
that claimed so many of our people. A feather headdress is
a small gift in exchange.*

She could scarcely breathe as she watched the Pu-tahi
proudly showing the gift to his men. There were murmurs of
approval all around. Then Ata-katinga removed his old
headdress, handed it to his attendant, and settled the new
one on his head.

"A worthy gift indeed," the Pu-tahi chief announced,
lifting his chin and stroking the fall of rich feathers down
the back of his neck. He took up his old one, fingering the
tassel of gold hair. For an instant, Tepua was afraid that he
would give the old headdress to Umia and expect the young
man to wear it. The moment passed and he handed it back
to the attendant.

After striding around and striking poses for his warriors,
Ata-katinga turned to the sailor. "And now the time has
come for our talk, Narrow-nose." Tepua watched Kiore's
face harden.

"Sit!" said the Pu-tahi, pointing to a mat. When Kiore
had arranged himself, the chief returned to his stool. Tepua
and Umia took the seats reserved for them.

Ata-katinga eyed the sailor with sharp suspicion. "Tepua
tells me that you came to these islands by mistake."

"It could be said so, yes."

"And that you disturbed my compound out of ignorance."

The sailor glared back sullenly, then gave an affirmative
grunt.

"A man who makes two mistakes can make another. Do
not be foolish enough to lie to me. I want to hear what you
know about the foreigners who invade our waters."

Kiore flushed with anger, and Tepua feared that he might
lose his temper and use his fists again, but he seemed to
remember why he was here. Carefully he began to speak.

He explained that the huge winged boats came from
several different lands, and that the people of these lands

often warred against each other. There were also raiders who stole cargoes from honest men.

"It is good that the foreigners fight among themselves," said Ata-katinga with satisfaction. "But someday they will tire of fighting each other and come after us."

"I see no reason for these people to disturb you," said Kiore. "There are rich ports on each side of the ocean, but nothing between."

Ata-katinga looked in puzzlement at Tepua, then back at the sailor. "Rich ports? Where?"

"Far to the east, but not so far as my country, sits a huge land that rises to the sky."

"A high island?" asked the Pu-tahi.

"Yes. Very rich and very large. There is a heavy kind of stone there that my people find pleasing. More pleasing . . . than fine feathers. It shimmers like sunlight on water. People make beautiful things from this stone."

Ata-katinga laughed. "I have seen the disks that foreigners treasure," he said. "They are useful only for children's games."

"My people think otherwise," Kiore insisted.

"Can the loud weapons be made of that same stone?"

"No. There is another kind, less rare, and far more useful for tools and weapons. I see nothing like it on this atoll."

Tepua bit her lip as the questioning continued. "Tell me about the weapons you brought with you," Ata-katinga demanded.

Kiore hesitated, glancing toward Tepua. In preparing for this meeting, she had urged him to describe the incident with the thunder-club. She knew now that Kiore's ill-fated companion had aimed his weapon at the sky, intending to harm no one.

Ata-katinga might accept this as a sign that Tepua's visitors were less aggressive than the foreigners he had seen. But if Kiore denied having any thunder weapons, the Pu-tahi would not believe him.

"We *had* a weapon," Kiore began cautiously. "Its

purpose was to make noise—to frighten people so they would not attack us." When he finished describing the death of his friend, Ata-katinga's eyes showed a glimmer of sympathy.

But the Pu-tahi grew curious about the fate of the dropped thunder-club, asking Tepua several questions about it. She answered truthfully, describing the failed search, and was relieved when Ata-katinga's attention finally returned to Kiore.

The sailor went on, describing the chiefs of the distant lands, the women, the foods, the animals. At last the conversation shifted to the events at Cloud Island.

"Are the evil foreigners who stopped there your countrymen?" Ata-katinga asked.

Tepua glanced nervously at Kiore. They had both hoped that Ata-katinga would not be so blunt. What could the sailor say now that would not anger the Pu-tahi?

"Perhaps you can help me learn the answer," replied Kiore cautiously. He spoke of the colored flags that identified the homelands of foreign vessels. Tepua saw sweat gathering on his brow as he waited to hear Ata-katinga's response. Beside her, Umia leaned forward in eagerness to hear.

Ata-katinga scowled, creasing the tattoos that covered his cheeks and brow. "You leave me with a puzzle, Narrow-nose. The vessel I saw remained for two days. I was able to examine it from sea as well as from land. Yet I observed no colors flying over its stern."

"That is troubling news," Kiore said, and Tepua could not tell if his expression showed relief or disappointment. "Honest men fly flags, to tell what chief they serve. If you saw none, then the foreigners you met were raiders, outlawed by my land and all others. It is no surprise that such men would attack you."

"Perhaps they were raiders," said the Pu-tahi chief. "They took everything that they wanted and gave nothing."

"They were not my countrymen," declared Kiore. "But

perhaps other boats have been seen off Cloud Island, some that did show colors.''

Ata-katinga shouted a question to one of his men. Someone brought an old canoe-master, who crouched at the feet of his chief.

"I heard of such a thing from a Cloud Islander,'' the canoe-master related. "In one corner it had stripes of red and blue and white, some straight and some crossed like this.'' He showed with his fingers.

Tepua turned to see Kiore gazing steadily at Ata-katinga, his face hiding whatever he felt. Last night he had described to her the emblem of his country, and this seemed to match. Yet she knew that Kiore did not trust Ata-katinga.

"That is not my flag,'' the outsider said quietly. "Perhaps your people have never seen my countrymen. If you ever do, I am sure they will give you a good welcome.''

TWENTY-ONE

Tepua slept well that night, warmed by the hope that Kiore might find some of his own people, fulfill his obligation, and return to her. But that would come later, after the Pu-tahi were gone. The alliance she wanted had yet to be worked out.

When she heard Ata-katinga's bellow again, Tepua thought for a moment that she was still asleep, dreaming of the uproar that Kiore had started on the previous night.

"Where is that narrow-nosed demon?" came a cry. "I will use his guts to bind my canoe! Where is that treacherous woman-chief?"

In darkness she sat bolt upright, her heart jumping. When she came out of her house into the pale, dawn light, she saw warriors on all sides, a crowd of angry men. Her own guards had formed a bristling wall to defend her. Ata-katinga and his warriors were trying to get closer, shouting fiercely and waving their spears.

"Stop this!" Tepua cried. "No weapons!"

The commotion halted for a moment, men breathing hard through flared nostrils. The sullen looks on their faces showed how they resented her intrusion. It was clear to her that both sides were spoiling for a fight. "Go back to your mat weaving, woman!" called one of the Pu-tahi. "Making war or peace is a task for men."

"Ata-katinga, does this filth speak for you?" she demanded.

The visiting chief pushed his way to the front of the crowd. He seemed twice as big as before; anger had inflated him. His tattoos appeared darker and more grotesque than ever, and his frown deeper. Behind him a thicket of Pu-tahi spears pointed directly at her.

"Mistress of treachery," said Ata-katinga. "This time your foreigner's offense cannot be excused."

"His offense?" Her knees felt weak. Kiore again? He had no further reason to trouble the Pu-tahi. He had assured her that he would stay away.

"Was it not you who sent the fair-haired thief to steal my headdress?" Ata-katinga narrowed his eyes. "Now I know why you gave me the other one. I am not stupid. I saw that the hair in the tassel was the same as the hair on that man's head. If I catch him, I will have two trophies!"

"I gave you my father's headdress in good faith. And yes, if you must know, I found yours offensive."

"Ah, so you admit— "

She interrupted, feeling her face grow hot. "Only that I found the sight of your war trophy distasteful. You came here to renounce war! I did not wish to insult you, so I offered another, hoping that you would put yours aside."

"So that it could be stolen and burned?"

Tepua's mouth dropped open. "Burned!"

With a growl, Ata-katinga thrust out a fist. He opened his hand, showing her a mass of soot-blackened feathers and shells. In the midst of the tangle lay the charred fringe of golden hair.

"Someone took this headdress from my guesthouse. I said nothing at first, because I did not wish to accuse you wrongly. Then my warriors found this at a campfire in the woods." He shoved the remains at her, so close that she could smell the singed feathers. "They found something else as well!" In his other hand he held up the leg coverings that Kiore often wore.

For a moment she could not breathe. Glancing around in

confusion and disbelief, she saw looks of fury on every Pu-tahi face. "I had no part in this," she protested.

"Am I to believe that the outsiders did this on their own? Good. Then I will deal with them myself. But you must find those men and deliver them to me."

Her heartbeat went wild. The Pu-tahi had found the headdress but not the men. Kiore had escaped, at least for the moment.

In fury, she stared at the Pu-tahi chief. She wanted to shout that his accusations were false, but misgivings kept her silent. Could Kiore have gone to Ata-katinga's guest-house, stolen the thing, and then flung it into his campfire? Perhaps he was capable of such a foolish act.

"I will find the foreigners," she offered in a tight voice. "If either is guilty, then I will deal out the punishment."

"No, Tepua-mua-ariki. If you value my friendship, you will bring *me* the foreigners." Without waiting for an answer, he gestured to his warriors, ordering them back to his compound. Several paused to shake spears at her, grimace, and shout threats before they departed. It was all she could do to keep her own men from replying.

She turned, and was glad to find Sea-snake behind her. It did not surprise her that the *kaito-nui* was absent at this crucial moment. "Find Paruru," she whispered as she drew Sea-snake aside. "Bring him to me if you can."

"And what of the outsiders? Should we do as Ata-katinga demanded?"

She sighed. "Yes, search for them. But if you succeed, keep the sailors hidden. I will talk with them first."

And then what? Turn them over to the Pu-tahi? She could not decide that now. She found Maukiri in the crowd, put her arm around her cousin, and staggered back inside her house.

The sun had barely risen and the shadows were still long. No breeze reached the humid interior of the island, where Paruru led the foreigners along a seldom-used trail. Sweat trickled down his nape and forehead and dampened the palms of his hands. The warrior shifted the heavy shark-toothed sword in his grip.

Paruru kept stopping, listening to every leaf that rustled, every bird that cried. No one was going to creep up on him. If a Pu-tahi spy found him now, he would slash open his belly and leave him for the crabs. If one of Paruru's own men appeared, he was prepared to do the same.

His warriors were taking Sea-snake's orders. Paruru remained *kaito-nui* in name only. Yet he had not forgotten his obligations. He intended to save the high chief from her folly, even at the cost of his own life.

Ahead along the trail he saw a place where the forest thinned. Confident that they could not be surprised here, he beckoned Nika and Kiore to catch up with him. When he reached a certain palm tree, recognizable by the double bend in its trunk, he paused. Yesterday he had pointed this tree out to Cone-shell.

Just above Paruru's head was a wrapping of sennit, barely visible against the rough surface of the trunk. *Three times around. Good.* Cone-shell had fulfilled his promise. Varoa's chief had sent for his warriors, and they had come during the night. Now he was ready to strike.

Paruru saw the sailors glance at the marking and frown with puzzlement. They knew nothing of his plans. When they saw Varoa's men, he would have some quick explaining to do.

Paruru heard a rustle in the undergrowth. *Only a rat,* he told himself, and wondered if he should take its presence as a sign. Why was he so uneasy? His actions today, he thought, would protect his people. The gods should be pleased.

He turned, carefully studying every low bush, but saw nothing out of place. Then he looked at Nika, who carried the foreign weapon in its mat wrapping. The thunder-club was prepared now, its load of stones tightly packed into its hollow. How Paruru's palms itched to hold it. *But not yet.*

Paruru had gained Nika's cooperation with a ruse. After hearing that Ata-katinga was asking about the missing thunder-club, Paruru embellished the news, adding that the Pu-tahi was planning to mount their own search for the weapon.

When the sailors doubted Paruru's report, he convinced them to leave their campsite awhile, then led them to where they could hide and watch while Pu-tahi crept up on it. The eels obligingly came. The foreigners did not guess that the Pu-tahi were seeking a missing headdress. After seeing savages tear their camp apart, Nika decided to flee with Paruru. Kiore, reluctant to lose sight of the weapon, agreed to follow. Since last night, the three men had been constantly moving from one hiding place to another.

"How much longer?" asked Kiore irritably as the *kaito-nui* led the way through dappled sunlight. "When will these Pu-tahi give up looking for us?"

Paruru gestured for silence. He pointed toward the path ahead, where marshy soil, littered with ferns, gave way to denser forest. As the men left wet ground behind, a Varoa warrior stepped silently onto the trail ahead. Kiore gave a cry of alarm.

"He is our friend!" Paruru hissed.

The *kaito-nui* turned, saw the look of mistrust in Kiore's eyes. Another Varoa warrior slipped behind the two foreigners.

"Nika—" Kiore shouted. Paruru heard a note of warning in his foreign words, and an angry rebuke from his companion. "What are we doing here?" Kiore demanded of Paruru. "Is it the Pu-tahi who want the weapon . . . or someone else?"

Once again the other sailor began to argue with Nika. There was no more time for games. At Paruru's signal the warrior nearest Kiore raised his club. . . .

Somehow the sailor sensed the movement. He knocked the man's arm aside and delivered a blow to his belly. Before the second warrior could get to him, Kiore dove into the thickest part of the brush. "Get him," ordered Paruru. The heavyset warrior charged after the vanished sailor, but his shark-toothed sword snagged on a branch, delaying him a precious instant. The other warrior recovered and followed his companion.

"They will get him," Paruru said confidently to Nika.

"But he—"

"Kiore is stubborn," Paruru tried to explain. "I told him what will happen if the Pu-tahi find us. They will use the thunder-club against Tepua, and their spears against the rest of us."

Nika seemed to waver and Paruru wondered if he would have to leave him behind. But if Nika did not carry the weapon, then Cone-shell might insist on taking it. "We must hurry," the warrior said. "Friends are waiting."

"Friends?"

"Just ahead, I have men waiting to stand with us. We will not have to face the Pu-tahi alone." He pointed down the trail. A muscle twitched in the sailor's jaw. Nika peered anxiously in both directions, but before he could make up his mind, a crowd of Varoa men emerged from the thicket ahead.

"What was the commotion?" asked Cone-shell, at the head of his company of warriors. The chief was arrayed for battle in a spiked headdress of coconut fronds and a war kilt. Paruru had never seen him like this. He recalled tales of long ago, when Cone-shell had led an attack on a neighboring island.

Paruru sensed Nika's fright at this sudden appearance of so many warriors. He moved closer, preparing to use restraint if Nika should bolt. But Paruru felt his own fears growing as well.

He gazed at Cone-shell with new respect. *I am a reef shark among the fish,* he thought, *but he is a great white shark that I have coaxed into the lagoon.* When Cone-shell was done feeding, he wondered, who would be left?

Whatever happened today, Tepua must survive. Paruru

had promised the gods that he would not let Cone-shell
seize her power. Now he began to doubt that he could keep
his word.

"Where is the other foreigner?" demanded Varoa's
chief.

Paruru struggled to get out his words. "He . . . ran off.
Your men . . . will catch him in the swamp."

"And if they do not?"

"He knows nothing that can hurt us . . . if we move
quickly."

"Then go!" At Cone-shell's signal his men fanned out
behind him, creeping silently through the undergrowth, their
spears held low. Paruru led them along the shortest route to
the Pu-tahi's compound. All the while he made certain that
Nika remained close beside him.

The sailor seemed terrified, his face awash with sweat,
his eyes shifting crazily. Paruru realized that despite Nika's
talk of battles and weapons, the young man was no warrior.
But Nika had done the important favor that his brother had
asked of him—preparing the weapon, teaching Paruru how
to use it.

The underbrush started to thin. Now the men were
drawing near Tepua's guesthouses, heading for the compound where the Pu-tahi would be gathered about their
chief. Paruru felt a growing dread as he advanced with the
others. His victory was almost at hand, yet it would be
Cone-shell's victory as well.

The *kaito-nui* gave a signal. The men crouched, taking
cover behind a stand of yellow-flowered *kokuru* shrubs.
Paruru could not see through the greenery to the compound
beyond, but he sensed an eerie silence there.

Keeping low, Paruru crept forward, parting the thin
kokuru stems to peer through. Ahead he saw the compound,
its neatly thatched houses, its clean yard, its low surrounding wall of white coral. Where were the Pu-tahi? Daringly,
he thrust his head farther out, until he could look to the side

in both directions. No one in sight. Yet it was too early for anyone to have left for assembly ground.

He listened to the distant boom of the surf and faint cries of birds. Why were no children splashing in the shallows? Why were no women greeting each other along the shore?

Then a frightening chorus of yells from behind made clear that he had been betrayed. The air was filled with heavy stones that struck heads and sent men sprawling. The remaining warriors of Varoa cried out in astonishment, rose, and charged into the open.

Paruru grabbed Nika's arm and dragged him forward, hurrying out of range of the slingers, then wheeling to face the foe. Only a fool would let the enemy keep its advantage of cover. Now the ambushers would have to show themselves if they wanted to attack again.

His blood pounded as he stood beside Nika, watching for the enemy to appear. For a long moment all was still again. An insect whined. A tropic bird flew overhead. Then he saw branches shaking, bushes parting.

Suddenly a forest of spears emerged from the shadows. Too many spears. They could not all belong to Pu-tahi. They did not even look like Pu-tahi spears.

Cone-shell's men stood with the lagoon at their backs. Paruru knew at once that his force was badly outnumbered. The attackers came closer, and he groaned in despair. Half were Ahiku warriors! The Pu-tahi dogs stood in one fierce line, the local warriors in another. And Tepua-mua-ariki, arrayed in her own spiked headdress, was leading her men in the charge.

With wild cries, the battle began, spear parrying spear, club striking club. Dust swirled, sun flashed on polished wood and the sudden brightness of blood when a man went down. In the midst of the onslaught, Paruru realized that Nika had slipped away from him.

He turned with alarm, but saw that the sailor had not gone far. Nika was behind him, crouching by the low compound wall. He had already unwrapped the weapon.

Paruru had wanted this used against the Pu-tahi, but now it would be turned against Ahiku as well. Even worse, Cone-shell seemed determined to deal the thunderous blow. Paruru saw him coming toward Nika as the sailor made his final preparations—cocking the beak, sprinkling powder in the bowl. Paruru felt a coldness in his gut as he caught the fierce glitter in Cone-shell's eyes. He had been *kaito-nui* for too long to give up his loyalties in a single day.

If Cone-shell seized the weapon and used it against Ahiku Clan, the damage would be far worse than anything Paruru had anticipated. The old ways of battle would mean nothing if a man no longer needed strength and agility, if a man could kill merely with a pull of his finger. Pu-tahi dogs deserved such a death. Ahiku men did not. Neither did Tepua.

Paruru's only hope was to reach Nika before Cone-shell did. The warrior felt as if he were moving in a strange slow dream, his legs weighted, his arms slow and heavy. As he threw himself into a lunge he heard a foreign shout behind him. *Kiore's voice.* Nika's eyes were wide with terror and he seemed not to hear.

Cone-shell was approaching from one direction, Paruru from another. Nika rose, staggered backward, then lifted the thunder-club. In seeming confusion, he pointed it first at the line of attackers and then at Varoa's chief. Everything around Paruru became a wild blur, but at the center, as if at the calm eye of a hurricane, he saw Nika's forefinger curl about the long tooth under the weapon.

"No!" Paruru cried, his hand reaching to stop him. *Too late!* The bird's beak fell. Sparks burst upward from the pan.

Paruru heard the roar at the same moment that he felt the pain, tearing down the outside of his arm. He fell, one hand clutching his wound, the other his head, where the echo of the terrible noise sounded again and again. Rolling over, he stared through clouds of drifting smoke and black patches that were closing out his vision.

He saw Cone-shell toppling, his hands clutching his breast, his mouth open in a scream that Paruru could not hear. And blood sheeted down Cone-shell's ribs like the ebbing tide running over coral.

TWENTY-TWO

Tepua watched with disbelief as Cone-shell and Paruru fell. The smoke cloud spread. Warriors cried out in panic. Varoa's men scattered, some diving into the lagoon.

Sea-snake grabbed Tepua's wrist, tried to drag her to safety, but she shook him off. "Wait!" she shouted, watching Nika where he crouched beyond the wall. His eyes were wild, his face slick with sweat. He staggered to his feet, swinging the weapon from side to side, showing its terrible mouth. . . .

"It must not speak again!" she cried. She charged forward, her spear aimed at Nika's belly. Then she saw Kiore running toward him as well—running right into her path.

She screamed a warning as she tried to aim high. Kiore ducked. Nika dodged and stumbled. The point missed both men, but Nika was down. With an enraged roar Kiore was on him, jerking the thunder-maker from his grip.

Kiore became a madman, smashing the weapon on the coral wall. The air rang with the sound of battering until pieces broke away and the rest fell, bent and twisted, to the ground. "The thing is dead," he said hoarsely, his chest heaving, his eyes bright with tears.

Tepua gazed at him in astonishment. He had destroyed the thunder-club, the work of his own people. "The battle is over!" she called to the dazed men who remained at the scene. "Let there now be peace among us."

Varoa's warriors held on to their weapons. Nervously they edged toward their fallen chief.

"No more fighting!" she shouted as Pu-tahi moved to cut them off. "We pledged our goodwill to the gods."

The Pu-tahi and the men of Varoa cast threatening looks at each other. "Come away," called Ata-katinga to his warriors. "We have no more business here," he said in disgust. "We are finished with these deceivers."

Tepua felt outraged by his words, but was glad to see the men following their orders. The Pu-tahi assembled about their chief. Slowly, one by one, the stunned warriors of Varoa put down their weapons.

A crowd had gathered about Cone-shell's remains. Tepua pushed her way through and looked down. Blood pooled in the gaping hole in his chest, welled up, and spilled over, staining the white sand. She gasped. Ata-katinga had told what the foreign weapons could do, but his words had not conveyed the horror.

"He is gone," said a warrior who knelt beside the body. "No one can help him." He began his wail of mourning, and others took up the cry.

Tepua turned, leaving the men of Varoa to their grief. She caught sight of Paruru, also lying still. "Send someone for Heka," she told Sea-snake. "She must know what has happened to her brother." Unwillingly she stepped around the mourners to look closer at the state of Paruru's body. She saw blood seeping from small wounds on his upper arm. . . .

Suddenly Paruru groaned and stirred. "He lives!" Tepua shouted. "Call a healer!" Paruru's hands went to his ears and his face twisted with pain. When she tried to speak with him, he did not seem to hear.

At last he looked in her direction. "Noise . . . in my ears . . ." he said weakly. "Not stopping." He clutched his head again. He was trembling all over and his face had gone pale.

He looked at her with wide, pain-filled eyes. "I cannot

hear you, *ariki*. But listen. This is . . . my doing. I planned it all. The burned headdress . . . and the weapon. Do not blame the outsiders.''

How can I not blame them? she wanted to ask. She motioned for Paruru to stay where he was until a *tahunga* could help him. There was no need to consider his punishment now.

At last she turned her attention to the sailors. Flanked by a pair of her warriors, Nika stood trembling beneath a palm tree. Guarded by another pair of men, Kiore sat on the wall, grimly watching the crowd. She wanted to believe that he had tried to prevent this violence. He had disarmed Nika and destroyed the weapon, but he was not blameless. None of this could have happened without the presence of these two men.

She approached Kiore, following his gaze as it went from Cone-shell's mourners to her stricken *kaito-nui*. ''May the gods forgive us,'' Kiore said quietly.

She had no words for him, no comfort. Her feelings were in turmoil. ''I must go,'' she said. ''I must deal with Ata-katinga now.'' She saw Kiore turn away in anguish, and wished she could stay with him.

Tepua tried to compose herself as she recalled the events of the morning. When news had reached her that warriors of Varoa were lurking in the forest, she had quickly conferred with Ata-katinga, agreeing that her men would fight beside his. For a brief while there had been an alliance between herself and the Pu-tahi chief. Now she saw Ata-katinga holding the ruined thunder-club, turning it over and over, his tattooed face dark with fury. Beyond him, she saw his men carrying their equipment from the guesthouses. They were leaving the atoll!

''Ata-katinga, I know what you are thinking,'' she said as she came up to him. ''But I was also deceived. I truly thought the weapon lost.''

He glanced up at her and tossed the ruined thunder-club aside. ''There is no more to say, Tepua. Whatever hopes I had are ended. I wanted you to stand with me against a common enemy, but I came to you too late."

"It is not so!" she answered. "Ata-katinga, my *kaito-nui* acted without my knowledge. It was his idea to attack you, not mine. Be glad that he relented at the last moment and tried to stop Nika from using the weapon. Otherwise you would be the one whose chest was torn out."

He eyed her fiercely. "How can that be?"

"Paruru has admitted everything. He could not stomach having your people as allies. Ask him how the weapon came to be here. And about the burned headdress as well."

"I may do that, Tepua-ariki. But it does not change anything." He gestured impatiently at his men to hurry.

"Ata-katinga, listen. I made a mistake and now I have suffered for it. I invited the foreigners to live among my people. We had never seen such men before. How could I know what they would do to us?"

"I do not fault you for that, *ariki*. Others have been fooled when they first met the many-colored men." For a moment he seemed lost in thought.

She searched his face, hoping to see a hint of softening in his deep eyes. He appeared implacable, but that was his way. She knew a gesture that might move him, only one. It would bring her more pain than she thought she could bear.

She remembered Kiore as she had just seen him, his hair dusty and rumpled, his face bristly. Yet his eyes, when he gazed at her, had gleamed with the same penetrating aquamarine that always made her breath catch in her throat.

She recalled the time she had spent close to him, enjoying his salty scent, warming to the gentle touch of his hands.

Tepua delayed a moment longer. Beyond the Pu-tahi chief and the cluster of houses the lagoon lay placid, a brilliant blue, unruffled by wind or by the troubles ashore. Wispy clouds hung overhead, but the tranquillity they suggested was a lie. There could be no joy for her here. Not now, or ever again.

When she spoke at last, Tepua's voice sounded strange to

her ears, as if another woman were speaking in her place, a cold, hard woman, a woman of ashes. "Ata-katinga, I am sending the outsiders away. Now. Today. They will leave this atoll and never be allowed to return."

The Pu-tahi eyed her for a long moment. "And what of those chiefs and elders of yours who still oppose our agreement?"

"There will be no more opposition. How can there be? When they see Cone-shell's body, they will understand everything you have said about the foreign invaders."

Ata-katinga drew in his breath. He turned to the left and then to the right as if seeking help from some invisible guide. Suddenly he barked a command that sent one of his men scurrying.

They were coming back! Tepua watched with astonishment and relief as the Pu-tahi began returning to the guest-houses. Her satisfaction lasted only a moment. Now she had to give the orders she dreaded. It was easier to let the woman of ashes speak instead.

"Bring the foreign boat!" she called hoarsely, sending someone to recruit the fifty men needed to move it from its hiding place ashore. "Tell the priests to release the sailors' goods. Fill the foreigners' water drum. Bring the provisions from their stockpile, and anything else we can spare."

Umia came forward, offering his help. She took his arm and walked with him back to the silent refuge of her house.

Paruru lay on a mat in Tepua's guesthouse. The *tahunga* was finished tending his wounds and Heka had ceased weeping over him. The noise was fading from his ears; he could understand some of what his sister said.

"What will you do now, brother?" she asked.

Paruru stared dully at the thatch above him. "I have no place on this atoll. I cannot stay."

"The gods played a cruel trick on you. If they had not sent the foreign boat—"

"Yes, sister, but I do not blame the gods for my fate." He

sat up slowly and found that his dizziness was almost gone. "I must go away, but there is still a small service I can perform. It cannot make up for my offenses, but I would like to do that much for Tepua."

Heka tried to stop him, but he pushed her hand aside and went to the doorway. When he stood outside in the open air, he felt more of his strength returning. The weapon had left painful wounds and burns on his arm, but the rest of his body felt sound.

He walked to the shore, where the foreign craft floated at anchor once again. The supplies were being loaded, boys handing up baskets of food. He saw the outsiders already aboard, glumly stowing their goods and readying their sails. Tepua was nowhere in sight, and neither were the Pu-tahi.

Glancing behind him, Paruru caught a glimpse of moving figures. He climbed a small knoll for a better view. Then he saw that a crowd had gathered at the assembly ground, Tepua and the chiefs meeting with Ata-katinga again. He groaned, knowing that now he was powerless to stop them.

Paruru turned his back on that troubling scene and once more approached the foreign boat. This time he went closer, wading out into the warm, shallow water. He knew that the sailors had every reason to despise him. Yet he had saved Nika's life, and perhaps also Kiore's, by concealing the turtle-killing offense. Perhaps they had not forgotten that.

"Nika! Kiore!" he called to them. The men looked up from their work, scowling. "You two cannot sail alone," Paruru shouted. "You need another hand." He knew that they had failed to find another crewman. Since Paruru had killed their original companion, it seemed fitting that he take the man's place.

The foreigners did not answer him. "Let me come with you," Paruru called. "I am strong, and I know the people of these atolls. I can show you how to catch fish and survive on the sea."

Still they did not reply. Paruru wondered if these two had learned anything at all during their stay here. He had made such an effort to teach them the customs of the atoll. . . .

"You are my brother," he called to the red-haired sailor. "We share everything. I have given you much and now it is your turn. I ask you for my share in the *vaka*."

The two foreigners glanced at each other, exchanged a few words. Paruru was aware that many people were watching him, listening to his pleas. But now he was nothing in their eyes, a man who had betrayed his chief. No one could be lower than that.

Paruru took a few steps forward, water lapping at his waist. Then Kiore gave a signal. "Come!" he said. Paruru threw himself into the lagoon. The burning of salt water on his wounds made him cry out but he managed to swim. With powerful kicks he reached the boat and let the sailors help him aboard.

Unsteadily he tried to find a place for himself in the foreign craft. At once he felt queasy, though the boat lay at anchor. The feel was nothing like that of the stable canoes of his people. The outlandish vessel seemed to roll whenever anyone moved, though it did not tip far.

"You are well prepared," he said with a false heartiness, looking around at the large collection of drums, the baskets of food, the heaped coconuts beneath the thwarts. In one corner he saw pearl-shell fishhooks that Nika had gathered. A roll of sailcloth lay near the mast. He glanced at it, remembering its strength. "We will go fast in this boat," he said. "And I will call on the spirits of my ancestors, who are Nika's as well."

He chattered on, but the men seemed not to hear him. He began examining the boat's gear, knowing he would have to learn how to use it. So much had happened since he first pursued this vessel and kept it from crashing on the reef. He had been eager then to learn the secrets of the strange rigging. Now, he feared, the knowledge would be hard won.

He sighed and looked out at the flotilla of canoes assembling around him. Paruru understood their purpose.

They were to make certain that the sailors got under way, and did not try to turn back.

And on the beach a crowd was growing, people coming from all directions to bemoan the departure of the foreigners. He saw Maukiri at the fore, wading into the water while she gashed her forehead with a shark-tooth flail. Others came behind her as the sailors pulled up their anchor. He saw Heka standing on higher ground, her own forehead glistening with blood. The moans and cries grew louder.

He felt tears gather in his eyes. A heaviness settled in his chest as he watched his sister. The proud frigate bird of Piho Clan would not let his disgrace weaken her, but she would always grieve for the loss of her brother.

But where was Tepua? Paruru blinked back his tears and tried to find the *ariki,* but she was out of sight now, undoubtedly still at the assembly ground. Did she care so little about the foreigners that she would not mourn their departure?

The mainsail's canvas filled and the boat began to pull away from the crowded shore. Planks groaned, ropes creaked, sails flapped, fittings jingled. What noises this craft made! He wondered how anyone could tolerate it.

The boat wallowed and lumbered in the light breeze. With longing, he watched the escort canoes skimming swiftly and silently over the lagoon. Then he forced himself to look away.

This life was finished for him. There would be another, but one that he could not imagine.

Paruru set his gaze forward. He did not look at the sailors, or the people along the beach, or the graceful palms that shaded the shore. He kept his attention fixed firmly on the pass as the boat sailed out of the lagoon.

TWENTY-THREE

Paruru had watched this boat sail on the ocean, but he had not imagined how it would feel under him. As the wind stiffened, the boat heeled over and spray flew from the bow. For a time Paruru did nothing but clutch the thwarts fiercely, convinced that he was about to be plunged into the waves.

The outsiders showed no such fear. They even raised a second triangular sheet in front of the mainsail. Paruru had never seen a vessel fly such an expanse of cloth. When the wind strengthened, the craft leaned harder, groaning and creaking more than ever. Paruru cried out in alarm but the sailors ignored him.

Slowly he began to realize that the vessel was supposed to lean like this, that the masts were in no danger of breaking, that the sails would hold. He would have to get used to the feel of this demon's boat . . . and to many new things.

When the shadows of sails had grown long on the water, Paruru noticed the flotilla making a change in course. He glanced at one of the accompanying canoes and saw someone pointing toward a speck on the horizon. Yes, he knew where they were headed now. They would spend the night at a small, uninhabited atoll called Beach-of-shells.

Running downwind, with sails flying out to either side like wings, they made good speed. The escort canoes kept up, with no apparent difficulty. Soon he made out the fringed tops of palm trees.

Beach-of-shells was a tiny gem, with a safe broad channel through its reef. Unfortunately, the islets were too small to support a permanent settlement. As the boat entered the lagoon Paruru noticed remains of temporary shelters made of sticks and coconut mid-ribs lashed together. He knew that this was a popular stopover for voyagers crossing between larger atolls.

The canoes glided up to the narrow beach, but the foreigners, with their deeper keel, stayed offshore. The outsiders threw out their hooked anchor, then lashed several short uprights in place to rig their hanging beds.

Kiore climbed into his and lay there swinging slowly, his arm dangling down. Nika brought out his little flute and began to play a mournful tune. For a time Paruru heard only the strange, sad music, and the cries of the birds that flew overhead. He noticed that someone ashore was building a cook fire while other men waded into the lagoon to spear the abundant fish.

The foreigners ignored these activities. Perhaps they intended to eat from what they had aboard. But why deplete their supplies, he wondered, when good food could be found here?

Paruru had offered to help these sailors survive. Now he felt he must prove himself. Gritting his teeth against the pain of salt water on his wounds, he flung himself into the lagoon and quickly reached the shallows. He strode ashore, curious to see what he could find.

He improvised a fish spear from a *mikimiki* branch and quickly caught more than he thought the sailors could eat. Using coconut husks and fallen wood, he built a small fire, setting the fish to cook on skewers. He broke open several coconuts, cut the meat out in chunks, and laid it on leaves. ''Come eat!'' he called to the sailors.

At first they merely scowled at him, but when he held up a chunk of roasted fish, he saw Nika lick his lips. Finally, the sailors stripped off most of their garments and swam ashore. "This island has good food," Paruru said proudly as he glanced down at the meal he had provided.

The men said nothing, but took their portions and began to eat. Paruru carried his own aside. Was this the way it would always be? he asked himself. Would these men ever again accept him as their friend? He ate quickly, disposed of his bones and other leavings, then went to take a walk on the tiny seaward shore. Glancing toward the southeast, with the setting sun warming his cheek, he fancied that he could still see his home atoll far in the distance.

Home? No. He must not think of it anymore.

Paruru blinked, then stared once again at the horizon. *Impossible.* Yet something was definitely there. As he watched, the speck grew larger, until he recognized it as a sail. A canoe was coming swiftly, heading directly toward him.

Tepua watched from the deck of her *pahi* as the silhouettes of palm trees grew larger against the pale orange sky. She felt an ache inside that she thought she might have to carry forever. Yet if she could have a few last words with Kiore, feel his arms about her one more time, then perhaps she could accept what she had done.

She glanced up at the billowing mat-sail. The winds had been good to her. Despite her late start she would reach her destination by sunset. Then she would have her chance—to make some small amends to Kiore for how she had treated him.

The leader of the flotilla had told her that he planned to stop for the night at this tiny atoll. What if he had changed course? As her canoe approached the pass she felt a cold surge of fear. If the sailors had not stopped here, then she would never see Kiore again. . . .

The island appeared deserted. Bracing herself against the pitching of the deck, Tepua stood for a better look. "What is out there?" Maukiri asked, coming up beside her. "*Aue!*"

Tepua followed her cousin's arm and suddenly cried with delight. Paruru, looking dumbfounded, was standing on a coral boulder at the edge of the channel. Evidently he recognized her, for he left his perch to pluck a small palm frond, then came back to wave it in welcome.

When her men brought her *pahi* into the tiny lagoon, the warriors ashore scrambled into the water. *"Maeva ariki!"* they cried, raising their spears to greet her as she stood on the deck. She acknowledged them, but her attention turned to the two men seated by a fire near the end of the islet.

Kiore stood up, staring at her in evident disbelief. Nika shouted to Maukiri and flung himself into the lagoon with a huge splash.

Tepua waited a moment longer as her canoe glided in. Then she jumped down to wade ashore through the shallows. Kiore's mouth still hung open as she approached him. Sorrow and longing warred in his eyes and in new lines that had appeared on his forehead. She wanted to smooth away the tracks of grief.

"Please listen," she said softly as she leaned toward him, pressed her mouth to his. His lips were warm, but unresponsive. His arms hung woodenly by his side.

She felt her hopes sink. Was he already gone from her, in spirit if not in body? "Oh, Kiore," she whispered. "How it hurts to want you, but not be able to have you!"

He stared at her in bewilderment. His eyes searched hers, and as they did, his sorrow seemed to ease. "That is the truth," she said. "I will not hide it any longer."

She felt his hand take hers, in the way a friend would touch as well as a lover. "Walk with me," she said.

Tepua led him to a place on the seaward side of the islet. The sun was setting, huge and red above the water. Close to shore, waves broke on the reef, erupting in plumes of spray.

"Tepua, you do not have to explain," Kiore said when they had seated themselves in a sheltered place. "I understand why Nika and I must go."

She gazed into his eyes, their color strangely muted by

the redness of the light. She answered softly. "I have thought about this awhile. All the trouble that you and Nika caused came from ignorance, not from bad intentions. I did not send you away as a punishment."

"For the sake of friendship with the Pu-tahi—" His voice held the sound of resignation, not bitterness.

"Yes."

"Are they satisfied now? Do you have what you want from them?" Despite the pain this had caused him, he seemed earnestly to hope for her success.

"Everything is settled," she said. "We have finally ended our fighting. There will be peace now between my people and those who used to raid our shores."

"That is good to hear," he replied, and an odd faraway look came into his eyes. "I have always thought fighting a poor way to settle arguments." He glanced ruefully down at the healing wounds on his arms, reminders of his bout with the Pu-tahi. "I often wished I could find another way." He lifted her hand, pressed her fingers gently.

"You are doing something important," he said. "Perhaps I was too shortsighted to see it before." He gave a short laugh. "If you keep this peace, you will accomplish what my people, with all their power, cannot."

"Yes—" She leaned closer, resting her cheek against his shoulder.

"I know," he said, stroking her hair gently. "The cost for us is high."

"I did not wish to send you away in anger."

"And I did not wish to be sent." Kiore turned his head, kissed her, and said, "I only wish we had met in a time and place where your people and mine did not find it so easy to harm each other."

"I hope that someday there can be peace between your people and mine."

"Then may the gods speed that day," said Kiore, pulling her closer. For a while they held each other in silence.

At last she asked, "Where will you go after this?"

"Not to Cloud Island. I cannot say if the islanders would welcome me or plunge their spears into my gut. We are heading far to the northwest, to a port where honest traders call."

"Will you take Paruru to your homeland?"

"If he wishes. Or he may find a place on one of the islands we pass."

"I wish no harm to come to him. We are all angry at Paruru, but his exile is punishment enough." Gently she began stroking the small of Kiore's back.

"Do not fret, Tepua. We three need each other to survive. We will put aside our differences, at least long enough to reach our destination."

"Then I am satisfied. I have asked the high priest to petition the gods, to pray that they help you safely over the water."

"I have also prayed to my own god," he said as he put his arm about her waist. They clung together awhile longer, until the light began to fade. "Come. We cannot stay here. The night air is cool."

Returning, they learned that Maukiri and Nika had found a nest for themselves in the forest. Tepua's men ferried her and Kiore out to the foreign boat. She stepped aboard. In the darkness she could just make out the shape of the hanging bed.

"Climb in!" he invited.

She put her hand on the long expanse of cloth and felt it swing away from her. "*Aue!* It will fall!"

"No. Try it."

At last he persuaded Tepua to get in. The sensation of swinging made her giddy. When he joined her, she heard the creaks of cords and spars, and expected the whole contrivance to come crashing down.

"See. It is warm and pleasant inside."

He was right. The cloth made a cozy shelter from the wind. She began to enjoy the gentle swaying. And yet . . .

Kiore seemed to sense her thoughts as he wrapped his

arms around her. "I am sure we can manage," he whispered.

"You have tried it before?"

"No, Tepua." He began nuzzling at her ear. "There are many things I never tried before I came to your atoll. This is one."

After that they had no need for talk.

The night had been far too short, and now it was gone. Tepua, drained from the grief of parting, sat on the deck of the *pahi* that was carrying her back to her atoll. In the morning light she watched the rise and fall of water, the surging whitecaps, the swooping terns. Somewhere far behind her Kiore was sailing in the opposite direction.

"Tepua, you need rest. We both do," said Maukiri, whose face was also wet with tears.

"There will be time for resting," said Tepua. "As long as I want. Umia will be chief soon." She looked out, watching for the first signs of land.

"That is so?" asked Maukiri with surprise.

"Faka-ora has been studying the signs. He told me that Umia's time has almost arrived. I will be released from my obligations."

"Then you should be glad. That is what you wanted."

Tepua blinked, and her own tears came again. Yes. She had carried out her duties. The gods should be pleased. . . .

"What will you do after this?" Maukiri's face was contorted with sorrow, and Tepua did not think this came only from the loss of her sailor.

"I will go back to Tahiti, of course. But this time I will not go alone." She stared at her cousin, watching her sadness ease a bit. "If I cannot stay here with my kin, why not bring part of my family with me?" She put her arm about Maukiri's shoulder.

"Tahiti!" Maukiri's mouth fell open in delight. "Yes, cousin!"

"You will find someone there. Someone to make you forget Nika."

Maukiri rubbed a glistening streak from her own face. "Perhaps—"

"You will forget him, cousin."

"And will you forget Kiore?"

Tepua had no answer. He would always be with her, she thought. But Maukiri was young, and light with her affections.

"You have told me so little about Tahiti," her cousin whispered.

"We will have time to talk along the way."

"But I want to know about the men. You said only that they were like ours."

Tepua sighed. "They are tall, well shaped, eager to please. You will be happy."

"I am not sure," said Maukiri. "You told me that outsiders have never been to Tahiti. The men there know nothing of foreign ways."

"And what do they need to know?" Tepua caught herself as she saw her cousin's sly grin. Was she hinting that the men of Tahiti might need lessons in *hanihani*?

Tepua peered at her cousin, her brows rising. She tried to imagine the impulsive Maukiri set loose among the stuffier Tahitian nobility. The prospect lightened her spirits. "Perhaps they have a few things to learn," she said cautiously.

Maukiri parted her lips, wiggled the tip of her tongue, and cried, "I am willing to teach them!"

Tepua laughed, but then a shout from the canoe-master made her solemn once more. Land had been sighted. Ahead lay the atoll of her birth. She peered out over the sunlit water, wanting to remember every detail of this last voyage home.

She tried to console herself. In the end, she had been the strong chief that her people needed, worthy of her ancestress, Tapahi-roro-ariki. Outsiders might come again, but now her people would be prepared. They would have allies, if needed, to stand beside them.

And they would have her brother, the high chief chosen by the gods. She had given Umia the confidence he needed to carry forward Kohekapu's rule. Umia would father the next chief. The wisdom of the ancestors would live on.

HISTORICAL NOTE

Tepua's atoll belongs to the group known today as the Tuamotu Archipelago of French Polynesia. Early navigators called them the Dangerous Islands because of their treacherous currents and underwater reefs. They lie in the central Pacific, below the equator, almost due south of Hawaii.

The Tuamotu islands are so numerous that some were discovered by the earliest European explorers. Several incidents of shipwrecks have been documented, and there were undoubtedly others, but history can tell us little about the fates of the stranded sailors.

Though these atolls were often sighted from ships, many remained isolated for centuries. Much of the early culture of some islands survived into the twentieth century. In the 1920s and 1930s, expeditions sent by the Bishop Museum of Hawaii collected a wealth of Tuamotuan material. Even today, one can still find people of these islands who remember the genealogies of their ancestors, all the way back to the gods and heroes of ancient times.

GLOSSARY

ari'i/ariki: a chief, or a person of the ruling class.

Arioi society: A cult devoted to worship of Oro in his peaceful aspect of Oro-of-the-laid-down-spear. In this role he also served as a fertility god.

aroha: compassion, deep sympathy.

atoll: a ring of coral islands that surrounds or partially surrounds a lagoon. The islands are typically low and flat.

aue: a cry of delight, surprise, or dismay.

ava/kava: a relative of black pepper. The roots and stems were used to make an intoxicating, nonalcoholic, drink. (Still popular today in the Fiji Islands and elsewhere.) *Piper methysticum.*

breadfruit: the staple food of ancient Tahiti. A single tree can produce hundreds of pounds of fruit. When eaten baked, it resembles the flavor and texture of yam or squash.

fai: the art of making string figures, popular throughout Polynesia; "cat's cradle."

fara: pandanus or screwpine. A principal source of food (seeds and fruit) for many atoll people. The leaves are an excellent source of thatch for roofs. *Pandanus tectorius.*

hanihani: to caress, fondle, stimulate.

high island: an island of volcanic origin, such as Tahiti or Hawaii. These islands have mountainous interiors.

kahaia: small atoll tree of the coffee family. *Guettarda speciosa.*

kaito-nui: mighty warrior.

kokuru: shrub of atoll shores, having narrow leaves and yellow flowers. The wood is very hard, useful for fishhooks and spears. *Suriana maritima.*

mana: sacred power, which was considered capable of transmission by touch. Humans as well as objects possessed *mana* to varying degrees.

marae: an open-air place of worship, usually a rectangular courtyard bounded by low stone walls, with a stone platform at one end. On atolls, the building material was coral.

maro: a narrow piece of cloth worn by men about the hips, made of bark-cloth or finely plaited matting.

maro kura: sacred red cloth wound about the loins of a chief at investment, and worn on a few other special occasions.

maeva ariki: salutation: "Exalted be the chief!"

Maui: one of several legendary heroes by that name.

mikimiki: small tree of the loosestrife family, common to atoll shores. Flowers are white. The hard wood was used for spears and fishhooks. *Pemphis acidula.*

motu: a low island created by the exposed part of a coral reef.

Oro: Polynesian god, patron of the Arioi in his peacekeeping aspect known as Oro-of-the-laid-down-spear. One of the major gods of Tahiti at the time of European contact.

pahi: a vessel built by connecting two canoe hulls side by side with poles, usually with a platform mounted above the hulls. This type of craft was used on long voyages or for carrying large numbers of people.

pahua: large tridacna clam, a mainstay of the Tuamotu diet.

pukatea: atoll tree that can reach heights of sixty feet. Considered sacred by some atoll dwellers. *Pisonia grandis.*

ringoringo: a spirit that was thought to give a warning cry at the approach of trouble.

sennit: cord made from softened fibers of the coconut husk.

tahunga: a healer; a specialist in some art or skill.

tamanu: a large tree of the mangosteen family. *Calophyllum inophyllum.*

Tangaroa: generally viewed as the god who created all else. Considered too far removed from human affairs to be addressed directly in worship.

tapa: bark cloth, made by pounding the softened inner bark of the paper mulberry, breadfruit, or hibiscus tree. (These are all high-island trees.) Cloth was often dyed or painted, the best colors being scarlet and yellow. Rolls of *tapa* were prized as gifts, not only for their utility and beauty but because of the amount of labor they represented.

Tapahi-roro-ariki: legendary atoll woman chief. (lit. "Brains-cleaving-chief.")

tapu: sacred, forbidden. Something that is restricted.

tiputa: a garment of woven leaf or of bark-cloth. It is much like a hoodless poncho, a rectangle of cloth with a hole in the center for the head.

taro: a cultivated plant of the atolls. The root, when baked, is somewhat like a potato. The cooked leaves resemble mild spinach.

Tepua-mua: lit. "foremost flower."

umu: shallow pit used for cooking. Stones within are first heated by fire. The food is then placed between the stones and covered to bake.

vahine: woman, wife, lover.

vaka: one-hulled canoe with an outrigger float mounted parallel to the hull

viavia: a coconut in its prime for drinking. The outer husk is still partly green and the meat within is soft. (Not available in supermarkets!)

SELECTED READING

Brooks, Candace Carleton, *Manihi: Life on an Atoll,* Ph. D. thesis, Stanford University, 1968.

Buck, Sir Peter H., *Vikings of the Pacific*, University of Chicago Press, Chicago, 1959.

Danielsson, Bengt, *Love in the South Seas*, Translated by F.H. Lyon, Reynal & Co., New York, N.Y., 1956.

Emory, Kenneth P., *Material Culture of the Tuamotu Archipelago—Pacific Anthropological Records No. 22*, Department of Anthropology, Bernice Bishop Museum, Honolulu, Hawaii, 1975.

Emory, Kenneth P. and Honor Maude, *String Figures of the Tuamotus,* Homa Press, Canberra, 1979.

Henry, Teuira, *Ancient Tahiti*, Bishop Museum Bulletin No. 48, Honolulu, 1928.

Moorehead, Alan, *The Fatal Impact*, Harper and Row, New York, 1966.

Stafford-Deitsch, J., *Shark: A Photographer's Story*, Sierra Club Books, San Francisco, 1987.

SPECIAL PREVIEW

If you enjoyed <u>Sister of the Sun</u>, you won't want to miss the continuing saga of Tepua and her return to Tahiti . . .

CHILD OF THE DAWN

by Clare Coleman

. . . an epic story of life and love, as beautiful and timeless as the islands themselves.

Here is an exclusive excerpt from the next captivating novel—coming soon from Jove Books . . .

Under a clouded, sullen sky, a two-hulled voyaging canoe neared the end of its journey. On the island ahead, mountain slopes rose steeply, vanishing into mist. Along the shore, black sand beaches spread beneath stands of coconut palm. As the sailing craft drew closer, cries rang out from everyone aboard—praises to the canoe-master for his skill, to the gods for providing safe passage.

Now their destination lay before them, rising from the sea—Great-Tahiti-of-the-Golden-Haze. The island wore a cape of feathery cloud, tinted gold by shafts of sun. A robe of green in an infinity of depths and shades covered her flanks. Her colors were strange to the travelers—mist-softened, lush, yet in places so fierce that it hurt the eyes to gaze too long.

The double-hulled canoe, the *pahi*, had come from the swarm of coral islands far to the east. Its hulls were pieced together from small wooden sections sewn with tough cord twisted from coconut husk fiber. A platform of lashed planks carrying passengers and cargo bridged the hulls. The two mat sails were plaited from strips of pandanus leaf.

Most of the men aboard—warriors, craftsmen, paddlers, had never seen the soaring peaks of a high island. Tugging at their sparse beards, or fingering the sturdy fiber of their loincloths, they spoke to each other with awe.

One of the female passengers, however, knew Tahiti well. Tepua-mua, a high-born woman of the atolls, gave a soft sigh. She remembered how long it had taken to get used to this new country—the valleys that cut so deeply into the tumbled hillsides, the still, moisture-laden air that seemed so heavy to someone from the wind-swept coral islands.

Now Tepua was returning to her adopted land after an extended stay with her family. Accompanying her was her cousin Maukiri, a sturdy atoll girl with a plump face and a fondness for mischief. Maukiri was stockier than Tepua, pleasant in appearance but far from beautiful. Her youthful buoyancy and spirit more than made up for any lack of physical charms. Tepua, on the other hand, had a wild atoll beauty that suggested her ancestors' struggles against wind and sea.

Dressed in a skirt and cape of finely plaited pandanus leaf, Tepua stood as tall as many men. Though she had the figure of full womanhood, her training as a dancer kept her as slender and supple as an atoll palm. Lustrous black hair with tints of blue tumbled down her back. Her skin was a luminous bronze, clear and smooth. She had a high forehead, an oval face with wide cheekbones, and a square jawline that came to a point at the chin. Her eyes were large, almond-shaped, and fringed with black lashes.

Tepua and Maukiri watched eagerly as the canoe approached the frothing line of surf, where the Sea of the Moon beat against the submerged barrier reef. Plumes of sea-foam spewed into the air, raining down as fine spray that wet their skin, salted their lips.

A gap in the arc of white surf marked the pass where ocean swells rolled through into the lagoon. The canoe-master shouted orders as the double-hull approached. Tepua and her fellow-passengers held on to anything they could grab as the *pahi* rose on the back of a long wave. For an instant it held there, the twin bows surging upward like two birds about to fly. Then the bows dropped as the wave gave the *pahi* a tremendous push that sent it hurtling through the pass.

Tepua leaned to one side as the double-hull turned in

response to the helmsman's powerful pull on the steering oar. Veering out of the wave just as it started to break, the *pahi* emerged into the glassy turquoise of the lagoon.

The crew took down mast and sails and began to paddle. Soon a stray land breeze enveloped the canoe with the island's breath. It was warm and lush with fruit and floral aromas, laden with moist perfume.

Tepua's thoughts turned to Matopahu, the man who had once meant so much to her. His house in the high chief's compound lay just ahead; she hoped she would find him nearby. How she longed to be ashore!

Yet something out there was amiss. Among the delightful aromas, she sensed a discordant note. The harsh tang of burning wood could not be hidden by anything else. *Cooking fires?* Had she forgotten how much smoke the many pit-ovens of Tahiti produced?

Curious, Tepua searched for an explanation. She saw many canoes drawn up on the beach but none in the water. Surely some great occasion was keeping everyone ashore. In the distance, above the coconut palms, smoke rose in a dark plume.

Maukiri turned, sniffing the breeze. "Someone is cooking a big feast. I hope they invite us to share it!"

Tepua eyed the smoke. Something about it seemed menacing, although she didn't know why. As she waited for the canoe to draw closer to the source of the fire, she began pointing out details in the scene to her cousin.

"That mountain is sacred to the high chief," she said. "And over there is his point of land—a place you must never go." Far ahead, where the shoreline jutted out, stood a majestic grove of Tahitian chestnut. In the deep shade lay the high chief's sacred courtyard, his *marae,* the site of rituals forbidden to women.

The view brought memories that made Tepua shiver. The *marae* was a somber and terrifying place. In its forbidding shadows, the gods alighted in the form of birds, eating the carcasses laid on the offering platforms, sacrifices of pigs, dogs, and—when the gods demanded—men.

Putting those thoughts aside, she gestured at the pleasant scenes before her, clusters of thatched roofs shaded by coconut palms or breadfruit trees. "All the people of our atoll could live in one district of Tahiti," she said as Maukiri's eyes grew round. She, too, had once been astonished at the sight of so many houses.

Just beyond the houses, the coastal plain ended and foothills began. Some dwellings were perched on the lower slopes, others at the mouths of narrow valleys that slashed like adze-cuts into the foothills, extending as far inland as the eye could see.

Though a rush of joy came over Tepua at the sight, she could not forget that she was giving up much to return to Tahiti. At home, by virtue of her birth as well as her service to her people, she was the foremost woman of the island. Here in Tahiti she would be treated with far less respect. She was returning to her life as a dancer in one of the lower ranks of the Arioi Society. Long ago she had pledged herself to serve their patron god, Oro-of-the-laid-down-spear.

While Maukiri gaped at the sights around her, Tepua went aft to where a bamboo cage was lashed to the deck. Inside sat a beautiful white dog with gentle eyes, upright ears and a plumed tail. Her name was Te Kurevareva, Atoll Cuckoo. Tepua gave the dog fresh water in a coconut shell. She put her hand through a gap and stroked the animal. The plumed tail wagged against the bamboo canes, and a wet nose poked out to nuzzle her face. She had brought this rare and valuable animal as a gift to the Arioi chiefs, though now she did not want to part with it.

Maukiri came up beside Tepua. "Stop playing with your dog and tell me where we are going," said her cousin in an exasperated voice.

"You will see soon enough," said Tepua, straightening up. She wanted to leave a few surprises for her cousin. What would Maukiri say when she discovered such common

Tahitian sights as rivers of fresh water flowing to the sea? At home, fresh water was found only in cisterns and a few brackish pools. What would Maukiri think of bananas, breadfruit, and a host of other foods she had never tasted?

"Then tell me about the people we will visit first," begged Maukiri, her brown eyes alight with anticipation.

"I have many friends," Tepua answered. She did not know where she would find a place for Maukiri, but the question did not bother her now. Tahitians welcomed guests, especially if they had good tales to tell. Some prominent family would take Maukiri in.

Eventually the two cousins would have to separate. Tepua would live with the performers and dancers of the Arioi. Maukiri would have to find other accommodations. "I will make arrangements for you," Tepua assured her cousin.

The younger girl turned, sniffing the breeze. "I'm not worried, cousin. Your friends must know how hungry we are. Smell the food!"

Again Tepua eyed the ashy haze that hung over the trees. Could all that have come from cooking?

"Feasting! Dancing!" Maukiri crowed. "What a good day to arrive."

The canoe made its way along the coast. Now the source of the smoke was much closer. Gray billows boiled into the sky with such violence that Tepua felt an upsurge of alarm.

"That is no cooking fire!"

Her cry drew the gaze of everyone on the *pahi*. The men began to shout and gesture.

Tepua shaded her eyes, squinting hard at the shore. In the shadows of the palm groves she saw figures scurrying. An orange ribbon of flame shot above the treetops.

"*Aue!* Something tall is burning." She clenched her fists as the realization swept over her. The only large structure in this area was the great high-roofed theater where the Arioi acted and danced. "*Aue, aue!*" she cried, her voice breaking.

The commotion grew aboard the *pahi*. The paddlers lost their rhythm, and the twin bows swung off course. "Head for shore!" Tepua shouted at the canoe-master.

She turned as a tall, tattooed atoll warrior left his place and came to her. This man was the captain of her escort guard, charged with bringing her safely to Tahiti.

"There may be trouble here," he warned. He stood beside her, arms folded, eyes narrowed.

"Maybe someone was careless with a torch." Tepua knew, even before the warrior scowled, that her suggestion was foolish. Who would use a torch in daytime? And cooking was done far from the performance house. No spark from the pit-ovens could have set off this blaze.

"We will see," said the escort captain. He was the best warrior her brother could spare to accompany her. Though slender, he was powerful, and he had five good men with him. Yet none of them had ever traveled this far from home. None knew the ways of high islanders.

Tepua heard screams from shore as more people, men as well as women, fled the fire. They wore wreaths of flowers and festive dress, but their celebration had been interrupted. As the people ran, their flower-crowns fell off and were trampled. Broken palm fronds and blossoms scattered to the breeze.

Maukiri began to moan softly. Tepua held her cousin's hand but the words of reassurance she tried to say died on her tongue. The white dog whined from inside her cage.

Tepua felt Maukiri start to shiver. "It is a bad omen. The gods must be angry," the girl wailed.

"Men have done this, not gods," Tepua answered firmly. She studied the growing turmoil on the beach. What had happened? Invasion? War? "You stay here," she told her cousin in a low voice. "I will see what the trouble is."

"Hold in the shallows," the warrior captain ordered the paddlers. Still a good way from shore, he clutched a long double-ended spear, leaped out of the *pahi* and splashed ashore. Tepua took a spear from another warrior and jumped down into the water that rose to her thighs. The men of her escort guard followed.

When she caught up with her captain he tried to dissuade her, saying that he would investigate the trouble. Tepua refused his offer, but allowed him and two of his men to follow as she plunged into the trees toward the site of the fire.

Crying children fled across her path. Then she saw people wearing distinctive garlands of yellow mountain plantain, sweet-scented ginger, or the sacred red and purple *ti* plant. Their tattoos were familiar, for she bore some of the same. Members of her Arioi lodge!

With a shock, she realized that the Arioi had been in the midst of performing, for their faces were smeared with red sap and their bodies blackened with charcoal. Some were hampered by oversized loincloths and other ridiculous costumes used in satirical performances. Her jaw tightened with rage even as her mind reeled with disbelief. What evil had interrupted the devotees of Oro in the midst of their celebration?

She looked for people she knew but could not recognize anyone under the face paint and costumes. "What is happening?" she called, but the fleeing performers were too panic-stricken to stop or answer.

She heard the harsh crackling of burning thatch. The smoke caught in her throat and made her gag. Then she was close enough to see the performance house ablaze, its high roof completely enveloped in flame. She groaned aloud in anguish. This was where the god Oro had inspired her, making her dance with such a frenzy that the Arioi asked her to join them. And now this great work of polished wood pillars and pandanus thatch was doomed!

As Tepua fought her way through the rolling clouds of smoke, worry for her fellow Arioi performers filled her thoughts. Where was her friend Curling-leaf? And Aitofa, the chief of the women's lodge?

At last Tepua emerged from the drifting haze and could

see the scene clearly. Now she understood why no one had tried to put out the fire at its start. Warriors bearing unfamiliar tattoos stood about the site, brandishing clubs and shark-toothed swords, threatening anyone who dared come close. No onlookers braved these fierce sentries. She saw Arioi and common folk watching with horror from the shadows.

"Tepua! Tepua! Is it really you?" She spun around. There stood another painted figure, as difficult to recognize as the others. She knew the voice. Curling-leaf!

Before the escort captain could prevent her, Tepua rushed into her friend's arms. "I am back. Oh, it has been so long!" Curling-leaf's embrace was strong, but Tepua felt the young Arioi woman quivering with rage and fright. "Who did this?" Tepua asked, searching her friend's eyes. "Who are those warriors? Why don't you have any weapons?"

Her own three guards clustered close about her, but she waved them aside. What could this handful do against so many others?

She turned back to Curling-leaf. "Tell me what happened."

"There is no time!" wailed her friend. "Everything has changed since you left. The high chief was cast down."

Cast down! Tepua stared at her friend, unable to make sense of the words. When she left Tahiti, Knotted-cord had been high chief over this district and several others. She remembered him as petty and irascible, but not arrogant enough to overreach himself. The only threat to his rule had been the popularity of his brother, Matopahu.

His brother! She closed her eyes, remembering Matopahu's ambitions as well as what he had meant to her. Had Knotted-cord been forced aside in favor of his reckless sibling? She forced herself to ask.

"No." Curling-leaf's answer made Tepua heave a relieved sigh, but the next words gave her a chill. "The chief's brother had to flee."

"But Matopahu was not hurt. He is alive, isn't he?" She clutched at her friend's arm, demanding an answer. It was for Matopahu as well as the Arioi that she had returned to Tahiti.

Curling-leaf looked regretful. "He is, but that's all I know. Someone told me he was here today, disguised as an Arioi. I did not recognize him in the crowd."

"Then, praise the gods, he is alive." Tepua's pulse began slowing and she felt steadier on her feet. "But who is the new chief, and why this outrage?" She gestured toward the burning performance house.

Her friend glanced apprehensively at the line of guards around the burning performance house. They were starting to notice the two women. Curling-leaf headed in the opposite direction, tugging Tepua to follow. "We can't stay. The new chief wants to destroy us." As Curling-leaf spoke, several other Arioi women emerged from the smoke, their garlands and costumes in disarray, flowers falling from their tangled hair. They rallied around Tepua.

"Go to my *pahi*," Tepua told them. "Straight through the trees and down the beach." She ordered one of her warriors to see that they got aboard safely. Ignoring the escort captain's pleas that she go with the departing women, Tepua plunged ahead with Curling-leaf and began to search for others who needed help.

She felt Curling-leaf take her hand and this time the grip was firm and steady. The spirit had come back into Curling-leaf's eyes. Now she looked more like an Arioi, despite her shredded garlands and the soot smudged over the red sap on her face.

"The others are hiding," Curling-leaf said. "We have to find them." She beckoned Tepua through a grove of breadfruit trees.

"Arioi? Hiding? Why aren't any of them fighting?"

"With what?" Curling-leaf answered angrily. "Our weapons are gone! While the whole troupe was performing, the creature who calls himself high chief had them stolen."

"Who is this man?"

"He was a minor chief. After you left, he led a rebellion against Knotted-cord. Now he takes the name of Land-crab and rules as high chief."

Tepua, bewildered, followed her friend across the leaf-carpeted grove. It surprised her that someone had risen against the former high chief. But this usurper Land-crab had done something far worse, something unheard of. Arioi were under the protection of their patron god and immune from attack, even during outbreaks of war. A covenant of peace reigned at all Arioi performances; this was a tradition that even the most exalted chief had never violated. Until now.

"The usurper chose a good name," said Curling-leaf bitterly. "He sits on us like a fat crab on a heap of coconuts, and tears us apart with his claws."

Well, this Land-crab would see what it was to anger Oro, Tepua thought, clenching her fists.